Praise for the novels of

JASMINE CRESSWELL

Secret Sins

"*Secret Sins* is romantic suspense at its finest
and places Jasmine Cresswell on the mantel
with the great ones such as
Jayne Ann Krentz and Judith McNaught."
—*Affaire de Coeur*

The Daughter

"A powerful romance, combined with seat-of-the-
pants tension and a surprising last minute plot twist,
make this fast-paced story another winner."
—*Publishers Weekly*

The Disappearance

"Cresswell's superb story matches her best work,
stretching nerves to the breaking point."
—*Publishers Weekly*

The Inheritance

"*The Inheritance* is a fast-paced, action-packed
romantic intrigue that never slows down to let the
reader catch his/her breath. The story line is filled
with excitement, sexual tension, and danger....
Jasmine Cresswell entertains the audience with a
non-stop romantic thriller."
—*Painted Rock Reviews*

Also available from MIRA Books and
JASMINE CRESSWELL

DESIRES & DECEPTIONS
NO SIN TOO GREAT
SECRET SINS
THE DAUGHTER
THE DISAPPEARANCE
THE INHERITANCE

Watch for the newest novel from
JASMINE CRESSWELL
Coming October 2001

THE
REFUGE

JASMINE
CRESSWELL

MIRA

ISBN 1-55166-608-1

THE REFUGE

Copyright © 2000 by Jasmine Cresswell.

Visit us at www.mirabooks.com

Printed in U.S.A.

To
Alexander, Grace and Caroline
Katie
Johnny and Annabelle
Emily and Dominic
With much love from Grandma

Prologue

June 1999, Stankovec Refugee Camp, Macedonia

The refugee camp was hot, dusty and stinking. In another few weeks the nights would turn bitterly cold. Snow would fall and the dust would vanish, but the foul odor would linger, the inevitable consequence of too many desperate people crowded into too little space.

Most visitors, especially those from the deodorized comfort of the United States, were overwhelmed by the smells, sights and sounds of so much human misery. Not Stuart Frieze. He had seen it all a dozen times before, and he strode between the rows of tents, displaying no reaction to the multiple assaults on his senses.

Despite his brisk pace and deliberately cultivated emotional detachment, he was aware of every detail of his surroundings. He skirted treasured cooking pots, tattered clothes drying on improvised racks, and cardboard boxes serving as makeshift cradles. He was careful to avoid looking into the eyes of the weary mothers who were struggling to bathe fretful toddlers in plastic bowls filled with tepid water, or provide other basic services for their shattered families. Stuart didn't need to look at the women to know the misery he would see. He already had enough haunting memories from his experiences at other refugee camps to fill the nightmares of several lifetimes. He had been a field director for the United Nations High Commission on Refugees for almost a decade, and he didn't think there was any form of human misery that he hadn't been forced to confront and deal with sometime during those ten long and frustrating years.

From his perspective, the camp at Stankovec was a typical example of the aftermath of a civil war fought with bitter intensity over land that most outsiders considered worthless. The war was officially over, but the victims of the war always remained long after government leaders declared a cease-fire. The outcome of the Serbian conflict with NATO had been utterly predictable, as far as Stuart was concerned. Both sides announced victory— in the media age, savvy international politicians realized there could be no public losers even if major parts of Serbia and Kosovo had been reduced to rubble. Then the TV news crews packed up and went home. The American public breathed a collective sigh of relief that the heartbreaking pictures of orphans and wounded senior citizens would now cease, so they could return to full-time preoccupation with Little League, the latest juicy murder, and the enticing crop of summer movies at their local multiplex.

From the American point of view, they had earned their right to indifference. After all, it was their tax dollars that had enabled democracy to triumph, leaving Kosovo safe for ethnic Albanians. Except for the minor point that Kosovo wasn't safe, and thousands of refugees remained destitute, wounded, orphaned, and widowed. The Kosovars had ravaged homes, no crops to harvest, and their shops had been looted. The few officials who attempted to point out these annoying facts met with the fate they deserved. They were ignored.

Stuart had learned to keep such cynical reflections to himself, and he certainly had no intention of returning to the States and trying to stir up public outrage with first-hand reports from the war zone. He'd been there, done that—and learned the true meaning of the word *frustration* in the process.

A dozen boys were playing soccer with a battered ball and improvised goalposts. He knew better than to create chaos by handing out candies to the lucky few who happened to be close to him, but he gave way to temptation and passed out the sticks of chewing gum he'd tucked into the pockets of his cotton pants. As he could have predicted, he was instantly surrounded by what seemed like a hundred waving hands. Mad at himself and the world, he had to call a security guard to disperse the crowd of disappointed kids.

Once a path had been cleared for him, he marched on, his brows drawn into a thick, angry line. What the hell kind of a world let kids waste years of their lives stuck on a barren hillside with no place to go, and nothing to do with their time but plot ways to find a gun, join the "liberation" army, and wreak vengeance on their enemies?

He knew the answer to his question, of course, even though he hated it. He shoved useless philosophical ruminations aside and concentrated on his search for the medical tent. He found it at last, and flashed his United Nations badge to gain admittance. He didn't actually work for the United Nations anymore, hadn't done so for three years, but security in the camp was laughably easy to breach for anyone with his years of bureaucratic experience. The checks on his documents at the entrance to the camp had been so cursory that a blatant forgery would have passed muster, and his forgery was pretty good.

Once inside the camp, security fell off even more, and the few remaining checkpoints could have been circumvented by any enterprising twelve-year-old.

"I have a meeting arranged with Dr. Mark Yarfield," he said to the orderly posted at the entrance to the medical unit. "Please tell him that Stuart Frieze is here."

He waited less than five minutes before a woman of about forty came out of the tent, stripping off a pair of surgical gloves as she came. She wiped the sweat from her forehead with a face mask before tossing it in the trash.

"Mr. Frieze?"

"Yes. I'm Stuart Frieze."

"I'm Dr. Riven. Carole Riven." She held out her hand and he shook it, returning her smile, even though alarm bells were sounding inside his head. This woman looked smart, and alarmingly astute. Not desirable qualities, from his point of view.

"I'm sorry, but Mark Yarfield was flown out of here last week," she said. "A medical emergency. Didn't they notify you?"

Stuart concealed a tiny spurt of relief. His information about Dr. Yarfield's hasty departure from the camp had been correct. A first small step in the right direction.

"I'm real sorry to hear about Dr. Yarfield," he lied, sounding convincingly worried. "I hope there's nothing seriously wrong with him?"

Dr. Riven grimaced. "He was diagnosed with TB. Once he's back in the States, it shouldn't be a problem." She paused, barely disguising a sigh. "Is there something I could help you with, since he isn't here?"

"Well, Mark and I were originally in touch because I wanted to make a donation to the hospital on behalf of the charitable trust I direct. The Wainscott Foundation, headquartered in Colorado. Under the terms of Mr. Wain-scott's will, the trustees agreed that I could provide some medical equipment to the exiled Kosovars that would help pregnant women and their babies. Dr. Yarfield suggested an incubator for infants needing intensive neonatal care, so that's what I arranged to have shipped here. It only took about a hundred hours of pleading with bureaucrats to get it added to one of the aid shipments..." Stuart gave a rueful smile before allowing his voice to tail off into a modest silence.

Understanding dawned on Carole Riven's expressive face. "Oh, yes, of course. The Wainscott Foundation—there's a plaque inscribed with that name on the incubator. It's already been a life saver several times over." She struggled valiantly to conceal another sigh. "We certainly appreciated the gift, Mr. Frieze, and I'd be happy to give you a tour of our neonatal unit, since Mark isn't here. You'll be pleased to hear that I've made arrangements to have your incubator shipped to Pristina as soon as our medical facility here closes down."

"You're a lousy liar and you wouldn't be the least bit happy to waste your time giving me a tour." Stuart gave her a cheerful grin. "You're cursing the fact that I've turned up in Stankovec and you're wishing you could get on with your work. You're also wondering why the hell rich benefactors can't just be satisfied with sending money, instead of constantly turning up on site and expecting to be thanked."

Carole looked startled, then laughed. A genuine laugh this time. "You sound as if you've been on the receiving end of one too many well-meaning official visits yourself."

"I have." Stuart grimaced. "Trust me, I understand what you're going through. It got so bad on my last U.N.

assignment that I literally broke out in hives whenever I heard that a delegation from the U.S. Congress was coming to visit one of the refugee areas I was responsible for.''

''I know exactly what you mean. Still, we need the publicity, I guess, or these people would just be abandoned. And the refugees remaining here are the most difficult cases, of course.''

Stuart scowled. ''The ones with no homes left, the ones whose families have been wiped out, and all their assets stolen, right down to grandma's old rocking chair. Four-hundred thousand refugees may have gone home, but it's the three-hundred thousand left behind we have to worry about.''

''You're so right.'' Carole gave him a sympathetic smile, a bond of trust forged between them, which was precisely what Stuart had intended. ''There's been an outbreak of chicken pox in the camp, and it's pretty hectic right now, but actually I'm glad to take a break for five minutes,'' she said. ''And since you provided the funds for the only reliable level-three incubator in this entire region, I guess I'm happy to spend time with you. Do you want to see our neonatal unit? That's a genuinely willing offer this time. For a field hospital, our facilities here aren't too bad.''

''I'd love to see it, but I'm afraid I don't have time,'' Stuart said. ''I have a busload of orphaned toddlers waiting to board a plane to the States, and I have to be out of here within the hour. The problem is, Mark Yarfield had promised to help me with another matter. I only stopped here because I needed his help. Urgently.''

''Well, I'll help if I can…''

''I think you'll be able to. It's a good problem, really. I've called in every favor I'm owed by the State Department and our immigration service, and I've managed to finagle temporary visas for two more adult refugees to come back with me to the States. Outside the regular quota, that is."

Carole Riven looked impressed. "That's great! At this point, given the devastation inside Kosovo, everyone we can get out of the region before winter is a blessing. How in the world did you manage to get two extra visas?"

Stuart grimaced. "Don't even ask. I licked so much shoe leather that my tongue still has sores on it. Anyway, the good news is that these two visas are valid immediately, and I have the authority to process the paperwork right on the plane. Dr. Yarfield figured that if I took a couple of young women who were pregnant, then I'd be rescuing not only the mothers, but the babies, as well. Four rescues for two visas, so to speak. The bad news is that I need to take the adult refugees with me on this plane, with the orphans, so they'll have to come right now. No time for me to make a careful selection. And no time for the women to indulge in long goodbyes to their families."

Carole frowned. "I don't think there are many Kosovar women who'd be willing to leave their families, even for the sake of starting a new life in the States."

"Dr. Yarfield told me he knew of some young women who'd been raped by a group of drunken soldiers who were supposedly guarding the camp." Mark Yarfield hadn't actually told him any such thing. In fact, his correspondence with Dr. Yarfield had been strictly limited to e-mail notes about the incubator. However, Stuart had read a British newspaper report about the rape of the young Albanian women, and his interest had immediately been caught. There had been half a dozen of them, terrified women who'd escaped from Serbian soldiers only to be attacked by the Macedonian guards who were supposed to be protecting them. Two of the women, virgins at the time of the attack, had ended up pregnant.

"I know the women you mean," Carole said, her voice hardening. "I was the doctor who treated them after they'd been raped. If they'd only come to me right away, I could have given them medication to make sure they didn't get pregnant. Of course, they were so ashamed of what had happened that they hid in the tents without seeking medical attention until we managed to find them a few weeks later. I offered them the chance of an abortion, but they wouldn't agree. Of course."

Stuart forced himself to sound casual. "They'd be ideal candidates for my emergency visas. And they'd probably be more than happy for the chance to have their babies in the States and start a new life there."

"Yes, I expect they would." Carole Riven looked almost cheerful. "This is great news. One of the few happy endings I've seen around this camp. I'll see if I can locate the women for you—"

"Time is really of the essence," Stuart said. "How long will it take you to contact them, do you think?" He glanced down at his watch and gave Carole Riven another of his rueful, appealing grins. "I can spare you about forty minutes if we're going to get them on the bus in time for us to make our plane."

I can't give her time to poke holes in my story. Once the women were gone, she'd be so relieved that she wouldn't give them another moment's thought. This visit would be entirely forgotten in the crush of her exhausting, eighteen-hour workdays.

Carole glanced at her watch. "Noon. Lunchtime, so they're likely to be eating or preparing food near their family tents. I'll get right on it. I should have details in my records of where they're staying. Can you wait here?''

"Don't worry about me." He smiled reassuringly, knowing that he looked like what he'd once been: a do-gooder who tried hard to get things done, a bureaucrat with a heart of gold. "I'll stay out of everyone's way so that your work isn't interrupted any more than it has to be."

Dr. Riven disappeared into the interior of the medical facility. She proved as efficient as Stuart could have hoped. She'd tracked down the two women—they were really no more than girls—within thirty minutes. The two bewildered refugees arrived at the medical tent, where Stuart was waiting, and stood with downcast eyes, clutching plastic shopping bags filled with whatever it was that constituted the remnants of their worldly goods. Beneath their light summer blouses, their pregnant abdomens were visibly swollen.

Stuart assessed them rapidly. Brown hair, blue eyes, smooth skin. Quite healthy looking, given the circumstances. They were just about perfect for his needs.

"Thank you so very much for your cooperation, Dr. Riven," he said, smiling at the girls warmly. They blushed and looked away. Poor things, they had been browbeaten by fate to the point that they had zero self-esteem. He resisted the urge to pat them reassuringly on the shoulders. After what they'd gone through, physical contact with a strange man wouldn't be comforting to them.

He switched his smile back to Carole Riven. "We need to get going, but I believe you've helped to make the future brighter for several people today. These women are going to enjoy a wonderful new start to their lives, and their babies will grow up safely in the security of the United States. This is great. Thank you.''

For once, Stuart meant every word he said.

One

Five minutes into the interview, Marisa already knew she wasn't going to get the job. She'd realized she was aiming high in applying for a position as assistant to the general manager at the Alpine Lakes Ski Lodge, but after six months of temporary jobs with low pay and no benefits, she was desperate to find something permanent that provided both paid vacation days and a medical plan. Right now, she and Spencer were only one medical emergency away from destitution. And if medical disasters were too unpredictable to worry about, she could give herself a fine case of insomnia fretting about what would happen when her paychecks from the mortuary came to an end on Friday. Because unemployment wasn't just something that might happen to her "one day." Unemployment was scheduled to drop its ax on her three days from now, on Friday.

Despite the drawback of having to cope day in and day out with a grieving clientele, Marisa had been deeply grateful for steady employment at Vincent's Funeral Home. She'd been working as a receptionist at the mortuary since Christmas, and liked her fellow workers, who were a cheerful bunch, rarely depressed by their somber profession. Other than the lack of benefits, she had no cause for complaint, and she wished the elderly owners hadn't decided to sell out to one of the national chains, causing an immediate elimination of her position in favor of a college-trained "grief counselor" who could double as front office clerk.

Newspapers and television commentators gave the impression the economy in Colorado was expanding so fast that just about anyone could find decent employment, but Marisa's string of temporary positions suggested otherwise. People with college degrees or specialized office skills might be urgently needed, but when you were a twenty-eight-year-old single mother, not to mention a high school dropout with no relevant work experience, the economy wasn't booming vigorously enough to keep you employed at anything close to a living wage.

Eight minutes into the interview, the general manager decided to quit wasting his time. He cut Marisa off in the middle of her halting explanation as to why she had dropped out of tenth grade to pursue a career as a fashion model, scarcely bothering to conceal his suspicion that "model" was a euphemism for something a lot less respectable. He rose to his feet, his smile polite but dismissive.

"Thank you for driving up from Denver to speak with me, Ms. Joubert. According to your current employer, you're a hardworking young woman and you've been popular with his clients, but I'm afraid you just don't have the skills or the experience I require. I need someone who can maintain a financial database and run spreadsheets showing projected occupancy rates and revenue generation in each major profit center—"

"I've had some experience with computers. My father—" Marisa stopped abruptly, remembering too late that mentioning her father was going to open up a whole new can of maggoty worms. She hastily switched tracks. "I'm very quick with figures."

"I'm sorry, Ms. Joubert." The general manager sounded impatient rather than regretful. "We're too busy at Alpine Lakes to take the time to train our employees in basic computer skills. New hires have to come on board ready to jump right into things, especially now that we're gearing up to promote our summer vacation packages. This is going to be a very busy season for us. Let me show you the way back to the main entrance. The corridors in this part of the lodge can get a little tricky."

Marisa came out into the Alpine Lakes parking lot to discover that the spring snow that had been threatening earlier was now falling in earnest. She picked her way across the slippery tarmac, trying not to ruin her one remaining pair of good black shoes. These were her interview shoes that teamed with the gray all-season fabric of her one and only interview suit, and, given the number of job interviews she had to go to in order to get hired, she needed to keep her outfit in the best possible state of repair. Remembering the hundreds of pairs of expensive shoes she'd casually tossed into Goodwill bags made Marisa cringe—although sometimes she wasn't entirely sure whether she shuddered with embarrassment at her past profligacy, or regret for her vanished wealth.

Her car, a two-year-old Saturn with snow tires still in place, would make it down the mountain roads to Denver just fine, but she felt defeated and incompetent after her humiliatingly brief interview, and in no mood to battle snarled highway traffic. When she noticed a trendy-looking café on Main Street, she decided to pull over for half an hour and give the snow plows a chance to clear the interstate. Spencer's daycare center didn't close until six, and it was now barely noon, which gave her more

than enough time to drown her sorrows in a foaming mug
of *caffelatte*.

She pushed open the door of *La Cafetière*, which was
shielded by a jaunty red-striped awning and had some
brave tulips trying not to look frozen in their window
boxes. The restaurant's efforts to look like a Parisian
sidewalk café were somewhat hampered not only by the
snow, but by the hardware store next door, which sent
out an earthy smell of grains and dried horse-feed that
battled with *La Cafetière*'s aroma of freshly ground coffee beans.

The café wasn't crowded, especially in view of the fact
that it was lunchtime, and the lone waitress quickly led
Marisa to a vacant table by the window. The waitress
appeared to be in her early thirties, and wore jeans,
teamed with a frilly white apron edged with lace. Marisa
wasn't sure if the combination of denim and lacy apron
was a sly joke, or if the waitress hadn't noticed the incongruity.

"My name's Kathleen," the waitress said, handing
over a single-sheet menu. "My husband's the chef, and
our menu changes daily. Everything's good, but the *pan-
ini* are our specialty."

It had been a long time since Marisa had eaten out
anywhere more sophisticated than Burger King, where
Spencer could indulge his passion for eating French fries
dipped into his carton of orange juice. She read the menu
with unexpected interest before finally selecting a *panino*
filled with prosciutto, artichoke hearts and sliced black
olives. She gave her order, and saved a few pennies by
asking for water to drink with her meal.

"Where are you from?" Kathleen asked as she came
back to pour ice water into a tall glass. She sounded
friendly rather than nosy.

"I was raised in Florida, but today I just drove up from Denver. How did you know I'm not one of the locals?"

Kathleen flashed a smile. "Folks who grew up around Wainscott don't order anything that can't be served with ketchup. I never did myself, until I went to New Orleans and met my husband. André is Cajun, and he thinks the definition of *civilized* is eating great food before spending the night dancing. He's going to transform the eating habits of Wainscott, or go bankrupt trying."

A group of three grizzled men in bib overalls came into the restaurant, and Kathleen excused herself before hurrying away to get them seated. The newcomers seemed to know everyone in the café and called out greetings as they sat down. Their collective gaze rested speculatively on Marisa before they all nodded to her politely and reached for their menus. Strangers in Wainscott, it seemed, were instantly recognized as such.

"What newfangled rabbit food has your husband got lined up for us today?" one of the men asked Kathleen, taking a pair of glasses out of his pocket but not bothering to put them on to read the menu.

"There's a tasty arugula and Belgian endive salad with walnut oil dressing, if you'd like it," Kathleen said with false innocence. She pretended not to hear the men groaning. "Or we've got a real nice chili with melted provolone cheese, if you'd prefer that by any chance. Of course, André'll make you all hamburgers and fries, if you insist."

Marisa smothered a grin, as the men all opted for the chili as if they were doing Kathleen a personal favor by not ordering burgers. Marisa's meal arrived soon after, grilled and seasoned to perfection, and she ate it with unexpected appetite.

"How's the sandwich?" Kathleen asked later, whizzing past with a coffeepot and a fistful of mugs for another table.

"It's wonderful," Marisa said. "You and your husband should do a roaring trade once word gets out that you're here."

"Yeah, we're counting on word-of-mouth. In the end, it's the only way to establish a restaurant. We had a good ski season with the tourists. Now we have to persuade the locals to eat here, too."

Kathleen returned after bringing the three men huge servings of apple pie and ice cream. "Would you like some dessert?" she asked Marisa. "André makes a fudge torte that's to die for. Or I can bring you a dessert menu, and you can choose your own caloric sin."

Marisa smiled and shook her head. "I've already exceeded my quota of sinning for today. I'll just have coffee, thanks."

"Regular, espresso, flavored? We've also got hazelnut decaf."

Marisa ordered a cappuccino to compound the indulgence of a lunch she couldn't really afford. It was depressing how her thoughts constantly circled back to money these days. Six months ago, it had seemed so easy to give away the $7.5 million she'd inherited when her father died, and even easier to put the money Evan had left into an irrevocable trust for her son's education. But a few weeks in Denver had been all it took for Marisa to realize that she'd vastly underestimated the difficulty of earning enough to support herself and Spencer.

Her sister Belle had seemed to have achieved financial independence so easily that Marisa had ignored the crucial differences between her situation and her sister's. First of all, Belle had a college degree and professional training. Second, Belle had no dependents when she broke away from the corrupting influence of the Joubert's illegal family business. And third, Marisa had a humiliating suspicion that her sister was just more competent than she was.

The net result of comparing herself to Belle was that Marisa had started her new life last October in a state of ignorance about finances that was either comical or offensive, depending on your viewpoint. She'd certainly had no idea how difficult it was for the average working family to make ends meet. When you grew up with an indulgent, multimillionaire daddy who just happened to be a crook, how money got into the family coffers wasn't something you were encouraged to think about. If you then married a rich husband who wanted you to be a combination slave and trophy, making every nickel do the work of a dime wasn't one of the skills you picked up along the way. Never rocking the boat, never provoking your husband's ferocious temper, demonstrating blind obedience in everything except your husband's dictates about your son—those were survival skills Marisa had down pat. But not how to survive on a poverty-level income. Nowadays, as she sweated out payment of her monthly bills, Marisa suspected she wouldn't have had the courage to give away her tainted fortune if she'd understood precisely what she was letting herself and Spencer in for.

What a moral giant she was, Marisa thought, stirring her coffee. So lacking in ethical backbone that she half regretted giving away money that had been accumulated entirely by treachery and criminal enterprise.

"The snow looks as if it's clearing," Kathleen said, returning to Marisa's table. "That's the worst thing about living up here in the mountains—spring takes forever to arrive, and then you blink your eyes and it's summer.

Still, the summer's gorgeous when it does finally get here. Lots of sunshine, no humidity, cool nights. And hours and hours of digging in my flower garden so that I have a good crop of petunias for the deer to eat.'' Kathleen laughed. ''Sometimes I don't know why I bother, but I got hooked on the gardening thing when I was in New Orleans and now I'm not smart enough to know when I'm defeated.''

''It must be beautiful up here in summer. I've often thought I'd like to live in the mountains.'' Marisa must have sounded more wistful than she intended, because Kathleen looked at her with sudden speculation.

''I don't suppose you're serious about moving, are you? Or looking for a job, by any chance? My sister's planning to get married, and she just quit as assistant to the general manager at Alpine Lakes. He's so desperate for a replacement, he'd hire you in a split second. They have great benefits, too. Three weeks' paid vacation your first year. If you stay right through ski season, you get a bonus. Lots of good stuff like that, you know?''

Marisa felt her cheeks flame. The general manager might be desperate, but not, apparently, desperate enough to hire someone as unqualified as her. ''I'm not looking for a job right now,'' she said stiffly.

Kathleen sighed. ''The job market's really tight these days, and nobody seems to be looking. It's a shame, because this town is full of old-timers and college kids just passing through from ski resort to ski resort. We need a few more people in the middle who want to stick around, especially women.''

''Are there a lot of jobs currently available up here?'' Marisa tried to sound casual, although she realized that the idea of living with Spencer in this small rural town was beginning to seem very appealing. Maybe losing the job at Alpine Lakes didn't mean the end of her dream of finding a job and establishing a home for Spencer in the tranquility of the mountains.

"There's lots of part-time and seasonal work," Kathleen said. "That's why we get so many college kids moving through. Wainscott used to be an agricultural center for the county. Then Colorado Properties bought the old lodge and turned it into a really upscale ski lodge, and the whole balance of the town started to shift. Then when old Grover Wainscott died—"

"The town was named after a person?"

"Yeah. The Wainscott family owned all the land for miles around, but the old man lived so simply that none of us had ever stopped to figure out that he was actually the driving force behind Colorado Properties and Alpine Lakes, much less that he had millions of dollars he was planning to leave to some weird charitable foundation."

"I don't understand. Is Alpine Lakes a charitable foundation? It looks just like a regular, for-profit resort—"

"Oh, no, Alpine Lakes is a regular resort. I'm talking about Wainscott Refuge at the other end of town. That's the place old man Wainscott—Grover Wainscott—left his money to." Kathleen bent forward, peering out the window, and pointed to indicate a massive brick building that formed an impassable bulwark at the end of Main Street. "You can see the old Wainscott mansion from here. See? If you can believe it, in this day and age, it's been converted into a group home for unwed mothers."

Marisa looked up, startled. "That's kind of a nineteenth-century concept, isn't it?"

"Sure, but you'd be surprised at how much need there seems to be for the services they're providing. It's always full to capacity, maybe because word's out that they do a terrific job at finding just the right adoptive parents for each baby. Stuart Frieze, the director, often comes in here for lunch, and I know he prides himself on the services they provide to the mothers after their babies are born. The women aren't just tossed out onto the street to sink or swim once their baby's been adopted. They can stay at the Refuge until they have jobs to go to, even if that takes a couple of months to arrange.''

The horrors of her marriage to Evan Connor had left Marisa with a large fund of sympathy for women whom she would previously have dismissed as foolish or incompetent at handling their lives. ''It sounds like a place that's providing a valuable service,'' she said.

''Yeah, it is. But they have even worse staffing problems than Alpine Lakes. I heard they had to hire on a janitor who's mentally retarded, and Stuart's been looking for office help for almost two months.'' Kathleen gave a wry chuckle. ''So far, he says the best candidate he's seen is a sixty-year-old woman who insisted on hanging up a banner behind her desk that said, 'God punishes fornicators in the everlasting fires of hell.'''

''Oh, my. That must have gone over well with the unwed moms.''

''Yeah. To Stuart's credit, she only lasted a day. Now he's back to using temps who can spell their own names, if he's lucky.''

Marisa disguised a sudden rush of hope by opening her purse and searching for the money to settle her bill. The director of the Refuge sounded desperate enough to hire almost anybody, even a high school dropout who was more than a little vague about the details of her past. Maybe her luck was finally about to change, and she would be able to snag herself a permanent job up here in Wainscott, after all. Apart from the relief of having an income, and the pleasure of living in a friendly small town, working with mothers-to-be would certainly make for a happy change after three months of arranging to inter corpses.

She would pay a visit to Mr. Frieze and Wainscott Refuge, Marisa decided. At this point in her life, she had nothing to lose.

Two

Stuart Frieze was obviously so desperate for office help that he was willing to hire anyone who could manage to sound coherent for the duration of a five-minute phone conversation. He answered Marisa's call himself, and asked a few questions about her previous work history. She knew her answers weren't impressive, but instead of sounding appalled by her lack of experience, his tone of voice became rapidly more cheerful as he realized that she was sober, hadn't just been released from jail, and had no mental illness that was acute enough to cause her to jabber incoherently into the phone.

He barely gave her time to finish her account of the simple tasks she was required to perform at the mortuary, before asking her to come for a personal interview.

"You said you're phoning from André and Kathleen's café, right? Can you drive over to the Refuge right now? We're only five minutes from the café, and it would be much easier to continue our chat face to face." Stuart Frieze paused for a moment, making no more than a token effort to disguise his eagerness. "I guess I could free up half an hour for an interview, if you could come immediately."

"Yes, I could drive over," Marisa agreed, afraid to allow herself to hope, despite Stuart's enthusiasm.

"Kathleen pointed out where the Refuge is located. I could be there in ten minutes or so, if that's convenient."

"I'll be waiting," Stuart said. "Just ring the front doorbell, and I'll let you in. We lock the outer doors because tourists keep wandering onto the premises thinking this must be the town hall. It's one of the few handicaps of working in a spacious old building, smack dab in the center of town."

Marisa walked back to the cash register and paid her bill, her stomach churning with a mixture of nerves and excitement. "I've agreed to interview with Mr. Frieze for the job you mentioned," she said to Kathleen. Protecting her pride in case she was rejected yet again, she gave a shrug. "I don't expect I'll take it, but this is a beautiful spot, and I have a free afternoon. I guess it can't hurt to check out what's available."

Kathleen's eyes lit up. "That's great! I sure hope Stuart can persuade you to stay. Small towns have their drawbacks, but I know you'd learn to love it here." She glanced toward the windows, saw that snow was still falling, and grinned. "I promise, it never snows after the end of May. Well, not most years, anyway, and where else could you find scenery like this?"

Marisa gave an answering smile. "Well, if you want an honest answer, I'd say in about half the mountain towns in the state."

Kathleen shook her head. "Uh-uh. Bite your tongue. Only in Wainscott. Even in Colorado there aren't that many places with a gorgeous natural lake, unspoiled mountain scenery, and a main street that still has a dozen buildings dating from the turn of the century. Wainscott is special."

"The Chamber of Commerce should hire you to do their PR," Marisa said, shutting off her smile to avoid any invitation to further intimacy. She felt drawn to Kathleen, but she was wary about appearing too friendly. Her whole life had been a harsh instruction course in the danger of trusting her instincts about people, and the fact that she intuitively liked Kathleen wasn't a reliable guide to anything. The truth was that she had lousy judgment. Witness that she'd loved her father until his dying day, despite the fact that he had made his fortune selling weapons to terrorists. Her disastrous choice of husband merely underscored her inability to assess a person's character.

Looking back, what bothered her the most about her marriage to Evan Connors wasn't that she'd fallen in love with him the moment she met him. Lots of women confused lust with love, and she could forgive herself for a brief attack of sexual insanity. What really stuck in her craw was the humiliation of having continued to love him long after they were married. She had been so slow to read her husband that it had taken her until after their son was born to realize that if it had become convenient, Evan would have killed her with less remorse than most people feel dropping a lobster into a cooking pot.

Even before her husband's violent death seven months earlier, Marisa had come to accept that she was one of those women doomed to love the wrong man. Nowadays, in self-defense, she avoided contact with people who provoked any strong emotion at all. Life might be dull that way, but it sure was a lot safer.

She said goodbye, sounding so stiff and aloof that Kathleen was visibly taken aback. Resisting the impulse to explain that she wasn't really standoffish, merely scared and a lousy judge of character, Marisa returned to her car. She brushed a fluffy dusting of snow from the windshield and drove slowly along Main Street toward

Wainscott Refuge, rehearsing ways she could describe her current employment so that it would sound marginally more impressive than file clerk and general dog'sbody.

Up close, the imposing Wainscott building looked more welcoming than it had from the café. Thick stands of pine and spruce on either side of the house grew far enough away to screen the side windows from the view of neighboring buildings without making the place appear gloomy. A weathered stone lintel over the entrance gave the date of construction as *Anno Domini* 1903. Having survived almost a hundred years of human folly, the weathered brick and stucco building exuded a sedate self-confidence that had largely vanished from domestic architecture somewhere between the killing fields of the First World War and the economic devastation of the Depression.

Above the lintel, a stained-glass window that looked as if it might be genuine Tiffany glowed through the falling snow. Lit from within, its design of pansies, daffodils and trailing ivy cast brilliant patches of color on the snowy stone steps, imparting a touch of fantasy to the otherwise stolid facade of the building.

Women who made the wrenching decision to give up their babies for adoption probably spent a lot of their time second-guessing themselves, Marisa reflected, but the Refuge was about as perfect a setting as you could imagine for waiting out an unplanned pregnancy. If you couldn't find serenity in these surroundings, you probably wouldn't be able to find it anywhere.

She would enjoy working in this gracious old house, and the town of Wainscott would be a wonderful change for Spencer after months of living in a cramped apartment in one of the most run-down sections of Aurora.

Bottom line—she badly needed to get this job. Drawing a deep breath to bolster her courage, Marisa rang the front doorbell.

The chimes had barely faded before the imposing double doors were yanked open to reveal a handsome man in his late thirties, who stood slap in the middle of the entrance, a pail of steaming water at his side. Dressed in jeans and a T-shirt that bore the logo Body by Nautilus, he wore big, old-fashioned glasses and clutched an industrial-size mop. He stared at Marisa with his head tilted in childlike curiosity, slowly absorbing the details of her appearance.

When he had finished his inspection, he apparently decided she was harmless. He dropped the mop into the bucket so that he could hold out his hand. "Hi. I'm Mr. James T. Griffin III. I'm the maintenance technician person at Wainscott Refuge." He enunciated "maintenance technician person" with great care, as if he'd had trouble learning how to pronounce the words. "Who are you?"

She shook his hand, which was damp and foamy with detergent. "Hi, James. I'm Marisa Joubert and I've come to see Mr. Frieze."

"People call me Jimmy." He looked at the soap bubbles he'd deposited on her hand and gnawed his lip anxiously. "I made you all wet."

"Just a little. There, I've wiped the soap off on this tissue. No problem."

"It's good manners to shake hands with people the first time you meet them." Jimmy passed on this piece of information without seeming to expect any response. Belatedly, he dried his hands by wiping them on the side of his pants, but he made no attempt to move his pail or open the door any wider so that she could walk inside.

On the contrary, he fixed his gaze on Marisa as if she

presented a difficult puzzle that he was required to solve. She tried not to stare back, but it was disconcerting to see such a well-developed body encasing such an obviously damaged mind. His features were almost as perfect in basic configuration as his body, but they were marred by lank hair that looked as if it needed shampooing, and an odd little beard that grew out of the center of his chin, leaving straggly hairs sprouting in several different directions. Behind his glasses, Jimmy's eyes were an unusually bright blue. They would have been attractive, if not for the fact that they were unfocused and slightly vacant even though he was looking straight at her.

His examination completed, Jimmy seemed to forget why he'd been staring at her. His gaze wandered as if he'd lost interest in figuring out what to do with her, and she had the impression he was about to close the door and shut out the problem. Her interview clothes weren't designed for snow, and Marisa was freezing her butt off, so she resolved to take the decision about what to do next out of James T. Griffin's hands.

"Could you move your pail so that I can come in?" she asked in the firm tone of voice she reserved for Spencer when he wouldn't clean up his toys. "Mr. Frieze is expecting me. We have an appointment."

Her voice had the desired effect of refocusing Jimmy's wandering attention, but he still didn't let her inside. "Mr. Frieze is in his office, but he didn't tell me you were coming. Besides, you can't come in because the floor is wet. I have to finish mopping the floor by two o'clock."

He examined his watch with a frown. "It's already 1:37. That means it will be two o'clock in…" He broke off, his scowl dissolving into a worried wrinkle. "That means it will soon be two o'clock, doesn't it?"

"You have twenty-three minutes," Marisa said gently. "Don't worry, Jimmy. That's plenty of time to finish washing the floor."

"Are you sure?" He stared at his watch with renewed anxiety. "Now it says 1:38."

"Even so, you have plenty of time, I promise. And I won't mess up anywhere you've washed already. Look, if I walk around the edges here, I can get to Mr. Frieze's office without treading on any of the clean tiles. "

"Okay, but don't slip," Jimmy instructed her. "Wet floors are slippery, you know." He finally scooted the pail and mop behind him so that she could come in.

"Thanks for reminding me." Marisa gave him a smile far warmer than she usually accorded strangers. Despite his imposing height and his Body by Nautilus muscles, James Griffin reminded her of Spencer. Her son had a habit of repeating her instructions with the same sort of solemn intensity that Jimmy had just displayed. Of course, Spencer couldn't speak in full sentences yet, but the similarity was there, and she found herself resisting the urge to pat Jimmy's arm and tell him he was a good boy for remembering the danger of wet floors.

"Is this Mr. Frieze's office?" she asked, when she'd successfully circumnavigated the patch of damp tiles and stood next to a closed office door to the right of the hall.

"Yes. Mr. Frieze is the director of Wainscott Refuge." James said the word "director" as if it signified a position of authority only marginally less awesome than that occupied by the president of the United States. "Are you going to knock on his door? If you want to speak to him, you have to knock on his door. No need to bang, he's not deaf."

Marisa smothered a smile. "Thanks for the tip," she said. "I certainly won't knock too hard and disturb him."

She knocked softly, as promised, and the door was opened at once. Another man, slightly older than Jimmy—and even better looking because he was well-groomed—stood framed in the doorway, a portable phone in his hand. He greeted Marisa with a firm handshake and a quick smile. The sharp intelligence in his brown eyes was a marked contrast to the vacant gaze of James T. Griffin III.

"Hi, I heard the doorbell ring, but I was on the phone. I'm Stuart Frieze, and you must be Marisa Joubert, right?"

"Yes—"

"Sorry to have kept you waiting, but I finally managed to get the regional director of the IRS on the phone, in person, and I wasn't about to hang up on him. It could be months before I ever track him down again, and if I had to speak with a machine one more time, I'd have totally lost it."

"I understand. The IRS isn't an institution to be trifled with. " Marisa was impressed that Stuart Frieze pronounced her last name perfectly. "Don't worry, your Mr. Griffin has been taking good care of me."

"I'm pleased to hear it. Thanks, Jimmy. Come into my office, would you?" Stuart radiated energy that was all the more noticeable in contrast to the shambling stance of the janitor. "There seems to be a brief opening in my insane schedule, and we need to take advantage of it before I get interrupted again."

"I'm mopping the floor," James interjected. "Do you see what I'm doing, Mr. Frieze?"

"You're doing a great job, Jimmy." Stuart Frieze smiled with no hint of impatience. "Now you need to move away from the front entrance and mop the other end of the hall."

Jimmy frowned. "I did that already. Can't you see I did that already?"

Stuart held on to his smile. "Yes, now that I look properly, I can see the other end of the hall is really clean. Great job, Jimmy. And thanks for answering the door when Ms. Joubert rang the bell. That was good thinking."

Jimmy grunted. "I still have to clean the middle of the floor, though. I've done both ends and that leaves the middle. Clean the corners thoroughly, and the middle will take care of itself—"

"You're right. Thanks, Jimmy. So get to work on the middle, okay? Then go and ask Mrs. Harlowe what you should do next."

"Okay. If I've finished by two o'clock, Mrs. Harlowe is going to make me hot chocolate. I like hot chocolate." Jimmy finally rolled the pail to a dry section in the middle of the floor and started to scrub the marble tiles with surprising speed and efficiency. He whistled beneath his breath as he worked, already oblivious to their presence.

Smothering a quick sigh, Stuart held open the door to his office and gestured for Marisa to go inside, but before they could close the door, a young woman—hardly more than a girl—came running down the hall, hands clutched to her very pregnant belly. She flung herself into Stuart's arms, sobbing, and poured forth a torrent of words that sounded frantic, even though Marisa couldn't identify the language the girl was speaking.

Stuart patted the girl's back soothingly, responding to her in simple English sentences and stroking her hair until the shuddering sobs died away, reduced to soft hiccups of distress. When the girl finally stopped crying, he disentangled himself, but still kept hold of her hands. He tucked her hair behind her ear in a comforting gesture as he nodded toward Marisa.

"Ms. Joubert is here to talk about coming to work at the Refuge." Stuart didn't introduce the girl to Marisa. "Can you go back to your room for a few minutes, Anya? I'll come and see you as soon as I've finished interviewing Ms. Joubert."

The girl barely glanced at Marisa. She nodded, giving Stuart a quick hug before walking back in the direction from which she'd come. He had succeeded in drying her tears, but her shoulders were still slumped in what looked like near total despair. She passed Jimmy without a glance, and he kept stolidly washing the floor, apparently no more interested in the girl's problems than she was in his.

"Sorry about that," Stuart said, when the young woman was out of earshot. "Okay, let's try again to start our chat, shall we?"

It didn't seem appropriate to ask a direct question at the start of a job interview, especially since Stuart hadn't introduced Marisa to the girl. In the end, though, concern got the better of discretion. "That poor girl seemed devastated," she said as she followed Stuart Frieze into his office.

"She was." Stuart hesitated. "Maybe it's just as well you saw her, because that sort of anguish crops up here all the time, and anyone who works at Wainscott Refuge has to learn to cope with it. Her name is Anya Dzhambirov, and she's from Chechnya, one of the former Soviet republics that has been struggling to win independence from Russia for the past ten years. For political reasons, the States has chosen to ignore what's going on there, but basically the entire province has been denied food and medical provisions, and as well is being bombed and strafed regularly by the Russians. Anya just heard that her brother was killed in a sniper attack. He was the only close relative she had left in the world.''

Stuart's voice had thickened, and he had to pause for a moment to gain control of himself. ''Not surprisingly, she's totally grief-stricken.''

Marisa thought how petty her problems seemed in comparison to Anya's. ''That's awful,'' she said. ''I'm so sorry.''

She winced as she heard her own voice. Despite her genuine sympathy for Anya, she knew that her words emerged sounding stilted and perfunctory. Evan had been such a master manipulator of her feelings that Marisa had spent the final year of her marriage training herself to eliminate every vestige of emotion from her speech patterns. Evan couldn't manipulate emotions that he couldn't detect, and the ploy had earned her a tiny bit of personal space to maneuver in. Unfortunately, she'd discovered in the months since her husband's death that it was surprisingly difficult to bring back the vivacity and energy she'd worked so hard and long to suppress.

She tried again to inject a note of concern into her voice, ruefully aware that the harder she tried, the more insincere she sounded. ''We're so fortunate here in America. It's shocking to contemplate how much some people suffer just because they're unfortunate enough to have been born in the wrong country at the wrong time.''

Pompous ass or glib hypocrite. Marisa couldn't make up her mind which phrase best described the way she must sound.

Stuart's gaze narrowed, but he gave no other indication that he had noticed anything untoward in the way she spoke. Perhaps she'd imagined the brief moment of scrutiny, since his reply suggested that he was taking her remarks strictly at face value. "You're so right about the unfairness of it all. Anya is only seventeen, and she's lost her parents, all four of her male cousins—and now her brother. Plus, she was dumped by her brute of a boyfriend as soon as she told him she was pregnant."

The magnitude of Anya's loss was almost incomprehensible. "Has the war wiped out all of her family?" Marisa asked. "Isn't there anyone left to help her? Cousins…aunts…grandparents?"

"No, that's why she's here. That's why all of our mothers-to-be are here, because they have absolutely nowhere else to turn. Still, the good news is that Anya's a very strong young woman, a real survivor. We'll see that she does okay despite this latest blow. Fortunately, we have experienced counselors on staff, and they work miracles on a daily basis."

"You say that the mothers-to-be staying here have nowhere else to turn. Why is that? Have their families turned them out simply because they're pregnant? I didn't think that happened very often nowadays."

Stuart's expression turned somber. "It happens more often than you might think, even with young women whose families have been in the States for several generations. But we don't have many American-born women staying with us at the moment. The terms of Mr. Wainscott's will instruct us to give preference to the young women most desperately in need, and that means many of our expectant moms are immigrants with horrific past histories of war and rape and brutality to cope with. Anya's story is all too typical of what our residents have been through, I'm afraid."

Stuart Frieze broke off. "But I don't want to depress you. Or myself, for that matter. We need to look on the bright side. Even though the news about Anya's brother is bad, by some reckonings you could say she's one of the lucky ones. The emotional issues may be tough for Anya to overcome, but in practical terms, she'll do just fine.''

"How can you be sure?'' She was going to lose this job, too, if she didn't stop sounding as if she were cross-examining her prospective boss.

"Because of our past record.'' Stuart smiled. ''Providing practical help is what Wainscott Refuge is all about. Did Kathleen tell you the story of how the Refuge got started?''

"She mentioned that a wealthy land developer named Grover Wainscott had left several million dollars to help unmarried mothers.''

"But Kathleen didn't tell you why Mr. Wainscott was so interested in the plight of single moms?''

Marisa shook her head. ''No, she didn't. She was busy serving lunch, and we only had the chance to speak briefly.''

"Then let me fill you in, because it will help you to understand what we're trying to do here. It's a sad story in some ways. Grover Wainscott and his wife, Sophie, had two daughters. Their elder daughter was called Prudence, but, unfortunately, she didn't live up to her name. She got pregnant when she was seventeen and still in high school. To make matters worse, the father of the baby skipped town rather than stand by her and face the consequences of what he and Prudence had done. This was back in 1972, when the only acceptable solution to an unplanned pregnancy was a quick wedding, especially in a family like the Wainscotts.''

"I'm surprised the boyfriend was able to get away with ditching her. In a small town like this, with a situation involving the most powerful local family—''

"The high school wasn't located here in Wainscott, which made a difference," Stuart explained. "As a matter of fact, there's still only an elementary school here in town. For the older students, we have a consolidated school district that brings in kids from all over the county. So the boyfriend wasn't from Wainscott, and Prudence wasn't nearly as well-known on campus as you'd have expected."

"Still, she must have been frantic when her boyfriend skipped town. What a rotten way for him to treat her."

Stuart looked sad. "Yes, but so typical of high school kids who are thinking with their hormones, not their heads. And then they get terrified when they find themselves facing adult consequences."

Stuart was too willing to provide excuses for the scumbag boyfriend. Job interview or not, Marisa couldn't suppress her sarcasm. "Forgive me if I can't work up much sympathy for the boy. Poor Prudence. I bet she felt she had absolutely no options."

"You're right. It was one of those typical teenage situations where Grover Wainscott had forbidden her to continue seeing the boyfriend, saying the boy was untrustworthy and after her money. Of course, the last thing Prudence wanted was to go to her parents and admit they'd been right, so she decided to get rid of the baby. Abortion was still illegal at the time, and in desperation she tried to perform an abortion on herself. I understand she used the traditional wire coat hanger."

Marisa flinched. "She must have been truly desperate."

"I'll say. And the story just gets worse. Prudence bungled the abortion—how could she not?—and her younger sister, Helen, who was only nine or ten, came into the bathroom and found Prudence bleeding to death on the tile floor.''

''Oh, my God!'' The scene Stuart painted was far too vivid for comfort, and Marisa shifted uneasily in her chair. ''Poor Prudence. And poor little Helen. What a nightmare for her to grow up with.''

He nodded. ''Especially since there's no happy ending. Understandably, Helen was terrified when she found her sister. She didn't understand what was going on, of course, but she knew it was something life-threatening. Her immediate reaction was to call her parents, but Prudence kept begging her not to, so Helen was left trying to staunch the bleeding. Apparently Grover Wainscott was a strict, stern father, and they were both quite scared of him, so Helen didn't attempt to override her sister's request. Eventually Prudence passed out, at which point Helen did go and find her mother. But by then it was too late, and Prudence died in agony a few hours later.''

''What a tragic story.'' Marisa's stomach was churning with sympathy, even though Prudence had died almost thirty years earlier.

''Yes, it is tragic, and Grover Wainscott never forgave himself for what he saw as his failure. I can understand that. Heaven knows, there was plenty of blame to spread around. Anyway, the upshot was that Grover became an active participant in the campaign to legalize abortions. Interestingly, though, he never expressed any special interest in the adoption process while he was alive, so it was quite a shock when he died and his family discovered that he'd left this house, and more than half his fortune, to set up the Prudence Wainscott Foundation to provide adoption services for unwed mothers. The Refuge was established six years ago to fulfill the requirements of his will.''

Marisa wasn't sure whether to feel more sorry for Prudence, who'd died, or Helen, who'd watched her sister bleed to death, or poor old Grover Wainscott, who'd been forced to live for a quarter of a century with the knowledge that his eldest daughter had been too afraid of him to ask for help. "This seems to be a story with no happy endings for anybody."

"Except you have to remind yourself that the fallout from those events has been positive in many ways. Fortunately, Mr. Wainscott took one of the few courses open to him that truly honors his daughter's memory. Because of her death, and his terrible sense of loss, several hundred women, their babies, and their adoptive parents have all found happy endings here at the Refuge."

It sounded like the wrap-up to a fund-raising speech, but Marisa was prepared to forgive Stuart his polemics. "It's a strange quirk of fate to think that Anya Dzhambirov from Chechnya is going to have her baby safely here in Colorado because of a failed abortion thirty years ago."

"It's very strange, but exciting, too. We have highly qualified adoptive parents already lined up and anxiously awaiting the birth of Anya's baby. A lovely couple from Wisconsin, with ancestors on one side of the family who actually came from Chechnya. In addition, when Anya finally leaves here, we'll make sure she has a decent job waiting for her. She's young, she's resilient and she has most of her life ahead of her—"

"But she's still lost her family and her baby."

"Her baby won't be lost," Stuart said sharply. "Anya has simply chosen to give her child the best possible start in life. A very wise and generous decision on her part."

"Yes, of course."

"You sound doubtful, Ms. Joubert. If you don't support the ideals behind the adoption process, I don't think you would be very comfortable working here.''

"Oh, I do support the idea of adoption. I know it's often the best possible solution for the mother and her baby, not to mention all those couples who can't have children and are longing to find a child to bring into their homes. I'm very much in favor of adoption.''

Marisa had spent more than two years trying to carry a baby successfully to term, and she'd thought a lot about the ramifications of adoption. Her response was entirely sincere, at least intellectually. It was also the correct one from Stuart's point of view, and he smiled at her approvingly.

"I'm glad you feel that way. We like to think that Wainscott Refuge is all about looking ahead. When the horror stories pile up—and they do—I have to remind myself that we need to focus on hope and the future, not despair and the past.''

He sounded as if he was quoting from an inspirational manual written for the Refuge's pregnant moms, but it wasn't a bad formula to live by, Marisa reflected. She should remember it next time she got ready to wallow in self-pity.

"How many pregnant women are living here right now?'' she asked.

"We have twenty-four pregnant residents at the moment. That's our maximum, and we've never had less than the full complement of young women here since I took over management of our program.'' Stuart spoke briskly. "We also have a full-time nurse-midwife, an aide for any medical emergencies that crop up overnight, and I live on the grounds in what used to be a guest cottage. Plus, we have the two counselors I mentioned who visit on Wednesday afternoon each week and are on call if there's a psychological emergency our midwife can't handle. We're also lucky enough to have an arrangement with a group of ob-gyn doctors from Estes Park. Each Saturday morning, one of the doctors from the practice makes the trip out here to conduct routine medical check-ups. The actual birth is about the only medical procedure we don't take care of here at the Refuge."

"It sounds very self-sufficient," Marisa commented.

"Yes. We pride ourselves on being highly efficient at delivering great medical care at reasonable cost. Unfortunately, we're not as well-organized administratively as we are medically. We've been short-staffed in the office for months."

Stuart pointed to the piles of paper stacked on every available flat surface. "You can see what a mess I'm in. My longtime secretary retired six months ago, and then we lost our clerk-receptionist when her husband relocated to Salt Lake City. With the booming economy in Denver, we've had a hard time finding permanent replacements. The temps we've hired do their best, but, to be honest, their best isn't good enough. At a certain point, unless there's somebody taking charge of filing and record-keeping on a regular basis, there's no system in the world that's going to stave off chaos."

Marisa tried not to sound breathless with hope. "I have quite a lot of experience dealing with filing systems and office administration. A lot of my current job description deals with record-keeping."

"That's great." Stuart's expression turned rueful. "I'm tempted to lie and say that you'll find this job a breeze. But I won't, because there's no point in hiring you and losing you the moment you find out the truth. Our office systems are on the point of meltdown, which would be bad in any organization. At the Refuge, it's a disaster. We're not dealing in widgets, we're dealing in human lives, and I live in dread that one day soon we're going to have a new baby arrive, only to discover that we've lost the address and phone number of the prospective parents.''

''I would enjoy meeting the challenge of reorganizing your office systems,'' Marisa said. ''I'm a very efficient person, and I'm trained to deal with families that are in emotional crisis.'' She managed not to blush at the exaggeration. After all, she had spent a lot of time at the funeral home dealing with grief-stricken family members. And for someone who had left school in the tenth grade and had no business training, she was quite efficient at routine office chores. Of course, in comparison to any high school kid who'd taken a couple of business courses at the local community college, she was clueless. But she would learn fast if given the opportunity—she knew she would.

She didn't want to give Stuart the chance to start probing her nonexistent qualifications. One question about spreadsheet programs, and she was a dead duck. To prevent him asking something terrifying about her accounting skills, or her familiarity with FICA forms, or a host of other hair-raising questions she had no idea how to answer, she launched into a description of her current job, managing to make her duties sound wide-ranging, if not exactly challenging.

''Plus, the timing is right for both of us,'' she concluded. ''My job finishes on Friday, and you need somebody who can start work right away.''

''I think you'd fit in very well with us,'' Stuart said. Her heart beat a little tattoo of triumph and relief.

''The job is yours if you'd like to take it. We're offering a salary of two thousand a month, payable every two weeks. I know the salary is low, especially in view of the current tight job market, but we're a nonprofit organization and our board of trustees is very conservative. However, I can offer a couple of advantages that you might not find at another organization, quite apart from the pleasure of living in Wainscott. First of all, we offer excellent fringe benefits, and employees are not required to make any contribution to our health plan. Second, I can get you a really good deal on an apartment. Helen Wainscott has inherited several pieces of property from her father, and, naturally, she's very supportive of the work we're doing here at the Refuge. When she heard that we were having difficulty finding reliable office help, she offered to make an apartment available for three hundred and fifty bucks a month. That's less than half what she could charge on the open market.''

Stuart leaned back in his chair, toying with a paper clip. ''Okay, that's the deal. Would you be interested, Ms. Joubert?''

Marisa swallowed hard. She earned less than twenty thousand at her current job and had to pay four hundred dollars a month for an apartment that wasn't even in a safe neighborhood. ''I'm interested,'' she said, trying to sound as if she were considering the possibilities, as opposed to being so thrilled that she was almost ready to jump across the desk and throw her arms around Stuart's neck.

She folded her hands in her lap, keeping them tightly knitted to contain her excitement. ''My apartment lease in Aurora expires at the end of the month, so there's nothing to stop me moving up here over the weekend. The fact that Ms. Wainscott is willing to rent me her apartment at such a reasonable rate makes the salary much more acceptable.''

"Wonderful." Stuart gave a smile. "I'll call and confirm the arrangement with her this evening. She currently lives in New York, but I have a number where I can always reach her—"

"Thank you. But there's one other thing I need to take care of. I can move this weekend if the apartment is available that soon, but before I can start work, I need to arrange for day care for Spencer."

"Spencer?"

"He's my son. Is there anywhere in town you can recommend?"

"You have a son?" Stuart stroked his chin. "How old is he?"

"He was two just a few weeks ago."

Stuart didn't attempt to find out if she had a husband, or an ex-husband, which many prospective employers did even though it was technically illegal. Far from sounding hostile to the idea of employing the mother of a toddler, he flashed her a sudden warm smile.

"You know, I'm starting to think we might be an exceptionally good match for each other, Marisa. I'm sure that finding good day care for your son has been a problem for you, right?"

She nodded. "It's been a big problem." One that she'd only partially solved in Aurora by putting Spencer in a super-deluxe child care facility that consumed a third of her take-home pay.

"Well, I have a really enticing offer for you. We have twenty-four young women living right here on the premises, and each of them is required to put in at least three hours a day of chores related to the well-being of our community. We've utilized their services to run an on-site day care facility for the past two years. I found that counselors and nurses are much easier to hire and keep on staff if we can offer high-quality, safe child care. We're licensed to have five toddlers on the premises, and at the moment we're only taking care of three. Your son would make four. And since he would be cared for by our residents, working to benefit the community, there would be no charge to you for the service. Which must make the salary I offered look a great deal more attractive.''

That was a major understatement. With subsidized rent and no child care costs, her salary would be verging on luxurious. Marisa felt her body relax from a tension that she only now realized had been intensifying for weeks. The prospect of having Spencer just down the hall while she worked was so wonderful that she was afraid to speak in case she said the wrong thing and blew this magnificent chance.

Stuart seemed to misinterpret her silence. ''I know the salary isn't great, but the fact that you don't have any child care costs would be at least four hundred a month to you versus any other job. Plus, I'm flexible on your work hours, within reason. If you want to come in nine-to-five one day, and eight-to-four the next, you just have to let me know, and I'll almost certainly be able to accommodate your needs.''

Marisa finally managed to get her vocal cords to cooperate. ''Thank you, Mr. Frieze, for your offer. The salary does become more attractive when it's combined with the other advantages. If you can arrange for the apartment rental you mentioned, then I would like to accept the job.''

''That's great!'' Stuart exclaimed. He stood up and leaned across the desk, extending his hand.

"Welcome aboard, Marisa. Let's take a tour of the facilities, shall we? I'm delighted that you're going to be joining us here at Prudence Wainscott Refuge. I know we're going to work really well together."

Three

On Monday morning, Spencer decided to be as un-cooperative as only a worried two-year-old can be. He didn't want to wake up, didn't want to get dressed, didn't want to drink milk or apple juice, and expressed his opinion of the oatmeal Marisa had cooked for his breakfast by dumping it all over the kitchen floor she'd only finished scrubbing at eleven-thirty the previous night.

Trying to react calmly so that she didn't increase Spencer's tension level, not to mention her own, Marisa did a half-assed job of wiping the oatmeal from the floor, and a slightly more efficient job of sponging the apple juice out of his curly blond hair. She reminded herself that a year ago she would have considered herself in heaven if she and Spencer had been living alone in their own apartment with no nanny to spy on them and no husband to torment her into submission. Evan's unexpected death had set her free, and she couldn't let mundane problems prevent her from focusing on the big picture. If she could just reach the point where she felt secure in her job at the Refuge, she was positive she and Spencer would be able to live happily ever after in Wainscott.

Fortunately, the weather was in a benevolent mood, even if Spencer wasn't. With a touch of springtime magic, the snow of the previous week had vanished from the town, although the mountain peaks were still capped with sparkling white. A warm sun shone from a sky of cloudless blue, and a few brave green leaves had risked unfurling on the sumac trees growing amongst the conifers that surrounded the perimeter of the small apartment complex. A great day for new beginnings, Marisa decided, even if her son did seem thoroughly spooked at the prospect of facing yet another change in his young life.

Bundling Spencer into his car seat and tucking his teddy bear onto his lap for comfort, Marisa kissed the crease of his neck where a tiny fold of baby fat still lingered. He rewarded her with a hug and one of his sweetest smiles. With a change of mood as unpredictable as the spring weather, he cheered up enough to sing *Pat-a-cake, pat-a-cake,* with tuneless enthusiasm, for the entire car ride. With no traffic to speak of, and no ice on the roads, the commute was short, which made Spencer's one-note serenade almost painless.

Arriving at the Refuge with eleven minutes to spare, Marisa allowed herself to hope that she wouldn't be late, after all. The walk from where she parked her car to the Refuge entrance should have taken no more than a couple of minutes. Unfortunately, Spencer's merry mood vanished when he realized that their destination was a huge building he'd never seen before. He decided that the multiple temper tantrums he'd already thrown that morning hadn't been sufficient to convince his mother that he was feeling big-time insecure. As soon as Marisa took his hand and started to walk him across the parking lot, he threw his teddy bear into what was probably the only remaining puddle of melted snow in the entire town of Wainscott. With typical two-year-old illogic, when he saw that he'd dropped his favorite toy facedown in the water, he burst into noisy tears, refusing to move.

"Bear durty. Bear need a baff," he insisted between sobs, watching out of the corner of his eye, as Marisa rescued the teddy and simultaneously tried to urge her son to start walking again.

She shook droplets of icy mud off Bear and grabbed Spencer's hand. "We'll give him a bath tonight. Come on, pumpkin, we have to hurry."

"No." Spencer's expression became mutinous. "Wash Bear *now.*"

"We can't bathe Bear right now, there's no clean water out here. And Mommy has to go to her new job. "

Spencer's wails increased to an ear-splitting decibel. Marisa hastily rummaged around in the bag of supplies she'd packed and found a baby wipe. Ignoring his protests, she cleaned the tears from Spencer's face, then rubbed the mud off the teddy as best she could.

"Look, he's clean now." She held out the teddy for her son's inspection.

"Bear *wet.*"

"Yes, but only a little bit. If you don't want to carry him, I will. Come on, pumpkin, we don't have far to walk. See, we're just going up the steps to the big house over there."

It was a major mistake to remind him of their destination. "No. No!" Spencer snatched his teddy and sat down in the puddle, hugging Bear to his chest and glaring at Marisa. Shivering from the cold, he nevertheless refused to budge.

He looked both forlorn and ridiculous, a heart-melting combination. Marisa knew that in other circumstances, she would have laughed and swept him into a giant hug. As it was, she experienced a humiliating urge to cry. If she picked Spencer up by force, he would wriggle and leave muddy streaks all over her skirt and jacket. Not to mention the fact that in his current mood he was capable of yelling in protest at the top of his lungs for the next several minutes—which was decidedly not the way she wanted to introduce her son to her new employers. On the other hand, if she continued to attempt to coax him out of the puddle by sweet reason, it looked as if they might still be here at lunchtime.

Jimmy the janitor rode up at that moment on a bike. He padlocked the bike to a stand next to the parking lot fence, then ambled across the lot toward Marisa and Spencer.

"Hi," he said to Marisa, poking his fingers into his scraggy beard. He appeared oblivious to her son, who was now drumming his heels in the puddle, sending muddy water flying. "How you doin', Ms....um, ma'am? Mr. Frieze says you're comin' to work at the Refuge."

"Hi, Jimmy. Yes, I'm starting work in the office this morning. Just as soon as I can persuade Spencer here to get his butt out of the puddle."

Jimmy stared down at Spencer, who stopped crying long enough to scowl back. Jimmy's ill-fitting glasses slipped down his nose, and he slowly pushed them into place, contemplating the puddle and its contents.

"Is he your baby?" Jimmy asked finally. "He looks like you."

People commented on Spencer's likeness to her all the time, and Marisa always felt a spurt of relief that her son hadn't inherited his father's looks, even though Evan had been very handsome. She hoped fervently that Spencer's character would owe as little to his father as his appearance.

"Yes, this is my son," she said. "His name is Spencer and he's two years old."

Jimmy's forehead wrinkled in puzzlement. "Why is he sitting in the mud?"

A darn good question, Marisa thought wryly. "Because he's scared of going to a new place and meeting new people, so he's behaving badly to let me know he's feeling scared."

Jimmy reached between the buttons of his quilted plaid shirt and scratched his chest while he assimilated this information, although Marisa wasn't sure he'd really understood her explanation. After a few seconds of scratching, he squatted down in front of Spencer. The pair of them eyed each other in silence, until Jimmy pulled off his glove and stuck his hand into the puddle.

He drew back sharply, shaking off icy droplets. "Gee, this water's cold," he said. "Why do you wanna sit in it?"

Spencer stuck out his bottom lip. "Bear inna water."

"What bear? Who is bear?"

Silently, Spencer held up his teddy. Jimmy gave the toy a quick glance, but he obviously wasn't up to inventing chitchat with a stuffed animal. Ignoring Bear, he looked back at Spencer. "You wanna ride on my shoulders, big guy?"

"No."

Jimmy paid no attention whatever to this response. He simply reached out and lifted Bear with one hand and Spencer with the other. He swung Spencer up over his head, depositing him on his shoulders, with Bear somehow squashed between Spencer's tummy and the back of Jimmy's neck. Spencer was too astonished to protest, and Jimmy strode off, humming under his breath, indifferent to the cold, muddy water seeping out of Spencer's pants and onto the collar of his flannel shirt.

Marisa ran to catch up, expecting howls of protest as

soon as Spencer recovered his breath. But far from protesting, Spencer appeared thrilled with his perch on Jimmy's shoulders and gave her a happy grin. "Look, Mommy! Me tall!"

"You sure are. You're nearly as high as the sky." She was very grateful for the janitor's help, even though his nonchalant attitude toward Spencer's physical safety was giving her fits. Spencer, of course, didn't mind in the least that there was nothing to keep him safely anchored except his own chubby hands and Jimmy's heart-stoppingly casual clasp around his ankles. Marisa repressed the urge to grab her son, but huddled close to Jimmy, ready to catch Spencer the second he slipped.

"Play horsey!" Spencer commanded, bouncing energetically on the janitor's shoulders.

"Okay." Jimmy broke into a snappy jog. Spencer shrieked with delight, and Marisa narrowly avoided a heart attack. She extended her hand in front of Jimmy's chest, and he stopped abruptly.

"Yes, ma'am?"

"Just slow down a bit, could you, Jimmy? Spencer isn't holding on as tightly as he should."

"Sure thing, ma'am."

Jimmy obediently walked a little slower, but in contrast to his usual ambling pace, he looked ready to break into a run again at any minute. Trotting to keep up, Marisa searched for a topic of conversation that might engage his attention enough to keep him safely slowed down, while they crossed the remaining few yards of concrete parking lot.

"Spencer isn't usually this friendly with people he doesn't know," Marisa said. "You're doing great with him, Jimmy. Are you used to spending time with little children?"

"Nope. I never had kids 'cause I'm not married. I earn good wages, though."

"I bet that's because you work hard. Do you have brothers and sisters, Jimmy?"

"I have one sister who's dead. She died in a car accident just a coupla months ago."

"I'm so sorry. You must miss her."

"I miss her real bad. She was a nice sister. Real smart, you know, but she was always kind to people. Especially to me." For a moment, Jimmy's voice thickened, then he seemed to cheer up again. "I have another sister who isn't dead. Her name is Lizzie, and she's forty-three years old."

"Is Lizzie married?" Marisa asked.

Jimmy nodded. "She sure is. She has a husband and two children. I don't see Lizzie very often 'cause her husband doesn't like me. He says I'm a 'freak of nature.'"

Jimmy enunciated the final three words carefully, but he seemed untroubled by his brother-in-law's disrespectful assessment, and carried on almost in the same breath. "I'm thirty-seven," he said. "My birthday is on next September the fourteenth, and then I'll be thirty-eight. How old are you?"

"I'm twenty-eight."

"That's younger than me." Jimmy's forehead creased into the scowl that she already recognized as indicating deep thought. "That's nine years younger than me."

"Very good, Jimmy. You worked that sum out just right. Thirty-seven take away twenty-eight leaves nine."

Arithmetic was apparently not a subject to hold Jimmy's attention unless he was the one doing the sums. "You have pretty hair," he said. "It's golden like a marigold. My sister Lizzie dyes her hair with brown stuff that comes out of a bottle. Do you dye your hair?''

Marisa found herself stifling a grin. ''Er, no. Actually my hair has always been this color. It hasn't changed much since I was a little kid.''

''My mom grows lots of flowers in her garden. Her garden is real pretty.''

Having a toddler helped her to fill in the missing connectors in Jimmy's conversation. Marisa guessed that his mind had leaped from hair the color of marigolds, to flowers in his mother's garden. ''Does your mom have a big garden, Jimmy?''

''Pretty big. She lives in Columbus, Ohio. My dad lives in Dallas, Texas. They're divorced. Are you divorced?''

''No. My husband's dead.''

Jimmy stopped abruptly. ''I'm real sorry.''

In the months since Evan died, Marisa still hadn't found an acceptable way to respond to people's sympathy. ''Spencer misses him a lot,'' she said, surprised to hear herself making the admission. Evan had been so unrelentingly cruel to her that she wanted to pretend he had no good points at all. But, in truth, he had loved their son in his own way, and she wondered why Jimmy, of all people, had provoked her to acknowledge that uncomfortable truth.

Jimmy seemed to sense her reluctance to speak about her husband, or perhaps he just got bored. With another lightning change of topic, he pointed out a magpie pecking in the dirt at the side of the parking area.

''See that big old magpie over there? He's busy searching for his breakfast. He eats worms and bugs. Oh, look, he's found a long squiggly worm.''

''Worms yukky!'' Spencer remarked.

"How do you know? Did you eat worms? I never ate worms." Jimmy seemed to feel that this omission made it impossible for him to pass judgment on their culinary appeal.

Spencer shot a glance toward his mother, almost as if he knew there was something strange about Jimmy's response. Oblivious to the exchange of glances, Jimmy climbed up the steps to the front door, whistling blithely.

"There's Delilah," he said, as they reached the entrance. "She always waits for me every morning. She's my friend."

Delilah turned out to be a scrawny tabby cat with only one ear and an expression even more haughty than that of most felines. She did, however, brush against Jimmy's legs and condescend to give a *purr* of welcome.

"She likes me a real lot," Jimmy said. Without dislodging Spencer, Jimmy bent on one knee so that he could scratch the tabby's remaining ear. "Hi, Delilah. Did you sleep well?"

"She sure seems to like you," Marisa said, as the cat's purrs increased in volume.

"Mrs. Harlowe says she likes anyone who gives her food, but I reckon she likes me better 'n most."

With considerable dexterity, Jimmy scooped up the cat and tucked her under his jacket. He then managed to stand up and ring the doorbell without dropping either of his wriggling charges. Apparently whatever caused his diminished IQ hadn't affected his physical coordination.

"Where's the kitty?" Spencer tugged on Jimmy's hair to attract his attention.

"Still here." Jimmy patted his chest. "I'm gonna give Delilah some milk for her breakfast when we get inside."

"Milk yukky." Regrettably, Spencer's conversation still seemed stuck in a negative mode.

Jimmy considered the comment carefully. "Milk isn't yukky if you're a cat," he said finally. "And Delilah is a cat."

"I a boy," Spencer said.

"Me, too," Jimmy said. "You're a boy and I'm a boy, but Delilah is a girl like your mom."

"I a boy, you a boy. Mommy a girl. Kitty-cat a girl." Spencer chuckled, for some reason vastly entertained by this cosmic insight into sexual differentiation. He was still laughing when the door was opened by a plain but pleasant-looking woman in her mid-forties.

Jimmy combed his fingers through his scrawny beard, smoothing down the wisps that stuck out. "Hi, Mrs. Harlowe. Nice sunny day, isn't it?"

"It sure is." Mrs. Harlowe gave the janitor a smile that was quite affectionate. "And who's this little guy riding on your shoulders?"

"He's..." Jimmy shuffled his feet and looked down. "I don't recall his name."

"This is Spencer, my son," Marisa said, stepping forward to rescue Jimmy from embarrassment. "And I'm Marisa Joubert. I'm starting work here today in the office."

"You want to take your kid back now?" Jimmy asked Marisa, before Mrs. Harlowe could reply to her. He leaned sideways, and Spencer slid down his arm onto the floor. By some miracle, Spencer landed feet first, still clutching his teddy. Marisa grabbed her son with one hand before he could run off, and extended the other to Mrs. Harlowe.

The housekeeper shook it briskly. "Nice to meet you, Marisa. My name's Fran, by the way." She patted Spencer's cheek. "Hi, little guy, how are you doing? That's a real nice teddy bear you've got there. I like the scarf he's wearing. What's his name?''

"Bear. Bear wet.''

"Is he? Never mind, he'll soon dry out in here.'' Fran smiled. "Gorgeous curls he's got,'' she said, brushing her fingers through Spencer's hair. "They almost seem wasted on a boy, don't they?''

Spencer submitted in silence to the indignity of having his hair ruffled by a total stranger. Which, at the rate things were going this morning, was about the best Marisa could hope for.

"Stuart told me you'd be starting work today if you could get settled into your apartment in time,'' Fran continued. "Glad to see you made it.''

"Just barely,'' Marisa admitted. "I had a hectic weekend getting organized, but the apartment was in great shape considering the previous tenant only moved out twenty-four hours before I moved in.''

Jimmy scuffed his toe at a crack in the tile, clearly bored by the conversation going on around him. "I used up all the hot chocolate in the cupboard at my apartment,'' he informed the housekeeper. "There's none left.''

"Never mind,'' Fran said. "We'll write it down on your shopping list, so's you remember to buy another box when you go to the store. Today's Monday, remember, and you always go shopping after work on Mondays.''

"Yes, I remembered. I brought my money.'' Jimmy patted his hip pocket. "Can I have hot chocolate for my morning snack, since I didn't have any for breakfast?''

"Sure you can, if you work hard. Run along into the kitchen, Jimmy, and I'll meet you there in a minute. I need you to help me clean the range. It's thick with grease.''

"Okay. I'll get my supplies."

"Tell Jimmy 'thank you' for the ride on his shoulders," Marisa instructed her son.

"Bye-bye," Spencer said, waving his hand. "Fank you."

"You're welcome." Jimmy walked off, hunched over, arms clutched around his stomach as if he was in acute pain.

Fran flashed a wry glance at Marisa. "He thinks I don't know he's got that darn cat hidden under his jacket. As if I'm not going to notice when he pours out half a pint of milk for the dratted critter every morning."

"He means well," Marisa said, somewhat surprised to hear herself springing to Jimmy's defense. "And Delilah probably helps to keep the mice down."

Fran made an impatient clicking sound, but she looked amused rather than annoyed. "You're another cat lover, are you? I can take 'em or leave 'em, myself. Oh, well, Jimmy's a good lad, for all he's got nothing upstairs. In case you were wondering, you won't get a spot of trouble out of him. You just have to get used to him asking all sorts of personal questions and the like, but you mustn't take offense if he asks something unsuitable. He doesn't understand that just because he wants to know the answer, that doesn't make it all right to ask the question."

"I'm sure we'll get along just fine," Marisa said. "Jimmy seems very polite in his own way."

"He is that. And better natured than a lot of people with twice his brains."

Marisa glanced at her watch and saw that it was a minute away from nine o'clock. "I'm sorry to run, but I really need to hurry and get Spencer settled into his new day care situation. Mr. Frieze did show me over the place when I came for my interview, but I don't quite remember how to get to the nursery. Could you point me in the right direction?"

"Sure. Go down the hall here, turn left at the end, and it's the second door on the right. Did you meet Janet McLaughlin already? She's the on-staff midwife, and her daughter must be right about the same age as your little guy."

"Spencer is two."

"And so is Janet's little girl, although she's coming up for three next month. Her name's Alicia, and she'll probably be glad to have a new playmate. Do you want me to come with you?"

"Thanks, but I don't want to take your time." Marisa gave the housekeeper a hurried smile. "It's been good to talk with you, but I know there's a pile of work waiting for me in the office and I don't want to be late on my first day."

Fran gave a friendly nod. "It's good to have you here," she said. "Stuart badly needs decent help in the office. Poor man—he works himself way too hard and he could use a break. Enjoy your first day at the Refuge. We're all very friendly here, and I'm sure you'll find this is a real nice place to work."

Four

At 4:45 in the afternoon, Marisa was still wading through the pile of papers left on her desk by the office temps who'd preceded her over the past several months. Some people might have considered the task tedious, but she wasn't at all bored. Not only was she thrilled to have gainful employment, but the sense of bringing order out of chaos was gratifying.

She couldn't kid herself that there was much scope for initiative or brilliance in what she was doing, but she was rather proud of her day's work. Heaven knows, if there was one thing that living with Evan had taught her, it was how to be compulsively neat and organized, and she figured she had lucked into one of the few jobs where she might actually be more efficient than any potential competitors.

She glossed over the thought of Evan with an ease she wouldn't have believed possible only weeks earlier. Maybe one day quite soon she would reach the point where she could hear his name spoken out loud without feeling physically sick. That was a goal worth striving toward, she thought, dusting off her hands.

She heard Stuart Frieze return to his office, just as she finished reorganizing a file drawer that was supposed to contain correspondence with various federal and state regulatory bodies but which actually had been crammed with every file folder for which her predecessors had been unable to find a home.

He stuck his head around the partition that separated her work space from his much more elegant office. "Marisa—you're still here. I'm so glad I caught you before you left for the day. Sorry I got tied up and abandoned you to your own devices all afternoon. I hope you didn't run into any major problems?"

Marisa shook her head. "On the contrary. Thank heavens, everything seems to be going smoothly."

In fact, she had been secretly grateful when Stuart hurried off to attend a meeting with a group of interns from Catholic Charities. She had worked much more efficiently alone, with nobody hovering over her and making her nervous.

"There were seventeen phone calls for you," she said. "I clipped all the message slips together and left them in the center of your desk. Once I've become more familiar with the systems here, I'm sure I'll be able to handle some of the calls myself."

"Phone messages clipped together and put on my desk?" Stuart raised his eyebrows in mock amazement. "Did you by any chance take down the names *and* the numbers of the people I'm supposed to call back?"

"Every one of them. And I asked the callers to repeat the phone numbers to be sure I didn't make a mistake."

"Be still my heart!" He grinned at her, eyes twinkling. "I can't believe I've managed to hire someone who understands that where phone numbers are concerned, *approximate* doesn't cut it. I'm almost afraid to ask—did you find time to file any papers in between taking all the phone messages?"

Marisa pointed to two of the in-trays on her desk,

which had been piled high at lunchtime but were now empty. "As you can see, I've made a start."

Stuart's expression transformed from friendly teasing to one of genuine astonishment. "Good heavens, that's great, Marisa. You've done more in one afternoon than the last three temps achieved the entire time they were with us."

"Filing papers away is pretty easy," she replied, coloring a little at the compliment. She smiled up at him. "The real test comes when you ask me to find a specific document, and I can actually do it."

"Stuart? Are you in there?" Janet McLaughlin, an attractive, petite woman with bright red hair, burst into Stuart's office. Marisa had realized quite early in the day that there was always some mini-crisis demanding the director's personal attention, and this just promised to be the most recent. Fran Harlowe hadn't been exaggerating when she said that Stuart was hopelessly overworked.

"Hi, Marisa. Have you seen Stuart? Oh, there he is. I'm so glad I found you!" Janet exclaimed. "I've been searching for you for the past twenty minutes."

"Naturally my office was the last place you thought of looking," he said dryly.

"Naturally." She flashed him a quick grin. "You have to get a pager, Stuart."

"I have a pager."

"Yeah, but the secret is that you have to press the little button that turns it on. Then people would always know where you are."

"Yes, they would, wouldn't they?" Stuart returned her smile. "Well, you're in luck, Janet. I just got back here a minute ago, and you're the first person to find me, so you get one-hundred percent of my attention, at least until the next person tracks me down. What's up?"

"I wanted to let you know that Katerina has started labor. She's getting pretty regular contractions every fifteen minutes or so."

"Katerina?" Stuart frowned. "That's early, isn't it?"

"Who knows?" Janet sounded resigned. "Maybe it's early. Or maybe not. She didn't notice she was pregnant for two or three months, and then she didn't go to the doctor because she hoped the pregnancy would just go away, so we don't have any reliable medical records about the beginning of her pregnancy. We're going strictly by the ultrasound we took in February. According to that, she has another three weeks to go before her due date."

"Hmm. Three weeks early shouldn't be too much of a problem," Stuart said. "Should it?"

"No, everything should be okay. Even if she's only at thirty-seven weeks, the baby's lungs should be functional. Hopefully. The pregnancy has been entirely normal so far."

"Good. Have you phoned Dr. Curtis to let him know Katerina is in labor?"

"Of course, and he's recommending that we transfer her to the hospital in Boulder right away. Since we're not sure of the due date, he wants us to be in the hospital if there should be any problems with the labor."

"Absolutely. Much better to be safe than sorry. So let's get going. I assume we don't need an ambulance to transport Katerina?"

"Oh, no. She's still in the very early stages of labor, and it's a first baby. She probably has anywhere from eight to twelve hours still to go."

"Then I'll drive her to the hospital myself, since I don't have any special plans for tonight. Help her pack an overnight bag, will you, Janet?"

"That's what I left her doing, but she should be through by now. I'll go check and be right back."

"Great. Bring Katerina here to my office whenever she's ready, and we'll get on our way to the hospital. We don't want to be caught short if this baby decides to put in an appearance quicker than anyone expects."

Janet gave a mock salute and left, zooming down the corridor like the Road Runner.

"I've seen Janet several times today," Marisa said. "But so far, I've never seen her walk anywhere."

"I don't think she understands the concept *walk*." Stuart gave Marisa a rueful smile. "We're really throwing you in the deep end on your first day here, aren't we. I wish I could pretend that today was especially hectic, but I can't. We have a resident going into labor every couple of weeks, so this sort of controlled chaos is pretty much what you can expect."

"I've enjoyed today," Marisa said. "And having worked at a funeral parlor for five months, it's a really pleasant change to wait for a baby to be born as opposed to helping people select coffins and headstones."

"I'll bet." Stuart shook his head. "That must have been a tough place to work. Whereas here..." He smiled. "You know, however many times I watch one of our residents go through this birthing process, somehow it never becomes predictable, and the baby's arrival is always a miracle that lifts your spirits."

A definite improvement on comforting the bereaved, Marisa reflected, even if she couldn't help worrying about how Katerina would feel next week when her baby had gone to its new home, and she was left to cope with the prospect of getting on with the rest of her life at a time when her body was flooded with postpartum hormones.

Still, according to Stuart, the Refuge didn't turn out its residents the moment they gave birth, so Katerina would have a few weeks more in this protective environment to find her emotional bearings. Marisa was glad for that.

Stuart broke into her thoughts. "I missed lunch and I'm going to grab a sandwich from the kitchen before Katerina and I leave for Boulder. I've eaten enough hospital food over the past couple of years to know that it's much better not to."

"Good thinking." Marisa smiled. "I'll see you tomorrow, then. With good news about Katerina's baby, I hope."

"Yes." Stuart swung around in the doorway. "Oh, before you go home, could you find the file for Katerina and leave it on my desk? Her last name is Tedescu. And I'll need the file on the prospective parents, too. Their name is Ringwold. If you could jot the Ringwolds' number down for me, I'll give them a call and let them know their baby's about to arrive in the world."

"That must be a nice part of your job," Marisa said, riffling through files in the cabinet drawers in search of ones bearing the relevant names.

"It's a terrific part of my job," Stuart said, his expression softening. "Our adoptive parents come from all over the States, so they don't always make it in time for the actual birth. Still, they usually get to meet their new baby within a few hours of its arrival. Talk about love at first sight—there seems to be an instant connection, as if God really did intend for each particular baby to end up with the specific set of parents we find for him or her."

He stopped abruptly and cleared his throat. "Anyway, we don't really have time to stand around and chat. I'm going in search of that sandwich. I'll be right back."

Marisa found the files without difficulty, since Stuart

had managed to keep the most important personnel records up-to-date and in alphabetical order, despite the administrative meltdown in the rest of the office. Katerina's file contained only the basic information that she had immigrated from Romania in 1999 at the age of eighteen, and that the father of her baby was the husband of the sister she had been living with in New York.

There was no name or address under the section headed Next of Kin, which saddened Marisa but didn't surprise her. Katerina was most likely being blamed as the worst sort of home-wrecker for seducing her brother-in-law.

The Ringwolds' file was much thicker than Katerina's. They had completed a lengthy application form and attached multiple photographs. The photos showed an attractive professional couple in their late thirties, living in a substantial colonial-style house in a leafy Cleveland suburb. Between the two of them, they earned almost a quarter of a million dollars a year, although the wife planned to quit work as soon as they adopted the baby, which would drop their annual income by eighty thousand dollars. Still, on $170,000 a year, Katerina's baby would be able to lead a comfortable suburban life with parents who had spent the past decade longing for a child. Marisa was as glad for the Ringwolds as she was sorry for Katerina.

The phone number for the prospective parents was written on the inside cover of the folder as well as on their application forms. Marisa copied it out onto a sticky note, attached it to the front of the file, and put the file and the attached note in the center of Stuart's desk. About to leave and collect Spencer, she noticed that the left-hand file drawer in his desk hadn't closed properly because a file hadn't been put away correctly and was sticking up, jamming the drawer.

She opened the drawer and pulled out the offending file. The name tab had torn and was likely to cause problems again unless it was fixed. Anxious to pick up Spencer, she debated just shoving the file back in the drawer, but her work ethic got the better of her. Using cellophane tape to do a quick repair, she was on the point of putting the file back in the drawer, when Stuart returned to the office.

"Success," he said, holding up a Tupperware sandwich box. "I'm provisioned for my stay in the hospital wilderness. I didn't expect to find you still here— Is that Katerina's file?" He reached for the file she was holding.

He glanced at the tab as he was speaking, then looked down quickly at the file drawer in his desk and saw that it was open. "What's this file doing out?" he asked.

His tone of voice was polite, but Marisa's stomach tightened into a hard knot. Her husband's worst fits of rage had always started with just that sort of cool, innocuous question. She felt her face freeze into the expressionless mask that had been her standard defense against Evan.

"Just as I was leaving, I noticed your desk drawer hadn't closed properly. I saw that the folder you're holding hadn't been put back correctly and the name tab on it had torn. So I mended the file with tape. I was just about to return it to the drawer, when you came back."

While she was talking, Stuart bent down and returned the file to the drawer, but it still jammed when he tried to close it. He reached inside, feeling toward the back of the drawer.

"Ouch!" He drew his hand back sharply after a couple of seconds, then straightened and gave her a smile that was both charming and rueful. "Thanks for spotting the problem. There's a piece of sharp metal hanging down and it's preventing the drawer from closing properly. Remind me tomorrow that it needs fixing, will you?"

"Certainly. I'll make a note." Marisa spoke coolly, although inside she felt anything but cool.

Stuart gave her a sympathetic glance. "You sound tired, Marisa. It's been a long day. Go home and enjoy a relaxing evening. You certainly deserve it after all the hard work you've done today."

"Yes, Spencer will be wondering where I've gotten to," Marisa said, walking back to her work station to collect her jacket and purse. "I hope Katerina's baby arrives safely and doesn't keep you up too late in the process of getting here. Good night, Stuart."

"Good night, Marisa."

"I'll see you tomorrow." She hurried out of the office, drawing in several large gulps of air to calm herself. She was overreacting, she told herself, because of events in her past that had absolutely nothing to do with her current situation.

Stuart had displayed no visible sign of anger just now, but Marisa couldn't quite convince herself that she'd read her boss incorrectly. Living with Evan Connors had turned her into an expert at detecting concealed rage, and she was convinced that Stuart Frieze had been furious when he returned to the office and saw her holding what must have been a highly confidential file.

The fact that Stuart had been perfectly friendly when he said good-night didn't reassure Marisa as much as it should have. Nobody could have been more charming than Evan when it suited him, which was usually when he was hell-bent on criminal deception. Still, she needed to stop viewing every man she met through the distorting shadow cast by Evan's pathological behavior. Stuart obviously enjoyed the respect and admiration of everyone at the Refuge. She shouldn't start suspecting double motives and a hidden agenda every time he frowned or hesitated for a split second.

She'd landed a good job that paid good money, and she wasn't about to work herself into a state because, for a couple of terrifying minutes, charming, gracious Stuart Frieze had reminded her forcefully of her late, highly unlamented husband.

Five

It was always a morale booster when one of the Refuge residents gave birth to a healthy baby, and Stuart felt in a particularly good mood as he drove back to Wainscott. Katerina's son had arrived shortly before two in the morning, after a routine labor and a quick delivery. He had weighed in at six pounds eleven ounces, a robust weight for an infant the doctors agreed was probably two or three weeks early. His lung function was normal, his vital signs were strong, and only the *vernix caseosa* coating his skin hinted at his slightly premature status. Katerina was apparently one of those fortunate women whose body adapted well to pregnancy and childbirth. A promising candidate for future projects, Stuart reflected, especially when a fifth of American women nowadays required C-sections to give birth.

Shortly after eight a.m., the Ringwolds arrived from Ohio to meet their new son. Stuart had experienced his usual high as he watched a teary-eyed Christine Ringwold cradle the baby in her arms for the first time. Larry Ringwold stood with his arm around his wife, unashamedly weeping. Eventually, Larry reached out and ran his forefinger softly across the downy fuzz on the baby's head. "We're going to call him Michael Christopher," he murmured to Stuart. "I think he looks like a Mikey, don't you?"

At that moment, Stuart had felt almost misty-eyed himself—an emotion that had nothing to do with the fifty-thousand-dollar donation the Ringwolds had already transferred to the Wainscott Foundation bank account. Truth be told, Stuart considered the Ringwolds something of a charity case, since most would-be parents donated a great deal more than fifty thousand to secure their right to one of the prime Refuge babies.

Like other clients of the Refuge, the Ringwolds would be on their way home to Ohio next week with the preliminary steps in the adoption process already taken care of. Best of all, they would carry with them a virtual guarantee that there would be no undignified legal hassles looming in their future. Stuart had honed the legal procedures to a point that maximized the convenience for the adoptive parents and minimized the pain to the birth mothers. Katerina had met the Ringwolds before she signed the forms waiving her parental rights, but she had been told only their first names, and she'd been given no hint as to where they lived.

Past experience convinced Stuart that this partial introduction of birth mother to adoptive parents made for the ideal compromise between old-fashioned closed adoptions and the current fashion for let-it-all-hang-out openness. Stuart had discovered that his mothers were more compliant if they knew that their babies would be well cared for by couples in stable marriages. Still, he was determined to discourage the dangerous precedent of allowing Refuge birth mothers to feel that they were entitled to keep tabs on a child that was legally no longer theirs. The Refuge couldn't afford to acquire the reputation of being an adoption center where birth mothers had inconvenient second thoughts.

In fact, Refuge adoption statistics were superb, and

Stuart always made a point of quoting them to prospective parents. Couples who acquired their babies through the Wainscott Foundation were never going to find themselves the object of lurid court battles, and they were in no danger of walking through the checkout at the supermarket and finding themselves making headlines in the tabloid press. Refuge mothers were so carefully selected that in the three years since Stuart had taken control, out of one hundred and seventy-three women who'd passed through the system, not a single one had reneged on her agreement to surrender her baby for adoption. Sometimes it had been necessary for Stuart to apply pressure, but in the end, all the women cooperated, and the troublemakers—no more than a dozen or so—had simply been excluded from further participation in his special programs.

There were a couple of twists in these statistics that Stuart preferred to gloss over, even in the privacy of his own thoughts. He didn't include the two Albanian refugees from Kosovo in his listing of Refuge mothers, for example. In fact, he tried never to think about those two women, or about Carole Riven. Carole had stuck her nose into business that didn't concern her and majorly fucked up his plans. He considered her death in a flaming car wreck a compelling example of divine retribution.

Fortunately, Katerina didn't have any friends or relatives hovering in the background, determined to find out what was happening to her. Stuart felt so confident that Katerina wasn't going to be a troublemaker that he was seriously considering her as his candidate for the Barnett project, which promised to be one of his most profitable undertakings ever.

Arthur and Jodie Barnett of San Francisco had been waiting six months for Stuart to assign a woman to carry Arthur's child. They wanted a surrogate mother who had the same petite stature as Jodie, along with Jodie's light brown hair coloring and unusually pink skin tone.

Almost as important as the physical characteristics, the Barnetts needed a woman who could be relied on never to reveal that the heir to Jodie's banking fortune was, genetically speaking, not hers. Jodie's grandfather had been a racist of the worst sort, a secret supporter of Hitler's eugenics program, and he had tied up his money in trusts that would only benefit his blood descendants.

Quite apart from the fact that they wanted their grandpa's millions, the Barnetts disapproved of his will on moral grounds. They were so determined to pretend the child was theirs by birth that Jodie planned to fake a pregnancy, timed to parallel the real pregnancy of the surrogate mother. Naturally, they were prepared to pay a great deal of money—a very great deal of money—to make sure that their deceit ran no risk of exposure or blackmail at the hands of the surrogate mom. Nowadays, with DNA testing available in home kits, people like the Barnetts knew that their only safety lay in never allowing the first hint of suspicion to be raised, so that an interfering judge was never tempted to order tests.

Stuart had noticed weeks ago that Katerina bore a quite remarkable resemblance to Jodie, but he'd said nothing. Always cautious, he had waited for Katerina to deliver a healthy baby before offering her to the Barnetts. He hadn't acquired his reputation for impeccable service by taking chances. He never proposed a deal without making sure he had all his ducks lined up in meticulously tidy rows, and his exacting standards paid off in generous profits and general happiness.

Glancing out the car window at the sun blazing behind the mountains, Stuart offered a heartfelt prayer of thanks for the miraculous way God kept sending him just the women he needed to meet his obligations. The money he got for arranging Katerina's impregnation by Arthur Barnett would pay a fully trained medical staff at his clinic in Zaire for an entire year. Despite genocidal neglect by America and other rich countries, hundreds of oppressed women and malnourished babies would receive life-saving medical care because he—Stuart Frieze—brokered a deal for the temporary use of Katerina's womb. As an added benefit, his negotiations would result in a child for the Barnetts who would be loved and pampered from the second it was conceived. Everyone would benefit from the deal—even Katerina, who would be generously rewarded for her assistance. And, God knew, with her total lack of marketable job skills and lousy command of English, she didn't exactly have a thousand other viable options for earning her living.

Thinking about the Barnetts switched Stuart's thoughts onto a less happy track. Marisa Joubert. Turning off the Boulder Turnpike, he mentally rehashed the scene from last night, when he'd returned to the office and found his new assistant holding his special project file. All the documents were encoded, so he knew she couldn't have read anything confidential, but his blood ran cold at the implications of what she'd been doing. Had Marisa's discovery of the secret compartment in his filing cabinet been as innocent as it seemed? He thought so, but he would have to watch her like a hawk until he was sure.

Stuart's stomach knotted with frustration. He was amazed at the problems posed by keeping the routine administration of the Refuge running smoothly. Who would have thought that with all the balls he was juggling, finding office help would pose his most constant dilemma?

When Marisa Joubert turned up on his doorstep last

week, she had seemed the perfect compromise hire—just smart enough to do the job; not smart enough to ask awkward questions. A high school dropout with almost no work experience, visibly unsure of herself, and obviously in dire financial straits, his decision to take her on had seemed inspired, especially when he learned that she was also a single mother. His experiences with Dulcie and Liz proved that there was nothing like having a child to feed and clothe for keeping an employee loyal. Loyal and not too inquisitive—exactly the way he wanted them.

At their initial interview, only two things about Marisa Joubert had worried him: she seemed too smart to have such a meager work history, and she was much too attractive to be so unsure of herself. In his experience, beautiful women had a natural self-confidence that came from a lifetime of being treated better than their plainer sisters. So why did Marisa Joubert appear withdrawn and...dull? No, *dull* was the wrong word. She seemed damped down, Stuart thought, as if she wanted to slide through life unnoticed.

He knew he was attractive to women, and yet Marisa Joubert had shown no awareness of him as a man. That wouldn't have bothered him too much—maybe he wasn't her type—but she hadn't emitted any sexual vibes at all. He was pretty good at taking a woman's sexual temperature, and Marisa's hovered right around freeze-your-balls-off.

She could be gay, of course. And there were a dozen harmless reasons why an attractive woman might lack self-confidence, which was why he'd ignored his niggling doubts and hired her. On the other hand, any incongruity in the person working as his assistant needed to be watched. As soon as he got a free moment, he would take Marisa out to lunch and probe into her background.

In high school, he'd been the typical self-centered jock, until he'd been taught a hard lesson in the consequences of mindless sexual conquest. Since then, he'd learned to be sensitive to a woman's needs. Nowadays, he had an uncanny ability to sense what it was women craved emotionally, eliciting all sorts of interesting confidences in the process. Still, it was going to be a time-consuming chore, and he resented wasting his valuable time on her. He only liked two types of women: rich and powerful, or poor and virginal. Marisa didn't qualify on either count.

Stuart turned into his parking space and slammed on the brakes, annoyed that his early-morning high was dissipating over the stupid problem of office help. He had so much to accomplish, so many people to help—he couldn't afford to waste time on trivial details like the disconnect between Marisa Joubert's attractive appearance and her lack of confidence.

He pocketed his car keys and took the path to the main entrance at a run. Enough of worrying. Time to refocus on the positive. He'd shaved and showered at the hospital, and he felt wide awake and alert. After years of being in charge of refugee camps in crisis spots all around the world, he prided himself on being able to go forty-eight hours without sleep. With that sort of conditioning, last night's wakefulness hardly created a blip on his energy levels.

He stopped at the bottom of the steps to draw in several deep breaths of pristine mountain air, feeling invigorated and ready to tackle whatever challenges the day threw at him.

"Hi, Mr. Frieze." The janitor called out to him from the corner of the building, where he was using a hose equipped with a special attachment to clean the windows.

"Hi, Jimmy, nice to see you." Stuart gave a friendly wave, glad of the chance to show kindness to someone so pathetically inferior. "How are you doing this morning?"

"I'm doing good. I'm washing the windows. I've washed twenty-three windows already."

"That's terrific. It's a great day to be outside, isn't it?"

Jimmy tugged at his beard, considering this. "Uh-huh, it's a nice day."

"It's going to be really hot this afternoon, I bet."

"Uh-huh. Could be." Jimmy returned to his original train of thought. "Did you know there are fifty-seven windows in this building? I've washed twenty-three already. That means there are thirty-four more windows to be washed. When I'm done washing them, you'll have a real good view out of your office into the yard."

"That's great," Stuart said. "I noticed yesterday that the windows really needed cleaning."

"Nobody told me to wash the windows. I figured out how to do it all by myself." Jimmy stood back to admire his handiwork and forgot to redirect the hose. A shower of water landed on his head, and he coughed and spluttered, choking on the spray.

"Oops, watch the hose, Jimmy." Stuart patted the janitor's back. "Turn the little lever on the nozzle to shut off the water. There, you got it. That's the ticket. Are you okay?"

"I'm okay, but the water's cold." Jimmy finally stopped coughing, and mopped his face and glasses with a piece of towel hanging from his belt.

"You need to come inside and change your shirt."

"Why?"

"Your shirt's wet," Stuart explained patiently.

Jimmy clutched a handful of his sweatshirt and

squeezed it a couple of times, but no water came out. "My shirt's not real wet," he said, turning the hose back on and squirting another window. "Just my hair got soaked real good, that's all."

"Well, the sun feels pretty warm already, so you should dry off fast. It sure is good to see the back of Old Man Winter, isn't it?"

Stuart had forgotten how literally Jimmy interpreted everything, and he watched in tolerant amusement when the janitor glanced over his shoulder as if expecting to catch sight of Old Man Winter speeding away. At least this time he remembered to keep the hose pointed at a window.

Jimmy shrugged, giving up on sighting Old Man Winter. "I like it when it's sunny," he said, and emphasized his comment by sending an extra powerful stream of water up toward a second-story window.

Stuart gave him a friendly thump on the back. "I'm with you there, Jimmy. Snow's fine as long as you can ski on it, or admire it from inside the house. It's a pain in the butt when you have to drive to work in it."

"I can't ride my bike when it snows."

"That's right, you can't. Well, I've got to get back to work. Enjoy the rest of the morning, Jimmy." Giving the janitor a final encouraging smile, Stuart went inside. It had been a lucky day for the Refuge when he'd hired Jimmy. He'd taken him on last month, strictly as a favor to Reg Donaldson, a fellow member of the United Way board who lived in Denver and ran an employment agency for people with disabilities.

As so often happened with acts of kindness, Stuart felt that he'd been rewarded several times over for his gesture. In the five weeks Jimmy had been working at the Refuge, cleaning standards had improved a hundred percent, and they'd actually saved money in the maintenance budget by cutting out subcontractors who'd been expensive and not very reliable.

As he crossed the entrance hall, Stuart heard the sound of two women's voices coming from his office. He recognized both of them, and quelled a surge of impatience. Marisa Joubert and Helen Wainscott. Damn! If Helen was in town, he could kiss goodbye the idea of catching up on his sleep. She was going to spend all night with him, talking and flirting for hours before she finally allowed him to coax and chivvy her into bed. Even when the sex was over, he still wouldn't get any sleep, since she liked to lie in his arms and ramble on at endless length about the latest antique doodad she'd acquired, or the vampire ball she was arranging as a Halloween benefit for the art museum…. Stuart yawned with boredom at the prospect.

Of course, he couldn't afford to offend Grover Wainscott's daughter, so he didn't show even a hint of his boredom as he strode into the office. Helen seemed to respond well to take-charge men, perhaps because her father had been such a hard-ass control freak. Stuart tossed his briefcase onto the desk, before walking over to her and taking her hand.

"Helen, my dear! How wonderful to find you here. What an unexpected treat."

"Hello, Stuart, it's nice to see you, too." She smiled at him shyly, her pale cheeks flushing bright red with pleasure. As always, she was expensively dressed in a designer outfit that did nothing to flatter her bone-thin figure. Still, better skinny than fat, Stuart thought. He recognized that his aversion to fat women was almost pathological in its intensity, but he couldn't stand the sight of pendulous breasts and flabby thighs. He didn't understand how so many American women could gorge themselves into obesity, when half their sisters around the world were starving.

He took Helen's hand and raised it to his lips. He'd discovered that she responded well to hand kissing and similar courtly gestures, even though he felt whenever he did it as if he were in a bad amateur production of *The Merry Widow*.

"You should have let me know you were coming. I hope you haven't been waiting too long."

"Oh no, I only just arrived. I'm on my way to Los Angeles, so I thought I'd stop off in Denver and pay you a visit."

The rich woman's version of being "in the neighborhood." Stuart smiled. "I'm very glad you did. You haven't been here in over a month, and that's much too long."

"I thought so, too." Helen's voice was breathy and girlish, despite the fact that she was galloping full tilt toward her fortieth birthday. They exchanged meaningful glances, and her blush deepened, as if she got turned on by the mere fact of making eye contact with him. She really was pathetic, Stuart thought, gazing deep into her eyes and trying out a soulful look intended to convey intense sexual longing.

With a little cough, Helen gestured hastily toward Marisa, as if to remind him that they weren't alone. "Your new assistant explained that you weren't expected back until right around lunchtime. She said you'd been up all night with one of the inmates."

Inmates? With considerable effort, Stuart refrained from openly correcting her choice of word. "Yes, one of our *residents* just had a healthy baby boy. I waited to meet with his new parents. They flew in this morning and they've already fallen in love with their new son."

"I'm so glad the baby arrived safely," Marisa said, speaking for the first time. "Is Katerina recovering okay? Was it a difficult delivery?"

"No, not at all. It was quite easy for a first baby, and Katerina's feeling pretty good this morning."

"She would be," Helen said. "Have you ever noticed that it's always these young girls who don't want babies who have them so easily? Whereas middle-class women who could afford to raise their children properly often can't get pregnant."

"I think that's one of those observations that turn out not to be true once you examine it more closely," Stuart said, wondering how Helen could have spent the past five years administering Wainscott Foundation funds and yet still be so ignorant of the basic facts about pregnancy and fertility in twenty-first century America.

"At least half my friends have had trouble getting pregnant," Helen insisted. "But did you ever hear of a teenager living in the inner city who had trouble getting pregnant?"

Stuart wanted to point out that her friends didn't constitute a reliable statistical sample, and that inner-city girls who failed to get pregnant were unlikely to be featured in the society journals that formed the backbone of Helen's reading program. Of course, he didn't make either point. Instead he smiled. Again. He did a lot of inward seething and outward smiling when he was with Helen.

"At least we can take comfort in the fact that the Refuge is doing a great job of finding loving homes for unplanned babies," he said. "Which is what your father instructed us to do in his will."

"Yes, it sure is. Those were his exact words."

"And good ones to take to heart." Stuart's cheek muscles were beginning to ache. He gave up and switched off his smile.

"Well, I don't know about you, Helen, but all I've eaten since last night is a sandwich. It's past noon already. Are you hungry, by any chance?"

"Yes, I am, rather. The food they served on the plane this morning was worse than disgusting."

"Good. Not that the airplane food was bad—but that you're hungry for lunch. Wainscott has acquired a really great new restaurant this past winter, and I think you'll be impressed. It's called *La Cafetière* and it's run by a woman who grew up around here and her husband, who's a chef from New Orleans."

"It sounds intriguing," Helen said.

"It's as good as it sounds. Why don't we walk into town and discuss over the daily special whatever business has brought you here?"

"That would be lovely," she said. "Actually, the official reason I'm here is that the trustees have been checking into the length of time inmates get to stay on at the Refuge after they've had their babies. We've gone over the records, and it seems that the average stay is almost two months post partum. That seems excessive to all of the trustees, so I said I'd talk to you about it and see if we can't find some way to get the women out of here a bit faster once they've given birth."

With remarkable self-discipline, Stuart avoided suggesting that the board of trustees go fuck themselves. Women stayed on at the Refuge because the most profitable part of his program occurred after the birth of a resident's first baby. Still, he needed to keep Helen quiescent and on side, so he gave her a look that said he understood where she was coming from and was grateful for the opportunity to consider her advice.

"I sure do understand why the trustees would be anxious to contain costs," he said, working on yet another smile. "On the other hand, you know I've always maintained that the greatest service we provide at the Refuge is giving our birth mothers the time to recover physically and emotionally before they leave here. But I'm always open to suggestions from the board. Very open. Let's talk about it some more over lunch and see if we can't brainstorm a creative solution."

"Yes, let's do that. I'm sure the trustees don't want to turn these women out onto the street before they've recovered. We're not heartless, you know, but we do need to keep tabs on expenditures—"

She was obviously gearing up for one of her standard speeches about the need for fiscal prudence. Stuart cut her off with a shake of his head and a chuckle so that she wouldn't feel reprimanded. Jeez, he'd forgotten what a high-maintenance project it was to keep Helen happy.

"No, my dear, not another word! Whatever the question, right now I haven't the vaguest idea how to answer you. I've been up all night, and I need coffee and food before we can have even a halfway intelligent discussion about finances or anything else."

"Of course. I'm sorry. I should have realized how tired you are—"

He silenced her by picking up her purse from the desk and hooking the strap over her shoulder; otherwise, they would have spent the rest of the day apologizing to each other. He put his hand under her elbow and guided her toward the door, pausing, when they were almost in the corridor, to check with his assistant.

"Marisa, I'll be back around two. I'm assuming there weren't any phone messages this morning that are too urgent to wait until then?"

Marisa shook her head. "No, there was nothing really urgent, at least as far as I can tell. It was a quiet morning, actually. I was able to get quite a bit of filing done, and I even conferred with Janet about setting up a flowchart that would show when each resident at the Refuge is due to have her baby, so that we'd know when we were likely to have our next vacancy."

"Great. I'll see you this afternoon, and we'll get caught up on everything then." He wasn't at all sure that he wanted Marisa and Janet conferring about anything behind his back, even something that sounded as harmless as a flowchart of estimated birth dates. Detailed statistics about Refuge operations could prove dangerous. At least, unless he'd generated them. But he couldn't worry about that now. He had Helen to take care of and get properly sweetened up before he could deal with the problem of Marisa's unexpected efficiency.

"Goodbye, Marisa, it was nice to meet you."

Stuart was surprised that Helen remembered his assistant's name. She wasn't exactly a woman who relished contact with the toiling masses.

"I'm glad Stuart finally has the help he needs to run the office smoothly," she added.

"Thank you." Marisa flushed very slightly, as if she was pleased by the small compliment. "Enjoy your lunch, Ms. Wainscott. You, too, Stuart."

The spring sunshine was so inviting that Marisa decided to eat outside with Spencer. The front of the old house abutted Main Street in the close-to-the-road style typical of pioneer buildings, but the backyard had a spacious lawn rimmed by evergreens and aspen. The trees formed a screen that ensured privacy and opened up only on the farthest western extremity of the property to provide a tantalizing glimpse of a lake that today sparkled azure blue in the sunlight.

Marisa had planned to lay out their impromptu picnic inside the gazebo that was built not far from the lake-shore, but as she and Spencer walked outside, they spotted Jimmy carrying a circular wrought-iron table across the grass to a small patio where a group of chairs had already been set up.

"Dimmy!" On catching sight of the janitor, Spencer gave a gleeful squeal and tore his hand loose from Marisa's, trotting toward his newfound playmate on stubby but determined legs. He could work up a fair old speed when he turned his mind to it, and Marisa had to sprint to catch up with him.

She grabbed Spencer's hand, then smiled at the handyman. "Hi, Jimmy, how are you? Do you need a hand with that table? It looks very heavy."

"No, thank you, ma'am. I can carry it. I'm real strong. I work out at the gym."

"Dimmy, be horsey." Spencer shook off Marisa's hand again, and clung to Jimmy's jeans, attempting to climb up the janitor's leg and—toddler fashion—paying zero attention to the fact that his would-be playmate was already carrying a weighty table.

Panting, Jimmy put down the table. "Hi, big guy." He gave Spencer a friendly pat on the head. "You want to take a ride on my shoulders?"

"Yep." Spencer beamed in delight.

"You have to wait while I carry this table over there." Jimmy pointed to the group of chairs already set out on the patio.

"Okay." Spencer wriggled in excitement and shook an imaginary pair of reins, as Jimmy hoisted the table back into his arms. "Play horsey," he said happily.

"Yeah, okay. We'll play horsey."

Spencer tagged alongside the janitor, giving a skip every two or three steps when the anticipation got too much for him. As soon as Jimmy bent over to put the table down, Spencer scrambled up onto his back, using the janitor's hair and handfuls of shirt to achieve his goal.

Giving Jimmy an apologetic smile, Marisa lifted her son off. "Spencer, be patient! You need to wait until Jimmy says he's ready. He's got a job to finish."

"I reckon it's pretty much done." Jimmy tipped his head to one side, looking at the table and chairs as if he couldn't quite believe that he'd arranged them so neatly. "I hosed them chairs down already before I brought them out. They look kinda nice, don't they? Makes you think of hot days and drinking lemonade."

Without waiting for Marisa to reply, he turned and hoisted Spencer onto his shoulders. "You ready to go for a ride, big guy?"

"Ready." Spencer nodded so exuberantly that he was in danger of sliding off Jimmy's back. The janitor repositioned him and set off around the garden at a speedy canter that had Spencer shrieking with laughter.

He was having so much fun that he completely forgot to hold on, but Marisa noticed that although Jimmy's hold on her son appeared casual, every time Spencer started to slip, Jimmy grabbed him. Even if the janitor's mental processes were slow, his physical reactions were apparently quick, which was reassuring, given the pace at which he was running around the yard.

"More horsey!" Spencer bounced up and down on Jimmy's shoulders, when the janitor finally slowed to a halt after they'd completed their fifth galloping circuit.

"I can't," Jimmy said, laughing. "I got no breath left. You bounced it all out of me." He took off his glasses, shook his hair out of his eyes, and wiped a bead of sweat off his forehead with the back of his hand. "Sorry, big guy. This horsey has no gallops left."

Jimmy looked across at Marisa as he spoke, and his gaze locked with hers. She could almost feel the heat of his body reaching out to envelop her, and the sensation was so powerful that she took an involuntary step backward. Her stomach clenched in an astonishing moment of gut-level sexual awareness. For a split second, she imagined herself pressed against his body, her head resting against his chest.

When she realized what she was thinking, she wasn't sure what shocked her more. The fact that her body had responded physically to a man for the first time in over two years. Or the fact that the man she'd responded to was—not to put too fine a point on it—mentally challenged.

Jimmy turned away, rubbing the lenses of his glasses with exaggerated concentration. Then he put his glasses back on and ducked his head toward Spencer in an awkward farewell gesture.

"I guess it's time for you to eat lunch," he said. "See you around, big guy."

"Dimmy, stay." Treating the janitor to a heart-melting smile, Spencer held out a section of peanut butter and jelly sandwich. "Here," he said, and patted the seat next to him. "Dimmy stay, okay?"

Jimmy hesitated, and Marisa knew that he was as aware as she was of whatever had passed between them. Moreover, he was embarrassed by—whatever it was. Since there was no way to avoid encountering each other two or three times a day, she realized that she had to make things comfortable again for both of them, since Jimmy certainly wasn't capable of smoothing things over.

Quelling her doubts, she looked up and gave him a friendly smile of the sort she normally reserved for Spencer's toddler friends. "Please stay, Jimmy. We have more food than we can eat, and we have grape juice to drink, as well. We'd love for you to join us, if you have time."

He swung his arms aimlessly back and forth a couple of times before replying. "Well, if you're sure it's okay, then I guess I'd like to eat lunch with you."

"That's great," Marisa said, hoping her enthusiasm didn't sound too fake.

The janitor sat down in the seat Spencer had indicated, and spread his hands over his knees. Since Spencer had long since eaten the square of sandwich he'd offered to Jimmy, Marisa put another sandwich and a couple of slices of apple onto a paper napkin and handed them to the janitor.

Jimmy took the food carefully. Perhaps she was oversensitive in thinking that he seemed super-anxious to avoid touching her. "Thank you, ma'am. This looks great. I like peanut butter and jelly real well."

"Please, there's no need for you to call me 'ma'am,'" Marisa said. "My name's Marisa."

"Yes, ma'am—I mean, Marisa." Jimmy kept his gaze fixed on his sandwich. "I never met anyone called Marisa before."

"Haven't you? I know a couple of little girls called Marisa, but I guess it was more unusual when I was growing up. When I was in school, I didn't know any other girls who were called Marisa."

She knew she was babbling, but she felt the need to fill the space between them with chatter. "My dad wanted to call me Marie Clothilde, after his grandmother, but my mom was tired of naming her babies after members of my dad's family. She'd already called my older sister Isabella to please her mother-in-law, and when I was born, she decided it was enough already. I have to admit, I'm glad my mom won that particular fight. Clothilde isn't exactly the name I'd choose for myself.''

Jimmy carefully wiped his fingers on his napkin. ''Do your parents fight a lot?'' he asked. ''My parents fought all the time.''

''My parents fought a lot, but it didn't mean anything. They were really in love, right up until the day my dad died. I never understood why they were so happy together, because they had nothing in common, as far as I could tell. ''

Jimmy squinted into the sun. ''I guess that means when couples fight all the time, they either hate each other and are going to get divorced, or else they love each other a lot and are going to stay together forever.''

She laughed. ''I guess so. Although those two choices cover quite a lot of ground.''

''Being married is hard,'' Jimmy said, after a moment of frowning concentration. ''If you're having a fight, how do you know what kind of a fight it is? The divorce kind, or the in-love kind?''

Marisa shook her head. ''Darn good question, Jimmy. Unfortunately, I have no idea what the answer is.''

''Dimmy, Dimmy, Dimmy!'' Spencer chanted, holding out a handful of squashed raisins. ''Here,'' he said. ''Dey waisins,'' he added helpfully.

''Thank you.'' Jimmy took the raisins and ate a mouthful, undeterred by their bedraggled appearance. ''Your mom is a good cook,'' he said to Spencer. ''This lunch is real nice. I'm a good cook, too. I can make spaghetti, and scrambled eggs, and chicken noodle soup, and grilled cheese sandwiches, and tuna fish salad—''

''Tuna fis!'' Spencer exclaimed, thankfully interrupting what promised to be a long listing of Jimmy's entire culinary repertoire. "Tuna fis is yummy."

"It sure is." Jimmy looked down at his feet. "If you like, I could make tuna fish sandwiches for lunch tomorrow. We could share them, like we shared your sandwiches today."

"Yay! Tuna fis!" shouted Spencer, who had never met a day that couldn't be improved by tuna fish sandwiches.

Marisa sincerely hoped that Jimmy's intellectual powers stretched to understanding what happened to tuna fish and mayonnaise that wasn't refrigerated. She gulped and crossed her fingers. "Yes, sure, that would be great. I'll bring some fruit and cookies."

"We can meet here," Jimmy said, sweeping the debris from their picnic into a plastic grocery bag. "I usually eat lunch right around twelve-thirty."

"Sounds good to me," Marisa said. She took a wet wipe from the supply in her purse and cleaned Spencer's face and hands. She had no luck in shushing his howls of protest at this cleanup job. He yelled loudly enough to convince any passerby that she was performing some barbaric form of ritual torture.

"Spencer, stop screaming," Jimmy said quietly. "Otherwise, I won't be a horsey anymore."

Spencer's howls stopped so abruptly, it sounded as if someone had thrown a switch.

Marisa stared at Jimmy in astonishment. "Thank you."

"You're welcome."

She hadn't intended to look at him, but somehow their eyes met, and the odd little flicker of awareness flashed through her nervous system again. Good grief, what was her problem? Obviously she wasn't attracted to Jimmy's scintillating conversation, or his charming sense of humor, so that meant she was attracted to his body.

The realization was uncomfortable. She had no idea where this sudden rush of hormonal enthusiasm was coming from, but Jimmy deserved better than to be turned into a sexual object.

Marisa drew in a shaky breath. "Well, I guess I'd better get back to work. I swear the papers in that office multiply every time I step outside the door."

Jimmy frowned, looking puzzled. "Papers can't multiply," he said. "Can they?"

"No, they can't," Marisa assured him, thinking what strange gaps there were in Jimmy's understanding. It was absolutely crazy that she felt physically attracted toward a man whose brain couldn't figure out simple metaphors.

"It was just a…" *Figure of speech,* she was going to say, then decided to change that to something easier for Jimmy to grasp. "It was just a way of saying that there are a lot of papers in Mr. Frieze's office, waiting for me to file."

"Just like there are a lot of windows waiting for me to wash," Jimmy said, pitching the litter from their lunch into a trash can, then swinging Spencer up onto his shoulders.

"Right." Marisa didn't risk looking in Jimmy's direction again. She walked at a brisk pace back to the office, listening as Spencer chatted animatedly to the janitor. No wonder Spencer and the janitor enjoyed each other's company, she thought acidly. They had about the same mental level.

Jimmy handed Spencer back to her at the door. "I'm not coming inside right now," he said. "I have to wash the windows. Goodbye, big guy. Goodbye…Marisa."

She absolutely was not going to let herself believe that

there was something special about the way he said her name. She looked away, momentarily unable to find her voice.

Spencer, thank goodness, wasn't similarly afflicted. "Bye, Dimmy." He waved enthusiastically. "Bye, Dimmy. Bye-bye-bye."

"See you tomorrow," Jimmy said, and walked off, hands shoved in his pockets.

Marisa was very happy to see him go.

Six

Marisa was getting ready to serve dinner and Spencer was already seated in his high chair, when the doorbell rang. "That better not be anybody trying to sell me stuff," she muttered, pushing the casserole dish back into the oven and shutting it with a *bang*. "I'm way too tired to be polite."

"Not tired," Spencer said quickly, anxious to ward off any mention of *bedtime,* that dreaded word.

"You're never tired," Marisa said with grim humor. Peeping through the spy hole in the front door, she was surprised to see Jimmy standing on the other side, scuffing the mat with the toe of his sneaker as he waited. She opened the door, and Spencer gave a crow of delight when he realized who had come to call.

"Hi, Dimmy!"

"Hi, buddy," Jimmy said, snatching off the Rockies baseball cap he was wearing and holding out Bear with his other hand. "I brought your teddy bear. I found him on the floor in the hall when I was cleaning up."

"Bear!" Spencer exclaimed, clapping his hands. "Hi, Bear!"

"Thanks so much for bringing him back to us," Marisa said. "I hope you didn't have to ride your bike too far out of your way to get here?"

"Kinda far. I live at number fourteen Kohler Ranch Drive, right next to the church."

"That's all the way at the other end of town, near the ski lodge. You shouldn't have come so far out of your way, Jimmy, but thank you."

He shrugged. "It doesn't matter. I like to ride my bike. Riding a bike gives you strong muscles in your legs."

Marisa ignored a sudden impulse to glance at Jimmy's thighs and check out his muscles. She buttoned Bear's sweater and dusted off his hat. "How did you find out where we live?" she asked, mostly to change the topic of conversation.

He scratched his head. "Uh...Mr. Frieze told me. He was working late, so I asked him."

"Well, thanks again for going to so much trouble, Jimmy. Spencer and I are both very grateful you brought Bear back to us. I can't believe we hadn't noticed he was missing, but Spencer would never have gone to sleep tonight without him, that's for sure. We'd have been in big trouble come bedtime. We really do appreciate it."

Marisa realized that she sounded completely fake, like a salesperson touting the benefits of a miracle cream guaranteed to erase wrinkles instantly. Jimmy gave her a speculative look, as if he sensed her insincerity even though he couldn't understand it. But why would he, Marisa thought, when she couldn't understand it herself?

Looking unsure of what he ought to do next, Jimmy gave an awkward bobbing nod of his head and turned to leave.

Spencer immediately protested. "Dimmy, stay!"

Jimmy stopped in the doorway, twisting his baseball cap in his hands. "I have to go, buddy. I'll see you tomorrow."

"No! Play horsey."

"Please stay." Marisa could hardly believe what she heard herself say. "We're just about to eat dinner. It's only macaroni and cheese, with fruit for dessert, but you're welcome to join us, if you'd like."

As soon as she issued the invitation, she regretted it. She and Spencer had already shared lunch with Jimmy for each of the past three days. It was flat-out crazy to be inviting him for dinner, as well. There was absolutely nowhere for their strange friendship to go, so for Jimmy's sake—not to mention her own—she needed to start imposing some realistic limitations on the time they spent together.

"Well, I didn't eat dinner yet..." Jimmy stared uncertainly into the distance. "But I guess maybe I should be getting home."

"Dimmy stay! Dimmy stay!" Spencer banged his spoon on the tray of his high chair in rhythm with his chant. "Dimmy stay. Dimmy stay."

Marisa rolled her eyes at her son. "Enough already, Spencer. We heard you the first time, okay?"

"Dimmy stay." Spencer gave a final emphatic *bang* of his spoon.

"Well, I guess you know how *he* feels," Marisa said, forcing herself to look straight into Jimmy's eyes. She felt perversely relieved that Spencer was providing all the enthusiasm she'd lacked in issuing her invitation. Heck, why not show that she liked Jimmy and enjoyed his company? It suddenly seemed mean to have been so lukewarm in her invitation, after he'd gone to all the trouble of bringing Bear back for Spencer.

"My son is a very persistent little person," she said. "He can keep that chant up for hours, you know, so you'd be doing me a real favor if you'd change your mind and join us."

Jimmy met her gaze for no more than a second or two. Then he turned away and made a performance of taking off his glasses and cleaning them. He dropped his Rockies cap in the process, and then dropped his glasses when he bent to pick up his cap. He shoved the glasses back on his nose impatiently, and they ended up slightly skewed, which had the unfortunate effect of making him look more feebleminded than usual when he finally straightened up to face her.

"I guess I'd like to stay, if you're sure it's no trouble," he mumbled.

"It's no trouble. It'll be a pleasure," Marisa said, speaking too heartily because she was lying and because she felt sorry for him. Jimmy was kindhearted, and she suspected he didn't have nearly as many friends as he would like. What harm could it do to share dinner on this one occasion? He and Spencer would eventually tire of each other, and in the meantime there was no reason not to allow them to enjoy each other's company.

"Come on in," she said, holding the door wide and smiling a belated welcome. "I was about to dish it up when you rang the doorbell, so we're all ready to eat."

Jimmy wiped his shoes on the mat with great care, and stepped inside. He looked around appreciatively as they made their way through the tiny entrance lobby, following her into the breakfast nook, which was nothing more than a linoleum-covered space wedged between the living room and the kitchen.

The contrast between this cramped alcove and the marble-tiled elegance of the dining room in the house she'd shared with Evan was so remarkable that Marisa had found herself comparing the two eating areas several times during the past week. Each time, she'd felt a soul-deep gratitude that she was no longer living in that hideous white palace in Florida, subjected to her husband's brutal demands for perfection and held hostage by her love for Spencer. Ever since Evan died, she'd felt like a poster child for the proposition that wealth could never bring happiness. The feeling had grown even more intense during the past few days.

"You've fixed this place up real nice," Jimmy said, shoving his hands into his pockets and rocking back on his heels as he took in all the details of his surroundings.

"Thank you. It's small, but I like it here a lot, especially after the apartment we had in Aurora. Somehow that apartment always seemed dark and gloomy, even on a sunny day. Here, it's the opposite. We have a great view of the mountains from the living room window, and we get sun all day long. Of course, you can't see any of the mountains right now because it's dark—"

Marisa broke off, realizing she was jabbering again. What was her problem when Jimmy was around, anyway? She couldn't understand why she felt this burning need to fill any moment of silence that ever developed between the two of them.

Spencer fortunately provided a distraction, so that her confusion wasn't too noticeable. "Sit here," he said to Jimmy, patting the air next to his high chair. "Sit here, Dimmy."

Jimmy looked across at Marisa. "Ma'am? Is that where you want that I should sit?"

"Yes, sure, sit by Spencer, if you can stand the noise. And watch out for stray pieces of macaroni. Spencer throws his food around when he gets bored. I'm trying to teach him that there are better ways to convey the message that he's finished eating, but so far I haven't persuaded him."

"I'll watch out for flying food." Jimmy slid into the

chair next to Spencer and tucked his baseball cap neatly behind his back. "Thank you, ma'am. This is real nice."

He'd remembered her name for the past two days, but for some reason, she chose not to remind him to call her Marisa, as if it were too disturbingly intimate in the confines of her own home. Which was crazy, given that everyone from plumbers to phone solicitors called her Marisa without any sensation of excessive intimacy on her part.

She laid Bear on the counter, taking another placemat and cutlery from the drawer and setting it on the table in front of Jimmy, then hurrying to serve the food. Fortunately, once they were eating, she didn't have to invent topics of conversation, since Spencer and Jimmy entertained each other very well. She could remain silent except for simple remarks such as asking Jimmy if he wanted pepper, or reminding Spencer to chew his food.

"That was real tasty," Jimmy said finally, pushing away his empty dish of fresh fruit salad. "Thank you kindly, ma'am."

"You're welcome." He had the oddest, old-fashioned way of speaking, Marisa thought. He sounded like a cross between Forest Gump and the Scarecrow in *The Wizard of Oz.* Maybe that's why she felt on edge when he was talking, as if she were waiting for him to drop nuggets of Hollywood-style folk wisdom into his conversation. Since this was real life as opposed to the movies, the folk wisdom never came, and she was left on tenterhooks.

"All done," Spencer said, squirming to get down. As soon as he finished eating, he regarded sitting in his high chair as a form of torture. "Play Dimmy," he said hopefully.

"Sorry, pumpkin, not tonight." Marisa wiped his sticky face and hands, sneaking up on him so fast that he forgot to yell. "It's late, and we have to get you to bed."

"No bed," Spencer said. "Play Dimmy."

"No, you can't play with Jimmy. He has to go home to his own house—"

"It's okay," Jimmy said. "I can stay for a while. I'll read Spencer a story. I can read pretty good. I can spell pretty good, too. At school, I won a prize for spelling."

"That's great, Jimmy." She sounded patronizing again. Marisa gritted her teeth and tried one more time to make the pitch of her voice normal. "What grade were you in when you won the prize, Jimmy?"

"I was in seventh grade. I had to learn twenty-five words every night, and some of them were real long. My sister helped me to learn them."

"I bet your mom and dad were very proud of you when you won."

"My mom was. My dad had left home already." Jimmy lifted Spencer out of the high chair and tucked him like an oversize football under his arm. Instead of protesting, Spencer started to giggle.

"Where do you sleep?" Jimmy asked, peering down at the bundle fidgeting under his arm.

"In my big boy bed."

"His bedroom's on the right, over there," Marisa said, picking up Bear and pointing to the door. "I'll come and get him undressed. While I'm doing that, why don't you look through his shelf of books and choose a story to read?"

Spencer seemed fascinated to have Jimmy in his bedroom. Instead of the usual nightly routine of squirms and wriggles, he was docile and cooperative, as Marisa changed him into his pajamas. He didn't even protest when she brushed his hair and rubbed baby lotion onto his face. He gave her a sleepy smile when she tucked him into his toddler bed, looking so angelic with his halo of curls that her insides melted into a puddle of love. She refused to think about the fact that he was past two years old and that she would soon have to take him to get those gorgeous baby curls cut off.

"The story I'm going to read you is called *Bert and Ernie Visit the Farm*," Jimmy announced, sitting cross-legged on the floor next to the bed, which was built low, and had plastic guardrails to prevent Spencer tumbling out while he slept.

"Yay! Bert and Ernie!" Spencer said.

"I like Bert and Ernie, too. And Big Bird and Snufalupagus." Jimmy had apparently been a *Sesame Street* fan in his youth.

"And Elmo and Grover!"

"Right." Jimmy opened the book and held it up, so that Spencer could see the pictures. "Okay, here we go. Have you heard this story before?"

"Only about a hundred times," Marisa said. "It's one of his favorites."

"Ernie on the train," Spencer said, citing his preferred part of the story. He tucked Bear securely into the crook of his arm and leaned back against his pillow, listening intently as Jimmy started to read.

To Marisa's relief, Jimmy didn't have any trouble sight reading. He managed to put quite a lot of expression into his voice and stumbled over very few words.

"That was great," she said, when he finished. "Thanks, Jimmy. You read well."

"The words in this story were real easy," he said, but he flushed at her compliment as if it had been more of a strain to read the book than he wanted to admit.

"Spencer, can you say 'thank you' to Jimmy for reading to you?"

"Fank you." Spencer's eyes were closing, but he forced them open again, determined to fight sleep until the last possible moment.

"Good night, big guy." Getting up, Jimmy bunched his fist and brushed it gently against Spencer's cheek. "See you tomorrow."

"Play horsey." Spencer's voice was fading into sleep.

"Okay. We will tomorrow. Good night."

"Look," Spencer said to Jimmy, gathering up his last reserves of energy and pointing to the solar system and scattered stars embossed on the plastic headboard of his bed.

"They glow in the dark," Marisa said, flipping off the light switch as she spoke. The sun, moon and planets shone with pale luminescence, and Spencer gave a sleepy sigh of satisfaction.

"I wish I had stars like that on my bed," Jimmy said. "They're cool."

"Cool." The word was a new one for Spencer, and he tried it out several times. "Cool, cool, cool. Cool."

Marisa leaned over and kissed him. "Good night, pumpkin. Sleep well."

Spencer popped his eyes open one more time. "Want duice."

Marisa shook her head. "Uh-uh. You had two big glasses of juice at dinnertime, and that's enough. 'Night, sweetie. See you in the morning."

She beckoned Jimmy out of the room, closing the door behind them. "Whew! I love my son to death, but it sure feels great when he's in bed, and I finally get a couple of hours to myself."

"I'll help you clean up from dinner," Jimmy said, carrying dishes from the table over to the sink.

"Thanks." Without Spencer to act as a buffer between them, Marisa was suddenly self-conscious again. She took the plates as Jimmy rinsed them, and stacked them in the dishwasher, wishing that he hadn't volunteered to help. They were working in such a cramped space that in normal circumstances they ought to have bumped into each other a dozen times, but they were taking such great care *not* to touch each other that they never once came into contact.

It was difficult to maintain this artificial distance while pretending it didn't exist, and soon the noise of rattling cutlery and running water wasn't loud enough to cover the tension taking on life between them. Every time she took a cup and avoided Jimmy's fingers, Marisa felt the tension grow more acute.

"Have you lived in Colorado for a long time, Jimmy?" She asked the first question that popped into her head, just so there would be some words filling the dome of silence that was expanding relentlessly around them.

Jimmy adjusted his glasses before he answered. "No, I just moved here. I used to live in Washington D.C." He turned around and leaned against the sink, shaking soap bubbles from his hands.

His eyes gleamed with sudden mischief. "Guess who I worked for. Go on, guess."

He was obviously trying to tease her, and she played along. Anything was better than the previous strained silence. "Hmm…let's see. Washington D.C. is the home of the federal government. Did you work for the government, Jimmy?"

"Kinda." He was obviously bursting to tell her where

he'd worked. He flicked a dish towel, making a loud snap. "I worked for the FBI."

For an instant, Marisa's mind blanked with shock. She had to swallow a couple of times before she could speak. "You worked for the FBI?"

He grinned, clearly delighted by her reaction. "Yes, ma'am. I cleaned up for all the most important people. I even cleaned up for Mr. Louis Freeh."

Marisa felt herself go limp. What the hell had she expected him to say, she wondered. That once he'd been an FBI agent, but now he'd decided to become a janitor? She drew in a deep breath, puzzled by her own reaction, and knowing that she needed to sound impressed by Jimmy's past place of employment, since he was obviously proud of it.

"Gee, that must have been an interesting place to work, Jimmy. Mr. Freeh is the head of the whole FBI, isn't he?"

Jimmy nodded. "He's the director and he's a very important man. More important than Mr. Frieze, even. But lots of people clean up for the FBI, and I'm the only person who takes care of keeping the Refuge clean. That means my job here is real useful. More important even than when I worked for the FBI."

"That's true. And I know Mr. Frieze is very happy with the job you're doing here. Does he know that you used to work for the FBI?"

Jimmy shrugged. "I guess he does. A teacher from my old school found this job for me. He's a friend of Mr. Frieze. I guess he told Mr. Frieze where I'd worked before."

"Why did you quit your job with the FBI, Jimmy? Didn't you like living in Washington?"

"Washington's okay. I used to like it there a lot." He

gave a slow smile. "I liked going to the Natural History Museum with my sister. Dinosaurs are cool."

"They sure are. Way cool."

Jimmy's eyes lit up. "Didn't you think *Jurassic Park* was just the greatest movie?"

"The best." Marisa had a secret addiction to sci-fi movies. Her sister, Belle, always accused her of having the taste of a twelve-year-old boy where movies were concerned.

"Which part did you like best? I liked it when the velociraptors chased the kids around the kitchen."

"That was exciting. But best of all, I liked the scene where the triceratops got sick. When I saw that, I believed for a few moments that I was watching real people trying to cure a real dinosaur."

Jimmy nodded. "Yeah, that was cool. I liked it when the baby dinosaur came out of the egg, too."

She realized they were smiling at each other as if they'd discovered something amazing about their shared interests, which was even more crazy than the rest of this crazy evening. A mutual admiration for the special effects in *Jurassic Park* was hardly the equivalent of discovering they were soul mates. Turning away, Marisa quickly bent to add detergent to the dishwasher.

"So if you liked living in Washington, what made you decide to move away?" she asked.

"I used to live with my sister," Jimmy said. "We had a real nice apartment with a balcony and everything. But after she died, I didn't want to stay there anymore. I missed her too much. She was my best friend in the whole world."

Jimmy's voice was tinged with desolation, and Marisa felt a surge of sympathy. She remembered he'd mentioned that his sister had died in a car crash, and she realized what a shock it must have been for him to lose his "best friend" without any warning.

Forgetting the space she'd so carefully maintained all evening long, she reached out and put her hand on his arm in an instinctive desire to comfort.

His muscles bunched under her touch. For a moment, his whole body froze into stillness. Then he jerked his arm away and quickly crossed to the table. Once he got there, though, he didn't seem to know what to do. He stood with his back turned toward her. His arms hung limply at his sides, but his hands, she noticed, were clenched into fists.

Dammit, she'd known he would react badly if she touched him. Marisa was angry with herself for putting an end to their pleasant conversation. Determined not to bring back the tension she'd worked so hard to banish, she spoke to him softly. "I'm sorry about your sister, Jimmy."

He didn't turn around. "I miss her. And that's why I came to Colorado."

"I understand why you wanted to get away from Washington, but why did you choose to come to Colorado? Do you have family here?"

"No," he said. "There's nobody. But Mr. Donaldson got me this job." He finally turned to face her again. He leaned against the table, arms crossed. "What about you? Do you have family here?"

"No. My sister and her husband have just been transferred to Washington, actually. My brother-in-law works for the government, too. Like you did." She didn't tell him that Sandro Marchese was one of the highest-ranking investigators in the U.S. Customs Service, in case Jimmy felt that his own former job with the FBI looked petty by comparison. "And my mother and brother are still in Florida."

"So if you don't have family here, why did *you* come to Colorado?" he asked.

She gave a wry smile. "To get away from my family, I guess. After my husband died, I needed to make a fresh start. In Florida, there were too many memories lurking around every corner, waiting to ambush me. Plus, my mother is one of those people who can turn a spoiled hamburger into a federal disaster, so when there's a real problem, her sympathy can be overwhelming to the point that it's exhausting."

Marisa had noticed previously that if she got too elaborate in her answers, Jimmy simply returned to another version of his original question. He did that now. "Do you miss your husband a lot?" he asked.

She could have lied. In the months since Evan had been killed, she'd glossed over the sordid realities of their marriage so many times that there was no reason why she couldn't do it one more time. But for some reason, Jimmy's simple directness seemed to force a truthful response from her.

"No, I don't miss him," she said quietly. "My husband had a vicious temper, and I couldn't trust him. That doesn't make for a happy marriage—or for good memories."

"Did he have an affair?" Jimmy asked. "My dad had sex with another woman and that's why my mom divorced him."

She'd forgotten Jimmy's tendency to ask questions that other people might like to ask, but knew they shouldn't. She wasn't sure how to answer him. Could she explain to a person with no experience of a sophisticated adult relationship that, in retrospect, Evan's unfaithfulness seemed a relatively minor offense in comparison to the cruelty with which he used their own child to blackmail her into silence about his criminal activities?

She tried to find words that were honest and yet simple enough for Jimmy to understand. "Evan had sex with lots of women after we were married, but he did other bad things, too. Really bad things that were against the law. If he hadn't died, he would have gone to prison."

Jimmy didn't seem shocked by her revelation. He looked at her consideringly. "You're smart," he said. "And you're pretty, too. Why did you marry a bad man?"

"That's a really dumb question," she said angrily.

He flushed. "I'm sorry. I guess I ask a lot of dumb questions, huh?"

She was immediately mortified that she'd said something hurtful just because she didn't like the direction in which his questions were leading her. She wrapped her arms around her waist and discovered she was trembling. How had their conversation traveled so fast from dinosaurs to questions that probed some of the most troubling aspects of her personal history?

Still, she had no right to blame Jimmy for the sore spots in her psyche. She drew in a shaky breath. "I'm the one who should apologize. I'm sorry, Jimmy, I didn't mean to snap at you."

"That's okay." He hesitated a moment before adding, "What did I say wrong? You *are* pretty. You *are* smart. Anyone can see that."

"You didn't say anything wrong, Jimmy. Really."

"Then why are you mad at me?"

"I'm not mad at you. I'm mad at myself."

"Why?"

The truth burst out in an angry rush. "Because I spent

five years married to a man who was a criminal, and for the first three years, I didn't even realize there was a problem. Now that Evan's dead, I keep asking myself why I was so blind. And why I couldn't find a way to stop him before he destroyed so many lives.''

And that was the painful truth she'd been running from ever since Evan died, Marisa realized. She could forgive herself for marrying him, since she'd been young and vulnerable and he'd been expert in his psychological manipulations. What she couldn't forgive was the fact that she'd been so obsessed with getting pregnant and carrying a child to term that she'd ignored a hundred different clues that Evan wasn't the man he pretended to be. And by the time Spencer was born, it was too late for wisdom. With the birth of his son, Evan had the hostage he needed, and he exploited his advantage with ruthless brutality, holding her to ransom while he tried to seize control of her father's smuggling empire.

Jimmy looked as if he wanted to say something comforting, but didn't know how. ''Mean people don't always look mean,'' he said finally. ''You shouldn't be mad at yourself because it took a while for you to find out your husband was only pretending to be nice.''

She smiled at his simple wisdom, albeit a tad ruefully. ''You're probably right, Jimmy. In fact, I'm sure you're right. I need to stop obsessing about what happened in the past. I can't change it, so I might as well accept it.''

Jimmy looked at her without smiling and touched her hair with the tips of his fingers. ''You're real pretty when you smile,'' he said. ''You don't smile very often, do you?''

Marisa's cheeks grew hot, and she found herself breathing quickly, as if the room had lost its oxygen. She realized, suddenly, that what she really wanted to do was take Jimmy's hand and run it slowly down her body, and she sprang back from him as if scalded.

What in hell was the matter with her, anyway? It was flat-out perverted that she was having sexual fantasies involving a man whose body might be spectacular, but whose mental age was prepubescent.

"You have to leave now, Jimmy." She'd done all the pretending she could manage for one night. She couldn't find any way to gloss over what had just happened—her reaction to his physical presence. She could only hope that Jimmy was blissfully ignorant of her fantasies, and that his feelings wouldn't be too badly hurt by her abrupt dismissal.

"Okay." He reclaimed his baseball cap and put it on with exaggerated care. Marisa knew him well enough by now to be sure that the fact he wasn't looking at her meant that he understood he'd offended her in some way. Dammit, she'd really messed this evening up. He didn't deserve to feel bad about something that was strictly her problem.

"Jimmy..."

"Yes, ma'am?"

"Thank you for having dinner with us tonight. Spencer and I both enjoyed your company a lot."

"It was my pleasure, ma'am."

She realized her hands were clenching the edge of the table as if she were in imminent danger of keeling over. She unwound her fingers and shoved her hands into the pockets of her pants. She even managed to dredge up a smile.

"Jimmy, we're friends. You should call me Marisa. Remember we talked about that before?"

"I remember," he said. They'd reached the front door, and she opened it, hoping that they'd managed to get their strange friendship more or less cobbled together again.

Jimmy paused in the doorway, and the cool mountain air blew in, making her shiver. He looked down at her in silence. He held himself motionless, and his face was without expression, but for one hysterical moment she thought he was going to kiss her.

Her imagination, thank God, was working overtime.

He stepped outside and turned back to give her a military salute goodbye. "Good night, Marisa. Sleep well."

"Good night."

She didn't wait to see him walk to the stairs. She slammed the door shut and leaned against it, shaking. She was not going to analyze what had just happened, she decided. There were some dark places it was safer not to explore, and her attraction to James T. Griffin III was definitely one of them.

Seven

Driving to work on Friday morning, Marisa renewed her resolve that she would avoid spending too much time with Jimmy and that she certainly wouldn't eat lunch with him today, however much Spencer pleaded. Her sleep had been restless, and sometime during the long night she'd reached the satisfying conclusion that she could blame Evan for her weird attraction to a man who—to put it bluntly—was several bricks short of a load. During the final year of their marriage, Evan had completely traumatized her, both emotionally and sexually. As a result, she was apparently unable to feel even a twinge of reawakening sexuality except in the company of a man who could never become a sexual partner. Since Jimmy was barely a mental adult, her subconscious must have qualified him as too ineligible to represent a threat, hence the extraordinary flashes of intense physical attraction.

Of course, she blamed Evan for almost everything that was wrong with her life, from hangnails to her anemic bank balance, so she wasn't entirely convinced by her self-analysis. Still, since no better rationalization came to mind, Marisa resolved to run with this one.

Her decision to avoid Jimmy was easier to stick to than she could have expected, because of a crisis at work. She and Spencer arrived at the Refuge fifteen minutes early, but she found Janet already in the nursery, playing a game of building blocks with her little girl, Alicia.

"Hi, Alicia." Marisa gave Janet's daughter a friendly pat on the shoulder. "Your hair looks so cute today. I love your barrettes. Are they new?"

Alicia nodded her head. "They're elfants. Their tails move, and their trunks."

"Wow," Marisa said, tugging off Spencer's jacket and helping him to hang it on his hook. "They sure are pretty." She turned to Janet. "What's up?" she asked in a low voice. "Where's Elsa? Isn't she assigned to the first day care shift this morning?"

"Yes, but she's in the bathroom," Janet replied. "She was very upset, but I'm sure she'll be fine in a minute or two."

"What's wrong? Not problems with her pregnancy, I hope?"

"No, nothing like that." Janet pulled a face. "It's Anya. Anya Dzhambirov. She's gone. Disappeared. She left last night, when everyone was sleeping."

Marisa's head shot up as she was retying Spencer's shoelaces. "Anya's *gone?* You mean, she just packed her bags and left? Without telling anyone?"

"Yep, that seems to be pretty much what happened. Fran Harlowe discovered she was missing first thing this morning." Janet pushed a pile of building blocks toward Spencer and helped him to start stacking them into a low wall around the tower Alicia had already built.

"We encourage all the pregnant moms to eat something when they get up, so when Anya didn't come down for breakfast, Fran went up to her room to check out what was going on. When she saw that the bed hadn't been slept in, she called Stuart, and he came in right away. They searched the entire building, which took a while, as you can imagine, but they concluded about fifteen minutes ago that Anya's not here. Stuart's talking to the other girls now, but as far as I can make out from what Elsa was telling me, nobody saw Anya after ten o'clock last night.''

"But where's she gone?'' Marisa asked. She shook her head. "No, ignore that dumb question. What I meant was, where *might* she have gone? I thought that was the whole point of the Refuge—that the women who come here have no money, and no place to turn.''

"You're right, and Anya is more deprived than most of our residents. She doesn't have any family even in Chechnya, let alone here in the States.''

"She doesn't have a car, either, so how did she get away? Presumably, she was lugging a suitcase, and it must have been fairly heavy. What did she use for transportation? And why on earth would she leave in the middle of the night? I mean, for heaven's sake, did she think somebody here was going to tie her to the bed and forbid her to go?''

"Who knows? Maybe if you've grown up in a police state like Anya did, then it takes a while to break the habit of secrecy. If she decided she wanted to keep her baby, she might have been afraid to tell us.''

"Would people here have tried to dissuade her from keeping the baby?''

"You betcha,'' Janet said without hesitation. "Anya's in no position to become a mother right now, either financially or emotionally. We'd have tried to persuade her that adoption was the best choice, but that doesn't mean anyone would have forced her to give away her baby. How could we do that, anyway, even if we wanted to?'' Janet pinched the bridge of her nose, as if trying to ease a headache. "I think the real problem is her boyfriend.

Anya received a long-distance phone call yesterday evening, and after that, Elsa says, she seemed upset. If the call really was from the father of her baby, that's definitely bad news.''

"Why? Have you met him? Is he nasty?"

"Very nasty. I haven't met him, but from what Anya has let slip from time to time, he's not only a convicted felon, he's also the controlling type, and physically abusive. The sort of guy who only feels really macho when his little woman is cringing at his feet after a couple of hefty slaps upside the head.''

"Well, that's just great." Marisa's stomach knotted at the images Janet's words conjured up. "What are we doing to try to find her?"

Elsa came back from the bathroom before Janet could answer. She looked pale, and her eyes were red-rimmed.

"I just heard the news about Anya," Marisa said to her. "I'm so sorry."

Elsa sniffed into a tissue. "I don't know why she go. She promise me we share an apartment when we leave here." Elsa's voice sounded thick with tears. "I thought she my good friend, but she not tell me she vant to leave."

"We'll find her, you know we will. Try not to worry, Elsa." Janet put her arm around Elsa's shoulders, sounding a great deal more confident than she had a couple of seconds earlier when talking to Marisa.

Elsa probably knew how much Janet's promise was worth, but she snatched at what comfort she could get. Straightening her shoulders, she made a visible effort to cheer up, aided by Spencer and Alicia, who started squabbling and forced her to pay attention to them. Marisa and Janet stayed long enough to help her get the children settled around the table with tubs of modeling clay and plastic shape-cutters. Then they both left to go to their respective offices.

"I'd better get ready for a marathon day," Marisa said. "Stuart must be twice as busy as usual, and his schedule was already jam-packed."

"It always is. I've no idea where he finds the time and energy to do all he does—"

"Oh, there you are, Marisa. Hi, Janet." Stuart came down the corridor almost at a run. Despite his brisk pace, he looked exhausted, which was no surprise under the circumstances. "How's Elsa?" he asked Janet.

"Medically speaking, she's just fine. Emotionally, she's doing okay. Not great, but okay."

"Good. Have you checked on Lili? She's another one of Anya's friends, and Fran Harlowe said she was crying all through breakfast."

Janet shook her head. "No, I haven't seen Lili this morning. I'll go and have a word with her now. Thanks for reminding me."

"Keep me informed if any of the girls don't seem to be coping."

Janet nodded. "Yes, I sure will. Darn it! I just can't understand why Anya felt the need to leave this way. Didn't she realize how upset all her friends would be?"

"I'm very much afraid we're seeing a textbook case of what happens when an abusive boyfriend goes to work on a vulnerable woman like Anya," Stuart said.

"Men," Janet muttered under her breath, heading toward the stairs. "Personally, I'm about ready to vote for sperm banks and a phased elimination of the male sex."

"I'll pretend I didn't hear that," Stuart said, managing a tired grin.

"If only Anya hadn't taken that phone call yesterday,"

Marisa said as she accompanied Stuart down the hallway to their offices.

"I was thinking the same thing," Stuart said. "But I'm not about to start monitoring phone calls. This place is supposed to be a safe haven for women who've had a rough time. It's not a prison."

"It's a difficult line to draw," Marisa said. "Anya's so vulnerable, she almost needs enforced protection from outside pressures."

"Yes, she does. But bottom line, in this day and age, we'd never get women to agree to come here if they weren't left with a healthy dose of personal freedom."

"Speaking of freedom, should I notify the police that Anya's missing?" Marisa asked.

"No need. I already did that as soon as we were sure she was gone."

"Will they even try to look for her, do you think? After all, she's an adult, legally allowed to live wherever she pleases. Nobody here has to give her permission to leave."

"That's not quite true," Stuart said, as they turned into his office. "Anya's only seventeen, and she's in the United States on a refugee visa, which makes me her official guardian. That means by law she was required to let me know her new address when she left here. If I file a complaint, the Immigration Service is supposed to go looking for her."

"Will they?"

"No, of course not." Stuart sounded angry, but Marisa realized his anger was directed at the situation, not at her. "According to whose figures you want to believe, there are anywhere from one million to three million illegal immigrants living and working in this country on any given day. Anya is just one more."

"You don't think the fact that she's still a minor might spur the authorities to take action?" Marisa asked.

"Dream on." Stuart was openly impatient with such a naive hope. "The streets of every city in this country are filled to overflowing with underage girls who've run away from home, and a lot of them are a hell of a lot younger than seventeen. Try eleven or twelve, if you want the police to sit up and take notice."

"Then there's not much hope that we'll get any help from the police or from the INS in searching for Anya."

"Realistically, they're going to do nothing."

A dead weight settled in the pit of Marisa's stomach. Memories of Evan were still painfully close, and she couldn't bear to think of Anya at the mercy of an abusive, controlling man. "Maybe there's some information in the files that might give us a clue where to start looking for her," she suggested. "How about an address for this rotten boyfriend of hers?"

Stuart sighed. "I've already started a search through all the relevant paperwork, to see if I can come up with any useful leads. We have an address for the baby's father, but I've tried calling the phone number that's listed, and the phone's been disconnected."

"He could be living there still and just neglecting to pay the phone bill."

"It's possible." Stuart didn't sound even marginally optimistic. "Frankly, I suspect the address is a fake, but we'll ask the police in New York to physically check it out, of course. If we're real lucky, they might get around to doing that within the next couple of weeks."

Marisa tried not to feel totally dejected. "What about the adoptive parents for Anya's baby? Will you have to notify them that Anya's changed her mind?"

"No, thank goodness. Fortunately, I've made it a rule

never to tell prospective parents the name of the birth
mother until their baby's safely here. But I do need to
get busy and reassign babies to prospective parents.
Anya's baby was provisionally matched with a Wisconsin couple, and I need to find them a substitute child right
away. They've been on the waiting list for almost two
years, and it's definitely their turn to become parents. The
trustees of the Wainscott Foundation come into town for
a board meeting next week, and I'm going to be tied up
with meetings and presentations, so I'd like to get this
shuffling around taken care of today. We need to get
busy.''

The morning flew by, even more hectic than usual, as
Marisa worked with Stuart to clear up the administrative
confusion left by Anya's precipitous departure. At Stuart's request, she called various charitable organizations
that had worked previously with the Refuge, letting them
know there was a vacancy for a new admission. Several
agencies were anxious to take advantage of the unexpected space for a mother-to-be, and she made a list of
those agencies, together with appropriate details, so that
Stuart could decide which lucky woman was going to be
offered the safe haven Anya had spurned.

The police arrived shortly before noon, in the guise of
Officer Bob Penney, who represented one-quarter of
Wainscott's entire law enforcement establishment. He
looked too young to be shaving regularly, and his normal
duties consisted of such demanding tasks as ticketing
tourists for parking in front of the fire hydrant during ski
season.

What he lacked in investigative experience, however,
he seemed willing to make up for in persistence. Fueled
by copious infusions of Fran Harlowe's iced tea and oatmeal raisin cookies, he interviewed every mother-to-be

and every employee at the Refuge with dogged dedication, but his questions elicited no new information, and certainly nothing that would justify his taking up more police time to pursue an active search for Anya.

At Stuart's request, Marisa listened in when Bob Penney reported back after three frustrating hours of questioning. "If your moms-to-be know anything about how and why Anya left, they're not talking," he said. "In fact, they seem real reluctant to talk to me about anything, let alone Anya."

"A lot of our residents have had bad experiences with the police in their native countries," Stuart said. "To be honest, I was hoping against hope that the sight of your uniform might scare them into cooperation."

"Well, it didn't." Bob Penney closed his notebook with a defeated *snap*. "That's always assuming they have anything to share. My best bet is that Anya decided to leave, then kept her own counsel about why she wanted out and where she was going."

Stuart was drumming on the table with his pencil. He realized what he was doing and laid it down, clasping his hands together before he spoke. "Anya has gestational diabetes and she speaks quite limited English. The diabetes has to be controlled by a strict diet and constant testing. If it's controlled, there's no problem, and she'll have a fine, healthy baby. If it's not controlled, the worst-case scenario is that she and the baby can both die. For her own sake, she really needs to be found."

"I sure do wish I could do something to help..." Officer Penney's voice trailed away.

Stuart's expression was bleak. "I know I'm asking a big favor, Bob, but could you check out the boyfriend's address in Brooklyn, as soon as possible?"

"Sure." Officer Penney was visibly relieved to grant

the favor. "I'll send a faxed request for an officer from the local precinct to check out the address. I'll tell him it's urgent for humanitarian reasons, but that's the best I can do. I'll let you know what we find out—if anything. But don't hold your breath."

"I'm not. I know too much about the immigrant underground to hold any false hopes. Anya can bury herself with no visible trace to outsiders." Stuart rose and shook Officer Penney's hand. "Thanks, Bob. I appreciate all you've done. I know you could have blown us off with a phone call."

"You're welcome. We weren't busy today." He gave a disconsolate shake of his head. "I just wish I could have been more successful in finding a few clues as to where she's gone."

Marisa and Stuart were both depressed after Officer Penney left, and the day didn't improve. Suzie, four months pregnant and a recent arrival at the Refuge, started to spot blood and had to be rushed to the hospital in Boulder. A couple of hours later, the doctor called to report that Suzie was miscarrying and seemed distraught to be losing her baby, despite the fact that she had never wanted to be pregnant in the first place.

"I'd better go and see her," Stuart said. "Do you think you can hold the fort here, Marisa?"

"I think so, yes." She gave a weak smile. "With luck, we won't have any more major disasters before the weekend."

"Don't count on it. Babies and pregnant women have no respect for weekends." He gave her a rueful smile that contained a new hint of intimacy. "Thanks for all you've done this week, Marisa. God knows how I would have managed these past few days without you here."

She flushed with pleasure at his compliment. The

knowledge that she really was coping well with the demands of her job was a huge morale booster. She already felt like a different and more competent person than the insecure woman who had barely scrounged up the courage to come for an interview. And the more courage she acquired, the more she noticed ways to expand her role and increase her usefulness.

"It's good to know I've found a job where I can make a real contribution," she said.

"That's an understatement. You've single-handedly held the office together this week." Stuart chuckled. "And to think I was hoping we might have a break in the schedule today. I wanted to ask you to have lunch with me so that we could have a chance to get to know one another a bit better. So far, we've barely spoken, except to exchange information about some emergency or other."

"Even without Anya's disappearance, you wouldn't have had any spare time today. We should just hang a sign on the outside of your door, Crisis Central."

He pulled a face. "That's too true to be funny. Oh well, let's hope that we can find at least one free hour to have lunch together next week."

He left for the hospital, and Marisa wondered if she'd imagined the faint suggestion of personal interest that she'd detected on Stuart's part. She hoped she was imagining it. Stuart was single, hardworking, dedicated, humane, handsome, and liked by everyone he met. However, instead of being pleased that he was showing signs of being attracted to her, Marisa felt only a mild exasperation. She wanted Stuart to admire her work, but she had no interest in him as a man.

Which made perfect sense, she reflected. Why would her crazy, mixed-up libido feel attracted to a normal, intelligent, good-looking man like her boss, when it could waste its time getting heated up over Jimmy Griffin?

The last two hours of the workday were free of major emergencies but filled with mini-crises that everyone seemed to expect Marisa to resolve since Stuart wasn't there. While it was great for her ego to realize that the rest of the staff at the Refuge already considered her an adequate substitute for the director, by the time she collected Spencer from the nursery, it was almost six, and she was so exhausted from trying to cope simultaneously with three different calamities that she couldn't face the prospect of going home to cook dinner.

"Would you like to go to Burger King?" she asked Spencer, buckling him into his car seat.

"Yes!" He punched his hand into the air, a gesture he'd learned from his uncle Sandro during a Christmas visit. "Burger King!"

Wainscott didn't boast fast-food restaurants, so Marisa drove a couple of miles to the interstate, where various pizza and burger joints vied for the privilege of loading cholesterol into the arteries of their customers. She ordered Spencer's favorite chicken nuggets, French fries and orange juice, adding a burger and salad for herself. The second she reached into her purse for the money to pay, she remembered that her change purse was sitting in her desk drawer at the office, where she'd shoved it when the phone rang right as she was reimbursing Janet for a diet cola.

So much for her new and super-efficient self, Marisa thought wryly. She had her wallet with her driver's license and credit cards, but Burger King didn't accept credit cards, and without her change purse she couldn't pay for the food she'd just ordered.

Embarrassed, she explained the situation to the server

behind the counter. The server called the manager, who asked where she worked. When she told him the Refuge, he pushed the tray across the counter toward her.

"Go ahead and enjoy your meal," he said. "You can bring the money in after you've eaten."

Since Spencer was hungry and beginning to whine, Marisa gratefully accepted the offer. "I'll drive back to the office as soon as we've finished eating," she promised.

"That's okay. Take your time and enjoy your dinner." The manager flashed a sympathetic grin. "You look as if you've had a rough day."

"The pits," she admitted.

She and Spencer both cheered up as they ate, and Marisa drove back to the Refuge deeply involved in a discussion with her son about how to make Teletubby custard. She let herself into the Refuge, holding Spencer's hand because the lights were dimmed for the night in this nonresidential section of the building and she didn't want him to run off.

But Spencer was scared by the flickering shadows and a silence that seemed oppressive after the lively babble he was accustomed to hearing during the day. His fingers tightened around hers, and he clung to her skirt, reluctant to move.

Bending down, Marisa swept him up into her arms. "Come on, pumpkin, I'll carry you."

Stuart's office was dark, and she flipped on the lights. The connecting door to her workstation was closed, but she could hear the muffled sounds of someone moving around in her office, shutting a file cabinet drawer. Probably Stuart back from Boulder and working late, Marisa thought.

But if it was Stuart in there, wouldn't the lights have

been on in his office? What if it was an intruder? She couldn't risk investigating, not when she had Spencer with her. To heck with paying Burger King. She'd come back and reclaim her purse tomorrow morning. Heart thudding, she started to move silently out of the office.

"Mommy!" Spencer began to whimper.

Marisa clapped her hand over Spencer's mouth, but it was too late. The door between her workstation and Stuart's office was thrown open.

"Dimmy!" Spencer gave a happy squeal of greeting. "IIi, Dimmy!"

"Hi, big guy." Jimmy smiled. "How you doin', buddy?"

"Burger King!" Spencer said, wriggling to get out of Marisa's arms so that he could run to greet his friend. She tightened her hold on him.

"What are you doing in my office at this hour of night?" she snapped.

He looked down, arms hanging limply at his sides, and she realized she had spoken with real aggression.

"I'm helping Mr. Frieze," he said.

"How?" Marisa's heart was still thumping.

"I'm copying the newsletter," Jimmy said. He turned and walked back to the copying machine that stood on a credenza in the corner of her office and that was, she now noticed, humming busily.

"The newsletter has to be out by Monday, because it's the newsletter for May, and May will soon be over. On Monday, it will be May the fifteenth, and then it's only two more weeks before it's June."

"Why didn't Mr. Frieze ask me to run the copies?" Marisa had no idea how she expected Jimmy to answer that question, or why she still felt this churning suspicion that Jimmy wasn't telling her the truth.

Jimmy considered his answer for a long, silent minute. "I don't know why Mr. Frieze didn't ask you to copy the newsletter," he said finally.

"Play, Dimmy!" Tired of being squashed in Marisa's arms, Spencer gave a giant wriggle and managed to escape her hold. He launched himself at Jimmy's knees, and hugged them tight. "Hi, Dimmy."

Jimmy tousled his hair. "Hi, Spence."

"His name's Spencer," Marisa said crisply, in no mood to be tolerant.

"Okay."

Marisa took her son's hand. "Come on, Spencer, we have to go home. It's late, past your bedtime."

He came reluctantly, and she was halfway to the door when Jimmy called her. "Marisa! Er, ma'am!"

She turned. "Yes?"

"How come you came back to the office tonight?"

Her purse! Good grief, she'd nearly walked out of here without her purse. A mind was really a terrible thing to lose.

She crossed to her desk and found the change purse that had caused all the trouble. She'd pushed it into her shoulder bag, then stalked back to the door without saying anything.

"Night, Dimmy!" Spencer's manners were better than hers, it seemed.

"'Night, big guy. See you on Monday."

Marisa still didn't speak. Right now, there was absolutely nothing she wanted to say to James T. Griffin.

Eight

Marisa had no desire to spend time alone with her thoughts, so she made sure that Saturday was jam-packed with activities, including house cleaning, laundry, a trip to the grocery store, and an afternoon excursion to the butterfly pavilion in Boulder. Spencer enjoyed having her undivided attention for hours at a stretch, even if he had to jump into the basket of clean laundry to get it; and the trip to the butterfly pavilion was a major success. Spencer was thrilled as delicate flocks of butterflies swooped and danced above his head, and Marisa was even more entranced than her son.

By the time they got home and ate dinner, it was time to bathe Spencer and put him to bed. Only minutes after he was asleep, Belle called from Washington, a regular Saturday ritual. Marisa's sister normally took a close interest in every detail of Marisa's life, but on this occasion she was, for once, totally self-absorbed.

"Where've you been all day?" she demanded, the instant Marisa picked up the phone. "I've been trying to call you for hours."

"Spencer and I went on an outing to Boulder. What's up? Is everything okay with you and Sandro? And the baby-to-be?"

"We're fine, all three of us. Great, in fact."

"You sound excited."

"I *am* excited." Belle's exhilaration bubbled across the phone wires. "I had another ultrasound, yesterday and this time the baby cooperated—"

"And the technician could tell you the sex?"

"Yes. Guess what we're going to have!"

Marisa smiled. "Hmm...I have so many sexes to choose from. This is very difficult—"

"Rizzie—"

"Okay, okay. I'm guessing it's a girl."

"Wrong," Belle said happily. "It's a boy! Oh, Rizzie, I had no idea what an amazing difference it would make once I knew the sex of the baby. It was always wonderful to be pregnant, but now it's electrifying. Suddenly, the idea that we're going to be parents seems so much more real. It's not some unknown baby growing inside me anymore, it's our *son*, and in another couple of months he'll be here."

"I know exactly what you mean. I felt the same way when I found out about Spencer. Is Sandro pleased the baby's going to be a boy?"

"Ecstatic. He's pretending he would have been just as happy if it had been a girl, but I know he's thrilled. He insisted we had to stop at the toy store on the way home and buy a stuffed rabbit dressed in a baseball outfit. Although, according to him this has nothing to do with sexual stereotyping. Oh, no. By sheer chance, it just happened that a cute blue rabbit wearing a sports uniform caught his eye."

Marisa laughed. "Right. I hope you didn't even pretend to believe him."

"Hey, what could I do? The guy was over the moon. I had to cut him some slack."

"Spencer will be almost as thrilled as Sandro. He's just beginning to realize that people are divided into two sexes, and he'll be relieved to know his first-ever cousin is going to be a boy just like him. Have you decided on any names, now that you know the sex?''

''We're working on it.'' Belle gave a chuckle. ''I have a list of my ten favorite names, and so does Sandro. Unfortunately, none of my favorites are on his list and vice versa. His number-one pick is Tom, and mine's Sebastian, so you can see, we have a few rounds of negotiation to get through before the baby is born.''

''That could be interesting. I'm not quite sure how you compromise between Tom and Sebastian.''

''They're not exactly close kin, are they? But we'll come up with something.'' Belle sounded supremely confident, and Marisa thought wistfully how secure and grounded her sister's marriage was. It had taken Belle and Sandro seven years to get together, but when they finally made the commitment, they seemed to fit together with no rough edges to grind against each other and create discord.

She chatted with Belle for another twenty minutes, filling her in on some of the details of her new job, before hanging up. Naturally, she didn't mention Jimmy. There was no reason in the world why she should want to talk to her sister about the office janitor.

Passing through the kitchen to get a diet soda, Marisa checked on Spencer, who was nose to nose with Bear and sleeping peacefully. Then she settled down to watch some television. Saturday night was the only opportunity she got to watch TV without Spencer around, and she usually enjoyed these few hours of entertainment chosen strictly to please herself. Her son was the light of her life, but there were only so many times you could watch *Teletubbies* before wishing that a spacecraft would swoop down and take Tinky-Winky and friends back to the planet they'd come from.

Tonight, though, no drama, comedy or news programs could hold her attention. Finally she gave up, muted the TV, and allowed herself to do what she'd wanted to do all day, which was to obsess about her encounter the previous night with Jimmy. Jimmy the handyman, otherwise known as James T. Griffin III, former office cleaner for the FBI, possessor of a powerfully developed body and sadly weak mind.

She had this compulsive need to chew over the details of their encounter because there had been something off-key about it, Marisa reflected. Something more than her nervousness at coming across Jimmy so unexpectedly in a darkened and empty building. Something more, even, than the disconcerting fact that she had once again reacted to his presence with a tremor of sexual awareness.

Trying to pinpoint what had bothered her so much, she mentally reviewed their conversation. She could remember what had been said with word-perfect recall, a fact that was odd in itself. After all, discussions with Jimmy didn't exactly sparkle with wit and wisdom. In explaining why he needed to work late, Jimmy had rambled on about the date and the fact that the Wainscott Foundation newsletter was overdue. There was nothing strange about that, since Jimmy seemed to be mildly obsessed about times, dates and numbers, as if he oriented himself to a world he didn't fully comprehend by keeping track of as many numerical facts as he could.

It was Jimmy's manner of speaking when he'd spoken to Spencer that really bothered her, Marisa realized. When they'd met in the parking lot on her first day at the Refuge, Jimmy had treated Spencer warily, as if he wasn't used to dealing with young children. But last night, he'd ruffled her son's hair in a casual, self-assured way that reminded her of the easy confidence her brother-in-law showed when playing with Spencer.

Surely that sort of bone-deep self-assurance wasn't something you could acquire in a week, just because he and Spencer had played horsey a couple of times? And when she'd snapped at Jimmy for using the nickname "Spence," his reply to her had been tinged with a sort of irony.

That's it, Marisa thought, sitting up straighter in her armchair. Last night she had never quite believed Jimmy was telling her the truth because she'd picked up on a subtle note of self-mockery in his voice. Why would Jimmy have found the situation ironic? More to the point, wasn't irony one of those higher order functions of the brain that could never be grasped by people of less-than-normal intelligence? So was she misinterpreting Jimmy's tone of voice, or...

Or what?

Or nothing, most likely. Marisa scowled into space, impatient with her meandering thoughts. The problem was that marriage to Evan had made her paranoid, causing her to see subterfuge and deception where none existed. She was leery of Stuart because she suspected him of having a raging temper that he kept concealed from the world. One small incident over a file was all it had taken to arouse her misgivings, and now she viewed her boss with distrust, as if keeping strict control of your temper were somehow a bad thing. And on top of harboring doubts about Stuart, she now suspected poor kindhearted Jimmy of...

Of what?

Her thoughts chased each other in narrowing circles until she gave up in disgust and took herself off to bed.

Climbing under the covers, she told herself with great firmness that she was going to put the events of Friday evening out of her mind—and was perfectly well aware that she was lying.

On Sunday, still in the mode of major activity to produce minimal thought, Marisa decided to take Spencer to ten o'clock mass at the local church. St. Anne's was located at the opposite end of town, near the Alpine Ski Lodge. By coincidence, it was also no more than a couple of minutes' walk from Kohler Ranch Drive, where Jimmy had mentioned he lived. Marisa was quite sure that the church's proximity to Jimmy's apartment had nothing to do with her decision to attend mass. It was time she and Spencer got back into the habit of attending church regularly.

With the fickleness typical of May in the Rocky Mountains, the weather had changed yet again during the night, and the sky was now overcast. At this elevation, it was always cold when the sun wasn't shining, and she and Spencer both needed to wear heavy sweaters to ward off the morning chill.

Spencer didn't seem in the least depressed by the gray skies or his return to winter clothing. He chattered happily all the way to church, and was only a little shy when she took him to the nursery where four other preschoolers were already playing. He settled down quickly with a giant pot of paste and a sheet of construction paper, while she gave her name and address to the Sunday School teacher.

Her son seemed to find the move to Wainscott entirely to his liking, Marisa reflected thankfully, as she watched him stick his sweater and the occasional colored cutout to his piece of paper. Since his tantrum on the day she started work, he had been exceptionally content and cheerful for a toddler in the thick of the terrible twos.

Waving goodbye, she followed the landscaped pathway toward the main entrance to the church, moving briskly to stay warm. But at the door, she turned abruptly and walked off in the opposite direction, offering a silent apology to God as she went.

God, presumably, wouldn't be surprised at where she was heading, since Marisa had finally acknowledged to herself that she'd been intending to go to Jimmy's apartment ever since she'd gotten out of bed this morning.

Jimmy had mentioned that he lived at number fourteen Kohler Ranch Drive, right next to the church. Number fourteen turned out to be a slightly dilapidated building, three stories high, with a weed-strewn path leading to the front door. The six mailboxes suggested that each floor had been converted into two apartments, and a label on one of the mailboxes indicated that James T. Griffin III lived in apartment 3B.

The outer door to the building had a frosted glass window, and, peering inside, Marisa got a distorted view of a shabby lobby and a bare wooden staircase. There was a bell on the door as well as a knocker, but when Marisa tried the handle, it turned easily. In small-town Wainscott, the crime wave seemed very distant, and security systems were deemed unnecessary.

Rap music blasted out from one of the ground-floor apartments, deadening all other sounds. She climbed the stairs slowly, and when she reached the dimly lit third-floor landing she almost turned around and went downstairs again.

What was she going to say to Jimmy, even if she found him at home? She heard her own breath pumping fast and shallow out of her lungs, and recognized her behavior as having passed beyond strange and into the realm of comedy. Still, she didn't do the sensible thing and retreat down the stairs. Instead, she rapped sharply on the panels of Jimmy's door before common sense could take hold and compel her to behave rationally.

"You're early," Jimmy said, as he opened the door. He did a double take when he saw who was waiting on the other side. He had been toweling his hair dry, but at the sight of Marisa, he stopped rubbing and let the towel drop around his neck.

"Oh, it's you. Hi, Marisa." Presumably he'd just gotten out of the shower, because he wasn't wearing a shirt and he didn't have his glasses on. The lack of glasses seemed to bother him, and he rubbed his hand across the bridge of his nose as if searching for them. But instead of narrowing his gaze to see more clearly, his eyes hazed and lost focus, his expression changing to one of vacant distraction as he absorbed the fact of her presence.

"Hi, Jimmy. I hope I didn't disturb you." He was wearing jeans, but he was barefoot as well as being naked from the waist up. Viewed this close, without a shirt, his body seemed to be composed of solid muscle. Marisa wondered who he'd been expecting to see. Someone he didn't feel the need to wear clothes for, obviously.

"I'm not dressed yet. I'm not wearing my shirt."

"I can see you're not dressed. That's okay, Jimmy." She found his tendency to state the obvious endearing, and gave him a little smile of encouragement. He seemed uneasy and dropped his gaze, shifting from one foot to the other and crossing his arms over his chest. As he moved, he ended up positioned so that he completely blocked her view into his apartment.

"I'm sorry if I came at a bad moment," Marisa said, made uncomfortable by Jimmy's embarrassment. He'd only been living in Wainscott for six weeks, so who did he know well enough to greet half dressed? He was stunningly good-looking, and she couldn't avoid the thought that she might not be the only woman who found herself attracted to his powerful body and sweet smile.

She despised herself for speculating about something that was none of her business. Jimmy was a self-supporting adult with a right to entertain whomever he pleased, whenever he pleased. She shoved her hands into the pockets of her sweater, suddenly feeling as out of place as a high school sophomore who'd been dared to ask the captain of the football team out on a date and now couldn't find any words to complete the dare.

"I was just in the neighborhood." She flushed bright red at the pathetic excuse. "If you're expecting someone else, I can leave."

"I have a friend coming real soon." Jimmy didn't open the door wider, or make any move to invite her into his apartment. She felt her blush expand to cover her entire body. She'd intruded on his privacy without any credible excuse, and Jimmy clearly wasn't happy about it.

"Then, I won't keep you," she said, recovering her dignity as best she could. "See you at work tomorrow."

"Yeah. Say hi to Spencer. Where is he, anyway?"

"At Sunday School." She turned to go, took a couple of steps toward the stairs, then swung back, needing to say something more that might justify her intrusion—not so much for his sake as for her own. "Jimmy, I'm sorry—"

Her apology died stillborn. In walking toward the stairs, the angle of her vision had shifted relative to where Jimmy was standing, giving her a narrow but clear view straight into his living room. Now she could see what his body had previously obscured: the corner of a pull-out desk of the kind that could be concealed behind closet doors, and on the desk a computer monitor that displayed a screen filled with columns of numbers.

If she'd turned around even a second later, she would never have seen the numbers, because, as she watched, the computer defaulted to a screen-saver program that marched colored dinosaurs across the monitor.

Jimmy noticed the direction of her gaze and realized at once what she'd seen. He swung around, and she was convinced his mouth gave an almost imperceptible twitch of relief when he saw the dinosaurs. "My mom gave me that computer," he said. "I like to play games on it."

She was one-hundred-percent sure that he was lying. Superficially, there was nothing incongruous about his remark—but at that moment Marisa knew beyond a shadow of a doubt what she'd been groping her way toward almost from the moment she first met Jimmy.

He wasn't mentally retarded. She'd stake her life on it.

Her stomach lurched, not with shock but with the realization that she wasn't really surprised at all. Jimmy had made a big mistake in trying to justify having a computer in his living room. If he'd kept quiet, she might have come up with a rationalization for its presence all by herself. She might even have found a way to explain away the columns of figures as just another example of his addiction to numbers. As it was, the moment he started to respond, she started to doubt. If Jimmy were the man he pretended to be, he wouldn't have interpreted her questioning gaze so swiftly. In fact, he wouldn't even have realized that he needed to justify having a computer. His immediate explanation that he had it just to play games was simply one more odd reaction in a string of odd reactions over the past week.

"I have to go now," Jimmy said, closing the door. "'Bye, Marisa."

"Wait." She stuck her foot in the door, no longer bothering to pretend she'd come on a social visit. "That's a very fancy computer your mother gave you just for playing games. What games do you like to play, Jimmy?"

"Lots of games. All different ones." He stared at her foot, seemingly willing her to move it. "I need to go now. 'Bye."

She kept her foot right where it was. "Name one game you enjoy." She spoke softly, but it was a demand nonetheless.

He blinked. "Dune."

"Bad choice, Jimmy." She was tired of playing straight-man in a comedy act she hadn't agreed to participate in. "I don't believe Dune is the computer game of choice for mentally retarded adults—"

"I like Solitaire, too. I like numbers."

It was true, he did like numbers. She had a momentary qualm, then shook her head. "It's no use, Jimmy. If you wanted me to believe the low-IQ shtick, you should have picked one of the shoot-'em-up games like Duke Nukem or Mortal Kombat."

"I do like Mortal Kombat. I like Dune and Solitaire, too. I don't understand what you're saying, Marisa. Are you mad at me?"

The fake naiveté of his question rubbed her nerve endings raw. "You bet I'm mad at you, Jimmy-boy." She felt her anger mounting, spewing up from the dark place where she'd stored all her rage and grief over the past few years. She was sick to death of men assuming that she would be too stupid to see through their chicanery.

"Let's quit with the Forrest Gump impersonation, okay? Who are you? And what's the real purpose of this scam you're running?"

"You know who I am. I'm James T. Griffin III—"

She snorted. "Right, and I'm the Easter Bunny."

"Are you? Then where's your basket of eggs?"

"'Cute' absolutely isn't going to cut it, Jimmy. I want answers, and I want them now."

"There is no scam, I swear."

"So what's going on here?" She feigned sudden enlightenment. "Wait, I've got it! You're a famous actor and you're just playing Jimmy the Retard to practice for a Broadway role. Wow! I wonder why I don't believe that?"

His eyes narrowed, and she could almost see him debating what lie to tell her next. At the last moment he must have changed his mind, and he looked away. "Go home, Marisa. For Spencer's sake, pretend you never came here today."

Marisa's anger boiled over, then coalesced into ice-cold rage. Evan had used Spencer to manipulate her behavior, and she'd succumbed to his threats, terrified to risk her son's safety. The results of her weakness had been disastrous. Instead of protecting Spencer, she'd put him and everyone else she loved in danger.

The lessons from those experiences had been hard-won, but she'd learned them well. She had vowed when Evan died in a hail of bullets that she would never again allow herself to be controlled through fear, and she wasn't about to break that vow.

"Don't you dare use my son to threaten me." She spat the words at Jimmy, making no attempt to hide her fury.

He wasn't wearing enough clothing to conceal a gun, and she figured any other threat to her safety she could take care of.

"Tell me what scam you're running at the Refuge, or I'm going to walk right out of here and call Stuart Frieze."

"Please don't do that." His voice was subtly different, deeper as well as infinitely more confident.

She let out a long, slow breath. "Well, what do you know? I finally caught your attention."

"I guess you did. How long before you have to pick up Spencer?" Jimmy ran his hand through his damp hair, pushing it away from his face.

Looking at him, she realized that in the past he'd deliberately left a limp strand drooping over his forehead. Along with the glasses and the scraggy beard, his disguise had been effective. Even so, she wondered how she could ever have been deceived into believing he was mentally handicapped, once she really started looking at him.

She glanced at her watch. "I have twenty-five minutes. Plenty of time for you to explain what the hell is going on."

"You'd better come in." He stood back, granting her access to his living room and shutting the door behind them. Belatedly, it occurred to her that she was being excessively trusting. She had no idea what sort of man Jimmy really was. The fact that he'd appeared amiable in his role as Jimmy the janitor meant nothing except that he was willing to deceive a lot of people in pursuit of his goal. Whatever that goal might be. With her record of misjudgment where men were concerned, there was a strong possibility she'd just forced her way into the home of an ax murderer.

She stood with her back pressed against the front door, and Jimmy sent her a look of wry understanding. "It's safe to come inside," he said. "I don't have designs on your life or your virtue."

"And I should believe you because...?"

"Because if I planned to harm you, I'd have done it by now. You came to me this morning, remember? I haven't lured you here by dint of my criminal cunning."

Jimmy extracted a T-shirt from one of the drawers and tugged it on, before sitting down on the sofa. "Join me? Sorry, there are no chairs, so this is your only choice if you want to sit."

His apartment consisted of a single whitewashed room with an attached kitchen alcove; and there was a door that presumably led to the bathroom. Furniture was minimal: a sleep-sofa, a coffee table, a chest of drawers, a TV, a few framed photos, and a pile of comic books on the counter that separated the kitchen area from the living space. With the doors to the closet that held the computer closed, the room would probably appear very much the sort of place that a mentally retarded adult might be able to maintain on his own earning power.

Marisa perched on the edge of the sofa, as far away from him as it was possible to get. "Whatever scam you're running must have the potential to make a lot of money," she said acidly, shifting to avoid a lumpy spring. "You look as if you're prepared to sacrifice quite a bit of personal comfort to keep up the fiction of Jimmy-the-halfwit-janitor."

"I've already told you, I'm not running a scam—"

"And, of course, I have no reason to doubt anything you tell me. Our relationship so far has been a model of truth and openness."

"No, of course it hasn't, but I'm not attempting to

scam anyone for personal profit. On the contrary, I'm conducting an investigation. And, for what it's worth, almost everything I've told you about myself is true.''

The fact that he'd deceived her really hurt, and her anger flared up again. "For what it's worth? Your word is worth *nothing!* All you've done is exploit my natural sympathy for someone I thought was handicapped and working hard to make a go of it. You've taken advantage of my friendship, and my son's friendship, and you haven't told either of us the truth about anything. Jimmy the janitor doesn't exist. He's one big lie—''

"No, he's not. James Griffin *is* my real name, and I *am* working as a janitor. Working damn hard, as a matter of fact. I told you that I used to work for the FBI, which is the truth. I still do work for them under contract from time to time. My parents had a nasty divorce when I was in my teens, and I really did share an apartment with my sister in Washington D.C.—until she was killed in a car crash this past February.''

Marisa refused to feel renewed sympathy over the loss of his sister, and she expressed no interest in his work for the FBI—assuming he wasn't twisting the truth about that to suit his own purposes.

"All those biographical facts are irrelevant, and you know it. Since you apparently have what passes for normal brain function, you should be smart enough to figure out that if little pieces of the truth are hidden inside a giant lie, the snippets of truth lose their meaning.''

"The fact that my sister Carole was killed in a car crash isn't irrelevant at all,'' Jimmy said quietly. "It's the whole reason I'm working as a janitor at the Refuge.''

"I'm sorry about your sister, but I see absolutely no connection between her death and your offensive masquerade.''

"The connection is straightforward. I believe Carole was murdered because of something that happened at the Refuge. Unfortunately, the police don't agree with me, and I haven't been able to persuade them to conduct even a cursory investigation."

There had been so much violence and death in her recent past that Marisa responded to the word *murder* with an instant emotional shutdown. Her instinctive reaction was to get up and leave Jimmy's apartment, to distance herself from the grief she could hear in his voice when he said his sister's name. It demanded a significant act of will on her part to remain seated, and another act of will to offer even a minimal expression of sympathy.

"I'm sorry about your sister," she said. "Her loss must be painful for you."

Jimmy looked at her intently, and she knew he'd picked up on the flatness of her tone. Without his glasses, his eyes appeared very blue and his gaze was penetrating, now that he wasn't deliberately sending it out of focus.

"I'm sorry if talking about my sister's death brings back bad memories for you, Marisa."

She'd confided details about her marriage to Jimmy when she'd assumed he wouldn't really be able to grasp the complexities of a relationship such as she'd endured with Evan Connors. It didn't improve her mood one bit to realize that Jimmy had understood precisely what she'd endured. Had understood well enough, in fact, to extrapolate and interpret accurately what she was feeling right this minute. Marisa had protected herself for so long by keeping her emotions hidden that she felt exposed and defenseless in the face of Jimmy's insights. She was deeply resentful that he possessed information she would never have shared if she'd known the truth about him.

Getting to her feet, she walked over to the window and

averted her gaze from him, looking out over the weed-filled backyard to the parking lot of the church. Even so, she didn't feel as if she'd put enough distance between them.

She was sure Jimmy understood why she'd moved away, but he came and stood on the opposite side of the window, anyway, invading her space and leaving her no privacy in which to rebuild the barriers of her comfort zone.

"Why are you so sure that your sister's death wasn't just a tragic accident?" she asked, avoiding a direct response to his comment.

"There are several reasons, but the first thing to make me suspicious was the fact that Carole left a message on my telephone answering machine a couple of days before she died. She'd just come back from a conference, and I was working on an out-of-town assignment, so we hadn't talked for a while, and she seemed upset at missing me. She said that she needed to discuss some worrying problems she'd discovered in connection with Stuart Frieze and the Prudence Wainscott Refuge. She asked me to get in touch with her as soon as I got home. When I finally got back from Dallas and heard her message, I tried to call her at the hospital—"

"At the hospital?"

"Yes, she is…she was…a doctor, an emergency care specialist. She's head of—she *was* head of Emergency Medicine at Georgetown University hospital. Early in 1999, though, she took a leave of absence and volunteered to work with the Doctors Without Borders organization. She spent six brutal months working in the Kosovo refugee camps in Macedonia."

"It sounds as if your sister was a remarkable woman." Marisa couldn't help feeling a reluctant interest.

"She was not only an outstanding physician, she was a wonderful mother—"

Marisa's stomach jumped. "She had children?"

"Just one. A daughter, Molly. She's nineteen now."

"I'm sorry. Your niece must feel the loss terribly." Against her will, Marisa felt her sympathy genuinely engage. "Is Molly's father still alive?"

"Yes, and he's been great since Carole died. He's South African, a heart surgeon, and Carole married him when they were both still in college. But she refused to live in South Africa under the apartheid regime, and Peter Riven wanted to go back there, so, in the end, they split up."

"That must have been hard on Molly. It's tough to arrange sleep-overs at dad's house when he's thousands of miles away."

"You're right. Carole and Peter tried not to fight about custody and visitation, but of course they did. But last year, with the political system in South Africa completely changed, Molly's father invited her to live with him for a year before she started college. Wanting to know the other side of her heritage, Molly accepted the invitation. Ironically, it was partly because she was missing Molly so much that Carole volunteered to go to Macedonia."

Marisa rubbed her hands up and down her arms, warming a sudden chill. Life's ironies, she'd discovered, had an unpleasant habit of rearing up and biting you when you were least expecting them. She had a grim suspicion that Jimmy was about to demonstrate the proof of this once again.

"This is a digression," Jimmy said impatiently. "I was explaining why I called Carole at the hospital. Unfortunately, we didn't connect. She was with a patient and couldn't come to the phone, so we never spoke. The next news I had about Carole was that she was dead."

"I really am sorry, Jimmy. Your sister sounds like a person who really made the world around her a better place."

"Yes, she did. I'd miss her whatever the circumstances of her death, but it's eating at my gut to know she was murdered and that her killer is walking around without a hint of suspicion trailing after him."

"But how did she die, exactly? If you're so sure she was murdered, why aren't the police conducting their own investigation? Or are they?"

"No, they're not. She was killed when her car slid off an isolated stretch of road in Maryland." Jimmy shrugged. "A tragic accident, according to the police."

"And you don't accept their verdict?"

"No, I don't. I believe the so-called accident was in fact a carefully planned murder. Her car was forced off the road."

Marisa understood why Jimmy didn't want to accept that his sister's life had ended so pointlessly, but nothing he'd said so far persuaded her there was anything more than dire misfortune involved. "Surely if somebody had forced your sister's car off the road, the police investigation would turn up evidence? Paint from another vehicle on her car, something like that."

Jimmy frowned. "No, her car was totaled, so there's nothing much left to check. I'm guessing her car was pushed by a heavy truck, with rubber padding on its bumpers. Carole's car smashed into a tree and rolled over twice. You'd have to search hard for evidence of what precipitated the rollover, and the police didn't search at all, let alone hard. It was pouring with rain the night she died—a really torrential downpour—and there were a lot of accidents that night. The state troopers were over-worked, undermanned, and predisposed to consider this just one more sad mishap on a rotten night. They only gave the accident scene minimum scrutiny, and when one of Carole's colleagues mentioned that she'd complained the week before of her brakes being faulty, they basically ended their investigation right there. Her car hydro-planed, the brakes failed. End of story."

"If there was a problem with her brakes and the road was slick, that might have been all it took," Marisa suggested.

"Yes, it might have been, but it wasn't. I know my sister, and she was one of the world's most organized people. If she mentioned a brake problem to one of her colleagues, you can bet your life she would already have made an appointment to get the brakes fixed."

"Did you check with the garage where she usually took her car for maintenance?"

"Yes." Jimmy spoke curtly. "They said she'd called and requested an appointment, but they were totally slammed with work, so they couldn't take her until the following week."

Marisa didn't say anything because the conclusion seemed obvious to her, and it wasn't the one Jimmy wanted her to reach. He looked at her, clearly saw what she was thinking, and his frustration boiled over.

"You're wrong, Marisa, and so are the police. I know my sister. She absolutely wouldn't have driven around for an entire week with failing brakes. If her regular service garage was too busy to take her, she'd have gone somewhere else. She was an excellent driver, as comfortable on dirt roads in the Caucasian Mountains as she was on superhighways in the States. But she wasn't ar-rogant or careless enough to take a Mercedes SL 600 sports coupe with failing brakes out for a long drive on a night when the rain was emptying out of the sky.''

He paused for emphasis. "Take it from me. Carole found somewhere else to get her brakes fixed, but short of calling every repair shop in the greater D.C. area and forcing them to check through their appointment schedules for the entire week prior to her death, I've no way of proving that.''

"Even the most careful people sometimes act out of character and take risks they shouldn't," Marisa said.

His smile lacked mirth. "You sound remarkably like the detective who told me to stop obsessing about Carole's death and pay her the respect of getting on with the rest of my life.''

"I'm sorry, Jimmy, but just because the detective was a jerk, it doesn't mean your sister was murdered. Horrible accidents do sometimes happen.''

"Would you be more inclined to believe I'm not inventing wild conspiracy theories if I told you that I set about tracking down the young woman Carole had been driving to meet—and it turned out she died the same day as Carole?''

Marisa gulped. "My God! How did she die? Another car accident?''

"No. She snorted too much cocaine and gave herself a heart attack. The odd thing is, I can't find anyone who was aware that the young woman in question had a drug habit. She'd only been working at the motel for a couple of months, so people there didn't know her all that intimately. Still, they were shocked when they found out how she'd died. They insisted there had been no signs of drug use, and she'd had a pre-employment drug test that had come back clean. The police shrugged. They pointed out that first-time users can die just as easily as long-term addicts if they're unlucky enough to get too pure a powder, or snort too much, or if their heart is weak to begin with.''

Marisa perched on the window ledge, her interest finally engaged to the full. ''Do you have any clue why your sister was going to see this woman?''

''Only guesswork. Her name was Ardita Spiri, and she was a refugee from Kosovo, a young woman who'd come to the States from the Stankovic camp in Macedonia. That's the refugee camp where Carole was working last summer.''

''If there is a link between your sister's death and this woman's death, don't you think it's more likely to be something that happened in the camp than something that's going on at the Refuge?''

''That was my immediate reaction, but when I couldn't convince the authorities that there might be a link, I started my own investigation. Which isn't as strange as it sounds, by the way. I'm an investigator by trade—''

''You really do work for the FBI?'' Marisa asked.

''Not anymore, although I was an agent with the Bureau until six years ago. Then a couple of colleagues and I left to form our own company. We're a partnership, based in the D.C. area, but we take on assignments all over the world. My partners consult with companies to help them secure their systems against technological espionage and the theft of business secrets. My area of special expertise is the investigation of corporate crime.''

He was looking at her as he spoke, and he broke off, grinning. ''You'd make a lousy poker player, Marisa. Your face shows exactly what you're thinking all the time. You're saying to yourself that my work predisposes me to see crimes and criminal activity where it doesn't exist. You think I'm taking a couple of sad coincidences surrounding Carole's death and blowing them out of proportion.''

Most people considered Marisa's face impossible to read. Evan had driven himself into paroxysms of rage over his inability to guess what she was thinking, and she'd clung to the defense that a carefully cultivated blank expression provided. When nothing else in her life had been under her control, keeping her thoughts to herself had been the only privacy she could lay claim to. She wondered how it was that Jimmy had seemed able to guess what she was thinking from the moment they first met.

"I'm trying to keep an open mind," she said. "But I still don't see any link between those two deaths and the Refuge."

"I'm getting to that. Once I realized that Carole and Ardita probably met in Macedonia, it was only a few hours' work to discover that Ardita was over here on an emergency refugee visa. She arrived in this country last May, along with a planeload of orphans brought in from the Stankovic camp by Stuart Frieze. What's more, Ardita went straight from the airport to Wainscott Refuge. She'd been raped by Macedonian soldiers who were supposed to be guarding the camps—and she was pregnant.''

Marisa flinched. "Life is sometimes seriously unfair, isn't it? That poor girl was hounded from her home by war, she was raped by the people assigned to protect her, she had to give up her child and she was trying to start a new life alone in a foreign country. And then, just when she's getting back on her feet, she dies."

"Her life was certainly tragic, but that makes me all the more determined to find out the truth about how she died. And I sure don't believe it was from a self-administered drug overdose.''

"You said you couldn't find any friends who knew Ardita had a cocaine habit, but have you found anyone at all who agrees with your theory that her death might not be accidental?"

"Like I mentioned, Ardita got on well with the people she worked with, but she'd only been at the motel for a few weeks when she died, so she didn't have any close friends on the staff. They're busy, hardworking people who don't have either time or any real interest in probing for the truth in the death of a woman they barely know. Fortunately, the manager remembered from Ardita's initial job interview that she'd come to Maryland because she had an old friend from Kosovo working in the area. It took me a while to track the friend down, but I eventually found out which motel she was working at. Her name was Darina Becolli, and she was working in Towson, about forty miles from where Ardita was employed. I went to talk to her—"

"And what happened?" Marisa was afraid she knew what Jimmy's answer was going to be.

"Nothing happened. We never spoke." Jimmy's gaze was agate hard. "She died two day before Ardita. Another unfortunate accident, of course, and in a different police jurisdiction, so nobody made any connection between the two cases."

Marisa's mouth was so dry, she had to swallow before she could speak. "What happened to Darina? More cocaine? A car accident?"

"If you can believe it, she was run over by a garbage truck. Imagine surviving the horrors of a bombing attack by the Serbs and rape by Macedonian soldiers, and then dying when a municipal garbage truck in Maryland backs up and flattens you."

"How do you get run over by a garbage truck?" Marisa was incredulous. "Surely the police suspected foul play at this point? I mean, garbage trucks aren't usually moving at the speed of light, especially when they're reversing."

"There were no witnesses, unless you count the crew on the truck, but Darina's blood-alcohol content was .12, way over the limit, and the cops concluded that she was lying passed out in the alley behind her apartment building when the truck started to back up. The driver wasn't even charged with a traffic violation, but he was so upset when he discovered what he'd done that he's in therapy, unable to get behind the wheel of a vehicle or return to work. Oh, and in case you're wondering, yes, Darina was also at the Refuge. Another rape victim. She had her baby ten days before Ardita."

"The deaths *could* all be coincidences," Marisa said, but she didn't even believe it herself.

"They could be," Jimmy agreed. "But I'm damn sure they weren't."

"Did you give the information about Ardita and her friend to the police?"

"Yes, and that's when Det. Sgt. Flynn told me I really needed to get a life. Stuart Frieze spent ten years working for the United Nations High Commission on Refugees, and at the time he resigned, he was considered the most efficient and honest director in the entire organization. He's currently on the board of four major international charities, and there isn't a single breath of scandal regarding his running of Wainscott Refuge. The actual funds aren't really in his hands—they're dispensed by the trustees. And anyway, the accounts are a matter of public record. Mr. Frieze is so much admired that he's received a personal letter of thanks from the governor of Colorado for the work he's doing in furthering the cause of adoption. In fact, I've decided he's the perfect candidate to succeed Mother Theresa.''

"Then why are you still here in Wainscott investigating him? He is the primary target of your investigation, right?''

"He sure is. Front and center.''

"Jimmy, I have to say this. You're a professional investigator with a lot of experience, but Carole was your sister, and you have a heavy emotional investment in the outcome of this case. I know from personal experience that when a person's emotions get involved in assessing criminal activity, good judgment usually flies out the window. Despite the links to the Refuge, it's a whole lot easier to believe that Carole, Ardita and Darina were murdered because of something that happened in the Stankovic camp than because of something that happened at the Prudence Wainscott Refuge. The fact that those two young women from Kosovo both delivered babies there doesn't justify concluding anything about Stuart Frieze being involved in something illegal.''

Jimmy opened the door of the avocado-green fridge and helped himself to a cola. "You want something to drink?''

"No, thanks. I have to go and collect Spencer in five minutes. Jimmy, answer me. Have you found out *anything* to link Stuart Frieze directly to the death of your sister or the other two women?''

"No, but that's because he's a real smart guy, not because there's nothing to find.'' He finished his cola and crumpled the can, then pitched it into the trash.

"There's too much to explain in the five minutes left before you have to pick up Spencer, and I need to find out what's happened to my friend who was supposed to have been here over an hour ago. Can I come around to your apartment tonight? We still have a lot to discuss.''

Marisa still wasn't sure that Carole's death had anything to do with Stuart Frieze and the Refuge, but she had put herself in a position where she had to make some hard choices. She either had to persuade Jimmy to give up his investigation, or go along with his masquerade, or report him to Stuart Frieze. Before she made her choice, she needed a lot more information.

''Come at eight o'clock, after Spencer's in bed,'' she said, walking to the door. ''And, for the record, I'm still mad as hell at the way you deceived me.''

''For the record, I'm mad as hell that you found me out. I guess that makes us even.'' Jimmy held open the door for her. ''I'll see you at eight.''

Nine

When Jimmy was twenty-two and a hotshot student at Yale Law School, he'd fallen hopelessly for one of the undergraduate women on his college tennis team. Leeza Johnson had a gorgeous body, long lithe legs, a cute retroussé nose—and she struggled hard to maintain a C-minus average. Her attitude toward life was fun-loving, and she had a throaty laugh that provoked Jimmy to a state of instant lust every time he heard it. When Leeza was anywhere in the vicinity, he could only stare at her in a state of mindless longing until she acknowledged his presence with one of her enticing little smiles and a teasing flutter of her lashes. When Leeza wasn't around, he obsessed about where she was and how soon he'd be able to find her.

The hours they spent in bed were spectacular, and, floating on a permanent sexual high, it wasn't at all difficult for Jimmy to convince himself that he was deeply in love. He maintained the illusion by refusing to notice how little he and Leeza agreed about anything on those few occasions when they quit making love and attempted to have a meaningful conversation. This state of blissful infatuation lasted just long enough for them to get married.

Within weeks of his wedding, Jimmy woke up from his lustful daydream. He discovered to his dismay that married couples couldn't spend twenty-four hours a day in bed, and that when he and Leeza weren't having sex, they found each other alternately boring and infuriating. They couldn't even play tennis together, since Leeza always cried if Jimmy beat her and cried even harder if he let her win, complaining that he never treated her seriously and wasn't respecting her as a competitor.

She was absolutely right, of course. In retrospect, Jimmy acknowledged that Leeza with her C-minus average had always been smart enough to see their relationship with a great deal more clarity than he, the straight-A whiz kid.

Their relationship continued to spiral rapidly downward. Six months into the marriage, the rosy haze had totally burned off, leaving behind a pile of ugly dead ashes. Leeza's retroussé nose had long since stopped looking cute and had begun to appear ridiculously childish. Her throaty laugh turned into an infuriatingly harsh giggle, and her gorgeous body so lost its ability to turn him on that having sex with her became a nightmarish duty that occurred less and less often.

Jimmy wondered why he'd never noticed *before* the wedding that the woman he'd fallen in love with existed only in his own overheated imagination. The real Leeza was another woman entirely.

The only slim credit Jimmy could claim for his behavior during their marriage was that he never sank to the level of trying to regain his lost sexual prowess by having an affair. On their first wedding anniversary, Leeza saved him from falling into even that sorry pit by giving him the perfect gift—she asked for a divorce.

Jimmy granted her request with profuse apologies and heartfelt gratitude, guiltily aware that the failure of the marriage was entirely his fault. Leeza had never pretended to be anyone other than the person she was. He had invented his Leeza out of whole cloth, propelled by the twin forces of passion and the desire to establish a home of his own, in compensation for the teenage years he'd spent shuttling between bitterly warring parents.

After their divorce, Leeza quickly moved on to a happy second marriage. Every year she sent Jimmy a Christmas card, with pictures of her two pretty daughters enclosed. He'd never been able to decide whether the cards were an in-your-face insult intended to show how much better off she was without him, or a simple gesture meant to convey the message that she bore him no ill will.

He might be no closer to understanding what motivated Leeza than he had been on the day they married, but their failed marriage had taught Jimmy an important lesson about himself. He enjoyed the company of women, in bed and out, but he despised the testosterone-soaked lust that had pushed him into marrying Leeza. After his divorce, he had enjoyed mutually satisfying relationships with several women, but he had never again initiated a sexual relationship without knowing the woman in question well enough to be sure they liked each other when they were vertical as well as horizontal.

Three years ago, he had hoped he'd finally found another woman he wanted to marry, but Meredith had a dazzling career as a litigator and wasn't prepared to slow down her race to senior partner by having children.

Jimmy thought long and hard about whether he was willing to have a childless marriage. He and Meredith enjoyed each other's company, and since they were both workaholics, their professional lives meshed rather well. In the end, however, he decided that having children was significantly important to him. With a lot of regret on both sides, he and Meredith parted.

The three years since their split had sometimes left him wondering if the scriptwriters for *Ally McBeal* were using his life for comic material. Only one constant had remained through all his post-Leeza relationships—even the end-of-the-millennium weird ones. Jimmy could honestly claim that since his divorce, he'd never again made the mistake of allowing sexual desire to overcome his powers of rational decision-making.

Until Marisa.

Marisa Joubert was not only the most beautiful woman Jimmy had ever encountered, but she was also the sexiest, her sensuality reaching out to him with even greater intensity because it was so rigorously suppressed. Ten days ago he'd opened the door to the Refuge and—for the first time since seeing Leeza on the tennis court—the impact of a woman's physical presence had been so forceful that he felt as if someone had rammed a fist into his gut.

The day had been overcast, and Marisa was wearing gray, but her dark clothes and the waning light of the wintry afternoon merely emphasized the stunning brightness of her hair and the creamy perfection of her skin. Snowflakes had caught in her hair and on the ends of her lashes, glittering as they melted. With her cheeks nipped pink by the cold, she looked like a lush Victorian painting of a fairy, simultaneously ethereal and erotic.

Jimmy's rational brain function had been instantly suspended. He swallowed hard, counted to twenty, and reminded himself that the middle of an investigation into his sister's murder wasn't the best moment to rediscover the power of lust to fry his brain. But his reaction to Marisa had been visceral, and his self-lecture didn't have much effect. A primitive gene kicked in, sending him into instant macho-man mode. He fought the urge to puff out his chest, snatch off his blank-lensed glasses, and plunge headlong into a seduction routine.

Only training and discipline had kept him in character at that first meeting. Then he'd been thrown for another loop when he met Marisa and Spencer in the parking lot on Monday morning. He hadn't expected her to start work so soon after her interview, and he wasn't mentally prepared for the encounter.

The presence of a toddler who was obviously hers had been another unwelcome surprise, since the possibility that Marisa might be married had never crossed his addled mind. A prime example of the ruinous effects of desire on brain activity, because establishing the marital status of a woman who attracted him was normally the first point on his agenda.

Cursing every step of the way, he'd shambled across the parking lot, amused at Spencer's stubborn refusal to get out of the puddle, and wishing like hell that he didn't know precisely what he had to do to maintain his role. As he mumbled a greeting to Marisa, the first thing he noticed was that she didn't wear a wedding ring. The second thing he noticed was that his relief at this discovery was way out of proportion to its importance. His current mission made any possibility of a relationship out of the question, so Marisa's marital status shouldn't— couldn't—matter.

Jimmy had worked undercover in a dozen different situations, both for the FBI and, more recently, on assignments for his own company. He'd never before been tempted to blow his cover. Until Marisa arrived at the Refuge, he'd actually found a certain gratification in playing the role of Jimmy, the slow-witted but good-natured janitor. Quite apart from a new understanding of the insults routinely leveled at people with mental handicaps, he'd sure as hell acquired a whole new respect for the hard work that went into keeping an office building clean and well-maintained.

He'd given himself another stern lecture about the importance of keeping in character as he extracted Spencer from the puddle, and over the past week he'd been on constant guard, never deliberately allowing Marisa to penetrate his disguise. Still, he couldn't deny that he'd engaged in a series of high-risk behaviors where she was concerned, ranging from eating lunch with her three days in a row, to returning Spencer's teddy bear to her apartment.

Having dinner with her had been courting disaster, and a couple of times during the evening he'd barely avoided it. In truth, despite his determination to pursue his investigation, there had always been part of him that wanted Marisa to see behind the facade of Jimmy the janitor. He recognized the selfishness of his wish. Having been raised as the daughter of fabulously wealthy parents, Marisa was now a struggling single mother who needed her paycheck from the Refuge. It was unfair to burden her with information about Stuart's activities that might make her reluctant to continue working for him.

Ethical issues aside, however, Jimmy had to admit that he'd felt a rush of relief when Marisa finally outed him. The struggle to maintain his role had become nearly impossible in her presence.

Which brought him to the present moment, and the fact that he had been standing on the doorstep of Marisa's apartment for at least two minutes and he still had no idea what he was going to say to her when she opened the door. He was carrying the file he'd built up on Stuart Frieze in one hand, and a bottle of Merlot in the other. He was suddenly afraid that it was terminally tacky to bring a gift that suggested he was thinking of this as a social occasion. When meeting to discuss violent death, was it acceptable to bring wine?

He scowled at the bottle, then shrugged. What the hell. There were no social rules that covered the niceties of explaining that he suspected Stuart Frieze of exploiting the young women who came to him for protection, and then murdering any of them who dared to protest. Tucking the file under his arm and squaring his shoulders, he rang the bell.

He heard the approach of quick, light footsteps, and then Marisa opened the door. She was wearing jeans and a nondescript T-shirt. Her fabulous mass of hair was scraped back from her face into a haphazard knot, and she wore no makeup, as far as he could see. She looked, if possible, even sexier than when she was dressed more formally.

She didn't smile at him, and he felt the loss. He'd become addicted over the past week to the radiant smiles she reserved almost exclusively for Spencer, but occasionally bestowed on him. He almost envied Jimmy the janitor the warm spot he'd found in Marisa's well-guarded heart.

"You're right on time," she said, giving an impatient push at a strand of hair that had fallen across her forehead. "Come on in."

Jimmy wanted to touch her hair. He wanted to hold her. He wanted very badly to kiss her. Hell, no. What he really wanted was to take her to bed and spend the rest of the night making slow, passionate love to her. But kissing her would at least be a small step in the right direction.

His fantasy didn't seem likely to be fulfilled at any point during this lifetime. Not only was Marisa unsmiling, but the look she aimed toward him was less than friendly. He had the disconcerting impression that she could tell exactly what he was thinking and found his adolescent lechery somewhere between pitiful and offensive.

"Are you planning to stand on the doorstep all night, or could you be persuaded to come inside?"

"Oh, I'll come in. Sorry." Reduced to a humiliating replica of his twenty-two-year-old self, Jimmy held out the bottle of wine. "This is for you."

As a witty line of dialogue, it was hard to imagine anything less inspired. There had to be something scintillating he could say to show her that James William Griffin, high-powered international investigator, was a fascinating guy who bore no resemblance to poor, retarded Jimmy T. Griffin. Unfortunately, right at this moment he couldn't think of another single word to utter, much less one that was scintillating.

Marisa took the bottle of wine with a polite murmur of thanks. "Spencer's asleep, so we need to be quiet, please. He's pretty good about sleeping through the night, but once he's disturbed, it's hard to settle him down again."

"I'll keep my voice down." He followed her into the living room, stuffing his hands into the pockets of his jeans and rocking back on his heels, while she went into the kitchen and searched through the drawers for a corkscrew. Then he remembered that rocking on his heels was a habit he'd invented for Jimmy the janitor, and he hurriedly pulled his hands out of his pockets and stood so straight that he looked as if he expected a military honor guard inspection at any moment.

He drew in a deep breath and let it out slowly. His behavior, he realized grimly, was truly pathetic.

"Success," Marisa said, holding up a corkscrew. "I wasn't sure I had one, it's been such a long time since I had any wine."

"I hope you like wine. That particular Merlot is from one of my favorite vineyards." Now he sounded like a pompous ass—not much of an improvement over sounding moronic.

"Oh, yes, I really enjoy the occasional glass of wine, especially Merlot." Marisa finally relented and gave him a small smile. "I sometimes think about treating myself to some wine with dinner, but since I always eat with Spencer, it doesn't seem the ideal drink. What would be the tasteful wine choice to accompany chicken nuggets and fish fingers, I wonder?"

"A robust Burgundy?" he suggested, returning her smile. "Or maybe an unpretentious Chardonnay?"

"I think I'll stick with diet cola until Spencer's menu selections get a bit more sophisticated."

"Don't hold your breath. My niece and nephew are in school already and they'll still only eat food that can be speared on the end of a fork and dipped into ketchup. It makes for limited dining choices."

She found two wineglasses and rinsed them under the tap. "How old are they? Your niece and nephew, I mean."

"Charlie is six and a half and Emma is almost five."

"They're still young. I would have expected them to be older. You told me when we met in the parking lot that your sister is forty-three."

"Yes, she is, but Lizzie didn't marry until she was in her late thirties. I'm surprised you remembered my sister's age."

Marisa turned away to throw the seal from the bottle

of wine into the trash, and he could no longer see her face.

"I have a knack for remembering trivia," she said. "The more useless, the better I seem to remember it. For example, I recollect that I felt sorry for you when you said your brother-in-law considers you a freak of nature. Although I suppose that was just another of your lies..."

"Trust me, I spoke the absolute truth." Jimmy grimaced. "My brother-in-law disapproves of everything about me, from my politics, which are too liberal because I didn't think execution was the appropriate punishment for President Clinton, all the way to the fact that I like snowboarding better than skiing."

"My sympathy is entirely with your brother-in-law."

He tilted his head. "You think poor old President Clinton should have been executed?"

"Don't joke." Marisa's cheeks were flaming. "I hate what you're doing at the Refuge, Jimmy. It's bad enough that you faked friendship with me and tricked me into confiding details about my life that I'd never have shared if I'd known who you really are. Somehow it's even more offensive that you took real facts about your family and distorted them to create a totally false impression of your personal circumstances. You were playing mind games with me—with everyone at the Refuge. I keep imagining you going home at night and laughing at us. Congratulating yourself on how stupid we all are to believe that you're mentally handicapped—"

"Never that. Not with anyone, and especially not with you." Jimmy put down the heavy file binder he'd compiled on Stuart Frieze, and went into the kitchen. He leaned against the counter, facing her. It required physical effort on his part not to reach out and fold her into his arms.

"Marisa, I'm sorry if you feel I've deceived you—"

"*Feel?*" Her voice was unsteady. "I don't feel that you deceived me, Jimmy. You *did* deceive me."

"If I did, it was for a just cause." He willed her to understand. "This isn't a trivial investigation, Marisa. It's very important to me. My sister dedicated her life to helping the sick and the underprivileged, and I'm one-hundred-percent sure the world is a lesser place for her absence. Not only is Carole dead, so are two young women who hoped the United States would provide them with a chance to start their lives over. What I'm doing at the Refuge has nothing to do with playing mind games, or any sort of games, for that matter. On the contrary, it's deadly serious. I'm attempting to prove that Stuart Frieze is the driving force behind a triple murder. Sometimes you have to remember the goal and forgive the methods used to get there."

"The end justifies the means? You'll never convince me of that," she said bleakly. "I grew up listening to my father make that excuse. I didn't accept it when I was a child, and I don't accept it now, from you."

The mention of her father gave him an opening, and Jimmy seized it. "You've mentioned your family and your past often enough that it's obviously an issue with you. You're asking for honesty from me, so at the risk of making you seriously angry at the invasion of your privacy, I need to let you know what I've done."

"What you've done? What are you talking about?"

"I ran an extensive background check on you, Marisa. It was nothing personal. I ran the same sort of check on all the other employees at the Refuge. I needed to know if you—and they—were who and what you said you were. These days, it doesn't take long to get a life history on almost anyone who has a Social Security number and a credit card—''

''In that case, aren't you worried that Stuart may turn the tables and run a check on you?''

Jimmy shook his head. ''There's no reason for him to be suspicious of me, because he isn't paying close enough attention to pick up on any minor inconsistencies in my character. Haven't you noticed that although Stuart's very kind and sympathetic, he doesn't really see people as individuals? I'm some sort of generic Handicapped Man, as far as he's concerned.''

''I think you're staking a lot on Stuart's presumed lack of perception.''

''Not really. One of the advantages of my line of work is that I have lots of experience in going undercover. I've changed my middle initial from W to T and given myself a different Social Security number. The biographical trail attached to that number is copiously documented and completely fake. If Stuart decides to have someone check me out for any reason, they'll find nothing to alarm them.''

Marisa moved away from him with fast, angry steps. ''Fake Social Security number, fake personality, fake IQ problem. Do I know anything about you that's for real, Jimmy?''

''You know that I want to find proof that Stuart killed my sister and two other innocent women.'' Jimmy let out a long breath. ''Every deception flows from that one simple fact.''

She brushed her hand across her forehead, and he wasn't sure if she was appeased. ''You were saying you'd run a background check on me...''

''Yes. 'Marisa Joubert' is an unusual name, and your family has been prominent in the Miami area for two generations. Do you want me to tell you what I found out?''

"I can guess," she said, and he admired the fact that she was able to keep her voice coolly controlled despite the fact that he would bet good money the Joubert family history was a painful subject for her. "You've discovered that my father, Marc Joubert, was a major international criminal, an arms dealer who traded stolen weapons and stolen technology to very unpleasant people. You've undoubtedly discovered that my husband, Evan Connors, was killed by gunshot wounds last fall. Did you also find out that my former father-in-law is serving a federal prison sentence for kidnapping and extortion? And that another ex-partner of my father's committed suicide rather than stand trial? And how about the juicy fact that my brother, Tony, barely avoided indictment on charges of racketeering and income tax evasion?''

"Yes, I found out all that—"

She didn't give him the chance to say anything more. "Did you manage to ferret out how Evan died?" she asked tightly. "Maybe not, because my brother-in-law cashed in a lot of favors so that the sordid details of Evan's death were kept pretty much out of the media—"

"I didn't only search published reports, so I know that Evan was shot in your home in Florida, and that the shooting was ruled accidental—although I couldn't find any record of who fired the fatal shot—"

"Maybe you're wondering if it was me. For the record, I didn't shoot my husband. But there were plenty of occasions when I would have been quite glad to pull the trigger, if only I could have put my hands on a weapon and found some way to keep Spencer safe—"

She was visibly shaking, and Jimmy found it agonizing to listen to the anguish in her voice.

"Enough," he said, putting his hand on her arm in an instinctive gesture of comfort. "Enough, Marisa. Evan Connors was a monster, and he treated you very badly—"

She shook off his hand, too proud to accept comfort from someone she was angry with. "It's never enough where my family's concerned," she said harshly. "There's always more—more past, more problems reaching out into the future. There's lots more dirt out there for you to find, Jimmy. However good you are at digging your way through the trash cans of the Internet, I can guarantee you've only scratched the surface of the garbage waiting to be exhumed about the Joubert family. Would you like me to tell you about the bombing of the British Embassy in Afghanistan, and how I think my husband may have provided the missile launchers that did the deed? Or how about the African dictator who wiped out one-fifth of his population by a combination of starvation and guns supplied by the Joubert Corporation? I calculate that my father made at least a couple of million on that hideous little deal."

"You weren't involved in those deals, or any others cooked up by your father and Evan Connors."

"No, not directly, but I never made any effort to help the authorities put my husband or my father behind bars. At least my sister had the courage to reject the Joubert family and everything it stood for. I ran off to New York, but when Evan needed help from me to gain access to the Joubert company, he persuaded me it would be better if I reconciled with my father. And I was so infatuated with Even that I meekly agreed."

It was painful to watch her. "That doesn't make you

responsible for the behavior of your father or your ex-husband. You were the victim of their crimes, not a perpetrator.''

"Where my father's concerned, you may be right.'' Marisa's voice was weary, as if she'd gone over this ground many times before and never yet found forgiveness for herself. "But nobody forced me to marry Evan. I chose him entirely of my own free will, and I'm responsible for having made such a rotten choice.'' She gave a bleak smile. "Do you know why I agreed to marry him so enthusiastically?''

"Why?''

"For the sex.'' Her voice was harsh with self-loathing. "When you get right down to it, I chose that despicable asshole to be my husband because he was terrific in bed. I always thought that you needed to love someone for the sex to be really satisfying, but my relationship with Evan is living proof of the fact that you can have absolutely wonderful sex with a man who doesn't love you in the slightest.''

"How do you know Evan Connors didn't love you?'' Jimmy asked quietly. "Just because he was a murdering son-of-a-bitch doesn't mean that he didn't love you.''

She gave a slight shudder. "The idea that he might have truly loved me doesn't make me feel better,'' she said tautly. "Being loved by a man like Evan Connors isn't exactly a tribute to any woman.''

Jimmy thought of Leeza. He'd made a terrible choice of partner when he was young, and yet there had been almost no lasting harmful consequences for anyone. A couple of bruised egos, and that was about it. Marisa had made a similar bad choice—no more foolish than his and Leeza's—and yet the consequences had been devastating. Several people had almost lost their lives, her son would have to be shielded from learning the truth about his dead father, and she herself was racked by guilt. In the face of such genuine tragedy, any comfort he could offer was almost insulting. Still, he had to try.

"You made mistakes, Marisa, but you learned from them. You did your best to put things right, and now you're doing everything in your power to move on and make a good life for yourself and Spencer—"

"How do you know that?" she demanded. "Given everything you've learned about my past, why do you assume that I'm one of the good guys?"

She probably wouldn't consider the fact that his heart turned over every time he looked at her a persuasive argument, Jimmy thought. In normal circumstances, neither would he.

"Personal judgment," he said. "I'm a professional investigator and I have to trust my instincts. Besides, when I researched your family, I found out a lot more about you than the fact that your father and ex-husband were crooks. I also discovered, for example, that you and your sister Isabella donated the money you inherited from your father to charity. Your father left an estate in excess of thirty million dollars, and your husband left you another three million. Your combined inheritance from the two of them was over ten million dollars. Every cent of that money is now locked away in a charitable trust. If you're one of the bad guys, clearly you're not motivated by money."

"Successful criminals are rarely motivated only by money. I should know. I've lived with two of the most successful. And the thrill of the deal meant every bit as much to them as the power and the money."

"But Stuart Frieze has nothing to offer you *except* money. And if ten million inherited bucks didn't tempt you, Stuart certainly can't lay his hands on enough to bribe you into cooperating with his schemes."

"As it happens, you're right about Stuart not being able to bribe me into cooperating. Not that he's tried. I've worked closely with him over the past week, and I've never seen the smallest sign that he's trying to hide anything." She hesitated for a moment, and he jumped at her hesitation.

"You just remembered something."

"No," she said quickly. Too quickly? "No, I didn't. It's too trivial to mention."

"Tell me, anyway. Please, Marisa."

For a moment, he thought she would refuse. Then she capitulated. "Okay, but it's nothing. In the last year of my marriage, I learned to be hypersensitive to even the smallest hint that Evan was about to lose his temper. That sensitivity hasn't left me, I guess. Just as I was leaving the office one evening last week, I happened to notice a folder sticking out of the file drawer in Stuart's desk. The name tab was torn, so I took out the folder and repaired the tear with tape. Stuart came back when I was at his desk, about to return the file to the drawer it had come from. I got the impression he was absolutely furious that I'd been snooping in one of his confidential files. And I mean almost-out-of-control furious, although he concealed his rage well. I guess it was the fact that he concealed his temper that bothered me. It was almost as if he'd had a lot of practice in hiding his rage. The fact is, he reminded me of Evan."

She gave an embarrassed shrug. "There, I told you it was nothing. The whole incident probably reveals a heck of a lot more about my personal hang-ups than about Stuart's possibly dark secrets."

"Do you remember the name of the file?" Jimmy

asked. "Did you even glance at what was inside while you were making the repair?"

She furrowed her brow, visualizing the folder. "'Postpartum 1999.' I think that was the name. As for the contents, it was columns of figures, as I recall, grouped under various date headings. It was nothing unexpected or out of the way."

Jimmy retrieved the ring binder from her coffee table and flipped through the contents until he found the header "Postpartum 1999."

"No wonder Stuart was annoyed," he said, showing her the entry. "You took the file that details all the special projects he worked on last year."

"Special projects?" she asked.

"A euphemism he uses constantly. Which I guess brings us back pretty much to the point where we left off our discussion this morning." Jimmy took the two glasses of wine that stood neglected on the kitchen counter and handed one to her, waiting for her to take a sip before drinking from his own.

"Explaining what Stuart is up to could take a while," he said. "Why don't we sit down?"

They moved into the living room and sat in the two armchairs placed on opposite sides of a small coffee table. The chairs were attractively covered in a cheerful butter-yellow fabric, but they were obviously inexpensive, and there was no sofa. A TV console, a cheap particleboard bookcase filled with paperbacks, and a couple of lamps completed the sum total of the room's furniture. When Marisa rejected her inheritance, Jimmy reflected, she'd rejected it totally, and he could only admire her stubborn determination to make it entirely on her own, without the comforting cushion of a float from her family's illegally acquired millions.

"Okay, let's hear it." Marisa slipped off her shoes and tucked her feet onto the seat of the chair.

Jimmy was chagrined to discover how much willpower it required to focus his attention on the subject they were discussing, and not on Marisa's legs or any other section of her anatomy. He cleared his throat and told himself to keep his eye on the goal, not the delectable diversion.

"For starters, Stuart Frieze isn't running a legitimate nonprofit adoption service. My best estimate is that he's selling slightly more than two-thirds of all Refuge babies to the highest bidder."

Marisa looked troubled. "That's a terrible accusation to make unless you're sure. *Are* you sure?"

Jimmy nodded. "Carole's phone message to me was too short to provide a lot of details, but she indicated that selling babies was part of what was going on at the Refuge. Being forewarned, once I started work there, I was struck by how many of the mothers-to-be at the Refuge are women from eastern Europe who don't speak much English."

"And that's significant because...?"

"Because Stuart wants young women who are isolated and alone, and therefore easier to hold in his power, and a language barrier helps to guarantee that. As for why he trolls for prospective mothers in eastern Europe, that's easy. He does that not only because women there are often desperately poor, or the victims of civil war, but also because many ethnic groups in the Balkans and the Caucasus have light brown hair and gray or blue eyes. And that's precisely the type of woman he's searching for."

Marisa's mouth wrinkled in distaste. "Are you suggesting that he only wants babies born at the Refuge who are fair-skinned and blue-eyed?"

"That's exactly what I'm suggesting," Jimmy said. "Our society is still prejudiced enough that blond, blue-eyed infants bring the highest price on the black market, so Stuart is carefully selecting his sales stock to meet market demand. It's an unpalatable fact, but it is a fact."

Marisa shook her head, rejecting his claim. "You're reaching too far and too hard, Jimmy. You're glossing over evidence that doesn't fit into your sister's theory about what's happening at the Refuge. The mothers-to-be aren't all from war zones in eastern Europe, and they certainly aren't all blond and blue-eyed. There are at least two African-American girls in residence right now. Danielle's from Detroit and Sharnia's from Chicago. And what about Kim Sung? Her brother brought her over here from Korea a couple of years ago, but he threw her out of the house when he found out she was pregnant. And Consuela Arnez is Hispanic. That's four women who don't fit your profile, right in the current group of residents."

"You're right, and you've just demonstrated how smart Stuart is," Jimmy said. "He has the board of Wainscott Foundation to answer to, and if he couldn't show some ethnic and cultural diversity in the roster of clients he serves at the Refuge, there would soon be a lot of irate trustees asking very awkward question. Out of twenty-four residents, four are women of color. Of the remaining twenty, sixteen have fair hair, and blue or gray eyes."

"That could be a coincidence. Maybe the next batch of incoming residents will have a completely different set of racial characteristics."

"No, I've checked the available information on all the residents for the past three years. The profile is always pretty much the same. There's another fact about the four

women you just mentioned that's very important,"
Jimmy said. "They're not really women, they're young
girls. Kim is fifteen. Danielle and Sharnia are fourteen.
And little Consuela is only thirteen. She doesn't turn
fourteen for another couple of weeks."

"They're all very young," Marisa agreed. "But I
don't see anything sinister about that. Sad to say, a lot
of single moms are very young. No surprise there. Young
girls tend to have unprotected sex more often than mature
women in their thirties, so more young girls tend to get
pregnant by mistake. Plus, older women who do get pregnant often decide to raise their babies themselves.
They're established, they have a little money in the bank,
they figure they can make it work. They don't want any
part of the adoption process."

"You're right. And since there are many more young
single moms than older ones in the general population,
Stuart needs to demonstrate that he's serving the youthful
sector of his potential client base. It's interesting, though,
that the women of color all happen to be underage,
whereas the blond, blue-eyed eastern European women
are all at least eighteen."

"Why is that interesting? What difference could that
possibly make?"

"Because it enables Stuart to kill two birds with one
stone, so to speak. The babies of the young women of
color are adopted by a strictly legitimate, aboveboard
process, with no money changing hands. When these
young women have had their babies, Stuart provides a
couple of weeks of aftercare, then he finds halfway
houses for them and sends them off into the world with
his blessing. He actively encourages them to go back to
school and make a fresh start on their lives. For these
girls, everything about the Refuge works exactly the way

Grover Wainscott intended it should. Meanwhile, Stuart is quite happy to have these young kids passing through the system, because they ensure that his statistics present an acceptable profile. Acceptable, that is, unless you break it down and do a very specific analysis. Plus, if Wainscott Foundation trustees ever want to talk to ex-clients to make sure their policies are being carried out, Stuart has plenty of satisfied Refuge moms to trot out on display for them.''

"And you're persuaded that this legitimate adoption process isn't what happens with the moms from eastern Europe?"

"Nope. Unfortunately, those poor women not only get their babies sold off to the highest bidder, but they also get signed on for the darker side of Stuart's operation—his money-making schemes involving other aspects of pregnancy and reproduction. And Stuart is smart enough to make sure that these women do sign on, literally. Which is why they need to be legal adults, over the age of eighteen.''

Marisa frowned. "Are you sure you aren't making Stuart out to be way more Machiavellian than he really is? Anya is from Chechnya and she's blond and blue-eyed, so according to your theories, she ought to be over eighteen. But I happen to know she's only seventeen, because after she ran away, Stuart and I discussed the fact that she's still a minor.''

"It's true Anya's seventeen right now. But she'll be eighteen by the time her baby's born. In other words, by the time it matters to Stuart, she'll be a legal adult.''

Marisa drained her wineglass and walked over to the sliding door that led to the balcony, staring out into the night. "The ethical lines in the adoption process are so blurred, Jimmy, and I'm not sure I'm in any position to pass judgment on Stuart, even if he is walking on the wrong side of that line.''

''I would have expected you to find his practices as appalling as I do.''

''I do. In abstract.''

''But?''

Marisa drew in a shaky breath. ''I had two miscarriages before Spencer was born. It took me three years and five surgical procedures before I succeeded in carrying a baby to term. At one point I was advised by my obstetrician to look into the possibility of adopting. I did start the initial steps of the process, and I'll be honest with you, Jimmy. If the surgeries had failed, and I'd gone the adoption route, I want to believe I'd have been ethical enough to put my name on a list and wait my turn, however many years it took. But there's a real shortage of healthy infants available for adoption, and if someone had offered me a chance to jump the queue by paying a few thousand dollars up front, I'm afraid to think what my answer would have been. After the third surgery failed and I had a second miscarriage, I was getting pretty desperate, and about the only thing I had at my disposal in those days was money. What better way to spend it? I can hear all the rationalizations I'd have used to excuse myself ringing inside my head right now.''

Jimmy came and stood behind her. A slight tug at her shoulder was all it took to persuade her to turn around to face him. ''You need to stop blaming yourself for every marginally selfish thought you've ever had, Marisa. Thoughts aren't crimes until you turn them into deeds. Besides, parents looking to adopt a baby are emotionally vulnerable, and that leaves them wide open to temptation. That's precisely why nonprofit adoption agencies like

Wainscott Refuge need to have strict guidelines in place to prevent illegal transactions.''

"But the Refuge has those guidelines. I've seen them in the handbook that's sent to all prospective parents."

"It has them," Jimmy said. "Stuart routinely circumvents them. You've only been working in the office a week, but I bet you can already see how the need for confidentiality makes it easy for him to manipulate the system without anyone else at the Refuge having the faintest idea what's going on."

He handed her his file on Stuart, realizing as he did so that he was entrusting her with the power to destroy his investigation. Not to mention the power to get him arrested on various unpleasant charges, such as illegal search and entry, theft of his employer's property, and invasion of patient privacy.

"Read these tonight after I've gone and see for yourself," he said. "But please make sure nobody else has access to the file, okay? That material could be dangerous in the wrong hands."

She took the file from him. "I'll make sure it's safe. What's in here?"

"Copies of original documents that are in Stuart's files, plus charts and analyses that I ran, some of them fairly complex. Study those, and you'll see for yourself that Stuart's doing much more than simply selling babies. He's into every aspect of pregnancy and procreation that can make a profit. Which means just about every aspect you can imagine."

"Such as?"

"For example, one third of the women who give birth at the Refuge go on to have eggs harvested from their wombs. He harvests anywhere from ten to twenty eggs per woman, per procedure, and he pays the woman a thousand bucks, tops. The going rate for prime eggs from young women at the Refuge starts at around seven thousand dollars apiece. At that price, even after he's paid medical expenses, the net profit to him is often in excess of $150,000 per procedure, per woman. Multiply that by twenty or more harvests a year, and you can see he's really raking in the bucks.''

Marisa shuddered. ''It's horrible. Egg retrieval is a painful and risky procedure, plus it's potentially dangerous health-wise. As you can imagine, I read a lot about infertility when I was trying to carry a baby to term, and stimulating a woman's ovaries to produce twenty eggs at a time creates a high risk for ovarian cancer.''

''Yes, it's surprising that so many of the women at the Refuge agree to submit to the procedure,'' Jimmy said grimly. ''But when you're as poor and defenseless as these women, a thousand bucks paid today can seem like great compensation for the increased risk of ovarian cancer when you're fifty. And selling eggs isn't all that Stuart's up to in the fertility field. He's also in the market for renting out wombs. I've tracked at least seven cases where women who gave birth at the Refuge went on to be impregnated by clients of Stuart's whose wives were infertile or unable to carry a pregnancy to term. Stuart apparently prides himself on matching the physical characteristics of the mother and the wife so precisely that the parents never have to reveal that the baby is only half theirs, genetically speaking.''

Marisa looked doubtful. ''In this day and age, when absolutely everything even faintly scandalous seems to end up on the front page of the *Enquirer,* I don't see how Stuart would manage to keep this sort of activity secret.''

''It's easier than you might think, when all the parties involved are anxious for secrecy. If the surrogate mom is paid well—by her standards, and if the adoptive parents are anxious to pass their new baby off as theirs by birth, rather than by adoption, then everybody connected to the deal has a strong inducement to keep quiet. So Stuart gets to carry on with his illicit schemes, safe from discovery or scandal—''

Marisa grimaced. ''If Stuart's doing such a great job of keeping the details of his activities secret, how did you find all this out, Jimmy?''

''It was simply a case of looking at what was happening at the Refuge from the perspective of expecting to find irregularities, as opposed to assuming everything was legitimate and aboveboard. Once I got an idea of what was going on, there was plenty of documentation in his files to prove my case. Stuart uses various basic codes to encrypt the information concerning his money-making schemes, but it wasn't especially difficult to break the codes. After that, it was just a question of going back to my apartment with the raw data and running some sophisticated analyses and compiling detailed statistical tables. Not a very exciting way of trapping a criminal, but effective.''

''Sale of body parts is illegal, I know that, but it isn't illegal to sell sperm or eggs, is it? And for sure it isn't illegal to act as a middleman for surrogate moms and prospective parents. Some lawyers specialize in brokering that sort of baby deal.''

''You're right. It's perfectly legal for men to sell sperm, which means that women can sell their eggs, too, even though procuring the eggs is a much more risky procedure. That's the beauty of the operation Stuart's running. Everything he's doing is at least borderline within the limits of current law. I think he sometimes pressures hard in order to get the agreement he needs from the women at the Refuge. But he does get them to agree eventually, because I've seen the signed consent forms. Selling babies is illegal, of course, but there's absolutely no money trail that I've been able to find so far that would prove what he's doing.''

Not speaking, Marisa rested her head against the cold glass of the sliding door. ''What is it?'' he asked. ''What's bothering you?''

She sent him a troubled look. ''Think about what you've just told me. If nothing Stuart has done is illegal, why in the world would it matter if Carole found out what he was up to? Why would he need to kill your sister even if she did threaten to reveal what was going on?''

''Because Stuart isn't worried about going to jail,'' Jimmy said. ''He's worried about having the money spigot turned off. The Wainscott Foundation trustees would fire him in a heartbeat if they knew what he was up to, and Stuart would lose a million dollars a year in illicit income if his operation were exposed. That amount of tax-free income a year wouldn't tempt you, perhaps, but it's more than enough to entice some people into committing murder. Obviously, Stuart is one of those people.''

''I guess so.'' Marisa sounded dubious. ''But what is he doing with the money? He lives in a modest house here in Wainscott and he drives a Dodge Durango. That's a nice car—but he's single, with no dependents, and he could certainly afford it on his regular salary. He works fifty- and sixty-hour weeks, splurges on the occasional lunch at *La Cafetière*, and—according to Janet—on his last vacation he went to a refugee camp in Africa. Not exactly high living.''

''I don't know what he's doing with the money,'' Jimmy admitted. ''Maybe he's one of those criminals who just needs to know that he has millions piling up in the bank. Maybe he's secretly addicted to gambling. Maybe he flies off to weekend orgies and drops a hundred thousand a weekend on booze, luxury hotel suites and high-class hookers. Anything's possible, but speculation isn't going to get us anywhere with the police. I have to show them the money trail.''

''Why wait until you have proof before you contact the police? Wouldn't it be better to bring in law enforcement and get some help from them right now? After all, they have the legal power to subpoena Stuart's financial records. You don't.''

''Catch-22. The police don't believe they have any reason to subpoena Stuart's financial records. Besides, can you imagine Officer Bob Penney going up against Stuart Frieze? It's not even a close contest. I'm a pretty good hacker and I've already checked Stuart's local bank account and his credit record. They're both squeaky clean. Wherever he's stashing the money he makes, it isn't in the States. And if I can't find the money—and tracking hidden money is part of the way I make my living—then I guarantee the police wouldn't find a thing. All we'd do is warn Stuart that he's under suspicion, and send him even deeper undercover.''

''Then you're stymied.''

''Not really. I suspect he has a nice offshore account somewhere like the Cayman Islands. But even if the money's safely on an island in the Caribbean, there has to be a paper trail right here in Wainscott. He isn't keeping records on his computer, either at work or at home, so he has to have a written record of his account number, or the current balance—something that would give us a lead into his account. If I could just find those records, I'm pretty sure I'd be able to access his account even if it's heavily encrypted. After all, as I just said, that's what I do for a living.''

"I thought you *prevented* people from accessing other people's bank accounts.''

He smiled. "Same thing. I have to know all the criminal techniques. The only difference is, I don't steal the money once I find it.''

Marisa frowned. "Jimmy, if you informed the trustees about what you've discovered, they'd be forced to investigate. Surely you already have enough hard evidence to convince them that the Refuge urgently needs a new director? Then you wouldn't have to find the sort of financial evidence that would convince law enforcement to take an interest.''

"Yes, I have more than enough evidence to convince the trustees that Stuart needs to go. But I'm not interested in getting him slapped on the wrist and fired. That would put a stop to his exploitation of women at the Refuge, but losing his job doesn't seem much of a punishment for a man I'm convinced murdered three women. Unfortunately, I can't prove he killed Carole and Ardita and Darina. I may never be able to prove that, because I assume the evidence has long since been destroyed. But at least I want him to do some serious jail time.''

"Is that realistic?''

"Yes, if I can collect evidence that he's committed fraud. The law doesn't care if he's auctioning off women's eggs and renting their wombs, but trafficking in human beings is illegal, and so is ripping off a charitable foundation. So I have to prove that Stuart is selling babies and pocketing the profits. And in order to prove that, I need your help, Marisa.''

"*My* help? What do you need from me?''

"I need you to carry on at work as if nothing has

changed. I need you to treat me just as you did when you thought I was mentally handicapped. And I need you to do and say nothing that will put Stuart Frieze on his guard. Will you do that? Not for me, but for the sake of all the women at the Refuge he's exploiting.''

"Well, of course I could do that," Marisa said. "But I'm not sure that I want to."

Ten

Before she could say anything more, Marisa heard Spencer crying. He woke up less often these days than in the weeks immediately after his father's death, but his nighttime cries still had the power to galvanize her into immediate action. She hated to imagine what horrific images from the past rampaged through his dreams, and she ran into his room, scooped him into her arms and rocked him gently back and forth until his terror subsided. He clung to her, his nose buried against her neck, his sobs gradually fading to the occasional hiccup.

"It's okay, pumpkin. Mommy's here. You're safe." She murmured the comforting words over and over again, more in hope that the sound of her voice would soothe him than for any meaning attached to what she was saying.

"Bang! Bang, bang!" Spencer's attempt to recount his dream was drowned out by another sob.

"Don't worry, honey. Mommy's here, Mommy and Bear. Nobody's going to hurt you." Marisa pointed to the row of stuffed animals lined up next to his bed. "See, all your friends are right here, too."

Spencer snuggled against Marisa, his fear obviously still remaining.

"It was just a dream, pumpkin. You're just fine." Marisa stroked his head, distressed by the fact that however incoherent Spencer's accounts of his nightmares, he would sometimes mimic the sounds of a gun being fired. She didn't need a degree in psychiatry to warn her that her son was still trying to work through frightening suppressed memories of the day his father was shot.

A wave of fierce anger washed over her, and she hugged Spencer extra tight. She would never understand how Evan could allow his son to be traumatized this badly. In his own way, Evan had truly loved Spencer, but it was typical of his selfishness that on the day his life ended, her ex-husband had cared more about salvaging a computer disk than about keeping his own son safe. He had deliberately put Spencer into harm's way because he knew this would be the most efficient method of keeping Marisa quiet and cooperative.

Just thinking about how Evan had treated Spencer was sufficient to send adrenaline surging through Marisa's body. She sprang to her feet, Spencer still in her arms, and had to pace the room to work off some of her rage. She patted his back soothingly, the anger pushed down deep inside, where she'd learned to keep it more or less contained.

Eventually she felt Spencer relax. "Okay, pumpkin." She kissed the tip of his nose. "I think it's time to go back to sleep. Would you like a drink of water?"

Spencer nodded. He took a couple of small sips, then pushed the cup away, rubbing his eyes sleepily.

She kissed his forehead. "Are you ready for Mommy to put you back into bed now?"

"No." He was sleepy, but he'd have to be a great deal more exhausted than this to acquiesce to being banished to bed. He shook his head vigorously. "No bed."

"Yes, pumpkin. It's bedtime for you."

"No. No bed." He suddenly wriggled, twisting around in her arms. "Hi, Dimmy! Story?"

"Hi, Spence." Jimmy let his knuckles scrape softly across Spencer's cheek. "How're you doing, kiddo?"

"Not sleeping."

"Hmm, I noticed. But it's nighttime. I think you're supposed to be asleep."

"No sleep. Read story."

Marisa shook her head. "No, Spencer, not now."

Spencer looked at Jimmy, a gleam of calculation in his eyes. "*Goodnight Moon?*"

"Sorry, buddy, no can do. You heard what your mommy said. It's time for you to go to sleep. I'll read you *Goodnight Moon* tomorrow."

Spencer's mouth set into a mutinous line. Before he could make any more demands, Jimmy held out his hands, and Spencer—to Marisa's surprise—climbed eagerly into them.

"Hi, Dimmy." Spencer patted him affectionately on the top of his head, a goodwill gesture he usually reserved for Bear or Peter Rabbit.

"Hi, Spence." Jimmy knelt alongside the bed and unwound Spencer's hands from his neck, depositing him onto the mattress. He pulled up the comforter and tucked Bear and Peter Rabbit under the covers, before leaning over to give Spencer a kiss.

"Good night," he said softly. "Your mommy and I are going to be right here, so you can close your eyes. We have everything taken care of."

Now that he was actually back in his bed, Spencer's resistance to the idea of sleeping seemed to be fading. "Mommy?" He directed a glance toward Marisa, his eyelids heavy.

"I'm right here. Go to sleep, pumpkin."

Marisa was pleasantly astonished when Spencer obediently closed his eyes. Sometimes after a nightmare, it took him as long as an hour before he was ready to fall asleep again. He twitched a couple of times, then rolled over onto his side and used Peter Rabbit's ears to tug the toy into a snug position against his tummy. Within moments, he was asleep.

Marisa started to tiptoe out of the bedroom. As she moved, she realized that Jimmy had his arm around her waist and that she had been leaning against him, totally relaxed, as she watched her son fall asleep.

Jimmy seemed to realize the same thing at the same moment. They both froze, without speaking, then sprang away from each other as though someone had detonated an electric charge between their bodies.

Marisa marched out into the living room, her stride all the more aggressive because inside she was shaking. Jesus, would she never learn? What was it with her and men, anyway? Why did she have this highly developed talent for always picking just the wrong one to get involved with? It was hard to imagine anyone less suited to her than a man who investigated white-collar crime for a living, unless she wanted her entire life to be an exercise in irony.

"We might as well talk about it," Jimmy said, following hard on her heels out of Spencer's bedroom. "What we feel for each other isn't going to go away just because we refuse to discuss it."

She didn't pretend not to understand him. There was no point in denying the obvious. "There isn't much to discuss, Jimmy. I seem to experience some weird chemical reaction when you're around and you apparently have the same reaction to me."

"'Weird chemical reaction'? Is that what you call it?"

"Yes." She spoke firmly, refusing to be distracted by the derisive glint in his eyes. "Your pheromones are hot for my pheromones. If we were teenagers, we might feel tempted to do something about it. Since we're both mature adults, we realize it's a shallow physical reaction that has no true importance."

"It feels damn important to me," Jimmy said.

"That's because sex always feels important to men, even when it's really meaningless."

"Sex is always *exciting* to men. It isn't always important. Big difference." He came and stood in front of her, too close to be ignored, and Marisa swung away from him, her heart pounding.

"Jimmy, last week I thought you were a mentally retarded janitor. Now I realize you're a high-powered investigator with a law degree. Whatever I may feel when you're around, I can't take my feelings for you seriously."

"Why not?"

"Surely you don't need to ask?" She wasn't sure if her frustration was directed at him, or at her body's stubborn refusal to heed the good sense of her own arguments. "I'm not attracted to the person you are. I can't possibly be—you've been two totally different people in the few days I've known you. I'm attracted to your body. Embarrassing, but true. However, not all attractions have to be acted on, so let me spell this out for you—I have no intention of having sex with you just because my hormones seem to have lost their powers of discrimination."

He smiled, and her heart did a quick back flip. Jimmy the janitor had a sweet smile. Jimmy the investigator had a smile that slaughtered her common sense. "Actually, I don't recall asking you to have sex with me," he said.

She flushed. "You're right. I apologize for leaping to

conclusions. My mistake. I assumed you were rapidly approaching that point.''

"Nope. Although I was hoping that eventually we might make love. I still hope that.''

"People can't 'make love' when they've only known each other for a few days.''

"Sure they can. Romeo and Juliet, Tristan and Isolde, Mickey and Minnie Mouse—''

"Mickey and Minnie Mouse?''

"Yeah, why not? Seventy-five years together and still going strong. Why should they be excluded from the annals of great lovers of history just because they're rodents? What has our society got against mice, anyway?''

She couldn't help it, she laughed. And wondered how long it had been since she'd found anything about the subject of sex amusing. Her laughter faded when Jimmy reached out and cupped her face with his hands.

"You're always beautiful, Marisa. You're spectacularly beautiful when you laugh.''

Marisa had grown up listening to people tell her that she was beautiful, as if that were the only significant thing about her. Her career as one of New York's highest paid models had emphasized the importance of her looks. For years, compliments about her appearance had simply made her impatient. Tonight, though, Jimmy's comment made her cheeks feel warm.

To cover her embarrassment, she spoke flippantly. "Is that your personal version of 'You're beautiful when you're angry'?''

"No. It's the simple truth.'' He brushed his thumb across her lips and lowered his mouth to hers with slow deliberation.

Alarms rang in her head, reminders of how sexual passion in the past had led her frighteningly astray. But the warnings floated away, unheeded. She had time to pull back from him, but she didn't. Time to say no, but she didn't. Part of her was fearful of ending the safety of her chaste, sexless existence, but another part longed to be kissed by him. In the end, desire overcame fear.

His kiss was devastating. Marisa would have expected him to be skillful, and he was. She would have expected him to be passionate, and he was. What she hadn't anticipated was the tenderness, or the subtle hint of vulnerability in his touch, as if kissing her was as threatening to his emotional equilibrium as it was to hers. Jimmy's expertise didn't impress her. In her modeling days, she'd been kissed by the world's best. It was his vulnerability that totally disarmed her.

When they broke apart, Jimmy's eyes were hazy and his breathing was as rapid as her own. She knew they'd just demolished a barricade that could never be rebuilt and that she ought to be feeling apprehensive. Instead she felt oddly exhilarated.

"Hot damn," Jimmy said softly.

She rubbed her hands up and down her arms, feeling the goose bumps. She forced herself to be sensible. "That was a mistake. I'm not ready to deal with this."

"That kiss was a lot of things, but a mistake isn't one of them. And I've learned the value of patience. I can wait."

She didn't ask what for. "I'm not sure if I'll ever be ready." She drew in an unsteady breath. "Past experience isn't encouraging in my case."

"Or in mine. We can take this as slowly as you want." He sent her a look that was lazily amused. "That way we can overcome our neuroses together."

"I can't help thinking my neuroses are likely to prove more difficult to overcome than yours."

"Could be. Hey, I'm not a competitive kind of a guy. You can win the who's crazier contest if you want." He was smiling at her again—the warm smile that melted her insides—and Marisa realized that she didn't want to win the contest or the argument. What she wanted was for Jimmy to kiss her again. She swayed toward him, the movement barely perceptible. Even so, he saw and responded at once.

His arms went around her, but he didn't drag her against him, as if he knew that he had to leave a crucial inch or two of space if she was to remain within her comfort zone. She lifted her mouth to his, the movement tentative, but an invitation nonetheless. His lips met hers, his touch light, almost delicate.

From some almost forgotten reservoir, she drew the confidence to relax and lean against him, not a passive recipient, but a willing participant in whatever might happen next. Jimmy's body pressed against hers, alien in shape and texture after months in which Spencer had been the only person she'd held or been close to. She felt rigid muscle, rough skin, the scrape of his wispy Jimmy-the-janitor beard against her face. Beneath it all she felt his strength, and a subtle restraint. A quality that had certainly never been present with Evan, even in the earliest days of their relationship.

For a while, their kiss remained gentle, and her pleasure was soft and languid, like warm sunlight on a summer afternoon. Without warning, her pleasure exploded into something fierce and hungry. No longer warm sunshine, but a torrential thunderstorm, complete with lightning strikes. If their first kiss had been passionate, this one was ravenous. Her mouth burned beneath Jimmy's, and her hands were all over him. In response, he grabbed her hips and pulled her hard against him, his hold suddenly as aggressive as it had previously been casual.

Her heart performed a swift somersault before steadying and starting to thud heavily against her ribs. Hot blood raced through her veins, carrying desire to every part of her body. Once upon a time, before Evan, she had been a passionate woman, but that had been a long time ago, and the speed and intensity of her arousal caught Marisa unawares. Her body erupted, seeking the sexual gratification that had been missing for far too long. Desire passed back and forth between her and Jimmy, growing hotter and more powerful with each exchange.

The remnant of her brain that was still functioning sent out a final warning, and Marisa realized that they were heading fast—very fast—in a direction she wasn't ready to go. Panic squeezed the air out of her lungs, and she gasped for breath. She put her hands on Jimmy's chest, pushing against him, suddenly frantic to break free of his hold.

He let go of her at once, but it took a moment for his gaze to focus. "What's wrong? Did I hurt you?"

She fought for breath. And calm. "No, not that. I'm sorry, Jimmy." She knew she was in no state to search for the right words to explain the god-awful mess that had been her marriage and the fears that resulted from her experiences with Evan. The nightmare of sex used as a weapon of subjugation. The sadistic pleasure her husband had taken in denying her the right to spend time with Spencer. The control he'd exercised over every aspect of her life, right down to the color of her lipstick and the clothes she was allowed to wear. Rigid independence was her way of fighting the demons, and she wasn't ready for the implicit surrender that was an integral part of any sexual relationship. Especially one that generated such intense, out-of-control sensations as this one.

She offered Jimmy the only explanation she was capable of at this point. "I can't do this. Not now. Not...yet." The tacit admission that one day they might actually make love was shocking to her.

"I told you I'd wait. I will." Jimmy's voice wasn't entirely steady. He stood still for a moment, fists clenched. Then he turned away, combing his hands through his hair and fastening his shirt. He tucked the ends inside his jeans and closed the zipper. The evidence of how far they'd progressed before she called a halt alarmed Marisa all over again. Starting a relationship with Jimmy Griffin struck her as a very high-risk venture.

If she'd never met Evan Connors, she might have been intrigued by the uninhibited responses of her body. But she'd seen up close and personal how meaningless sexual attraction was in terms of basic compatibility, and how threatening passion could be to happiness. She'd lived with the consequences of desire run amuck, and she had no desire to revisit that particular scene. Before she ever made love again, she needed to know that the man partnering her was someone she would trust with her life. And with Spencer's, which was a hundred times more precious to her.

"Any chance of a cup of coffee?" Jimmy asked.

She hesitated.

"I can't leave yet," Jimmy said, picking up on her reluctance. "We still need to talk."

She shook her head. "I'd rather not discuss this, Jimmy. Not now. I have to work some things out for myself—by myself—before we...before we make any decisions about where this might be heading."

"I wasn't planning to discuss anything personal. But we do need to talk about Stuart and the Refuge."

"Oh. Stuart."

"Yeah, Stuart." Jimmy gave a grim smile. "You remember him, don't you? He's the guy you work for who might be a triple murderer."

The realization that she'd completely forgotten why Jimmy had originally come here tonight wasn't exactly reassuring. To put it mildly, her priorities seemed to be severely scrambled.

"You're right," Marisa said. "We do need to talk. We never resolved the problem of what to do about Stuart."

"No, we didn't. So—is there any chance of a cup of coffee?"

"Sure." She went to the kitchen, glad to have a practical task to perform. Maybe a routine chore would send her brain back into functional mode. Or, at least, an approximation thereof. "I have decaf or regular, whichever you'd prefer."

"Let's go for the real stuff. I could use a shot of caffeine." Jimmy watched her spoon grounds into the filter. "Marisa, I really do need your help with Frieze. I realize you find my investigative methods offensive, so I understand why you said you couldn't help me—"

"I never said that. Or at least, I didn't mean to." She slid the basket into place and flipped the switch to brew. "What I said was that I wasn't willing to keep silent and do nothing—"

"If you don't keep silent about who I am and what I'm doing, that's the equivalent of refusing to help," Jimmy said. "Obviously, I have a lot of experience with white-collar crime and workplace fraud. Trust me, if you go to the Wainscott Foundation trustees, or to law enforcement officials, and tell them what I'm doing, it's as likely that I'll get arrested as that Stuart will. The very best outcome you can hope for is that Stuart will be fired. Not much of a punishment, do you think?"

"No, it wouldn't be. I'm sorry if I gave you a wrong impression earlier on. As I recall, what you actually asked me was, would I be willing to keep silent and carry on exactly as if nothing had changed. And I said probably not. What I meant was that I'm not willing to sit back and do nothing. I've tried doing nothing when I'm surrounded by criminal activity, and I've concluded that as a coping method, it sucks."

"You wouldn't be doing nothing—far from it. You'd be cooperating by your silence."

She shook her head. "It's not enough. If Stuart's guilty, he needs to be in prison. If he's innocent, he deserves to have your suspicions laid to rest. The only way to move forward from here is to find the file where Stuart keeps financial records for his illicit deals. If it exists."

"Agreed, and I'm working on that right now—"

"I know you are, but it would be much better if I took over that chore. Assuming the file is in his office and not at his home—a big assumption, by the way—I'm the logical person to go looking for it."

"No, it's too risky. I can't allow you to—"

"I didn't know you had to give me permission," Marisa said tartly. "How is it risky, anyway? Taking care of the files is a major part of my job description. I have the perfect excuse to ferret around Stuart's office and look for anything incriminating."

"Which is why we have to assume that Stuart doesn't have the information stuck in a file drawer, neatly labeled 'Financial Records of Illicit Deals.' If he did, he wouldn't have given you free run of his filing system. If records of his illegal profits exist, searching for them is a major project. It's definitely not something you can accomplish on your lunch break.''

"That's true, but I'm still willing to take it on to the best of my ability. Although there must be a good chance the records you want either don't exist, or else are stashed somewhere in Stuart's house, not in his office.''

"They could be at his house, but I don't think they are,'' Jimmy said. "It's actually been easier for me to search his home than his office. When he's at work, or away on a business trip, his home is guaranteed to be empty, and I've managed to do a pretty thorough job of searching the place.''

She quirked an eyebrow. "Breaking and entering?''

"Fortunately, there was no need to 'break' into anything. Stuart has the same casual attitude to home safety as the rest of Wainscott. He routinely leaves windows unlatched, and once I even found the door unlocked. The fact that he lives so close to where he works probably makes him careless. But he might as well have the place barricaded like Fort Knox for all the good it's done me. He's lived in the same house for three years, ever since he became director of the Refuge, but there's not a damn thing there to indicate how he spends his leisure time. He takes *Newsweek* magazine, and the daily newspaper. No subscriptions to specialty magazines. He has no videos, and his collection of CDs looks as if they're castoffs from Muzak, they're so bland. The carpet is beige, the walls are off-white, and the only personal photos are from his time at the United Nations—Stuart standing in front of various refugee camps with VIPs from Congress and the U.N. Not a family shot anywhere in sight. For a man to be that cautious, he has to be hiding something. ''

"Maybe he's an orphan.''

"Maybe." Jimmy sounded as frustrated as he looked. "Or maybe he's just damn clever at covering his tracks."

Marisa wanted to offer some encouragement. "Since his money-making schemes are all connected to the Refuge, it would make more sense for him to keep the financial records in the office there, don't you think?"

"I would have expected them to be in his home, but since they're not, his office at the Refuge has to be my next bet."

Marisa pulled a couple of coffee mugs down from the shelf. "You said you haven't had much chance to search through the files at the Refuge?"

"I've done my best, but it's been really hard for me. Unfortunately, the Refuge is never empty, day or night. Even when the office section is officially closed for the night, I'm always worried about encountering some hungry expectant mom who's come down to the kitchen for a midnight snack."

"Or an office clerk who's forgotten her purse."

"That, too." Jimmy gave her a smile. "I have to say, you seriously destroyed my powers of concentration on Friday night."

"You were taking a big risk going into Stuart's office so early in the evening."

"Not really. It's safer than a midnight trip. If I went into his office in the middle of the night, I probably wouldn't run into anyone. But if I did, I'd be dead meat. What excuse could I give for being there? At least in the early evening, if someone finds me, I can explain away my presence. The fact that the copying machine is in your office makes a great excuse, because everyone knows that Stuart has been so short of office help these past few months that he taught me how to use it."

The coffeemaker spluttered to a halt, its task complete,

and Marisa went to the fridge for milk. "How do you drink your coffee? Do you need sugar?"

He shook his head. "No, thanks. I drink it black."

She poured him a mug and handed it to him, adding milk to her own. "Well, that's settled, then. You've already checked out Stuart's home and found nothing, and it's too difficult for you to invent excuses to rummage through the files in the office. That means I need to do the searching. Next week will be the perfect opportunity. Stuart has an all-day meeting with the board of trustees of Wainscott Foundation on Tuesday. They're having a board meeting at the Alpine Lodge, and he's not coming into the office at all. There's still more than enough paperwork waiting to be organized—nobody will think anything of it if I spend all of Tuesday filing. Anyway, everyone else is too busy keeping up with their own work to pay attention to me and what I'm doing."

Jimmy didn't look happy. "It sounds easy, Marisa, but I'm convinced there are solid reasons to believe this man is a murderer. If I'm right, Stuart is a man who has no hesitation in killing to protect himself. You need to think carefully before volunteering to do something that might cause him to conclude you're a danger to him, or to his schemes."

"I'm not ignoring the danger," she said quietly. "But I spent too many years of my life looking the other way when I suspected terrible crimes were being committed by people I loved. I found out the hard way that avoidance and determined ignorance eventually create more problems—and much bigger problems— than stepping up to the plate when I know it's my turn. When Evan died, I swore I was going to create a new life for my son, and that it wouldn't be based on any sort of moral or ethical compromise. I'm not about to renege on that promise this soon.''

"You could just quit your job," he said softly. "This isn't your fight, Marisa. You have no obligation to help me put Stuart Frieze behind bars."

"Maybe I don't have an obligation to you, but I feel a strong obligation to all the young women Stuart is bringing to the Refuge and then exploiting for his personal profit. I know what it's like to feel powerless in the face of your circumstances, and I hate to think that Stuart's taking advantage of the women who come to him when they've nowhere else to turn. Quite apart from the death of your sister and the other two women, if he really is doing even half of what you claim, I want to help bring him to justice. I'm going to do this, Jimmy. I need to feel that for once in my life, I wasn't too cowardly to do the right thing."

Eleven

Marisa stayed up until the early hours of the morning, reading the information Jimmy had collected on Stuart Frieze. Seeing the incriminating data laid out in black and white, with supporting charts, graphs and tables, removed any lingering doubt she might have entertained about Stuart's guilt in regard to his exploitation of the young women who came to the Refuge.

Jimmy's accusations of murder were less convincing. None of the information he had gathered directly supported his contention that Stuart had killed Carole, or the two refugees from Kosovo. A case could be made that Stuart had strong motives for silencing them—except that there was no proof any of the three women had threatened to reveal what was going on at the Refuge.

In fact, there was only Jimmy's word for it that Carole Riven had ever claimed to be investigating irregularities in the operation of the Refuge. With damaging honesty, Jimmy had included a notation in his file that a search of Carole's papers after her death hadn't revealed a single reference to Stuart Frieze. Jimmy could, however, prove that his sister had spent a week's vacation at the Alpine Lodge in Wainscott in February, although Ardita and Darina had already left the Refuge at that point, so she couldn't have spoken with them. Jimmy speculated that something in Wainscott had aroused Carole's suspicions, and that she'd sought out the two refugees, making contact with them later in February. What was beyond dispute was the fact that by the middle of March, all three women were dead.

The evidence that Stuart had had ample opportunity to commit the murders was slightly stronger. Jimmy had copies of expense account records showing that Stuart had been in Baltimore the week the deaths occurred. Supposedly, he'd flown there to attend a national conference of adoption providers, but he hadn't stayed at the official convention hotel. Instead, he'd booked into an inn located inconveniently far from the site of the conference. The inn was, however, at the apex of a geographic triangle that would have given Stuart swift highway access to each of the three places where the deaths had occurred.

A district attorney would never consider taking such a feeble case to court, but Marisa could understand why Jimmy was so sure that his sister had been murdered by Stuart Frieze. Marisa reserved judgment. The fact that Stuart was a sleazeball profiting from other people's desperation didn't constitute proof that he was a murderer. Her own brother was a perfect example of a man whose ethical code needed major reworking, but who would never be willing—or decisive enough—to commit murder.

With so much unpalatable information about Stuart at the forefront of her mind, Marisa didn't look forward to returning to work and being forced into close proximity to a man she now cordially despised. Still, she had plenty of experience in hiding her feelings, and she schooled herself not to let her disgust show when she walked into Stuart's office on Monday morning.

She needn't have worried about Stuart detecting any subtle differences in her manner toward him. He was finishing up a phone conversation just as she arrived, and he acknowledged her greeting with an agitated nod of his head, barely glancing in her direction.

"That was Bob Penney from the Wainscott sheriff's office," he said, hanging up the phone. "The police in Denver have notified him that they may have found Anya Dzhambirov."

Stuart's grim expression was sufficient to warn Marisa that this wasn't good news. "Is she...hurt? In trouble?"

"I'm afraid it seems likely that she's dead. Apparently, the body of a young pregnant woman was found in a motel in Denver early this morning by the cleaners. The body—the woman matches the description of Anya, and the police want me to make a positive identification."

A leaden weight settled in the pit of Marisa's stomach. "Was she—" Her voice cracked, and she had to swallow before she could continue. "How did she die?"

Stuart ran his hand over his chin, avoiding Marisa's gaze, as if eye contact were too threatening to his composure and couldn't be risked. "It was what I was so afraid of when I heard she'd run off with that damn boyfriend of hers. She was beaten to death."

"Oh, no!" Marisa felt sick. Poor Anya, whose short life had been an endless litany of brutality, and whose death, apparently, had been more of the same. She swallowed hard. "Have the police arrested anyone for the murder? Her boyfriend?"

"Not as far as I know, but Bob Penney didn't have many details." Stuart sounded both weary and depressed. "I really have to start the drive down to Denver right away, before I lose my nerve. I've seen too many dead bodies in my life, and this isn't a task that's going to get any better for waiting."

He grabbed his briefcase and snapped it shut with a

burst of angry energy. "That poor, foolish girl. Why the hell didn't she stay where she was safe?"

Stuart grabbed his car keys and left, without waiting for an answer to his own question. Marisa walked through to her office, fighting an urge to cry. She sat down at her desk and turned on her computer, her mind churning with bittersweet images of Anya, and the baby who'd never had the chance to be born.

Her desktop program flashed a reminder of the day's most urgent tasks, and she blinked at the screen, called back to awareness of her surroundings by the flicker of colorful icons. But instead of responding to the prompt on her monitor, her thoughts coalesced into a sudden gruesome realization about Anya's death.

Stuart could easily be the person who had murdered her.

A few hours ago, Marisa had been willing to give the director of the Refuge the benefit of the doubt, but now she wasn't so sure. Had his grief just now been genuine, or a nauseating example of hypocrisy? Anya had rebelled and left the Refuge, planning to raise her own baby and depriving Stuart of a profitable sale. Not to mention losing him a crop of valuable eggs. Within three days of running out on him, she was dead. She hadn't been the victim of a supposed accident, as had Carole Riven and the women from Kosovo, but from Stuart's point of view, a woman beaten to death in a motel was almost as good as an accident. Marisa would be willing to bet next week's wages—which she couldn't afford to lose—that Anya's death would be followed by no more than a cursory police inquiry.

From Stuart's point of view, he was as safe as if the death had been declared accidental. The police investigation of Anya's murder was going to focus exclusively on her brutal ex-boyfriend, Alex Makhmedov. Who, now that Marisa thought about it, was known to exist only because Stuart claimed that he did.

Had any independent observer ever seen Makhmedov? As far as Marisa knew, nobody ever had. According to the biographical details provided by Stuart, Anya's boyfriend was an illegal immigrant, a member of the Chechen Mafia. What a perfect suspect! Nobody would be surprised if Makhmedov proved impossible to find, since illegal immigrants tended to hide themselves in big cities even when they were basically law-abiding. If they were wanted for murder, they'd dig themselves so deep into the underbelly of the city as to be invisible. The police wouldn't be surprised if Makhmedov couldn't be found at his last known address. Stuart had already forewarned everyone that the address and phone number he had on file were most likely fakes. And since there was no physical description of Makhmedov for the police to go on, their investigation would soon grind to an inconclusive halt.

All of which would leave Stuart free and clear to pursue his profitable schemes at the Refuge. Auctioning off babies. Selling eggs. Renting wombs. Profiting from people's suffering.

Damned if I'm going to let him get away with it.

Marisa pushed back from her desk so quickly that she knocked over her chair. She didn't even notice. She ran out into the hall, and only slowed down when she bumped into Fran Harlowe.

"Hey, where's the fire?" Fran gave her a friendly smile.

"Sorry." Marisa searched for an acceptable excuse for running like a loon. "I've got a ton of work to get through, and the light in my office has gone out. Do you know where Jimmy is? I can't find any spare fluorescent bulbs. Besides, I need a ladder to reach the fixture.''

''Jimmy's in the kitchen, mopping the floor. I'll tell him what the problem is and send him to you.'' Fran's smile dimmed. ''Have you heard the news about Anya? It's terrible, isn't it? I'll never understand why that poor kid thought she needed to run away. And now look what's happened to her.''

''I heard the news,'' Marisa said. ''Stuart was talking to the police about identifying the body, when I arrived. Poor Anya.'' Her eyes welled with tears, and she dashed them away, afraid that if she started crying she might not be able to stop.

''Maybe it isn't her.'' Fran was apparently a certified optimist.

''Let's hope. I guess there's more than one pregnant young woman in Denver who matches Anya's general description. Brown hair, gray eyes, medium height, medium build.'' Marisa tried to share Fran's optimism.

''Anya always seemed so attached to Stuart. I can't understand why she'd run out on him like this. Can you?''

There was no honest answer she could give to Fran's question, and Marisa felt her tension levels rising. It was less than a year since she'd been knee-deep in lies and deceptions. She hadn't expected to find herself revisiting the same nightmare scene ever again, let alone within months of Evan's death.

''I guess pregnant teenagers aren't noted for their wise decisions,'' she said. ''Anya was terribly upset about her brother. Who knows what was going on in her mind? Anyway, I really need to get back to my office. Send Jimmy to me as soon as you can spare him, will you?

I've got a pile of stuff to get through today, and I can't work without a new lightbulb.''

"Sure thing. I'll send him right away. The kitchen floor can wait. I'm making a real simple lunch today, so there's time to spare before the floor needs to be mopped."

Jimmy arrived in her office a couple of minutes later. He was carrying a small stepladder that he set down with exaggerated care. He scratched his chin, his gaze puzzled as he stared at the ceiling and its blazing fluorescent lights.

"Mrs. Harlowe said your lights aren't working. She was wrong. All your lights are working real good. You don't need a new bulb." He picked up the ladder and turned to leave.

"No, don't go, Jimmy. I need you to stay." It was unsettling to watch the man she had nearly made love to the previous night revert to his role as Jimmy the janitor. If she'd thought about it, she would have realized that he couldn't possibly maintain a successful impersonation if he flipped in and out of character every time he saw her. Still, she wasn't prepared for the shock of seeing how deeply he immersed himself in his role as a mentally challenged person.

His gaze roamed the office, never meeting hers. "I'm real busy this morning, miss. Is it important?"

"Yes." Marisa closed the door between her office and Stuart's, leaning against it to be sure that nobody could come in. "I need to talk to you about Anya," she said, her voice low.

"You always leave the door to your office ajar," he said, his voice even lower than hers. "Open it again. Quick."

She moved to open it.

"Wait. " He put out his arm, stopping her. "Damn, when I'm around you I can't think straight." He flipped the light switch, plunging her windowless cubicle into semidarkness.

"What on earth are you doing?" she asked.

"Giving myself a valid excuse to be here. Your office is supposed to be too dark to work in, remember?" He climbed the ladder at high speed and removed a ceiling panel so that he could unscrew a fluorescent bulb from its fixture, then climbed down and opened her office door.

"Okay, now you have a lighting problem. We have about ten minutes, maximum, before I have to be out of here." He spoke softly, positioning himself so that he could see Stuart's office and the entrance to the lobby. "What's the problem?"

Despite Jimmy's claim that he couldn't think clearly when she was around, he gave no sign that he was in any danger of blowing his cover. Marisa didn't find his skill entirely reassuring. After Evan, how could she ever learn to trust a man who displayed such an easy mastery of deception?

He leaned forward and gripped her hand. "Marisa, we don't have much time..."

"Sorry." She drew in a steadying breath. "Did Fran Harlowe tell you that the police have found a young pregnant woman in a motel in Denver? She's been beaten to death, and they think it might be Anya Dzambhirov. Stuart's gone to Denver, supposedly to identify the body. But it occurred to me after he left that Stuart himself might very well be responsible for killing her. The way she died seems to fit the pattern of your sister's car accident, and the deaths of the two women from Kosovo. Anya refuses to comply with Stuart's demands. She doesn't tell anyone about her problems, which is the same as Ardita and Darina. Instead, she runs away in the middle of the night—or so we're led to believe, although nobody actually saw her leave. Then a couple of days later she's found dead in circumstances that are unlikely ever to be investigated seriously. Doesn't that sound as if her death could be Stuart's handiwork?"

"It's close enough to be worrying," he said grimly. "I had the same thought. Let's hope we're both wrong and that this young women in Denver isn't Anya."

"Okay, I'm hoping. Hoping very much. But Jimmy, if it does turn out to be Anya, I can't continue to keep silent about what you're doing here. It was one thing to agree not to talk to the police when we were dealing with three deaths that happened months ago and are beyond solving at this point. It's another thing to tacitly aid and abet Stuart in covering up for Anya's murder."

"I agree," he said. "However, it's too early to abandon hope that we may yet find Anya alive. Don't let's make any firm decisions until we know exactly what we have to deal with. It's possible that she really did run off with her boyfriend, you know. I spoke to her one-on-one a few times, after she heard the news that her brother had been killed in Chechnya, and that death changed her mind completely about giving up her baby for adoption. She was the last surviving member of her family, and she couldn't bear to think of her child growing up among strangers, never knowing its true heritage."

"She confided all that to you? Thinking you were mentally retarded?"

Jimmy shrugged. "Anya speaks limited English. From her point of view, I guess it didn't make much difference whether she was stumbling through a conversation with me or with anyone else. Let's hope her boyfriend came through for her, and she's with him right now."

Marisa pulled a face. "Is it any better to hope that she might have run off with her boyfriend? According to Stuart, Makhmedov is a violent, brutal man. If he's telling the truth, Anya didn't do herself any favors if she went back to him."

"But there's no reason to expect Stuart to tell the truth. We have no way of knowing anything at all about Makhmedov."

Marisa pressed her fingers to her forehead, where a headache had started to pound. "This is so frustrating. Almost every biographical fact we know about Anya comes from Stuart, or from files Stuart has had ample chance to alter. If Anya's dead, Stuart can manipulate the police into believing just about anything he pleases concerning her past history."

Jimmy removed her grinding fingers and replaced them with his thumbs, massaging her temples. "But if we voice our suspicions to the police, at least they'll start looking for evidence that Makhmedov may not be exactly the man Stuart Frieze is making him out to be. And we have to hope that once the police start asking questions, something will start to unravel, and implicate Stuart."

"And if we could get Stuart indicted for Anya's murder, we wouldn't have to work so hard to find financial records that could get him indicted for fraud."

"That's true." Jimmy tucked a strand of hair behind her ear. "Feeling better?"

She nodded, then stepped back, disconcerted that she was already regretting the loss of his touch. Even more disconcerted to find that she wanted him to close the damn door and kiss her.

"If you lose your job as a janitor, I recommend you train as a masseur. You have the touch. Thank you."

"You're welcome. Bottom line, we need to wait for

Stuart to return from Denver before we decide what to do next."

"I'm likely to hear before you do whether it's Anya who was killed. As soon as I know, I'll make an excuse to come and find you—"

Jimmy shook his head. "Bad idea. When we're at work, we should avoid speaking to each other. I'll come around to your apartment tonight. It's too risky to—"

He broke off in mid-sentence, transforming into Jimmy the janitor before her eyes. He dropped his head forward, and his shoulders rounded into a sloppy hunch, leaving his arms hanging loosely at his sides. He took a clumsy step toward the ladder, tripping over her wastebasket as he went.

"Oops. Sorry." He bent down to stand the basket upright again, and nearly lost his glasses in the process. He rescued his glasses and picked up a couple of balls of crumpled paper that had tumbled out of the wastebasket.

"There was a bumblebee caught in your fixture, miss. Or maybe it was a wasp. How do you tell a wasp from a bumblebee when they're dead?"

"I don't know, Jimmy. I can't even tell them apart when they're alive."

"I don't know, either."

He took the fluorescent bulb from her desk, where he'd set it earlier. "I cleaned everything real good, so this light should work okay now."

"I sure hope so. But you said that ten minutes ago, Jimmy." Marisa broke off, pretending that she'd just caught sight of the woman who'd come into Stuart's office a full minute earlier.

"Oh, Ms. Wainscott, I'm sorry. I didn't notice you. You should have said something."

So if you didn't notice her, how would you know she's

been waiting there, not saying anything? Marisa realized that she was out of practice in the art of duplicity after a mere eight months of honest living. Hoping Helen Wain-scott hadn't noticed the inconsistency, she fixed her face into welcoming smile and walked into Stuart's office.

"Stuart will be very sorry to have missed you, Ms. Wainscott, but I'm afraid he had to go in to Denver."

Helen Wainscott looked flustered. "Oh, have I got my dates wrong?" She pulled a slender address book out of her Coach purse—five hundred bucks worth of dark brown leather and brass trim that managed to clash quite badly with the subtle blue undertones of her forest-green suit.

She flipped through the pages of her diary, frowning. "No, I'm not mistaken. It says here that Stuart and I were supposed to meet at nine-thirty to go over the agenda for tomorrow's board meeting."

"I'm very sorry. Stuart didn't have a chance to tell me about his schedule for today. He was called away unex-pectedly—"

Helen sighed. "Don't tell me. Another baby is about to arrive in the world?"

"No, not a baby. I wish it had been something that pleasant." Marisa had noticed before that Helen Wain-scott had an ambivalent attitude toward Refuge mothers and their babies. But remembering the horrific story of how ten-year-old Helen had found her sister bleeding to death after an illegal abortion, she could understand.

"I'm afraid it's a rather worrying emergency," Marisa said. "Stuart's had to drive in to Denver. The police want him to help identify the body of a young woman who was found in a motel early this morning."

"Why in the world would the police need Stuart to drive to Denver for that?"

"Unfortunately, there's some possibility that the dead body…that it might be one of the young women who was living here at the Refuge."

"My goodness, I'm sorry to hear that." Helen sounded as if she was more perturbed about the scandal that might possibly attach itself to the Prudence Wainscott Foundation than she was about the murdered woman.

"How did the young woman die?" she asked. "Not a drug overdose, I sincerely hope?"

"No, not drugs. She was beaten to death."

"Oh, dear." Helen touched a slender white hand to her throat. "Oh, my. She was pregnant, of course, or she wouldn't have been living here at the Refuge."

"Yes, she was."

"So the baby's dead, as well. That's really too bad. What a tragic loss." Helen reached into her purse again, then stopped abruptly. "It's at moments like this that I wonder why in the world I decided it would be a good idea to give up smoking."

"Smoking is bad for you," Jimmy said from the top of the ladder, making them both jump. The lights in Marisa's cubicle flickered on, as he repositioned the fiberglass panel in the suspended ceiling. "Smoking makes you cough. Smoking turns your lungs black and frizzled. Smoking makes you smell bad—"

Marisa's gaze met his. She saw the glint of mischief in his eyes, and had to smother an almost irresistible urge to laugh. She spoke repressively. "Thanks for the warnings, Jimmy, but Ms. Wainscott knows all about the dangers of smoking. That's why she gave it up."

"I don't smoke," Jimmy said smugly. "My lungs are pink and healthy." He climbed down from the ladder. "Your light's fixed now, miss."

"Thanks, Jimmy."

"You're welcome. There was a fly in your light fixture as well as the wasp. Or maybe it was a bee. I don't like wasps. Or bees. I don't like spiders, either. Or beetles." He turned to her, his brows drawn into a slight scowl. "I'm going to mop the kitchen floor."

Helen Wainscott watched him leave, her mouth pinched. "Sometimes one has to wonder if Stuart's obsession for helping the less fortunate doesn't get carried to extremes."

"Jimmy's a very good worker," Marisa said blandly.

"He'd have to be. Just pray that you don't get electrocuted this afternoon when the light fixture explodes because he screwed the bulb in back to front." Helen returned her purse to her shoulder. "Well, there doesn't seem to be much point in sitting here waiting for Stuart."

"No, I imagine it will be early afternoon before he's back."

"I'm staying at the Alpine Lodge. Have Stuart give me a call when he gets back from Denver, will you? Remind him that he's supposed to be joining me and the other board members for dinner tonight."

"I'll do that," Marisa said. "Is there anything I could do to help in the meantime, Ms. Wainscott?"

"No, thank you, my dear. I'm sure you have a lot of work to get through, and I wouldn't want to intrude." Helen Wainscott probably meant to sound kind, but merely sounded patronizing. "Just make sure you don't forget to pass on my messages to Stuart."

Stuart called from the police station in Denver, just as Marisa was leaving to take Spencer for lunch. "It wasn't Anya," he said. "I'm over the moon. It wasn't Anya."

"That's wonderful news," Marisa said. She felt her

face break into a giant smile. So much for imagining Stuart was a murderer. Anya wasn't even dead!

"I'm so glad you have good news," she said. "Except that there's still a woman who was beaten to death, of course. Since it isn't Anya, do the police have any leads as to who it might be?"

"They know who it is. Right as I was being taken to the morgue to identify the body, a man turned himself in to the police. Said the woman in the motel was his wife. Tracie Riccardo. She was a dental hygienist and—according to her husband—she'd been having an affair with her boss. Apparently, he followed them to the motel and broke in on the pair of them. The husband planned to beat up the boss and take his wife back home. But the boss—obviously a true hero—ran away. So the husband took out his frustrations by beating his wife to death. Of course, he's now overcome with remorse, swearing he never meant to hurt her." Stuart made a noise of disgust. "Having seen what he did to his wife, I hope the D.A. gets him locked up for life."

He sounded entirely sincere, but Marisa had lots of experience with criminals who were genuinely outraged by other people's crimes, while totally excusing their own. "It's horrible to think of how that woman died," she said. "But, thank God, Anya's safe."

"We hope." Stuart's voice sobered. "There's still that brute Makhmedov to worry about. Anyway, I called right away because I was sure everyone at the Refuge would be worrying. Pass on the good news, will you?"

"I sure will. Oh, by the way, Ms. Wainscott was here this morning. Apparently you had arranged a meeting with her to discuss the agenda for tomorrow's board meeting."

"Damn! I completely spaced it. I'll call her, make profuse excuses. You know what it's like at a nonprofit organization. We need to keep the board chairperson happy, or she can make life impossible for us all. Is Helen staying at the Alpine Lodge? Her family used to own it, you know—'' Stuart broke off rather abruptly.

"Yes, that's where she's staying."

"I'll be back by two-thirty. We'll have to work hard to get the agenda for tomorrow's meeting printed and copied with all the back-up documents before five. But I'm sure we can make it. I feel energized just knowing that we don't have to start making arrangements for Anya's funeral. I'm sure you do, too."

Either he was genuinely relieved that the body he'd just examined wasn't Anya's, or he was a brilliant actor. Marisa wished like hell she knew which it was.

"I'll clear my desk so that I'm ready to work on the agenda the moment you get back," she said. "If you don't have any more instructions, I'm going to hang up so that I can get busy telling everyone that the woman in the motel wasn't Anya. It's great to be the bearer of such good news."

"Go to it. See you this afternoon." Stuart hung up the phone.

Twelve

Stuart enjoyed his dinner at the Alpine Lodge with the board members of the Wainscott Foundation. After so many years spent bullshitting the bureaucrats of the United Nations in order to keep funds flowing and refugees eating, his ass-kissing skills were well-honed. By contrast to the hard-nosed and frequently corrupt bastards who ran the U.N. refugee supply centers, the Wainscott trustees were a bunch of naive do-gooders, endearing in their own gullible way. Keeping them happy was easy enough to be amusing. From doddery old Bishop Jefferson, who had marched alongside Martin Luther King in the glory days of the civil rights movement, to Leonora Cassidy of the Gay Women's Adoption Coalition, the trustees were so busy pursuing their own narrow agendas that he could drive a Mack truck through the gaps they left in their oversight duties.

Aside from the satisfaction of manipulating the trustees, the dinner offered the earthier satisfaction of eating a good meal. The Lodge had a talented new chef, and Stuart had seen enough starvation to appreciate gourmet food when it was put in front of him. However, it had been a long, difficult day, and by the time the meal ended, he was ready for bed.

Unfortunately, so was Helen, and the fluttery breathlessness of her manner indicated that there would be no reprieve tonight from his duties as in-house stud. The subtle but unmistakable signals she was sending indicated to him that she was bound and determined they would spend the night together.

Having sex with Helen brought back uncomfortable memories, but keeping her happy was the most important way to safeguard his fund-raising activities, and Stuart prided himself on being too smart to fight the inevitable—so he waited for the other board members to go to their rooms, then turned to her with a small, intimate smile. In the interests of keeping his African clinics operational, the least he could do was fake desire.

"Alone, at last," he murmured. "Are you ready for a nightcap?"

"That would be nice." She blushed. "But the bar is so crowded, don't you think?"

It was his cue to suggest retiring to her room. Jesus H. Christ! They'd been having sex regularly for the past two years, ever since her divorce from Senator John Crowland became final. He wondered why in hell she still needed to be seduced every damn time. As far as he was concerned, the ritual foreplay had gotten old a long time ago.

Still, he might as well try to enjoy it. He dropped his voice to a husky purr. "There are a lot of people at the Lodge for this time of year, aren't there? Your suite would be more private—if you don't mind inviting me up."

Her blush deepened. "Well, since you suggested it... Shall we go up now?"

"Yes, let's. Having a nightcap with you would be the perfect end to a very long day." He voiced the lie with smooth charm. Thank God, she'd succumbed quickly. With luck, this wouldn't be one of those nights when

Helen played hard to get for five or six hours before falling on him like a sex-starved escapee from a women's prison.

The Lodge had only three floors, and Helen's suite occupied the most attractive corner on the top floor, a palatial set of rooms with a westerly view of the mountains and a southern view of the lake. Although her father had developed Alpine Lakes into a resort and built the Lodge, Helen had lost her controlling shares in the property during the complicated divorce settlement that ended her marriage.

Stuart thought the current management of the resort was generous in making the suite available to her whenever she came into town. But old habits died hard, it seemed, and the Wainscott name was still one to conjure with in this part of the Rocky Mountains. Helen continued to receive as much fawning attention from Alpine Lakes managers as if she still owned the place.

Helen liked their seductions to follow a pattern chosen by her, and the stage for tonight's scene had been set before she went down to dinner. The suite had recently been redecorated in a sleek art deco style, and the lamps had been left on, set to cast muted pools of light onto the shiny chrome-and-glass surfaces of the occasional tables. A bottle of vintage VSOP Remy Martin cognac rested on the main coffee table, alongside a silver platter of chocolate truffles.

Sex with Helen had its minor compensations, Stuart reflected with sardonic appreciation. That was a hundred-dollar bottle of cognac, if ever he'd seen one.

She flashed him a look through half-closed eyes that he guessed was intended to be sultry. "Help yourself to a brandy while I slip into something more comfortable," she said, her voice chirpy.

She wasn't trying to be funny, and Stuart knew better than to laugh, but he did have to stifle a groan. Even Marlene Dietrich would have had difficulty getting away with that line. In Helen's schoolgirlish voice, with her hands fiddling uncertainly with her purse, it was both pathetic and comic.

To cover his reaction, he picked up the bottle of Remy Martin with an exaggerated flourish. "Take your time. We have all night." *Unfortunately.* "Shall I pour one for you, too, my dear?"

"That would be nice. Thank you."

Helen returned from the bedroom quite quickly, wearing a satin robe with a sash tie, and high-heeled mules trimmed with swansdown. She had obviously decided that tonight's seduction was going to be in keeping with the art deco furniture—a reenactment of a sleek Hollywood drama from the nineteen-thirties. Stuart would be expected to play the suave, sophisticated seducer, a cross between Charles Boyer and Rudolph Valentino. Until the moment that they tumbled onto her bed—at which point she would expect him to transform instantly into aggressive-but-sensitive Millennium Man.

Helen sat on the sofa and crossed her legs, sending him another one of the tremulous smiles that damn near drove him crazy. Although not in the way Helen hoped. Still, she had great legs, and he eyed them appreciatively. If he was going to be forced to perform tonight, he might as well enjoy those parts of the scenery that turned him on.

"Would you like that cognac now?" he asked.

"Mmm. A really fine cognac is one of life's greater joys, don't you think?"

"Absolutely. And these chocolates look like the perfect accompaniment."

"They're from Belgium. Forget about the Swiss and the Austrians, Belgians make the best chocolate in the world. They have some of the world's finest restaurants, too. Did you know that?"

"No. I've not spent much time in Europe, actually. Except for eastern Europe, of course."

"We should take a trip together sometime soon. I'm sure you'd enjoy it."

"I'm sure I would. Unfortunately, time is always at a premium for me."

She directed a slightly impatient glance at him. "Your girls are still going to churn out their offspring whether you're there or not, Stuart. Being director of the Refuge doesn't mean that you have to be on site three hundred and sixty-five days a year. You need to learn to relax a little more."

She leaned forward and took one of the truffles, then bit into it with exaggerated enjoyment, licking her lips slowly, leaving them glistening and wet.

She'd seen one too many movies where the lovers seduced each other over a meal, Stuart thought, mildly turned off. She had an uncontrolled passion for chocolate, and he often wondered if she was bulimic, because otherwise, he couldn't understand how she kept her figure.

He handed her the glass of cognac he'd poured, then sloshed a generous serving into his own glass. By morning, he was sure he would have earned every sip of his five-star brandy.

Helen patted the cushion, and he obediently seated himself next to her. He took her hand and stroked her fingers before turning her hand over and pressing a light kiss into her palm.

"I think the dinner tonight went well," he said. "Your menu choice was perfect. Delicious without being a budget-buster. I wouldn't want the board to think we were extravagant with the Foundation's funds.''

Flattery always worked well with Helen, and she visibly softened. "I'm glad you approved of the menu. You were in good form yourself. You always do a wonderful PR job with the board, and you seemed to handle things particularly well tonight." She leaned back, her head tilting to rest against the pillows, and he took that as his cue to kiss her.

She tasted of brandy and chocolate—not a bad mixture—and he deepened the kiss, relieved when she once again responded without making him work too hard. It really looked as if tonight was going to be relatively easy going. They might even get to sleep before midnight, which would be an unexpected treat.

He finally had to come up for air, and she drew away from him, pushing the lapels of her robe together. "Have you done a thorough background check on Marisa Joubert? And, if so, what did you find out about her?"

"What?" Stuart blinked, trying to regroup; his thoughts had already moved into full seduction mode. Asking a specific question about his running of the Refuge was definitely not part of Helen's normal routine, especially when they were about to have sex. She rarely focused on details of how the Refuge operated, and he certainly wasn't accustomed to having her take an interest in a boring subject like staffing.

"That woman you've hired as your office assistant." Helen spoke crisply. "Have you run a background check on her? It's something that needs to be done." She bit into another chocolate, eyes closing in pleasure as the filling oozed onto her tongue.

"I haven't run a check as yet." He was annoyed that he had to admit this. The power in his relationship with

Helen was delicately balanced, and her intrusion into personnel decisions in regard to the Refuge seriously upset the tacit agreement whereby he kept her flattered and sexually satisfied in exchange for her cooperation in keeping the board happy.

"It didn't seem a matter of any special urgency," he said, annoyingly aware that he sounded petulant.

"On the contrary. Checking on Marisa Joubert should have been an obvious priority—"

"I can't imagine why."

"You can't? Didn't you notice that Marisa Joubert is one of the most beautiful women you could ever expect to see outside a movie theater?"

"Well, yes, I guess I realized she's quite attractive in a rather overstated way—"

"She's not 'quite attractive.' She's stunning. And she's not overstated, whatever you mean by that. She's gloriously vibrant. What's more, on the two occasions I've met her, she seemed exceptionally competent. With that combination of talents, did it never occur to you to ask yourself why she's content to work for low pay at a home for unmarried mothers?"

"Of course it did." In fact, he was irked that he'd been troubled by precisely the same things as Helen, but that since it had been a hectic week, he'd allowed the need for action to get buried under the pleasure and convenience of having an assistant who knew what she was doing.

He defended himself. "Marisa has a young son, and she's a single mother. Her employment options are limited. I'm providing free day care for her son. I'm positive that was a big inducement for her to accept the job at the Refuge."

"You seriously think day care was enough to persuade

her to bury herself in a home for wayward teenagers? When she could be making ten thousand bucks a shoot on modeling assignments?'' Helen looked incredulous.

''Then why did she apply for the job? And having heard the salary, why did she take it?''

''My best guess is that she's an investigative reporter, looking for a story.''

He couldn't let the implications of that remark pass unchallenged. ''What would she be investigating, Helen? There's nothing newsworthy about the Refuge, unless she wants a warm, fuzzy human-interest story. And she doesn't need to go undercover for that. In fact, I've been considering approaching *Sixty Minutes* or one of the other TV newsmagazines and asking them if they'd like to do a show shaped around one of our young mothers and her experiences at the Refuge.''

This time the look Helen sent him was genuinely admiring. ''Great idea, Stuart. Really. Go for it. But while you're waiting for Morley Safer to come calling, Marisa Joubert needs to be investigated. After all, she has access to a lot of very confidential documents. We need to know she's a woman who can be trusted. Totally.''

''You're right.'' No point in denying the obvious, even if it enabled Helen to score points. ''I'll call Phil tomorrow and get a background check started.''

''While you're at it, have him run a check on that janitor person, too.''

''On Jimmy?'' Stuart laughed. He couldn't help it. ''Come on, Helen. I respect your desire to protect the integrity of the services we provide at the Refuge, but what conceivable reason would I have to run a background check on Jimmy Griffin? He came to us from Donaldson and Associates in Denver. They specialize in finding employment for the developmentally challenged, and they provided a sheaf of references for him."

"Did you check them out personally?"

"As a matter of fact, I did. I was wary of hiring somebody with learning disabilities in a tightly knit community like the Refuge, and I spent a great deal of time talking to Reggie Donaldson before he persuaded me to give Jimmy a chance. And the references all checked out. Anyway, what the hell do you suspect Jimmy Griffin of doing? The guy has trouble finding his way inside out of the rain."

"You're probably right." Helen took a sip of her cognac. "Even so, have Phil run a detailed background search. And that's an order from the chairperson of the Refuge to her director of operations."

"I'll see to it this week."

"Not this week. Tomorrow."

Stuart smiled and gave a mock salute. "Yes, ma'am." Sometimes he really hated Helen Wainscott.

She leaned over and kissed him full on the lips. No girlish hesitation this time. Her tongue thrust into his mouth, and her hand went straight for the zipper of his pants.

"I made you angry," she whispered.

"No—"

"You're so desirable when you're angry." She untied the sash of her robe, letting it slither off her shoulders, leaving her naked to the waist. Stifling a sigh, he obediently took his cue.

The sex was over more quickly than he could ever remember. She got up to take a shower within seconds of reaching climax, standard procedure for Helen. She emerged from the bathroom with her hair coifed and her face made up again. Stuart was almost relieved to see that the pattern established over two years wasn't all going to be tossed aside in a single night.

She sat down, but not on the sofa. She took a chair across from him. "It's my birthday in two weeks' time. I'm going to be thirty-eight."

"I remembered." He smiled. "If you can manage to come in to town again on the appropriate day, we must do something really special to celebrate."

"I agree," she said. "We should try to get pregnant."

Stuart choked on his cognac. Get pregnant? *Has she lost her fricking mind?* He put down the glass, spluttering.

Helen watched him cough, her gaze cool.

It took him a while before he could speak. "My dear, it's a lovely suggestion, and I'm flattered at being chosen as the prospective father, but do you think single motherhood is an adventure you want to embark on?"

"Of course not. If I'm going to have a baby, I need a husband." She paused for just a fraction of a second. "Will you marry me, Stuart?"

He stared at her, his hands resting limply on his knees, his vocal cords incapable of producing a sound. What the hell was he supposed to say now? Jesus, he'd thought this day had brought its worst when he had to drive down to Denver, wondering if the end of the journey would bring him face to face with Anya's mutilated body. After Ardita and Darina, he'd been so nervous...

And Helen was waiting for him to respond. He cleared his throat. Then cleared it again. "My dear, have you thought about what you're suggesting? Is it wise—?"

"Naturally, I've given it a great deal of thought." Her gaze narrowed. "You aren't as enthusiastic as I'd hoped, Stuart."

The image of Helen as anyone's wife was hard to bring

into focus. Stuart had never felt a moment's surprise that Senator Crowland had decided to divorce her—only that the two of them had stayed married for almost eight years. If it was hard to visualize her as Crowland's wife, the thought of her as *his* wife—as the mother of his child—was beyond the bounds of Stuart's imagination.

The irony of her reaching such an extraordinary decision at precisely this moment wasn't lost on him. Why now? Why the hell did she have to ask now? Marriage to Helen could never have been less convenient. But he knew he had no choice. Helen was perfectly capable of having him fired from the Refuge if he refused, and he would never be able to find such a perfect setup again.

His stomach roiled, and he was afraid he might vomit. Nevertheless, he prided himself on rolling with the punches and springing back to his feet still fighting. He'd cope with this disaster just as he coped with everything else. With grace and dignity.

He rose to his feet and crossed to Helen's side, drawing her to her feet and kissing her tenderly. "My dear, if you're sure this is what you want, I'm thrilled. In fact, I can't imagine why I didn't come up with the idea myself."

She returned his kiss with equal tenderness. "You're such a charming liar, Stuart. I really do believe we're going to be very happy together."

Thirteen

By Tuesday afternoon, Marisa's fingers were black from riffling through Stuart's files, and her mood was blacker than her fingers. Apart from ink-stained hands, all she had to show for six hours of intensive searching were bleary eyes and an aching head. She had found precisely nothing in the way of incriminating financial records.

As a minor consolation, she had managed to perform an impressive blitz on the legitimate filing, so she would be able to justify how her time had been spent, if Stuart chose to inquire. His desk was now completely clear of papers. Her own desk still had small piles of documents waiting to be filed, but that was because she needed an excuse to continue rummaging through the cabinet drawers, not because she genuinely was unable to find homes for these last few sheets of paper.

Her failure to find any documents dealing with illicit financial transactions was frustrating in the extreme. If she'd been Spencer, she'd have been throwing her toys and drumming her heels long before now. She couldn't shake the sensation that Stuart was laughing at her from afar, mocking her for being unable to come up with a single piece of damning evidence.

Oddly, the fact that she had so far failed to find any proof of Stuart's wrongdoing didn't convince her that it wasn't there to find. She had plenty of past experience dealing with criminals, and she knew that even the smartest of them kept notes and records that, rationally, should never have been allowed to see the light of day.

Something about the criminal personality seemed to require danger in order to feel fully alive. Her husband had been so convinced of his invincibility that he'd become careless, and ultimately given her the chance to bring him down. Her father had been even more of a compulsive risk-taker than Evan. Marc Joubert had done more than keep records that were damaging; he'd spent his life playing come-and-get-me games with law enforcement for the sheer, reckless excitement of it.

Stuart Frieze didn't strike her as a reckless man, but he must share some of her father's hubris or he wouldn't have left half a dozen damning files in unlocked file cabinets where Jimmy, or any other investigator, could find them. And if the records of Stuart's baby sales and egg harvests had been stored here in this office, it seemed quite likely that his financial records would be here, too.

Having lectured herself into a burst of fresh enthusiasm, Marisa yanked open another file drawer. This one contained minutes of board meetings, correspondence with individual trustees, Christmas card lists going back to 1996, a record of the small gifts that Stuart had given to staff members on various occasions, along with his expense accounts for the past eighteen months.

She wasted fifteen minutes pouring over the expense reports before concluding there was nothing in them to raise even a spark of interest. The sums of money involved were too small to be conccaling major profits, and, unfortunately, there were no offshore bank statements slipped in among the standard Refuge expense forms.

Marisa shoved the drawer shut with considerably more

force than necessary. She had been naive—not to mention infected with a touch of the Joubert family arrogance—to assume that in a single day, disrupted by phone calls and a dozen other duties, she was going to locate documents that would immediately reveal how much money Stuart had syphoned off from the Refuge and how he was laundering it.

Her mood was gloomy enough that she was almost relieved to be interrupted by the phone. She took a message from the obstetrician's office in Estes Park and made a notation for Stuart to call Dr. Needham. Seconds later, Janet poked her head through the office door, wanting to discuss a problem concerning medical records that she couldn't persuade the New York Health Department to provide. Then one of the counselors called from Denver with a reminder that she had been summoned for jury duty the following week and needed to change her regularly scheduled visiting hours.

Marisa made the appropriate notes and added more messages to Stuart's pile, no longer grateful for the interruptions. The workday was almost over, and she was getting nowhere at high speed. Tomorrow Stuart would be back in the office, and she wouldn't be able to roam at will through his files. She needed to find evidence of his wrongdoing today, while she still had free access to the entire system.

Refusing to let the pressure get to her, she doggedly worked her way through the budget files and the records of petty cash expenditures for the current year. She had always been pretty good with figures, but, as far as she could tell, the petty cash records couldn't have been more pristine if they'd been prepared by the IRS director in person. Her stomach churned with frustration as she confronted yet another dead end.

Muttering rude epithets at her absent boss, Marisa linked her hands behind her neck and stretched muscles that were protesting too many hours spent hunched over files. She hadn't yet examined every file folder in the office, but she was rapidly approaching that point and she felt angry with herself for being unable to psych out Stuart's system. Always assuming he *had* a system. She could no longer ignore the possibility that her failure to find anything useful was due to the fact that there was nothing incriminating to find, at least in this office.

She blew upward, lifting a piece of hair that had fallen over her nose. In addition to an aching head and bleary eyes, she felt hot, sweaty and irritable. Since logic seemed to be getting her nowhere fast, maybe she should stop searching through the financial files and start hunting for one with a name tag that was completely unrelated to money. How about "Recipes," she thought. Or "Theater Tickets." Or "Snowmobiles."

Marisa stopped massaging her neck and sat up straighter, arrested by the realization that she had already seen files with all those names. Not exactly subject headers that she would have expected to find, which was why the names had stuck in her subconscious. It was worth double-checking, she decided. She had pursued so many dead ends today, it wouldn't hurt to go back and give those oddly-named files a second look.

She found the "Recipe" file first. It contained a sheaf of brightly colored pages, headed with names such as Klara's Apple Pudding, Maria's Honey Sponge Cake, Theresa's Chicken with Paprika, and Margit's Onion Tartine.

Marisa wished she could convince herself that she'd found secret encoded sheets of data about Stuart's off-shore banking, but she couldn't. A note from Fran Harlowe indicated that it was a Refuge tradition for the residents to cook a favorite dish for the Christmas Eve holiday party, and for the recipe for each dish to be presented to Stuart as a token gift from the young woman who had prepared it. There was even a snapshot in the back of the file, showing last year's Christmas buffet table, with the moms-to-be lined up behind the dishes they'd cooked for the festivities. Fran beamed into the camera behind a snowy-white frosted cake decorated with giant red numbers: *1999.* It gave Marisa a jolt to realize that two of the smiling young women were Ardita and Darina, who must have left the Refuge only a week or two after the picture was taken.

Okay, so the "Recipe" file was full of recipes. So much for her brilliant flash of inspiration. But there were two more files to check out before she needed to get depressed. Marisa instructed herself to move on.

"Theater Tickets" contained details of a fund-raising project conducted jointly with the Denver Repertory Theater Group. The profits from a week of special performances were being used to fund educational programs aimed at reducing teenage pregnancy. There were plans already in the works for a repeat of the highly successful fund-raiser in February 2001. Unless Stuart had faked grateful letters from the school board and some twenty other supporting documents, this was a legitimate project. Another example, in fact, of how hard Stuart worked to prevent the problem of unmarried, underage mothers. Sighing, Marisa returned "Theater Tickets" to its appropriate niche.

The third and last file provided no more than the other two. "Snowmobiles" contained an exchange of letters between Stuart and a local snowmobile dealership. The dealer had offered to provide snowmobile transportation if ever one of the Refuge residents went into labor in the middle of a blizzard and secondary roads leading to the highway hadn't been ploughed.

Aargh! as Snoopy would say. Marisa thumped her fist against the elegant paneled wall of Stuart's office. In a movie, the panel instantly would have sprung open to reveal a secret hiding place stuffed full of jewels and money. In real life, she merely hurt her hand.

She plunked herself down behind Stuart's desk, nursing her grazed knuckles and scowling at a squirrel running across the grass. It looked annoyingly cheerful in contrast to her own deepening dejection. The squirrel disappeared into the high branches of a distant spruce tree. One minute it was there, a split second later it was gone, vanished from sight.

Just like the encoded files that were here in this office only last Friday. Marisa rose slowly to her feet, belatedly aware that in addition to not finding any files relating to Stuart's offshore bank accounts, she hadn't come across any of the encoded files that Jimmy had discovered during the preceding six weeks. She'd read Jimmy's transcription of the relevant files only two nights ago, and she remembered the six file names quite distinctly. "Postpartum 1999" had been one of them—the same file Stuart had been so angry to find her holding on the night Katerina's baby was born.

Marisa had a clear mental image of what had happened to that particular folder. Once the torn label was fixed, Stuart had returned it to the bottom left-hand drawer of his desk. She'd already checked through that drawer earlier today, but she didn't remember seeing the "Postpartum" folder there. Of course, she'd been looking for files with financial headers, not for files that Jimmy had already analyzed in minute detail, so she might have mentally glossed over it. But she didn't think so.

It took no more than a couple of minutes to confirm that "Postpartum 1999" was no longer where Stuart had put it last week. Just to be sure, Marisa double-checked every filing cabinet in Stuart's office and her own. The "Postpartum" file was nowhere to be found. Nor were any of the other five files that Jimmy had transcribed. All six of them had vanished from the Refuge filing system.

Only one explanation for their disappearance seemed likely. Unlike Marc Joubert, Stuart had no intention of daring the devil when he didn't need to. Despite the fact that the six files were encoded, he'd removed them the moment he decided they might prove dangerous. If there had ever been any record of Stuart's illegal financial transactions on file here, he'd undoubtedly removed those at the same time. Marisa faced the unwelcome fact that she could search the Refuge filing system from now until next year and would never find anything incriminating.

She paced the office, consumed by the wish that she'd started her search just a little sooner. The files had still been here on Friday, so Stuart must have removed them over the weekend. It was unbearably frustrating to think that a mere forty-eight hours earlier, she might have been able to find documentary evidence that Stuart was racking up illegal profits from selling Refuge babies.

Of course, forty-eight hours earlier, she had still thought Jimmy was a mentally handicapped janitor and that Stuart was a noble humanitarian, so her regret was illogical. But logic wasn't doing anything to cheer her up at this point. With all six files missing, and no proof of financial shenanigans, she and Jimmy might even have a difficult time persuading the trustees to dismiss Stuart.

Realistically, any hope of sending him to prison was beyond the bounds of possibility.

It was only a few minutes away from five o'clock, and Marisa was too tired and too depressed to start on a major new project. She caught sight of a flash of bushy tail as the squirrel ran down from the branches of the spruce tree and sat at the edge of the grass, eating a nut or seed with apparent relish. At least the squirrel seemed to be enjoying the day, Marisa thought morosely.

Despite her grouchy mood, the view from Stuart's office window was really lovely, even at this time of year when spring hadn't yet arrived in all its glory. In the distance, partially screened by a grove of budding aspen trees, she could see Stuart's little house, converted from what had once been a guest cottage in the days when the Wainscotts had been the social leaders of the entire county and needed accommodation for visiting dignitaries.

For all Jimmy's claim that searching Stuart's house had been relatively easy, Marisa knew that he had been downplaying the risks involved. The mere fact that Stuart could sit at his office desk and see straight across the lawn to his home—

Marisa's thoughts skittered to a dead halt. Her eyes grew wide, and she stared at Stuart's house fixedly, although she wasn't really seeing it at all. Stuart didn't own the house where he lived, a fact she'd had no reason to think about until right now. The guest cottage was provided for his use, rent free, part of his compensation package as director of the Refuge. Since the cottage was owned by the Wainscott Trust, Stuart didn't have a mortgage or property taxes to pay. But Marisa was quite sure she'd seen receipted bills for the payment of property taxes when she'd been hunting through the files.

If Stuart was paying property taxes, then he presumably owned property. Was this how he used some of his illegal profits? She'd bet it was. Jimmy had also mentioned how empty of personal belongings Stuart's home had seemed when he searched it. Maybe that wasn't because Stuart had an obsessive need to conceal his true personality. Maybe it was simply because Stuart had another house that he considered his real home. And was it too much to hope that his "real" home might be the place where he'd taken his encoded files and his financial records when he removed them from the Refugo filing system?

Energized by hope, Marisa made a beeline for the cabinets. She found the folder that contained Stuart's most recent income tax return and thumbed through the enclosed pages. No property tax receipts here, and no mention of a mortgage, either. Which was a good sign, since it suggested Stuart had paid cash for the property and didn't want to draw attention to his purchase. But where had she seen those damn property tax receipts? Maybe in the file that contained preliminary material for Stuart's next annual tax return.

She pulled the appropriate file and started searching. A sappy grin spread across her face when she found the slender bundle of receipts, neatly fastened with a tiny bulldog clip. *Yesss!* Here they were: six oversize postcards. Three years' worth of receipted property taxes for a house near Castle Rock, an area south of metro Denver that had recently grown by leaps and bounds, as the corridor from Denver to Colorado Springs became one giant builder's lot.

Stuart owned half an acre of land, plus a three-bedroom house, in a development called Mountain Pines. Lot number 124. Street address 437 Mountain Peak Lane.

How fortunate that when Stuart had removed his encoded files from the Refuge filing system, he must have forgotten about these few tax receipts—

"I'm back," Stuart said from the doorway. "Hello, Marisa. I didn't expect to find you still here. It's well past five, you know."

Thank God that living with Evan had made her an expert at hiding guilt and fear. Making no attempt to return the tax folder to the drawer, she swung around to face him. She fixed her mouth into a cheerful smile. "Hi, Stuart. I guess I lost track of time. How was the board meeting? Successful, I hope." She tried to sound as if she were absolutely delighted to have him arrive at precisely this moment.

"The board meeting was very successful. We managed to get quite a few thorny issues resolved. And the budget for the second half of the year is approved."

Despite this positive news, Stuart didn't look too happy. He walked over to his desk and did a double take when he saw the stack of messages waiting for him. "Good grief. I think it was almost better when half my messages got lost." He gave her a weak smile. "Just joking. Are any of these really urgent?"

"None of them is desperate, but a couple are important." Marisa went through the list of phone calls with him, convinced that at any second he would notice the bundle of property tax receipts lying on top of the filing cabinet alongside the open folder.

Fortunately, his attention seemed to be focused on his messages. "I can see you've done a great job of holding the fort while I've been gone. As usual." Stuart gave her another smile, and this time he managed to make it as warm—and as insincere?—as her own.

"My desktop is clear for the first time in months.

Amazing. I'd honestly forgotten what it looked like underneath all that clutter." His smile deepened. "I'm happy to see it's a very attractive shade of dark cherry. You've worked wonders, Marisa."

"Thanks. Well, as you can see, I was just finishing one last job, when you arrived back." She gestured to the open file drawer and hoped for the best. She'd found with Evan that directing his attention to something she wanted to hide was one of the best ways to ensure that he expressed no interest. She could only pray the same tactic would work with Stuart.

It didn't.

"So what are you working on right now?" he asked, looking over at the open file cabinet.

Her heart slid down into her shoes, but the lie came swift and smooth—a skill that she apparently hadn't lost in the months since Evan's death. "I just found the folder that has copies of the counseling schedule for the rest of the year. Since Rachel has jury duty next week and can't come in, I wanted to find this month's roster for you. That way, you'll be able to see at a glance who might be available to fill in for her."

"Thanks, that was a very useful thought. As you can imagine, our residents need a lot of help working through their problems, and I'd like to shuffle the counseling schedules so that everyone gets the chance to talk to someone they already know."

Marisa managed a casual stroll across the room to the filing cabinets. "I haven't found the sheet for next week's schedule as yet. It shouldn't take me more than a minute or two, if you can just hang on."

"Let me help. I might recognize the file more easily than you."

Oh, shit. Stuart wasn't waiting for her to bring the

schedule to him. He was walking across the room, determined to help. She had about five seconds before he discovered that the folder resting on top of the cabinet contained his tax return, not counseling rosters. Her lie had been quick and smooth, but it had been seriously dumb.

She was saved by a total fluke. Jimmy couldn't have known how badly she needed something to divert Stuart's attention, but he appeared at the entrance to the office just when she was about to abandon hope.

In a single movement, she swept up both the folder and the property receipts, managing to tuck them all under her arm where Stuart couldn't see the name tab. That bought her about another two seconds. She flashed Jimmy a look of desperate appeal, and he inclined his head in an almost imperceptible acknowledgment.

"Mr. Frieze!" He banged loudly on the office door. "You have a package, Mr. Frieze. It arrived this afternoon. I have it here."

"Okay, Jimmy. I hear you." Stuart, thank heaven, turned around. "You know, Jimmy, I'm fortunate enough to have perfect hearing. There's no need to bang the door down when you want to attract my attention."

"Sorry, Mr. Frieze. Where would you like for me to put this package? It's kinda heavy." The package was big, and Jimmy huffed a couple of times as he shifted the weight from one arm to the other.

"What is it, do you know?"

Jimmy shook his head. "No. I don't know. But it's real heavy."

"Bring it over to my desk, will you?" Stuart finally moved away from the filing cabinet, and Marisa shoved the tax folder back into the drawer. Quietly, she closed the drawer. Fortunately, the address of Stuart's property was easy to remember.

"This must be the new printer I ordered," Stuart said, searching in his desk for a pair of scissors to slit the packaging tape.

"Let me get that for you, Mr. Frieze." Jimmy produced a pocketknife and slit open the package. He managed to position himself so that he blocked Stuart's line of sight, and Marisa seized the opportunity to find the schedules she had supposedly been looking at all along. Fortunately, she knew her way around the filing system pretty well after today's intensive search, and it took her only moments to open the correct drawer and pull out the appropriate folder.

She strolled across the room and tapped Stuart on the shoulder to attract his attention. "Sorry to have to run," she said. She put the folder of schedules on his desk, opened to the counseling roster for May. "But it's five-twenty, and Spencer will be wondering where I am."

"Yes, you should go home. You've worked late almost every night since you started here. I don't want to take advantage of your enthusiasm." Stuart stared at the package Jimmy had just finished opening, but Marisa had the impression that he wasn't really seeing it.

"Well, I'll be going, then. Good night, Stuart. 'Night, Jimmy."

"Good night," Stuart said.

"Good night, miss."

She turned to leave, but Stuart called her back. "Wait! Before you go, Marisa, I have some good news to report to you. Personal news."

Stuart cleared his throat awkwardly. "Helen Wainscott has agreed to marry me," he said at last. "We're thinking of setting a date for the wedding sometime in early July. As you can imagine, I'm a very happy man.''

He and Helen Wainscott were getting married? Just in time, Marisa stopped herself from flashing a glance of utter amazement in Jimmy's direction. Hard on the heels of that amazement came concern for Helen Wainscott, followed by a rush of relief that the wedding wasn't scheduled to take place until July. She and Jimmy would have at least five or six weeks to prove the case against Stuart and save his poor bride-to-be from making a terrible mistake.

''Well, congratulations,'' she said finally, aware that she'd waited much too long to respond. ''What a nice surprise. Ms. Wainscott is such a great champion of the work you're doing here. I hope you'll both be very happy.''

''I'm sure we will be,'' Stuart said.

From his tone of voice, Marisa decided that smart money wouldn't bet on it.

Fourteen

The doorbell rang just as Marisa was getting Spencer ready for bed. Holding his hand, she walked with him to the door. She wasn't surprised to discover Jimmy standing on her doorstep, even though they'd made no specific arrangement to get together tonight. But she was surprised to feel her heart give an undeniable jump of pleasure at the sight of him.

"Hi, Jimmy." Her voice had a ridiculous huskiness when she said his name.

"Hi, Marisa." He smiled at her. Not a Jimmy the janitor smile, but a full-throttle, high-powered James W. Griffin smile. It was crazy, but damned if she didn't feel a little weak-kneed.

She cleared her throat to get rid of the huskiness. "Come in. We should probably avoid having anyone see you visiting me if we can manage it."

"You're right. There's no point in inviting questions." He stepped inside, then crouched down so that he could give Spencer a high-five. "Hi, Spence. How're you doing?"

"Hi, Dimmy. Baf wif bubboes."

"You look really clean. You smell good, too." Jimmy stood up again and handed Marisa the cardboard box he was carrying, which was stamped with the logo of *La Cafetière*.

"I brought us a couple of slices of Andrea's secret recipe fudge torte. It's seriously wonderful. And there's a *C-O-O-K-I-E* for Spencer."

"Cookie!" Spencer exclaimed, stretching out his hand. "Cookie, pweeze!"

Jimmy looked down at him, astonished. "Hey, kid, you're not supposed to know how to spell."

Marisa laughed. "Spencer has a highly developed talent for learning life's essentials. He knows how to spot crucial city landmarks such as McDonald's and Burger King from vast distances. He also knows how to spell *cookie*—and *b-e-d,* so that he can avoid it."

"No bed," Spencer said instantly. "Not tired."

Marisa and Jimmy exchanged grins. "A guy who knows how to prioritize like that is obviously going to become a man to reckon with." Jimmy ruffled Spencer's hair. "May I give him the you-know-what?"

"Yes, sure. Thanks for thinking of him."

Jimmy handed the cake box to Marisa after taking out a cookie shaped like a teddy bear, covered with glistening sugar sprinkles. "Here you go, big guy."

Spencer gave him a beaming smile. "Fank you." He examined the cookie with intense concentration, deciding where to start eating. That important decision out of the way, he took a crunchy bite of leg and reached up to take Jimmy's hand.

"New jammies," he informed Jimmy, as they walked into the living room. "Dey yellow."

"Hmm...I have to say, they look bright blue to me."

"Okay." Spencer was quite happy to agree that his pajamas were blue. Marisa had recently tried to teach him his colors with significant lack of success. In Spencer's world view, learning to distinguish between purple and pink had no value compared to the usefulness of spelling *bed*, or recognizing the logo for McDonald's.

Spencer ran off to his bedroom at warp speed and returned with his copy of *Goodnight, Moon*. He thrust the book into Jimmy's hands, before popping the last bite of cookie into his mouth.

"What do you have to say if you want Jimmy to read to you?" Marisa asked.

Tilting his head to one side, Spencer awarded Jimmy his most beguiling smile. "Pweeze, stowy! Fank you," he said.

Jimmy grinned and swung Spencer up into the air, tucking him under his arm like a football. "I'm not sure whether that was a genuine mistake, or whether you're incredibly smart to imply it's a done deal." He carried Spencer over to one of the armchairs and sat down. "Okay, let's do the story thing."

Spencer climbed up onto Jimmy's lap, squirming until he was comfortably situated with his head resting against Jimmy's chest and Bear tucked under his arm.

Jimmy read the story twice before pronouncing "The End" with considerable firmness. "Everyone in the book has gone to sleep now."

Undeterred, Spencer shot him a speculative look. "More stowy."

"Sure thing, buddy. Tomorrow I'll read you another story." Before Spencer could work up a protest, Jimmy rose to his feet, swinging him onto his shoulders as he stood. "Let's go for a ride, okay? Have you got hold of Bear?"

For answer, Spencer thumped Jimmy's head with his teddy. He and Jimmy dashed around the apartment three or four times, swooping under door lintels and swinging around pieces of furniture as if they were obstacles on a racetrack. Marisa felt an odd pang of wistfulness as she watched them.

"More horsey!" Spencer said, when they finally came to a halt in front of his bedroom door.

"Tomorrow." Jimmy tipped to the side, flipping Spencer from his back and catching him just before he hit the floor. It was the same maneuver that had nearly given Marisa a heart attack in the parking lot, when Jimmy and Spencer had first made each other's acquaintance. Seeing the split-second coordination that was necessary to make the move work without crashing Spencer headfirst on the floor, Marisa realized why her subconscious had been suspicious of Jimmy almost from the start.

It was approaching eight-thirty, and time to put Spencer to bed. Naturally, he didn't want to go. Marisa tried to steel herself to ignore her son's protests, but, as always, he managed to cajole her into extending their goodnight rituals for at least fifteen minutes. He'd conned her into a drink of water, two trips to the bathroom and several adjustments to the night-light and his selection of stuffed animals, before Jimmy intervened.

"'Night, Spence. Sleep well." He took Marisa by the hand, and led her out of the bedroom, ignoring Spencer's outraged howl as the door closed.

"I need to go to him. He's scared." Marisa was already halfway back to her son.

Deceptively casual, Jimmy interposed himself between her and Spencer's bedroom door. "You know he's not really scared."

"On the contrary. I know he has nightmares that terrily him."

"He has to fall asleep before he can have a nightmare. Right now, he's awake and not one bit scared. He's just angling for your attention."

"Don't!" she said tensely. "Don't tell me how I'm turning him into a sissy and how he has to get over it and learn to be a real man—"

"You're confusing me with your former husband. I hope I'd never say anything that stupid."

"Good. Then please excuse me while I check on my son."

Jimmy grinned. "Honey, it seems to have escaped your notice that he's already stopped crying."

She gritted her teeth. "He needs me—" She stopped abruptly when she realized Jimmy was right. Spencer had stopped crying and was entertaining himself by crooning a garbled version of the alphabet song.

She wasn't willing to be mollified just because Jimmy happened to be right on this particular occasion. Spencer was her son. *Hers.* After being excluded from the first eighteen months of his life, she sure as hell wasn't going to allow some stranger to waltz in and imply that she was an overindulgent mother. She turned away and walked into the kitchen, her spine stiff.

She heard Jimmy following her, but that didn't mean she had to acknowledge him. She reached into the cupboard and took out two small plates, pointedly avoiding looking at him. She would report to Jimmy on the property records she'd found in Stuart's files, while they ate the cake—and then he could leave. The sooner the better.

"There's still half a bottle of your wine left," she said coolly. "Would you like some with the cake? Or would coffee be better, do you think?"

Her formal courtesy was a subtle insult, but Jimmy ignored it. "Whatever you want." He stroked his hand over her hair, his touch light. "Okay, let's talk about this, Marisa. How mad are you?"

"I'm not mad..." She reached into the cupboard again

and pulled out a couple of coffee mugs, then banged them on the counter.

"Spencer is a great kid, and you're a great mother," Jimmy said. "Suggesting that it might be smart to leave him to cry for thirty seconds wasn't intended as a criticism—"

" Good heavens, Jimmy, I never thought it was." Her voice sounded brittle, and she tried to soften it. She wasn't going to give him the chance to accuse her of being prone to feminine hysterics. She found coffee and scooped it into the filter basket. "I'm not that sensitive."

Unfortunately, she spilled coffee grounds onto the counter because her hands weren't quite steady. Jimmy looked from the spilled grounds to her. "That bastard of a husband is always at the back of your mind, isn't he? You look at me but you see him. What's it going to take to get rid of him?"

Her stomach knotted. "This has nothing to do with Evan or you. This is about *my* relationship with *my* son." She used a damp paper towel to sweep the spilled coffee into the trash.

Jimmy made an impatient sound under his breath. "It has everything to do with Evan. You told me yourself that he needed to control you, and that he used Spencer as a weapon."

She avoided his gaze. "I told you a lot of things I shouldn't have."

There was an unexpected moment of silence, and she swung around to find Jimmy looking at her, his eyes dark and focused, his stance tense.

He spread his hands in a gesture of apology. "You're right," he said quietly. "I took advantage of the role I was playing to elicit confidences that you wouldn't have given if you'd known the truth. I'm sorry."

She'd been working up a fine head of steam, but his apology took her temper off the boil. She scowled at him. "How annoying of you. There's nothing like having a man apologize to take all the fun out of a good argument."

He shot her a wry glance. "In that case, while I'm at it, I may as well finish the job. Putting Spencer to bed is your business. I shouldn't have tried to impose my judgment over yours. If you wanted help, you could have asked for it. I won't butt in again."

It was a generous apology, and the last tiny knot of tension in the pit of her stomach dissolved. "I have to say, Jimmy, that when you eat humble pie, you do it with flair. Which means, darn it, I probably have to concede that you were at least half right just now. Spencer plays me for a sucker at bedtime."

"I guess most kids do. I've watched my sister and brother-in-law jump through hoops with their two. Maybe that's why I reacted strongly to Spencer's routine tonight."

"Speaking of Spencer, did you notice that while we've been busy apologizing to each other, he's stopped singing?"

"I noticed." Jimmy drew in a visible breath. "Do you want to check that he's safely asleep?"

She grinned, able to laugh at herself again. "Peacefully asleep as opposed to smothered by one of his stuffed animals, you mean? No, I'm okay. I'm not that neurotic about his safety." She moved past him to get cream out of the fridge, but he reached out and stopped her.

"God, Marisa, you're beautiful when you smile."

"You said that before, last time you were here." She wanted to sound matter-of-fact, but instead she sounded breathy and flustered.

"Did I? Well, it's difficult enough pretending I have a functioning brain when I'm around you. You can't expect originality, too." He cupped the nape of her neck, not exerting any pressure, just touching her. She wasn't sure why she didn't move away, but when she didn't, he closed the distance between them and bent his head to hers.

She'd become almost accustomed to the passion that exploded between them when they kissed, but she still didn't have the faintest idea how to cope with the sensation of soft yearning that stole over her each time she went into his arms. She could dismiss the fireworks—she'd experienced those many times before, and with more than one man. What she couldn't dismiss were the feelings of tenderness and warmth, the crazy suspicion that if she ever surrendered to Jimmy, the result wouldn't be simple submission on her part and domination on his, but something magically different. Something outside her previous experience. Something wonderful for both of them.

Marisa didn't like to think of sex and wonder in the same breath—it was too frightening after the debacle of her marriage. Made uneasy by her own pleasure, she stirred restlessly in Jimmy's embrace, and his beard scraped against her face.

"What's wrong?" His voice was harsh, and his eyes were clouded with desire when he looked down at her, and yet she still felt as much tenderness as passion in his touch.

He ran his thumb across the skin he'd scraped. "Damn this stupid beard. I hurt you."

"No. I'm fine. Really." Now that she'd put an effective stop to their kiss, she realized that she very badly wanted Jimmy to kiss her again. *Déjà vu* all over again, she thought. Wasn't this exactly what had happened last time they kissed? They were even standing in the same spot.

Except that this time she would call a halt before they ended up discussing her multiple hang-ups. Bad enough to be hauling around so much neurotic baggage, without having to talk about it all the time. She put her hand on Jimmy's shoulder, intending to push him away. Instead, her body refused to accept the command, and her fingers dug in, pulling him fractionally closer.

It wasn't much of an invitation, but it was enough. Jimmy swiftly bent his head and kissed her again, igniting a hunger so deep and immediate that she was knocked off guard. His mouth was demanding, and his tongue thrust hard against hers without any teasing foreplay. His hands reached for her with unexpected aggression, and she reached right back, relishing the sensation of his heated skin burning beneath her palms.

He pushed her shirt from her shoulders and trailed kisses down her throat to her breasts, igniting thrills of pleasure that were intense enough to be painful. She leaned back, closing her eyes as sensations ripped through her. The tenderness that intrigued her so much had long since vanished, burned away by raw physical need. She had never felt an ache this intense, an urgency this inexorable. She was drowning, spiraling down into her own desire, waiting for Jimmy to lift her up and take her to climax. A touch—he wouldn't even have to enter her—and she would be there.

And that, Marisa realized with sudden cutting clarity, was precisely why she couldn't give in. The desire Evan had once aroused in her had been tepid in comparison to what she felt now, and yet it had been sufficient to cause her to make unforgivable mistakes of judgment. Given the passion Jimmy was able to provoke with almost no effort, it was terrifying to contemplate the power he would exercise over her if they ever became lovers.

A couple of nights ago she had implied that one day, when they knew each other better, they might make love. Now she wondered if she would ever feel safe enough to allow that to happen. Safety required trust, and the feelings Jimmy aroused in her were too strong to be trusted.

Struggling for breath, she broke out of his arms. Trying to reassert control, or at least the appearance of it, she leaned against the counter, not sure that she would be able to stand without something solid to support her.

"I'm sorry," she said, tying the ends of her shirt together because her fingers had failed to manage the task of fastening buttons. "I'm sorry, Jimmy, but I can't do this."

A muscle flickered in his clenched jaw. "From my perspective, you seemed to be 'doing this' just fine."

A slight understatement, Marisa silently acknowledged. Heat flared in her cheeks, but honesty seemed the only way to go at this point. "Maybe I was. Apparently, I'm one of those women who really needs sex—"

"What the hell does that mean? Are you implying that what happened between us just now was simply because you've been deprived of sex for the past year?" For the first time she could remember, Jimmy sounded genuinely angry.

Expressed in those stark terms, Marisa realized she'd been suggesting something demeaning to both of them. She drew in a steadying breath. "What I was feeling just now...it scared me. I was about two seconds away from being completely out of control."

His tight expression relaxed somewhat. He took her hand, and she felt it tremble when he pressed a kiss against the pulse of her wrist. Amusement warmed his voice when he spoke. "Marisa, honey, people are supposed to lose control when they make love."

"Not...not like I do." She removed her hand from his, folding her arms tightly across her chest so that both her hands were tucked safely out of his reach.

His gaze narrowed. "This is about Evan Connors again, isn't it."

"In a way." She looked at him pleadingly, needing him to understand, and yet not sure if she would ever be able to find the right words. "When Evan and I first met, I wanted to have sex with him, too. Really wanted it."

"Not like this. Not like it is between us."

"No." Nothing had ever been quite like the way Jimmy made her feel.

He shrugged. "You were attracted to the wrong man. It happens. I was married once, briefly, and that was a mistake, too. Hopefully, I've learned from the experience and moved on."

Her hands twisted in frustration. Even the news that Jimmy had been married barely impinged on her consciousness. "You're deliberately not understanding. Evan wasn't just the wrong man as in, 'Oh dear, we aren't compatible. Bummer.' Evan was a criminal who coldbloodedly plotted to marry me and get me with child. He wanted a son or daughter who could be a living weapon to use in his power struggle to take over my father's empire, and he was prepared to hide his true character and manipulate me through two miscarriages and five surgeries to get what he wanted."

"He sounds like a thoroughly unpleasant kind of a guy. But that says nothing about you and less than nothing about our relationship."

"It has everything to do with us. I have to face the

fact that Evan got to me initially through sex.'' She looked away, ashamed to admit the truth. ''Don't you see? I'm susceptible. It was easy for him to make me want him.''

Jimmy crooked his finger under her chin. He eased her head back so that she was forced to look at him. ''You've convinced me,'' he said, an edge of anger in his voice. ''Evan Connors was a monster. It's a good thing he's dead, because I'd really like to kill him right now. However, you haven't said a damn thing that explains to me why you have any doubts about your own integrity. Evan was an expert deceiver. He manipulated you in the bedroom as well as out of it. End of story.''

Marisa finally allowed herself to express the fear that had haunted her for the past two years. ''But it isn't that simple, Jimmy.'' Even to her own ears, her voice sounded small and thin. ''If I'd been a normal woman, brought up in a family with normal ethics, don't you think I'd have noticed what Evan was really like, right from the beginning?''

''No, I don't. He was a talented con man, and you fell for the scam. Stop punishing yourself for being a victim.''

She wanted to believe him, but she couldn't excuse herself so easily. ''Shouldn't some protective instinct have kicked in? Why didn't some moral alarm go off, warning me that this man I had sleeping in my bed was a potential killer? I wasn't a naive young girl. Anything but, in fact. I'd been working in a tough, competitive industry for five years when I met Evan, and I prided myself on being able to sort out the scumballs from the reasonably decent guys.''

He didn't answer her in words. Instead, he took a wine-glass from the cupboard, poured out some of the leftover wine and pressed the glass into her hand. "Drink this," he said. "You look as if you're going to pass out at any minute."

"I'm not sure that drowning my sorrows in drink is going to help." But she took a few sips and actually did feel marginally better afterwards. The self-doubt was still there, but the alcohol dulled the intensity. Maybe this was why she didn't keep wine in the house, Marisa thought. Not because it didn't go well with Spencer's chicken nuggets and fish fingers, but because she was smart enough to realize that alcohol was both seriously tempting and the wrong answer to her problems.

She set the glass on the counter. "Thanks. I feel better now." She gave him a smile that was only half fake. "If you'd like to go into the living room, I can bring us coffee and cake."

"I'm not quite ready for social chitchat," Jimmy said. He put his arms around her, holding her just tight enough to prevent her escaping.

"Listen up, Marisa, because you need to hear this. You've implied several times that you feel guilty because of what Evan Connors did. That's crazy, and at some level you must know that. Adults are responsible for their own behavior, not for other people's."

"Yes, but I should have been able to stop him—"

"You didn't know he needed stopping until it was too late. You misjudged Evan. That's unfortunate, but it's not a crime. People misjudge other people all the time, for good and ill, sometimes out of prejudice and sometimes with the best intentions and the purest of motives."

"I didn't just misjudge him! I *married* him!"

"That was a mistake. Could it have been avoided? Possibly. But human beings make mistakes on a regular basis. As for what you seem to regard as your major sin, here it is. For a while, you enjoyed sex with Evan. That means he was a competent lover, not that you have defective morals. I married Leeza. That was a mistake, too. And, yes, I married her because the sex was absolutely great. So mind-blowingly great, in fact, that I forgot to notice I didn't much like her.''

"How many people has Leeza tried to murder?" Marisa asked bitterly.

"None, of course. As far as I know, she's a law-abiding citizen who's kind to dogs and respectful of senior citizens. But the point is, I'd have married her anyway."

Jimmy drew in a deep breath. "I don't want to trivialize what you went through with Evan, but at a certain point, you have to decide to accept what happened and carry on. Or not. But before you decide to stay mired in the past, wallowing in guilt, ask yourself if that isn't giving Evan the ultimate victory, one that he sure as hell doesn't deserve."

"You make it sound as if I enjoy wallowing in my guilt—"

"Do you?"

"Damn you, Jimmy, I don't deserve that comment."

"Maybe not. But if you're fixated on the past, it sure makes it easier to avoid confronting the future, doesn't it?"

"I hate people who play armchair psychologist," she muttered.

He pulled her closer and kissed her lightly on the forehead. "I'm open to suggestions for any alternative games you might want to play."

The look she sent him was troubled. "Jimmy, you're going to have to be really patient with me. I made myself a lot of promises when Evan died, and one of them was that I would never have sex again unless I was deeply in love with my partner and he returned my feelings completely. These last few nights with you have made me realize that I don't want to break that promise.''

''I guess that leaves me with two options. I can persuade you to change your mind—''

''Don't hold your breath,'' she said softly.

''Then I guess I'm stuck with my other option. I can persuade you to fall in love with me.''

The warm melting feeling in the pit of her stomach was almost as troublesome as her out-of-control response to his sexual advances. ''That's only half of what it's going to take to get me into your bed, Jimmy. You have to be in love with me, too.''

He leaned forward and brushed his lips over hers. ''You know, somehow I don't believe that's going to be a major problem.''

Fifteen

Now that she and Stuart were an engaged couple, Helen had apparently decided that she could dispense with the display of reluctance before they had sex. When Stuart arrived in the suite on Friday evening, he found his fiancée waiting for him, wearing a transparent black nylon negligee, black strap sandals, and nothing else. It seemed Helen's fantasies had moved up a couple of decades in movie history, from Mae West in the thirties to Marilyn Monroe in the fifties.

All too aware that Helen was going to be seriously upset by his report on Marisa Joubert, Stuart dutifully fulfilled his obligations in the bedroom before leaving his fiancée alone to take her ritual shower. He was starving after a day at the Refuge that had been too busy to allow time for eating, and he figured that the privileges of the engagement ought to work both ways. If Helen no longer needed to wait for sex, he no longer needed to wait to order dinner.

He picked up the phone and ordered a room service dinner for both of them, charged to her account. There was a minor satisfaction to be derived from making the selection from the menu without any reference to Helen, and then sticking her with the bill.

The room service waiter arrived with their meal, just as Helen emerged from the bathroom.

"Great timing," Stuart said, smiling at her. He was developing lockjaw from the number of fraudulent smiles he'd delivered in the past week. He hoped to God that business would soon call her to New York. Or San Francisco. Or the planet Jupiter, for all he cared. Anywhere but Wainscott. He needed some solitude to work out how the hell he was going to avoid going through with this farcical marriage. He was dedicated to his work, but there were some sacrifices he wasn't prepared to make, even in the interest of keeping his clinic in Africa funded.

The waiter was young and earnest. "Where would you like me to set up your dinner, sir?"

Stuart was smart enough to know that his engagement to Helen didn't entitle him to answer that question when she was standing right there. Helen merely needed sex on her terms, whereas he needed a hell of a lot more than that, which made him very much the junior partner in this relationship. Maybe that was part of the reason he disliked her so much.

He turned to Helen. "Where would you like us to eat dinner, my dear?"

She hesitated. "The table by the window would be nice, don't you think?"

In public, even if there was nobody around except a waiter, Helen displayed all the self-confidence of a sixth grader starting a new school. Stuart knew she wasn't genuinely shy, but he'd decided the various masks she donned had become so deeply internalized that she now no longer remembered they were merely acts and could be discarded at will.

"Perfect choice," he said. "Had you noticed it's a full moon? The view is especially lovely tonight." He did the smile thing again.

The waiter worked with quiet efficiency to set out their

food. "Enjoy your dinner, Ms. Wainscott. Mr. Frieze. Call when you've finished, and we'll send somebody to remove the dishes."

"Thank you." Helen signed the bill without even glancing at it. Why would she look at it? Stuart thought bitterly. Helen never thought for two minutes together about money and where it came from, unless she happened to be on one of her bitching jags, when she could deliver endless tirades on the evilness of lawyers and the way she had been ripped off by her ex-husband, the senator.

Helen's mood tonight was hard to read, but she ate quite a bit of the red snapper he'd ordered for her, before pushing away from the table and going to the bar to pour herself a brandy.

"Time for business," she said briskly. "My father's legacy is too important to be destroyed, and we can't afford to have years of work ruined because we don't pay proper attention to details. So have you heard back from Phil with a background check on your new assistant?"

"Yes." Stuart rose to his feet. "As always, my dear, your intuition has proven amazingly accurate."

She looked up sharply. "The Joubert woman doesn't check out?"

"I'm afraid that she isn't quite the person I assumed." Stuart poured himself a snifter of brandy. No point in missing the chance to drink VSOP Five Star when it was right at hand, even if his stomach was churning with the knowledge that Helen was going to be pissed as hell.

He cleared his throat. "You'll be pleased to hear that Phil has done his usual excellent research job—"

"That's what he's paid for," Helen said impatiently.

"Yes, well, he's found out quite a lot in a very short

time, since there was a great deal of information available concerning Marisa Joubert. She's the daughter of Marc Joubert, who died last year in Miami. Heart attack. The death was very sudden and unexpected.''

''If that's supposed to mean something to me, it doesn't. I've never heard of Marc Joubert.''

''There's no reason why you would have, my dear. However, Mr. Joubert was a superstar in certain very unsavory circles. His family ran an international smuggling ring for three generations. They started smuggling weapons and stolen technology during the Second World War and saw no reason to stop once the war was over. The original two Joubert brothers fought alongside General de Gaulle and the Free French, risking their lives to transport secrets they'd stolen from the Nazi forces occupying Paris across the Channel to England.''

''They were war heroes, then.''

''Yes, although that was the last time any of the Jouberts seems to have cared whether or not they were selling their stolen technology to the good guys. We're not talking Robin Hood here. For the past sixty years, the Jouberts have been earning themselves multiple-millions of dollars by selling the latest weapons to any purchaser who could come up with the necessary cash. No questions asked about where the cash comes from, or what the purchaser intends to do with the weapons.''

''And Marisa is part of this notorious family?'' Helen looked justifiably doubtful, since Marisa certainly didn't fit her preconceived image of a woman born into such a family. ''You're sure it isn't just a coincidental similarity of last names?''

''No. The Jouberts have been major social leaders in Miami for years now—''

''*Social leaders?*'' Helen took great delight in her role

as chairwoman for various exclusive charity events, and she didn't like to think that people who openly violated the law could make their way into the upper echelons of society.

Stuart gave a placatory smile. "I guess there are so many crooks operating in a city like Miami that nobody noticed or cared how the Jouberts made their money. It's not like New York, my dear, and the circles you move in. Anyway, the point is that Marc Joubert's funeral was a major civic event, and Phil found plenty of newspaper and TV pictures of Marisa, taken at her father's funeral. I have them here for you."

Helen took the pictures and looked at them intently. "This wasn't taken at her father's funeral, presumably." She held up a shot of Marisa looking both glamorous and sultry on a tropical beach.

"No, that picture was taken in 1995 for the *Sports Illustrated* calendar. Phil found literally hundreds of photos from an earlier life when she was a successful high-fashion model in New York. As you can see from those pictures, the Marisa Joubert working at the Refuge is unmistakably Marc Joubert's daughter."

Helen frowned, then remembered the danger of wrinkles and hastily smoothed her brow. "If the Jouberts are as rich as you say, why in God's name would she be working at the Refuge for a few hundred bucks a week?"

"I've no idea." Heaven knew, that was the simple truth. Obviously, Marisa wasn't there for any good purpose, but he couldn't for the life of him figure out what she was up to. "Marisa was married to a man named Evan Connors, who was wealthy in his own right. Nowhere near as rich as her father, but he had assets in the millions."

"She's divorced?" Marisa gave a bitter smile. "That

explains it, then. Her husband cleaned her out in the divorce settlement.''

"No, she's not divorced. Her husband died last fall, shortly after her father."

"How did he die? The husband, I mean."

"He was shot." Stuart saw Helen's expression and shook his head. "No, Marisa had nothing to do with it, according to Phil. The death was ruled accidental, and there doesn't seem to be any suggestion that Marisa was involved. Evan Connors's money was all tied up in trusts, as was Marc Joubert's, so there's no public record of exactly how much they actually left. However, Phil's checked around, and there's fairly widespread agreement that Marc Joubert left half his fortune to his wife, and split the remaining half equally among his three children."

Helen found her cache of chocolates and selected a truffle. "Then, how much did Marisa inherit?"

Stuart took a fortifying sip of brandy, waited for the blast. "A lot, actually. Phil's best guess is that she inherited a minimum of five million dollars after taxes. More likely, she inherited ten."

"*Ten million dollars?* Marisa Joubert has *ten million dollars* in assets?" Helen swallowed the truffle and coughed. She sank down onto the sofa, visibly stunned.

Stuart enjoyed seeing Helen's world order so satisfactorily turned upside down. Or he would have, if he didn't share her appalled incredulity. He couldn't think of any good reason why a woman with assets of five to ten million dollars would be working at the Refuge for twenty thousand bucks a year. In fact, he couldn't think of any reason at all why a woman that rich would be here in Wainscott. Why wasn't she in Aspen, if she had a thing for mountains? Or in the South of France, if she wanted heat and glamour?

"I knew her shoes were Ferragamos," Helen muttered. "They were old, but I could see they were Ferragamos. And her suit the other day looked like an Armani."

She rose and paced nervously up and down the room. "What does she want, Stuart? What's she doing at the Refuge?" She paced the room some more, not really expecting an answer. "Maybe she's in league with the janitor."

"In league to do what?" Stuart tried not to sound too impatient. "Besides, in accordance with your request, I asked Phil to review Jimmy's background and references. He ran a very thorough check, and, as I told you, we have no problems there. Jimmy Griffin is exactly what he claims to be. I've seen his school graduation record, and I've read the actual report from the special vocational college he attended for three years after high school. He couldn't manage to get certified as a plumber, which was what his family had hoped for him, and the counselor recommended that he go into janitorial services. His work record since then is glowing. He's been as popular in his previous jobs as he is here. I'd already checked all his references, of course, and Phil checked them again. They all stand up to scrutiny. As far as Jimmy's concerned, you can put your mind to rest."

"She must be a reporter," Helen said, bringing her attention back to Marisa. "With looks like that, she probably works for one of the big local TV stations."

Stuart shook his head. "She couldn't work within any major TV market without Phil finding out. If she's a reporter, she works somewhere so obscure that there's no record of it anywhere, and even that doesn't seem likely."

"Maybe she's trying to break into journalism with a scoop," Helen said, sufficiently worried that she actually ran her fingers through her hair, ruining the style. "The timing's right. Her husband dies, she's bored and restless. So she decides that being a TV newscaster would be fun. Maybe she fancies herself as the new generation's Barbara Walters. To her surprise, she discovers that on-air journalism is competitive enough that she can't buy herself a spot on any major network. So she decides to win herself a job by promising to bring them a major news story about the Refuge."

It didn't seem very likely, Stuart thought, but what better explanation was there for Marisa's presence at the Refuge? If you'd grown up with more money than you could spend, and married into a second fortune, obviously money wouldn't be much of a motivator, but fame quite possibly was. Marisa Joubert was beautiful, and he could see that most men would find her sexually appealing, even though she was too old for his taste. He reluctantly acknowledged that it was possible she was planning to use the Refuge as her springboard to fame and fortune in the field of television journalism.

Still, he wasn't willing to concede the possibility without testing it a little. "Superficially, it might seem plausible that she's an aspiring journalist," he said. "But when you think about it more deeply, that seems unlikely. What possible reason would Marisa Joubert have for deciding to investigate the Refuge? She's an unemployed social climber, from a very dubious Florida family, recently widowed. How would she know that there's anything going on at the Refuge that would be of interest to reporters?"

It was a measure of his concern that he let slip the

implicit acknowledgment that there was something illicit for a reporter to uncover.

"Hasn't it occurred to you yet that she's a perfect fit for the profile of the sort of woman you normally sell Refuge services to? Maybe she heard about your extra-curricular activities from one of her friends."

"Surely not. She's young and she has a son of her own—"

"Are you sure he's hers? Maybe he's adopted."

Stuart considered this for a moment, then shook his head. "No, Spencer looks very much like her. And it's not just coloring. In fact, their coloring isn't an especially close match. But they have similar bone structures, and their mouths are identical."

"Well, there's another possibility." Helen looked at him over the rim of her brandy glass. "Maybe Carole Riven spoke to her before she died."

Stuart looked at Helen in silence. The name *Carole Riven* was one that they both tended to avoid. Still, since Helen had brought it up, he pondered the possibility that Carole Riven might, indeed, have spoken to Marisa before she so conveniently took herself into the next world in a flaming car wreck. Such a contact on Carole's part would only make sense if Marisa really was a journalist, and Carole had known that fact.

He swallowed nervously. "I'm not sure we want to mention Carole Riven's name to Phil."

"Why not?"

"I think that's obvious. At the moment, nobody knows Carole has any connection to the Refuge, even if it is a very slight one. It's better we keep it that way. If it weren't for that problem, I'd ask Phil to check and see if there's any way Carole and Marisa might have met."

"Don't ask Phil. I have someone I can ask. He's good,

he's quick—at least if you catch him when he isn't high—and he won't ask any awkward questions. Since he has a major coke habit, he's always willing to work for cash, and he isn't likely to acquire a sudden urge to pass on information to the police.''

"Ask him, then. In the meantime, the bottom line is that I have to fire Marisa," Stuart said.

He barely repressed a sigh. Thinking about the blissful organization in his office, it was a real heart-wrencher to contemplate losing Marisa's services. "What the hell excuse am I going to use to get rid of her?"

Helen shot him a look of withering disgust. "Are you crazy? The absolute last thing you want to do is fire her, when we have no clue as to what she's been doing there."

Stuart had to acknowledge the wisdom of that although it made him nervous that Helen had abandoned her favorite role of simpering submission. "Good point. Well, then, I'll just have to keep a really close watch on her and see if I can get an idea of what she's up to."

Helen shook her head. "We're never going to find out what she's up to by observing her in the office, where she's going to be on her guard. We need to know what she does in her time off. Does Phil have anyone working for him who's able to do routine investigations? Surveillance, for example?"

"Yes, it's a big agency. I chose them deliberately, since I figured they were likely to have enough cases that they wouldn't pay much attention to the small jobs I assign them."

"A rare piece of smart thinking on your part."

Helen's open disdain infuriated him. He hadn't taken on the job at the Refuge in order to meet with scorn from an unattractive woman like her, even if she did provide him with cover from board scrutiny.

Resisting the urge to strangle her, he gave a sickly smile. "Thanks, dearest."

Helen gave no sign that she'd heard the sarcasm. She spoke crisply. "Tell Phil you want to arrange for Marisa to be followed. Tell him you suspect her of stealing petty cash, or selling confidential information from the files. Yes, that would be better. Something that directly affects the integrity of Refuge operations and gives you a legitimate excuse to pursue her. Make sure he understands that when she's not at the Refuge, you want to know where she is and who she's in contact with 24-7."

"What about phone calls? We need to cover those, too. And she may have a computer. She could be communicating with an accomplice by e-mail, and we'd never know."

Helen smiled tightly. "She's living in one of my apartments. I have the key. Assuming she hasn't changed the locks, I'll take care of bugging the phone on Monday, as soon as she goes back to work."

"And the e-mails?" Stuart's stomach felt queasy despite the brandy. "Jesus, Helen, she could have been sending daily reports to some fucking TV station, for all we know."

"Please, Stuart. You know how much I dislike profanity." Helen frowned. "Let's hold off on the panic. She'll be at the Refuge for at least eight hours on Monday. That's plenty of time for me to download the entire contents of her hard drive. If she's been e-mailing someone, we'll soon know."

Stuart didn't feel any better. "I'll call Phil on Monday and tell him we need Marisa followed. I'll ask him to put one of his colleagues right on it."

"And leave Marisa with this entire weekend to go wherever she wants? To make contact with whomever she pleases?" Helen picked up her cell phone and handed it to him. "We can't do anything about her phone, but we can make damn sure we know who she's meeting in her spare time. Call Phil now," she said. "Tell him you want a tail on Marisa Joubert's ass within the hour."

Sixteen

With Marisa's discovery that Stuart Frieze owned property just outside of Denver, Jimmy the janitor's lack of a car became seriously irritating for the first time since Jimmy had arrived in Wainscott. If he'd had access to transportation, it would have been easy to zip down to Stuart's house after work one evening and check out the lay of the land. As it was, lack of transportation kept him penned up in his apartment, suffering from an oppressive sense that time was beginning to run out on him and his investigation.

His generally gloomy mood hadn't been improved by the fact that he and Marisa had agreed it was unwise for them to continue meeting after work. Wainscott was a small town where people were always running into each other unexpectedly. Sooner or later, somebody would notice that the mentally retarded janitor from the Refuge regularly visited Marisa Joubert's apartment, and his cover only worked as long as people didn't seriously question it.

Since Jimmy was the one who proposed the limitations on the time they spent together, he couldn't really complain that Marisa agreed—but he sure as hell wished that she hadn't sounded so goddamn cheerful about it all. Couldn't she at least have *pretended* that she was going to miss him?

"It's a pity about the carpet," Reg Donaldson said mildly. "I've grown kind of attached to it over the years. Still, it probably needed replacing, anyway."

"What?" Jimmy looked at the man seated opposite him in the comfortable living room. The man who had gone to grade school with him, and who was now senior partner in a firm that devoted ten percent of its profits to finding employment for the physically and mentally handicapped. The man who had arranged for him to get a job at the Refuge. Reg had picked Jimmy up in Wainscott earlier this morning and driven him to his home in Cherry Creek to wait for the arrival of Marisa and Spencer.

Jimmy registered that Reg had said something about the carpet. He blinked and looked down at the floor. "What's the matter with your carpet?"

"Nothing, except that you're going to wear it out if you don't stop pacing." Reg took a long drag on his cigarette. He was a recovering alcoholic who hadn't touched a drop of alcohol since the day his wife left him ten years earlier, but he drank two pots of coffee a day, and Jimmy couldn't remember ever seeing him without a cigarette smouldering in his hand.

"Oh. Sorry." Jimmy cleared his throat. "I guess I'm anxious to get going."

"I can see that." Reg gave a friendly grin. "I'm looking forward to meeting the woman who's causing you to jump out of your skin every time a car turns into this street. She must be quite something."

"Jesus, Reg, this isn't about a woman." Jimmy realized he was about to start pacing again, so he shoved his hands into his pockets and planted his feet firmly in one spot. By the window, as it happened, where he could see the road, and Marisa's car the moment it arrived. Not that he was obsessing or anything. Dammit, he was engaged in serious business regarding his sister's death and the man who most likely killed her. He had a perfect right to feel tense.

He gave an impatient shake of his head. "This isn't about Marisa. It's about finding something that might actually help me to nail the smarmy bastard who's running the Refuge."

"Saint Stuart of Wainscott," Reg said, blowing smoke circles at the ceiling. "I hate to rain on your parade, Jim, but I'm guessing you'd have an easier job pinning your sister's murder on the Queen of England."

Jimmy spoke through clenched teeth. "I'm going to do it. Trust me on this." He broke off. "Here's Marisa. I was starting to get worried."

"I can see why. She's two minutes late."

Jimmy fell straight into the pit his friend had dug. "No, it's five minutes. We agreed ten-thirty."

He turned quickly to go and open the front door, and saw that Reg was looking at him with an expression that hovered somewhere between pity and amusement. He realized, too late to save his pride, not only that he had just admitted he was counting off the minutes until Marisa's arrival, but that he also had a sappy smile plastered onto his mouth and that his voice had softened into a husky murmur when he said her name.

Since there was no way to deny the truth, he shrugged and admitted it. "Okay, you've got me. I'm insane about the woman. I've known her less than three weeks and I'm already terrified that I might not be able to persuade her to marry me."

Reg wiggled his eyebrows. "Did I hear that right? I can't believe you let the *M* word escape from your lips."

"You heard it, Reg. You can start laughing now."

"I'm not laughing. I'm envious." Reg gave his friend a hearty thump on the shoulder. "Wait here. I'll let her in."

Jimmy stood by the window and listened to Reg greet Marisa. "Hi, there. I'm Reg Donaldson, Jimmy's buddy from grade school. It's nice to meet you, Marisa. Jimmy's been jumpy as a cat waiting for you."

Marisa's reply was warm with laughter. "Has he? He was probably afraid I would double-cross him and go to Stuart's house alone. We should tell him not to attribute his own sneaky intentions to other people."

"Hmm, could have been that, I guess. Anyway, come on in."

"Thanks. This is Spencer, my son. Spencer, can you shake hands with Mr. Donaldson?"

Pathetic soul that he was, Jimmy could actually feel his pulse rate accelerate at the sound of her voice. Dimly, he registered the fact that Spencer and Reg were exchanging a few words, and that Reg was inviting Marisa and Spencer to come into the living room.

Since it would be real nice if he could avoid making a total horse's ass out of himself in front of Reg Donaldson, he walked over to the window again, trying to find some way to arrange his limbs and muscles so that it looked as if he were casually enjoying the busy street scene outside, as opposed to craning every nerve to wait for Marisa's arrival. Her footsteps were approaching fast. Spencer was chattering. Jimmy's stupid heart was pounding.

And that little Ford Escort has just driven down the street for the second time in the last couple of minutes.

Jimmy watched, as the driver parked between two other cars on the opposite side of the street and waited. This was a residential neighborhood, with no shops, no obvious excuse for someone to park their car and then just sit in it—

"Hi, Dimmy!"

"Hi, Spence." His gaze fixed on the Escort, he reached down and scooped Spencer up in his arms, giving him an absentminded kiss.

The driver of the Escort got out of the car and looked straight across the road at Reg's house. Jimmy, fortunately, was standing to the side of the window, and probably couldn't be seen. He scrunched himself and Spencer back behind the drape, just to be sure.

Apparently satisfied that he was watching the right house, the driver snapped his fingers toward the rear of the Escort, and a large, splay-footed mutt jumped over the backseat and out onto the sidewalk.

Good cover, Jimmy thought. A dog in urgent need of a walk provided the perfect excuse for stopping the car in almost any location, and on a street with this much traffic, nobody was really going to count how many times the dog and its owner walked up and down.

The driver—medium build, medium coloring, no facial hair—walked briskly toward the end of the street, and then turned around and walked back again. As he passed Reg's house, he slowed down his pace just sufficiently to read the numbers on the mailbox. He pulled a little notebook from his pocket and scribbled a quick notation.

"What's up?" Reg asked. "What's the problem, Jimmy?"

"Keep away from the window. I'm pretty sure Marisa was followed. I don't want her tail to know he's been spotted."

"Which car?" Reg asked, squeezing next to him.

"The white Ford Escort parked two houses down on the opposite side of the street."

"Yeah, I see it."

"The driver wrote down the number of your house, and he's already walked that dog up and down the street twice."

"Do you think he was hired by Stuart?" Marisa asked, joining them at the window.

"That's a good question."

"So let's ask him." Marisa looked ready to breathe fire and roast the hapless tail.

Jimmy grabbed her when she was already halfway to the front door, handing off Spencer to her in the process. "What the hell do you think you're doing? Are you crazy?"

"Good morning to you, too, Jimmy."

He was momentarily diverted by the realization that he hadn't said hello, and that she looked even more stunningly beautiful than usual. She was wearing jeans and a deep yellow sweatshirt that reflected a golden sheen onto her skin and made her hair glow like a halo of sunlight. All in all, she looked just about good enough to eat.

Unable to resist, Jimmy bent and kissed her. The kiss was quick and reasonably chaste, since she was holding Spencer, and Reg was only a few feet way. Even so, it was enough to send his blood pressure soaring.

"Good morning." He let out his breath on a long sigh. "It's really good to see you, Marisa. Jeez, I've missed you. What idiot decided that we ought to stop meeting after work?"

She tilted her head back to look at him. "I believe that was you. Something about the need to preserve the integrity of your role."

He leaned his head against her forehead. "You know, sometimes I take myself much too seriously."

Spencer tugged at Jimmy's shirt. "What doin', Dimmy?"

"Um, actually, I was kissing your mommy."

Reg spoke from his post near the window. "Our dog walker has just gotten back into the car. He's pretending to study a map. I think we can safely assume he's waiting to see if Marisa is going to come out again. Are you going to confront him, Jimmy?"

"No. Much as I'd like to know when he was hired, and whether Stuart did the hiring, he's not going to tell us just because we ask. And presumably some of your neighbors might object if I beat the crap out of him in an effort to persuade him to be more cooperative. It's much better if we work out a way to ditch this guy without ever indicating that we've noticed he's there."

"Great idea, but how do you propose to lose him?" Reg took in a drag of smoke.

"You know Denver better than either of us—what do you suggest? Stuart's property is in Castle Rock, but we want to lose the tail before it's obvious where we're heading. Any ideas?"

"There must be twenty or thirty shopping plazas between here and Castle Rock. Maybe we could do a little creative dodging through one of them?" Reg tugged at his lower lip, thinking. "No, it's Saturday, and the malls will be crowded, which makes them too unpredictable. How about the car wash on Orchard Road and Quebec? That would give you quick access from I-25, both on and off, and you'd never have to leave the car."

"I don't see how a car wash would enable us to lose a tail," Jimmy said. "In a car wash, the vehicle isn't even under your control—"

"Yeah, it is in this place. I'm talking about one of those huge self-service places with at least fifteen bays for individual vehicles. And I happen to know that when you turn into this particular car wash from Orchard Road, there's a little alley you can drive along that swings around behind the cleaning bays and comes out on Quebec. But if you don't know the alley is there, it's hard to spot. By the time the guy in the Escort turns into the place and starts cruising the bays looking for you, you'll have exited onto a different street and be heading south toward I-25.''

Jimmy nodded. "That could work. Provided this alley you're talking about really isn't easy to see from the main road."

"It looks as if it leads to a brick wall. It's only when you actually drive right along the path that you realize it curves around and takes you behind the wall."

Jimmy frowned. "If the alley is that difficult to spot, will we be able to find it in time to give our tail the slip?"

"Probably not," Reg said. "I suggest I drive Marisa's car, and you take mine, Jimmy. Then, when we've ditched Marisa's tail, we'll rendezvous somewhere and switch cars. You can carry on to Stuart's house with Marisa, and I'll drive my van home."

"Thanks, Reg, that would be great. So I'll meet up with you and Marisa—where?"

Reg considered for no more than a second or two. "There's a grocery store on Yosemite, just a couple of blocks east of the car wash," he said. "It's a big plaza, and King Soopers is the anchor store. You can't miss it. Wait for me at the northwest end of the lot. I'll drive there as soon as I'm sure we've shaken off our tail."

"Okay," Jimmy said, impatient to put the plan into action. "Let's do it."

Reg started walking toward the kitchen. " I'll get my

car keys for you, and then Marisa and I will leave right away. You stay here until you see the guy in the Escort follow us.''

Jimmy saluted. ''Yes, sir.''

Marisa looked at Jimmy, her gaze troubled. ''This little caper is turning out to be more risky than I expected. I can't help drawing parallels to the situation when your sister was killed. She uncovered incriminating information about Stuart Frieze, and the next thing you knew, her car had been forced off the road. Now we've uncovered incriminating information about Stuart Frieze, and there's a man following me. Spencer is going to be in the car with us. It's one thing to make the choice to put myself at risk, quite another to put him in danger.''

If he called this one wrong, he would never forgive himself, Jimmy thought. He drew in a very deep breath. ''I'm sure the man in the Escort only has instructions to tail you,'' he said. ''If he were planning to stage a fatal accident, he'd be driving a truck or some heavy vehicle. In a Ford Escort, he could kill himself in the process of forcing you off the road. Plus it's mid-morning on a warm and sunny day, and the guy has no way of knowing where you're going, or what route you'll take. Those aren't the sort of conditions under which any professional killer would attempt to cause a fatal accident. He needs darkness, rain, ice, isolation—all the things that were present when Carole was killed, but none of which are present for us now.''

Marisa thought for a moment before nodding. ''That makes sense. Okay, if we're just being followed, I have no problem taking Spencer along.'' She smiled at him. ''I'll see you in a little bit, Jimmy. Hopefully, minus one trailing Ford Escort.''

"Just like that?" he said quietly. "You accept my judgment about Spencer's safety that easily?"

"Not easily," she said. "Where Spencer's concerned, nothing is easy for me. But yes, I trust your professional judgment. Absolutely."

Given her background, he would take any trust she was able to give him, especially when it involved Spencer. It was a start, Jimmy thought. A pretty damn good start.

Seventeen

"We did it!" Marisa exclaimed, turning to smile at Reg as he exuberantly drew her Saturn to a halt.

"Yeah, I think we did." Reg grinned at her. "Jesus, I need a cigarette." He unfolded his lanky body from the seat and lit up the second his foot hit the pavement, drawing a deep, satisfying drag. "I have to tell you, your no-smoking rule sucks."

Laughing and feeling decidedly pleased with herself, Marisa followed him out of the car. She reached into the back to release Spencer from his seat. "You've been really good, pumpkin," she said. "This has been a lot of boring driving for you, hasn't it?"

Spencer had noticed the fast-food place at the corner of the supermarket lot. Since he was being accused of good behavior, he decided to angle for a reward. "Go Burger King," he said hopefully.

"Well, it is almost lunchtime, I guess." Marisa saw Jimmy get out of Reg's SUV, which was parked a couple of spaces down from her. She waved to him. "How do you feel about eating fast food for lunch, Jimmy?"

"Sounds great to me. But not here. We'll turn off at the next highway exit, just to make absolutely certain our Escort guy doesn't get lucky and pick up our trail again."

"If you really feel you need to be that cautious," Reg said. "But we've lost him, that's for sure."

Jimmy smiled at them. "You look like cats who've shared a jug of cream—so I guess you didn't encounter any problems?"

"None. Whole operation went down smooth as a baby's bottom." Now that he'd had a hit of nicotine, Reg waxed enthusiastic. "The guy in the Escort did a good job of following us—always kept at least two cars between us and him, hid himself in among other white cars whenever he could—but we shook him at the car wash. Presumably he's still circling around, wondering where the devil we got to." Reg chuckled, well-satisfied with his plan and its execution.

Jimmy gave him a grateful pat on the back. "Thanks for your help, Reg, I really appreciate it."

"Glad to be of service. I had a good time, in fact. For a few minutes there, I was able to indulge in a real James Bond fantasy. I even had the requisite gorgeous sexy woman sitting next to me."

Marisa laughed, then realized to her chagrin that she was actually sneaking a look at Jimmy to see if he'd noticed the compliment. If that wasn't pitiful, she didn't know what was. Still, it wasn't Reg's fault that she turned into a certified moron every time James Griffin was around, so she gave him a dazzling smile and a friendly handshake.

"It was really nice meeting you, Reg."

"Likewise." Reg gave Spencer a high-five. "Catch you later, kiddo."

Jimmy held out the keys to his friend's SUV. "Thanks again, Reg. I'll see you early this evening. I'll call you if there's a change of plan for any reason." Jimmy swung Spencer into his arms. "Okay, Marisa, I'll belt this little guy into his seat, and then we need to get going."

Spencer was not happy to be deprived of a fast-food experience that had seemed practically within his grasp. They had barely turned onto the highway, before he announced that he was thirsty.

Fortunately, Marisa had that one covered. "There's a cup of apple juice in the bag right behind your seat," she said to Jimmy. "Could you get it out for him? It's in a no-spill cup, so he can't do any damage."

"Sure thing." Jimmy twisted around and just managed to grasp the diaper bag, which was stuffed with various provisions for Spencer. He pulled it up and searched for the apple juice.

"Got it." Jimmy turned around again to hand Spencer the cup. "Here you go, buddy."

Marisa realized that Jimmy's voice sounded abstracted, which was unusual when he was talking to Spencer. She also realized he was still slewed around, facing toward the rear of the car.

"What is it?" she asked with sudden foreboding.

Jimmy's response was terse. "Speed up a little, will you?"

Marisa accelerated to seventy-five. "I can't go any faster than this, Jimmy. I-25 is always crawling with cops—especially this stretch. What's the problem?"

"I'm almost sure we're being followed. I've seen this same car hanging on our butts ever since we turned onto the highway."

"But Reg shook the Ford Escort at the car wash, and that's ten miles away. How could he possibly have found us again?"

"It isn't an Escort following us this time. It's a blue Honda Civic. There must have been two cars on your tail this morning. You shook the Escort but not this one."

Marisa shook her head. "That isn't possible. Reg

checked very carefully when we turned onto Quebec. There was nothing following us, absolutely nothing. Are you sure about the Honda?''

"Pretty sure. He's stayed two or three cars behind us ever since we hit the highway, despite the fact that other cars have been constantly cutting in and out. And when you speeded up, so did he."

"It could be coincidence."

"It could be." Jimmy's voice indicated how unlikely he thought that was. "We could go off the road at the next exit and double back on ourselves, entering the highway in the opposite direction. If the Honda follows, we would be certain."

"Do you want me to do it?" Marisa asked.

"Probably not. Pulling a stunt like that is the equivalent of hanging out a sign warning the tail that he's been spotted."

"At this point, do we care if he knows we're on to him?"

"Yeah, because once he knows he's been spotted, it's going to be even more difficult to shake him."

Marisa pushed a strand of hair out of her eyes and squinted into the mirror. "I still want to know how in the world he managed to find us."

"Good question." Jimmy was silent for a minute. "Even if the driver of the Ford Escort called for backup the second he lost you, his partner wouldn't have had any idea where to go looking for you. It's too much of a coincidence for this new tail to have found us in the supermarket parking lot by sheer chance."

"If it isn't coincidence, then how did he do it?"

Jimmy's mouth turned down. "My best guess is that you have an electronic tracking device attached to your car. I don't see how else they could have found us so quickly."

"A tracking device?" Marisa took her eyes from the road long enough to send him a puzzled gaze. "But that makes no sense. If there's a tracking device on my car, then the Ford Escort shouldn't have lost us at the car wash. The fact that the driver couldn't see precisely where I was turning ought to have been irrelevant. I've watched all those spy movies, too, and I know how tracking devices work. My Saturn should have appeared as a flashing *blip* on his tracking screen."

"It probably did," Jimmy said. "I'm guessing that the driver of the Escort didn't really lose you—he just let you think you'd gotten rid of him. Your maneuvering tipped him off to the fact that he'd been spotted, so he called his partner and they switched off. The Honda became the primary tail, the Escort went on backup. Because they want you to carry on with your planned activities unaware that you're being followed, just like we want to shake them without letting them know for sure that we've identified them."

Marisa was quiet for a moment. "Electronic tracking devices. Two cars. Two men. A double tail like this would be pretty expensive, wouldn't it, Jimmy?"

"Yes, it would be." He turned to look at her. "We have to face the fact that Stuart knows you're suspicious of him."

"Then why doesn't he just fire me and be done with it? Why the tail?"

"Because he needs to know how much you've found out before he throws you out."

"This isn't good news, is it?" Marisa's voice was small. "Stuart isn't the sort of man who leaves loose ends dangling."

"No, he isn't." Jimmy's voice was edged with anger. "I'm tired of being followed. Let's cut this tail off our butt right now. Take the exit that's coming up just ahead. Put your indicator on so that the driver of the Honda knows we're going off the highway."

Marisa complied, then looked into the mirror. "He's moving over into the right lane. He hasn't turned his indicator on, though."

"Probably doesn't want to do anything to attract your attention."

"McDonald's!" Spencer cried happily, spotting the magic sign. "Go McDonald's!"

Marisa shot a quick glance at Jimmy. "Can we? If there isn't time, I have some cheese and crackers he can eat."

"No need. Taking him into McDonald's should work pretty well."

Marisa's gaze flicked to the rearview mirror again. "Honda Man's following us off the highway."

"Good." Jimmy surveyed the parking lot, as they drove off the exit ramp. "This place is full to bursting, which is exactly what I need. Hopefully, the guy in the Honda will follow you and Spencer into the restaurant, which will leave me free to de-bug your car."

"What if he doesn't follow Spencer and me into McDonald's?"

"Then I'll have to come up with Plan *B*." Jimmy swiveled around and took Spencer's empty juice cup. "Honda Man has found a parking spot on the far side of the lot from us."

"And there's a car vacating a spot right in front of us," Marisa said. "Shall I turn in here?"

Jimmy nodded. "Yep, grab it. Give me the keys before you get out of the car, will you?"

Spencer proved a godsend, as they walked into the restaurant. Hopping, jumping and chattering nineteen to the dozen, he didn't allow them to appear stiff or self-conscious. Just as they reached the entrance, Jimmy bent down and pretended to tie the lace on Spencer's sneakers.

"Honda Man's sauntering across the lot now," he said, straightening. "Shi—" he remembered Spencer "—I mean, *shoot!* He's stopping to smoke a cigarette, right where he can see your car *and* the entrance to Mac-Donald's. He's not going to go inside."

Marisa scooped Spencer into her arms. "So what do we do now?"

"You go and feed Spencer lunch, while I put Plan *B* into operation."

Marisa gave him a steady look. "You never expected him to follow us into the restaurant, did you."

"Probably not," he acknowledged.

"You aren't going to do anything foolish, are you, Jimmy?"

"Absolutely not." He grinned. "Well, not if I know in advance it's foolish."

"I'm not reassured."

"You should be." He gave her a swift kiss. To hell with what Honda Man would report back to Stuart Frieze. "You have nothing to worry about, honey. Go eat. See you in ten minutes."

Marisa took Spencer into the safety of McDonald's, and Jimmy walked back to the parking lot. So far this morning, he and the guys tailing Marisa's car had been playing a fancy game of bluff and double-bluff, but it seemed pointless to continue. His cover was well and truly shot the moment either of these guys phoned in a report to Stuart Frieze. Since bluffing was no longer go-

ing to cut it, he had nothing to lose by forcing a confrontation.

Ignoring the fact that Honda Man could see exactly
what he was doing, he started a methodical search of
Marisa's car. He knew the tracking device was going to
be small—no larger than a book of matches, and possibly
as small as a quarter—but it would be affixed to the ex-
terior of the vehicle, and in one of a fairly limited number
of places. Since he was confident it was there, it shouldn't
be impossible to find.

He searched for seven minutes without success, and
eventually had to lie flat on the ground, peering up into
the car's underbody, before he found the tracker mounted
high in the well behind the fender. He removed it and
stood up, brushing grit and dirt from his jeans.

Honda Man was still smoking, but he crushed the butt
under the heel of his boot and had started to hurry back
to his car when Jimmy held up the bug between his
thumb and forefinger and waved it at him, deliberately
taunting.

Jimmy didn't give him the chance to reach his car, or
his cell phone. He stepped into Honda Man's path and
held out his hand.

"Hi, I'm Jimmy Griffin. Nice to meet you. Who are
you?"

The man attempted to shoulder past, but Jimmy stuck
out his foot and grabbed the man's arm, twisting it into
a half nelson that was as effective as it was painful. He
dragged him to the side of the parking lot, where they
weren't so easily seen. Honda Man resisted, but made no
noise to attract the attention of passersby—confirmation,
if any had been needed, that his activities wouldn't with-
stand scrutiny.

Jimmy pushed him up against a giant trash container.

"You and your buddy in the Ford Escort have been following me all morning. Which makes me kinda pissed off, you know?"

"I didn't follow nobody."

Jimmy shook his head. "I wonder why I don't believe you? Let's stop playing stupid games, shall we? You saw me remove that cute little bug you were using to keep track of us, so you'd be real smart if you decided to answer my questions. What's your name?"

"Forget it, mister. You can't attack me in a public parking lot—"

"It seems to have escaped your notice that I just did."

"Yeah, well, now you'd better let me go, or I'll scream and get the cops on your ass."

"I don't think so, since if the police get called to settle our dispute, I'll be forced to tell them you attached an electronic tracking device to my girlfriend's car without her knowledge and consent. Which is, of course, illegal. Which I'm quite sure you know, because otherwise you'd have been hollering and screaming long before now."

"I didn't stick nothing on nobody's car. I don't know nothing about any bug you found on your car."

"Then, I'm sure you won't have a lick of trouble explaining to the police—and the state licensing board for private investigators—why you have monitoring equipment in the Honda, tuned to track this specific bug I just pulled off Ms. Joubert's Saturn. The bug that, according to you, you know nothing about."

Honda Man looked at Jimmy with unadulterated loathing. "You're a regular smart-ass, aren't you."

"I like to think so."

"I'm only doing the job I was paid for. It was nothin' personal."

Jimmy interpreted this as some sort of apology, but

instead of relaxing his grip at this sign of submission, he tightened it. "Well, since it's nothing personal, who's paying you to follow Marisa Joubert?"

"I don't know. And you can break my fuckin' arm, for all the good it'll do you. I don't know the client's name."

Jimmy, unfortunately, believed him. "Is it an old client? A regular? A new customer?"

"I don't know. I'm the hired help. I don't know nothin' about who's givin' the job orders."

"That's a pity, because if you don't have any information to give me, I really can't think of a reason in the world why I shouldn't report you and the firm you work for to the licensing board. Right after I break your fuckin' arm, of course."

For the first time, Honda Man looked really scared. Apparently the prospect of a broken arm troubled him a lot more than did a possible encounter with the police or the state licensing board. "Look, I don't want no trouble—"

"Then, listen up, buddy, because here's the deal. In just a couple of minutes, we're going to walk into McDonald's together as if we were best buddies. Then you're going to get in line and order yourself lunch. Then you're going to sit inside and eat it. You're going to take your time. In fact, you're going to take at least fifteen minutes. When you're done, you can call your boss and tell him or her we found the bug, removed it, and you lost us in heavy traffic. Or you can tell him the truth— that I spotted you and scared you shitless. But if I were you, buddy, I'd go for losing us in traffic. Your boss is going to take that better."

The man said nothing, and Jimmy ratcheted his armhold one painful notch tighter. "Do you think you have those instructions clear in your mind, old pal? Especially the one about sitting inside McDonald's for fifteen minutes?"

"Yeah. Shit, can you ease up on my arm?"

"In a while. Okay, let's go inside. Let's try this question one more time. What's your name?"

Honda Man paused for a long moment. "Lionel."

It was such an unlikely name that it might even be his real one, Jimmy thought. Not that he really cared. "Okay, Lionel. Now let's walk toward McDonald's. Make sure you smile. We're trying to look like best buds, remember?"

They walked into the restaurant together.

Marisa and Spencer were at a table right by the door. Jimmy spoke tersely to Marisa. "Take Spencer out to the car, then drive around and pick me up outside the main entrance. Be as quick as possible, okay?"

"Yes." Marisa didn't waste time asking questions. She wiped Spencer's fingers, pulled off his plastic bib, and then rose.

"Come on, pumpkin. I'll carry you, since there are so many people around." She lifted him out of his chair and walked swiftly out of the restaurant without sparing a glance for Lionel.

"Let's get in line," Jimmy said, propelling Lionel toward the order counter. He stood next to Lionel as the line snaked toward the counter, one eye fixed on the glass door to the parking lot. As soon as he saw Marisa draw up in her Saturn, he abandoned his lock on Lionel's arm and ducked out of the line, sprinting for the door.

"Drive as fast as you think is safe," he said to Marisa as he slid into the passenger seat.

"Drive where?"

"Not on the highway. Anywhere that leaves us options for shaking off Lionel if he decides to come after us."

"Lionel?" Marisa repeated.

"The guy driving the Honda. I think he's sincerely afraid I was going to bust his arm in multiple places, but I don't know how long the terror will last."

"I'm assuming from Lionel's miserable expression that you found the bug?" Marisa said, as they drove onto Yosemite, a busy thoroughfare with enough stores and shopping plazas on either side of the road to provide a dozen easy escape routes.

"Yes, it's here. Deactivated." Jimmy held it out on the palm of his hand. "Unfortunately, I couldn't find out who ordered the surveillance on you. I'm sure Lionel was genuinely clueless about who was paying for his services."

"It has to be Stuart Frieze, doesn't it?"

Jimmy hated to open old wounds, but he felt obligated to answer her question honestly. "Unless there's a reason why the tail could have been ordered up by one of your father's old associates. Or one of your ex-husband's."

She considered his suggestion carefully before dismissing it with a decisive shake of her head. "No, this can't be anything to do with Evan or my father. Sandro— my brother-in-law—made sure the word was leaked in all the right circles that I knew nothing about Evan's business activities, and that I'd given away all my money. I was afraid Spencer might become a target for kidnapping, so we made sure that the news of my poverty was spread far and wide."

"Then, I guess we can be pretty safe in concluding that our tails this morning came courtesy of Mr. Frieze."

Marisa was silent for a moment before giving him a wry smile. "I guess I'm making real progress in dealing with my various neuroses. I no longer seem to be obsessing about my criminal past. How can I spare the time, when I have a brand-new set of crimes to worry about, and a whole new cast of criminals out to get me?''

Jimmy felt a sharp pang of guilt, and couldn't return her smile. ''I never meant for you to get involved in this, Marisa.''

''You didn't drag me into this against my will. I involved myself. The way Stuart is exploiting the women who come to the Refuge really gets my goat. I want to see this guy behind bars almost as much as you do.''

The journey to Castle Rock was, thankfully, uneventful. Spencer dozed off, exhausted by a day of almost nonstop driving, and the traffic thinned sufficiently for them to cover the final ten miles of the journey in less than ten minutes.

''There's a map of the area in the glove compartment,'' Marisa said, when they exited the highway. ''It's last year's map, but I hope it's still reasonably accurate.''

Castle Rock had been settled since the early days of Colorado's statehood, but what had once been an isolated and hardy pioneer community was now bursting with commercial developments. A sprawling outlet mall vied with ranches that were being broken up into yuppie five-acre home sites, and bulldozed land seemed to sprout speculative housing construction almost overnight.

Stuart's house was part of a development called Mountain Pines that was bordered by a dirt road on one side, and a new four-lane road on the other. A sign advertised that there were thirteen lots left, and that home prices, including lot, started at $299,000.

They were nice homes, Marisa reflected, but certainly not pricey enough to account for a tenth of the money Stuart had squeezed out of his operations at the Refuge.

It was mid-afternoon when they drove toward Mountain Peak Lane, and there were plenty of signs of typical weekend activity. Several home owners were in their front yards planting summer annuals. A few men were washing their cars, and children rode up and down the narrow sidewalks on bikes and Big Wheels.

"I wonder why Stuart chose to buy property here," Marisa said. "This is the last sort of neighborhood you'd expect a single guy to want to hang out."

"I certainly can't imagine Helen Wainscott settling down here after they get married," Jimmy agreed.

Marisa laughed. "Good grief, I'd forgotten about Helen. I think she'd loathe it."

"Remember, Stuart bought this place a couple of years ago, so he and Helen barely knew each other at the time." Jimmy looked from the map to the street signs. "We're almost there. Turn right here, and then Stuart's street is the first on your right."

Marisa followed the directions onto a pleasant, grassy-banked street that looked indistinguishable from all the other streets in Mountain Pines.

"Stuart's house must be the one with the dark blue door and the clump of aspen in the front yard," Jimmy said.

Marisa slowed to a halt. As she did so, a woman came out of the open garage, carrying a tray of bright red geraniums. She walked over to an empty flower bed located close to the sidewalk. The woman was young and in an advanced stage of pregnancy.

"My God." Marisa let out a slow breath, hardly able to believe her eyes. Beside her, she could feel Jimmy turn rigid with shock.

"My God," he said, echoing her. "It's Anya. Anya Dzhambirov."

Eighteen

Jimmy had already leapt out of the car, while Marisa was still double-checking to make sure she'd put the vehicle in park. He sprinted across the sidewalk and caught up with Anya before she could run back into the garage. Panting, she doubled over, cradling her abdomen.

"Jesus, Anya, are you okay?" Jimmy wasn't sure whether to pin her to the garage wall or fan her flushed face. "Listen to me, will you? Don't be frightened. You have nothing to be afraid of as far as we're concerned, I swear. Please let us talk to you."

She turned her head. "No. I must go in."

Marisa had finally unlatched Spencer from his car seat and joined them in the garage. Spencer, remembering Anya as one of the women who had cared for him at the Refuge, gave her a friendly smile, seemingly oblivious to the tension. He had picked up a geranium flower from the garage floor where it had fallen from the planting pot, and he held it up to Anya, his gaze fixed on her face.

"Here," he said, pushing the flower into her hand.

Anya's expression softened, fear chased away by tenderness. "You are kind boy, Spencer. Thank you. Now, I go in. Goodbye."

Marisa wasn't quite as intimidated by Anya's pregnant state as Jimmy was, and she stuck her foot in the door. "Before you shut that door on us, you might want to consider your alternatives. The police are looking for you, Anya. Would you prefer to talk to them or to us?''

The blood drained from Anya's face so fast and so completely that Marisa was afraid she would faint. Cursing herself for forgetting that having the police looking for you in Chechnya was much more terrifying than knowing Officer Bob Penney was hot on your trail, she quickly backpedaled.

''I'm sorry, Anya, I didn't mean to scare you. You don't have to worry, I promise. The police aren't going to hurt you. They want to help you, that's all. Everyone at the Refuge is worried because you left without telling anyone where you were going.''

A faint trace of color returned to Anya's cheeks. ''The police will not deport me?''

''No, of course they won't,'' Jimmy said firmly. ''Anya, you're safe here in Colorado. Nobody's going to send you back to Chechnya.''

She gave him a weary, sideways glance. ''You give word too easy. I haf no Green Card.''

''That doesn't matter because you have a valid temporary visa,'' Marisa said. ''I saw the documentation in your file. You have every right to be in the States, Anya. Nobody is going to ship you back to Chechnya.''

Spencer had only ever seen Anya at the Refuge, in a day care center that was well-stocked with toys. Bored with a discussion he didn't understand and in which he played no part, he tugged on Anya's maternity smock.

''Me pway?'' he said. Noticing his mother looking at him, he amended his request. ''Pweese?''

Anya gave him a brief, tentative smile. ''I haf no toys, Spencer.''

''I have toys for him in the car,'' Marisa said quickly.

"I could get them, if you'd let us come in and talk to you."

Anya shifted her weight awkwardly from one foot to the other, her hand massaging the small of her back. "Stuart say I must stay inside house. Nobody can know I am here."

"But it's too late to worry about that. We already know you're here," Jimmy pointed out. "Anya, you must see that you have no choice. Neither do we, for that matter. If you don't talk to us, we'll have to notify the police that you're staying here."

Anya's expression was stubborn and fearful at the same time. "I am safe. Why you need talk with police?"

Since they weren't making any headway, Marisa decided to push a little bit harder. "The police won't deport you, Anya, but for sure they'll want to know why you left the Refuge and why Stuart pretended that he didn't know where you were. Stuart reported to the police that you were missing, when he knew that you were living in his house, perfectly safe."

Her head jerked up. "Stuart—he will be in trouble?"

"Yes," Jimmy said.

"Absolutely," Marisa agreed.

Anya's resistance crumbled at this threat to Stuart, and she walked abruptly into the house, leaving the door standing open behind her.

"Take Spencer and go in before she changes her mind," Marisa muttered to Jimmy. "I'll get his toys."

By the time she came back with Spencer's toy bag, Jimmy was sitting at a table placed near the window in a sunny, attractive kitchen, and Anya was helping Spencer choose a cookie from a brightly colored tin. At least Stuart wasn't keeping Anya in some bleak semi-prison, Marisa reflected. If the kitchen was representative of the rest of the house, Anya would be more than comfortable living here.

Spencer was so pleased to be out of his car seat that he was quite agreeable to being settled on the floor with a selection of his toys around him. To Marisa's relief, he was soon absorbed in one of his favorite puzzles.

Since she had no idea how long either Spencer or Anya would remain cooperative, she decided not to waste time in useless conversational foreplay. She walked back to the breakfast nook and asked her question without any preamble. "Why did you run away from the Refuge? Your friends there are very worried about you."

"I am sorry. Was…necessary."

Anya sat down across the table from Jimmy, looking at him curiously. "You speak different today. You haf not glasses. You are not…" She twirled her finger against her forehead, searching for the appropriate word. "You are normal man."

"Yes, you're right," Jimmy said.

"Why you…" Words failed her again. "Why you act like you haf not full brain?"

"I'm a private investigator. I pretended to be a janitor because I didn't want people at the Refuge to pay any attention to me. I needed to discover what was going on at the Refuge."

Anya looked blank, and Jimmy tried again. "I'm a detective. A private detective."

"Detective?" Even if the rest of Jimmy's explanation had gone over her head, that was a word Anya understood very well. Her cheeks lost their color again. "You are policeman?"

"No," Jimmy said quickly. "I'm not with the police, Anya. I'm a *private* investigator. That means I work for people or for companies that pay me to find out things. I'm not working for the government, or the police.''

Anya's gaze flicked to Marisa. ''And you? You are *private investigator* also?''

Marisa shook her head. ''No, Anya, I'm not. I'm just a single mom, trying to earn my living and make a good home for Spencer. I only met Jimmy for the first time when I started work at the Refuge.''

''Then why you are here? Why you are...'' She made an impatient sound as she sought the words to frame her question. ''Why you are coming after me?''

''We're not com—'' Marisa started to say, but broke off when Jimmy flashed her a warning glance.

''Marisa is helping me in my investigation,'' Jimmy said. ''We need to know why Stuart is hiding you here, Anya.''

''I am here because I am going to keep my baby.'' There was a faint note of defiance in her voice, but she didn't expand on her answer. She fell silent, her fingers twisting together on the gleaming tabletop.

''And Stuart has offered to let you stay here until the baby's born?'' Marisa suggested. Although given everything else she knew about Stuart, she would have expected him to toss Anya out onto the street once she no longer had a baby to sell. And if he was merely offering her a helping hand out of the goodness of his heart, why all the need for secrecy?

''Stuart always knew I never want to give away my baby. I come to Refuge, but when my brother is killed, I will not do it. Talk is over. Finished.''

''I understand completely,'' Marisa said. ''You have no family left, and you want to keep your baby. I would feel exactly the same way in your position.''

She reached across the table and held Anya's hands,

stilling the restless movement of the girl's fingers. "Don't worry, Anya, you'll do just fine. There are lots of people who will help you and your baby to get settled into a new life here in America. In fact, I can put you in touch with an organization that will be able to pay the rent on an apartment for you."

Marisa made a mental note to call her brother and arrange for the Joubert Trust to make a grant to Anya. It was really gratifying to think that a tiny portion of her father's ill-gotten gains—much of it made selling weapons to desperate people like the Chechen rebels—would finally be used for a peaceful and constructive purpose.

"Thank you, but I not need help. I am fine." The defiance in Anya's voice was more pronounced, and she looked straight at Marisa, daring her to show doubt. "Stuart will marry me soon. When it is my birthday."

Marisa drew in a startled breath and started to cough. Jimmy managed to avoid choking, but he stared at Anya in stunned disbelief.

"I am getting water." Anya rose, not pleased at this reaction to her news. She poured the glass of water and returned to the table to plop it in front of Marisa. "Stuart will marry me," she said. "I haf engagement ring." She reached inside her shirt and pulled out a gold chain, from which was suspended a traditional solitaire diamond in an attractive gold setting.

Jimmy found his voice first. "Have you thought this through, Anya? Don't you think Stuart might be a little old for you?"

"He is forty-four. I am eighteen. Is fine. But we must be married before we tell people of our plans, and it is…complicated to marry before I am eighteen. In June, I am legal adult."

"Are you in love with him?" Marisa asked.

Anya's eyes narrowed and her expression became more than a touch cynical. "In love?" She shrugged. "I am Chechen. In Chechnya, I haf no home, no family, no future. Only Russian bombs, Russian soldiers and Russian tanks. Stuart is my protector. Of course I love him."

Her protector? Marisa hoped to God that was true. She couldn't begin to imagine what Stuart's plans for Anya might really be. Could he possibly be planning to marry Anya? Since he'd just announced his engagement to Helen Wainscott, it didn't seem likely. More likely, the note of defiance in Anya's voice stemmed from a gut-level fear that Stuart's promises of marriage weren't worth very much, despite the shiny diamond engagement ring.

Marisa and Jimmy exchanged bemused glances, neither of them sure whether to start issuing warnings, or to congratulate her.

Jimmy was first to break the strained silence. "So when did you and Stuart first decide to get married, Anya?"

She shrugged. "When my brother is killed, I tell him it is time."

Sometimes it was difficult to decide if the odd impression Anya created stemmed from her broken English, or from something else. Jimmy obviously picked up on the same oddity that Marisa had noticed. "*You* told Stuart it was time to get married?" he asked.

Anya's smile was world-weary enough for a woman of ninety. "Does it matter if he ask me or I ask him? I will keep my baby, and she will have her father to care for her. We be happy living here in this house, my girl and me. And I will be good wife to Stuart."

An almost impossible idea began to form in Marisa's head. It was so impossible that she almost hesitated to ask. "Anya, who is your baby's father? Is he from Chechnya, like you?"

Anya got up from the table and walked over to the fridge. "I haf lemonade. You want lemonade?"

"My God, are you thinking what I'm thinking?" Jimmy murmured.

"I sure am. Tell me I'm crazy."

"You're not crazy." Jimmy got up and walked over to the counter, where Anya was busying herself pouring three glasses of lemonade. He took the jug out of her hands, then crooked his finger under her chin and tilted her head so that she was forced to look at him.

"Please tell us, Anya. Who is the father of your baby?"

She pulled away from him, wrapping her arms around her abdomen in a gesture that was both eloquent and protective. "Stuart is my baby's father," she said fiercely, as if daring him to challenge the truth of her statement. "I was virgin when he make love with me the first time. Now he will marry me."

Even though she'd been half expecting Anya to make the claim, Marisa still had a hard time absorbing it. "On your admission forms at the Refuge, you listed a man called Alex Makhmedov as the father of your baby, Anya."

"And so? Alex is my cousin. He is bad man, always hiding from American police. He beat me. I must work for him in his bar, but he pay no money. Alex says I haf big debt to him, because he buy me ticket to leave Chechnya. I am so hungry one day, I run away. Stuart find me when I am at counseling center for refugees in Brooklyn. Stuart is kind. He takes me to fancy hotel. I can use shampoo for my hair, and soap that makes me smell pretty. He buys me warm clothes, new shoes, and we have much good food to eat—''

''And then he makes you pay for the food and the clothes by having sex with him.'' Marisa's stomach churned with disgust.

Anya raised her head, eyes glittering. ''You are wrong,'' she said hotly. ''Stuart did not *make* me have sex. I chose to make love with him. He wanted me, I knew that—but he would not ask. And it did not seem much to give.''

Marisa turned away, so furiously angry that she didn't trust herself to speak. Of course, the saintly Stuart would never force a young, helpless virgin to have sex with him in exchange for food and clothing. Nothing that straightforward for him. He would simply ply her with kindness, along with the food and clothes, until her natural gratitude took over and she offered him her body, the only currency she possessed. Had Anya been any less raped because she didn't fully comprehend what Stuart had done to her?

Spencer, no longer willing to be ignored, decided to attract his mother's attention by throwing a plastic building block at the wall, and Marisa realized that he'd been calling her for the past several minutes. She'd been so wrapped up in what Anya was saying that she'd actually filtered him out, an unheard-of experience for her.

Apologizing to Anya, she crossed the room and picked him up, hushing his cries. He was feeling lonely and neglected, so she gave him a hug, deciding to leave disciplinary statements about throwing toys at the wall for another time.

''Can he haf more cookie?'' Anya asked.

''Thanks, but he's not hungry—just tired and bored with playing by himself. Maybe we could go outside into the yard? It's fenced in, so he could run around without getting up to too much mischief.''

Anya was not enthusiastic about the idea of extending their visit. '' We haf nothing more to say. You go now.''

''There are a few things you need to know before we leave,'' Marisa said. ''Please, Anya.''

It took quite a bit more persuasion before Anya reluctantly escorted them out onto the deck, and invited them to sit in the cushioned chairs grouped around a small patio table. By great good fortune, a neighbor's kitten jumped over the fence just as they got settled, and Spencer was delighted to entertain himself by chasing it around the bushes. An older cat would have rebelled and retreated back over the fence, but the kitten was as energetic as Spencer and seemed just as delighted to have found a playmate willing to remain in endless motion.

''It's really important for you to understand what I'm about to tell you,'' Jimmy said, talking to Anya's back since she was determined to ignore them. ''If I say anything that you don't understand—anything at all—you have to let me know, okay?''

It took a while to get even a grudging ''Okay'' out of Anya, and she kept her gaze fixed on Spencer and the kitten, refusing to meet Jimmy's eyes.

''First off, I can pretty much guarantee that Stuart isn't being honest with you. He may have said he's going to marry you—''

''He will marry me. As soon as I am eighteen.'' Anya touched the chain that held her ring.

''Maybe you're right, but I don't see how he can marry you, Anya. He's engaged to Helen Wainscott, the daughter of the man who founded Wainscott Refuge. Their engagement was announced in the newspaper just this week.''

Her face paled, then flushed. She finally swung around to look at them. "You lie!"

"No, Jimmy isn't lying," Maria said quietly. "I'm sorry, but he's telling the truth. Stuart is the one telling you lies."

Anya collapsed back into her seat. After a moment of silent brooding, she spoke fiercely. "Okay, so he is engaged to Helen, but he will marry me. He will."

"How can you be so sure of that?" Marisa asked.

Anya gave another of the cynical smiles that ripped at Marisa's heart. No seventeen-year-old should have the experience to produce such a smile. "In Chechnya, we grow up hearing that we are stupid. The Russians tell us we are criminals, that we are dirty, ignorant peasants. The Russians are wrong. Stuart believed I was stupid immigrant girl. Now he understands I am smart. Why do you think I am here, in his house? Because he wants me to be here? No. He would like me to be at the Refuge, giving my baby—his baby—away to strangers."

"Then why did he bring you here?" Jimmy asked.

"I am here because I told him that he will marry me, or all the world will hear that my baby is his baby. You will see. In the end, Helen Wainscott will not be Stuart's wife. Anya Dzhambirov will be his wife. Because he knows he must marry me if he wants me to hold silent about who is the father of my baby."

Marisa wasn't sure whether to be appalled or admiring of Anya's hard-nosed approach to getting what she wanted. Anya's logic would have been great if Stuart were the sort of man to respond meekly to blackmail. Unfortunately, Marisa was afraid that Stuart was as likely to murder Anya as marry her.

"Look at me, Anya." Jimmy leaned across the table.

"You think you have all the angles covered, but you're making a big mistake."

"I not understand."

"You've screwed up," he said. "Do you understand that? You've miscalculated."

Anya shifted nervously. "How I...screw up?"

"Do you remember Ardita and Darina?" Jimmy asked. "They were refugees from Kosovo who stayed at the Refuge."

"I remember them," Anya said warily. "They are glad when they must give their babies away, because they hate the fathers. They were raped by soldiers in Kosovo. Now they work in hotel."

"No, they don't. Ardita and Darina are dead." Jimmy was deliberately brutal. "I believe they were murdered."

A muscle twitched in Anya's jaw. "Murdered?"

"Yes," Jimmy said.

"Who..." She moistened her lips with her tongue. "Who killed them?"

"I believe Stuart did."

"No, you are wrong—"

"I'm sorry, Anya, but I'm quite sure I'm right. We think Ardita and Darina threatened Stuart—"

"Threatened—what is threatened?"

"They told him they would report him to the police."

Anya's mouth settled into a mulish line. "They have no reason to threaten Stuart. No cause."

"We believe they had a very good reason," Jimmy said. "Stuart wanted to give Ardita and Darina drugs that would make their ovaries produce a lot of eggs. Then Stuart planned to remove those eggs from their ovaries and sell them to women who can't have babies of their own—"

"What is so bad about that?" Anya expressed neither

surprise nor concern. "Ardita and Darina would get money. For few hours' hurt, they would have many dollars to start new lives."

If you'd spent the first seventeen years of your life struggling to find adequate food, clothing and shelter, Marisa supposed Anya's casual attitude was understandable. Ethical issues that might seem exquisitely complicated to philosophers holding well-paid jobs in American colleges probably seemed irrelevant to Anya and many of the other women who came to the Refuge. No wonder Stuart didn't have any trouble getting his victims to sign on the dotted line of his consent forms.

Jimmy was smart enough not to get drawn into a debate about the morality of Stuart's program. "If you want to donate eggs, then you're right, it's no problem. The important thing is that you and all the other women at the Refuge must be free to choose. We believe that Ardita and Darina didn't want to go through with the procedure and that they refused. When Stuart wouldn't listen to their refusal, we think they contacted my sister and asked her to help them."

Anya looked puzzled. "They contacted your sister? Is she also investigator?"

"No, she's a doctor. She knew Ardita and Darina when they were in the refugee camp, before they came to America."

"So did your sister help them?"

"She tried to help them," Jimmy said. "She didn't succeed. We don't know exactly what happened, because Ardita and Darina died, and so did my sister. They were all killed in the space of one week."

"I am sorry for you, Jimmy. To lose a brother or a sister is hard, I know that."

"Anya, I think you're trying not to understand what

I'm telling you. We believe that Stuart arranged to have Ardita and Darina and my sister killed because they threatened the safety of his money-making operations at the Refuge.''

Anya took a long swallow of lemonade before answering him. ''You haf no proof that Stuart killed your sister and those women.''

''No, but I'm quite sure he did.'' Jimmy leaned closer, forcing Anya to look at him. ''You threaten Stuart even more seriously than they did. That's why he's agreed to marry you. But the fact that he's engaged to Helen Wainscott suggests that he has no intention of keeping his promise to you.''

''Why you are telling me this?''

''Because we want you to understand that you're in danger,'' Marisa said, deciding this was no moment to pussyfoot around the truth. ''If Stuart doesn't marry you, how will he prevent you telling everyone that he's the father of your baby?''

''He cannot stop me,'' Anya said harshly. ''I will tell everyone what he has done.''

''Exactly.'' Jimmy paused for a moment to let his agreement sink in. ''Stuart can't afford to have you do that, Anya.''

Marisa rammed the point home. ''How did he stop Ardita and Darina and Jimmy's sister from telling everyone what was going on at the Refuge?''

''You think he killed them.'' Anya's voice was suddenly very small.

''Yes,'' Jimmy said. ''We think he killed them. Just as he will kill you.''

Nineteen

Stuart hung up the phone, noting absently that his hand was quite steady. Amazing, considering the report Phil had just given him. Christ, what was he going to do now?

Helen was in the kitchen playing domestic, giving him a blissful few minutes before he would have to face her. He wandered over to the window of his cottage, stared out into the gathering darkness. He'd never felt much attachment to the house provided for him by the Wainscott Trust, but he did love the view. The deep, dark mystery of the lake, the tranquil grandeur of the mountains, the quivering aspen—about as far removed from the sun-baked plains of Africa as could be imagined.

He would miss this view when he was fired from his job at the Refuge, as he obviously would be. Right this minute, he couldn't come up with a single idea as to how he might protect himself against the storm Jimmy Griffin and Marisa Joubert were about to unleash over his head, and Helen would be too busy trying to save herself to come up with any salvation for him.

Odd to think that his disgrace would come about because he'd tried so hard to relieve a tiny portion of the world's misery. If he'd kept some of the money he'd made, he'd have been able to hire a slew of fancy lawyers to protect him. But since he'd given all his money away, he would be forced to rely on public defenders, which meant that he was as vulnerable as a slab of overripe meat staked out for the vultures.

Stuart assessed the case against himself, trying to be analytical. The D.A. would have a hard time making stick the charge that he had sold babies. All the Refuge clients would lie through their expensively capped teeth, insisting that they'd made voluntary donations to a reputable charity. He gave a dry chuckle. Oh, yes, his clients would all know how to protect their well-toned asses. They'd claim that their huge "donations" were expressions of joy and appreciation for the marvelous work done by the Refuge. *Pay for a baby? Your Honor, we're shocked—* shocked—*that you could make such a suggestion.*

Unfortunately, he had no such fig leaf to cover his own, rather scrawnier, ass. The prosecutors would be able to get him on the charge of syphoning off the very funds that clients claimed they had donated to the Refuge in innocent good faith. Yeah, there was no way around it, Stuart decided. A jail cell looked as if it was going to play a prominent role in his future.

He shouldn't be surprised if his reward for providing health care to the indigent turned out to be imprisonment. During his time with the United Nations, he'd realized that do-gooders were reviled by the people they attempted to help, and squeezed by fat politicians in the rich countries providing the money. It seemed that there were few targets as satisfactory and easy to pick off as a person preaching harmony, cooperation and love.

Stuart had been teetering on the edge of a nervous breakdown when this total lack of respect and gratitude had first driven him to the decision to raise his own funds and deliver his help directly. For three years, he'd done a terrific job, even if he did say so himself. Every time he got discouraged by the difficulties of keeping the money flowing, he reminded himself of how much good his clinics were doing in bringing medical care to the women and children of Africa.

The AIDS epidemic was leaving an entire generation of orphans starving, illiterate and deprived of love. Unfortunately, nobody in the West seemed to give a damn. Western diplomats knew that the infrastructure of many African nations was unraveling, but they couldn't persuade their governments back home to take action. The few schools that had once existed were closing because the teachers had died. Hospitals offered aspirin to cure the multiple secondary infections of people suffering from the final stages of the disease. And men still believed that using a condom was part of some wicked American plot to sterilize them.

His clinic had been one outstanding exception to the misery running rampant through central and southern Africa. But now, in the wake of Phil's phone call, he didn't see how he was going to continue funding even this small beacon of hope.

Shit! Frustrated beyond endurance, Stuart crashed his fist into the wall, cursing at the way things had turned out.

How had it all gone so wrong? Until Ardita and Darina had chosen to ignore the service he'd performed by bringing them to the United States, his fund-raising had been difficult, but not impossible. For the past few months, though, he had felt as if he were lurching from one crisis to the next, with his operations at the Refuge constantly under siege.

Who would have thought, when he stood in the blistering sun in Stankovec, that the two women with downcast eyes and swelling bellies would cause him so much trouble? Truth be told, he'd been deeply hurt when Ardita and Darina went behind his back and contacted Carole Riven, bringing her hotfooting to the Refuge with accusations of exploitation—and worse.

Even now, Stuart couldn't understand their lack of gratitude. Without his generous rescue mission, the two women would have been rotting in a stinking refuge camp, shunned by their fellow exiles and condemned to raise babies whose fathers they hated. He'd saved them from misery, and their reward had been to stab him in the back. It seemed as if endless problems had flowed from their act of treachery, culminating in this current disaster. A disaster from which he saw no way out.

Helen came into the living room from the kitchen, interrupting his melancholy thoughts. She wore a dress with white collar and cuffs, accessorized by a single-strand pearl necklace and a perky little apron. In keeping with her sudden spurt of domesticity, tonight's role was apparently going to be Mrs. Cleaver from *Leave it to Beaver*. Stuart wondered what sex with June Cleaver would be like, then realized he wasn't likely to find out. Helen wouldn't be demanding sex from him once she knew about Phil's report.

Perhaps there was a minor blessing to Phil's news, after all, Stuart thought sardonically. At least Helen wasn't going to insist on marrying him when she discovered how badly he'd screwed up. Helen only had room in her life for winners.

"Dinner's ready," she said brightly. "Who was the phone call from, dear?"

Oh, yes. This was definitely *Leave it to Beaver* night. "That was Phil, from Denver Security. "

"The detective agency? He wasn't scheduled to report in until ten tonight, was he?"

"No." Stuart drew in a deep breath. Might as well get

the confession over with. "I'm afraid he called to report a failure. His men lost track of Marisa Joubert, and they haven't been able to reestablish contact."

"How could they do that?" Helen's voice was sharp. "They were supposed to be following her electronically, weren't they? Surely, any fool can follow a blinking light on a computer monitor."

"They were following her electronically, as instructed, but Phil claims there was some sort of malfunction, and they lost her."

"Were they at least able to guess where Marisa might have been going when they lost her?"

"Unfortunately not. She was in south metro Denver and she could have been going to a multitude of locations."

"Maybe she was simply going shopping. Isn't there some big new mall in that part of Denver?"

"Yes, but I don't think she was planning a shopping trip." Stuart knew there was no point in prevaricating, so he stumbled on. "Phil provided a full account of where Marisa had been prior to the moment his men lost her. Also a description of the two men she met up with in Denver."

"So who did the little witch meet?" All trace of Mrs. Cleaver vanished with the astringent question.

There was a certain welcome release in not having to pretend the situation could be salvaged, and Stuart found he could speak quite crisply. "Marisa left her home with Spencer this morning at 9:25. She arrived at her first destination in Denver at 10:35—"

"And that destination was...?"

"She went to the home of Reggie Donaldson."

Nobody could accuse Helen of being slow on the uptake. She remembered the name instantly. "Donaldson?

He's the man who runs the employment agency for cripples, isn't he?''

"He has an agency that serves handicapped people, yes."

Streaks of red color slashed across her cheeks. "He's the so-called friend from the United Way board who persuaded you to hire that cretinous janitor. And now it turns out he knows Marisa Joubert, too? So much for friendship."

"Yes, it seems Reggie deceived me." Stuart realized he must be in a state of emotional anesthesia, because the admission was barely painful. "Unfortunately, we have added confirmation of the fact that Reggie wasn't dealing honestly with me. I won't bore you with irrelevant details, but at some point later on in the morning, Reggie and Marisa Joubert met up with another man. From the description, it sounds like Jimmy Griffin."

Helen's breath expelled in an angry hiss, and Stuart dipped his shoulder in resignation. "I'm sorry, my dear, but I can't avoid the conclusion that he and Marisa have been working together all along and that Reggie Donaldson set me up. Jimmy was driving a minivan, although he told me he couldn't drive. Also, according to Phil's operatives, Jimmy didn't seem to be mentally challenged."

"Mentally challenged?" Helen exploded into movement. "God Almighty, Stuart, do you always have to be so damn politically correct? The guy pretended to be a moron, and all the time he was creeping around with his bucket and mop, he probably had a camera and a tape recorder locked onto you. The only question is whether he and that Joubert woman are poking their noses into Refuge business on behalf of law enforcement, or a TV station."

Stuart's stomach knotted, but he spoke quite calmly. "Yes, it seems likely that Jimmy Griffin has been having a fine old time at our expense. We have to assume that Marisa went through my papers, too. She had free run of the filing system."

"You surely aren't telling me that you were stupid enough to leave written records concerning your special projects open to her perusal?"

Stuart couldn't have been quite as anesthetized as he'd thought, because the scorn in Helen's voice left him smarting. "All the relevant documents were encoded. But it was impossible to keep track of everything—the schedules, the medications, the surgical procedures—without writing a few things down. We have to accept that a clever investigator would be able to break the code and compile statistical records that would be quite revealing."

"*We* don't have to accept anything," Helen said. She swung her arm back in a wide arc and hit him flat-handed across the face with all the power she could muster. "Jesus, Stuart, how could you have been so stupid? Jimmy the Moron is a genius compared to you."

The humiliation stung far worse than the actual blow, but, in the end, Stuart found he didn't really care enough to respond to either one. He'd needed somebody to cover for him with the Wainscott board, and he'd recognized early on that Helen was ripe for recruitment. Helen had been responsible for trolling the byways of the social elites, finding the clients who could afford to pay premium prices for quick solutions to their fertility and adoption problems. He could make a lot of trouble for her if he wanted to, but he wasn't a vindictive person, and he discovered that vengeance was beneath him.

Stuart knew exactly why Helen had hit him. She was

worried sick, and she certainly had cause to be. Since her divorce, they'd always split the proceeds from his activities fifty-fifty, and her chief source of income was about to vanish. Other women would have amended their lifestyles, but he didn't think Helen was capable of living in any style that was less than luxurious.

"You're right," he said wearily, massaging his jaw. "I haven't been smart in keeping my tracks covered, but you don't have to accept any blame for what's happened. There's no point in both of us going to jail. I'll make sure no hint of suspicion lands on you, Helen."

Instead of being grateful, she was enraged. "And what the hell am I supposed to live on while you're in jail? That bastard ex-husband of mine screwed me over, and my senile father left his entire fortune to make sure whores and idiot teenyboppers would go through with their pregnancies and dutifully hand over their babies to morally upright married couples. God forbid that they should have abortions! Do you know how many abortions I've had, Stuart? *Three.* And every time they vacuum another fetus out of me, I think, *Fuck you, Daddy.*"

Helen ripped off the Mrs. Cleaver apron and flung it to the floor. Stuart had never seen her lose her temper so completely before, and he watched with an interest that was detached enough to be almost clinical.

"Men!" she exclaimed. "Why do men always have to fuck everything up? Do you know what it was like growing up watching my father pretend that he wasn't responsible for my sister's death? He could never bring himself to admit that he was to blame. Oh, no, he had to blame everyone else. Prudence—because she'd lacked the courage to come to him and tell him she was pregnant. My mother—because she hadn't drummed the right values about chastity into Prudence's head. Me—because

I was ten years old but didn't manage to stop my sister bleeding to death.''

"It must have been very difficult for you—"

"Difficult? It was a nightmare. My father had always been strict, but after Prudence died, he turned into a monster. I was twenty-two years old before I went to college, because my father wasn't prepared to let me out of his sight in case I got pregnant like my sister. By then, he'd managed to make me so terrified of men that it was another two years before I worked up the courage to go out on a date. I still can't bear to remember how frightened I was the first time I had sex. Do you know what it's like to be swamped by images of your sister dying every time a man kisses you?''

Stuart was surprised to find himself feeling sympathy for Helen. She was one seriously screwed-up woman, but she'd acquired her neuroses the hard way as he had every reason to know. He roused himself from a growing sense of torpor to soothe her.

"Look, maybe things aren't as bad as we think. We don't know what Marisa and Jimmy are planning to do. We don't even know for sure what they've ferreted out.''

"Too much," Helen said curtly. "We can count on that.''

"Maybe, but we still have a little time. They don't know that we're on our guard, so they'll be in no rush to go to the authorities with anything they've discovered Maybe we should just cut our losses and catch the next flight to Mexico or Brazil, before the police start to close in on us. There are no irregularities in actual Wainscott Foundation funds, so the authorities here probably wouldn't bother to follow us just because I ran a profitable sideline.''

His suggestion seemed to calm Helen somewhat, although he knew she wouldn't consider fleeing the country an acceptable solution to their dilemma. If anyone fled the country, it would be him, traveling alone. Sweating out exile in Rio de Janeiro was not something she would contemplate. No, she would pile all the blame for what had happened onto him. When detectives questioned her, she would claim that she'd known nothing about what was going on, and she would build a wall of lawyers around her protestations of innocence. If hanging Stuart out to dry was what it took to save herself, Stuart would be well and truly hung out.

Perversely, he felt his spirits lift slightly. Every cloud had its silver lining, he thought with gallows humor. He bitterly regretted the loss of his clinics, but he could almost look forward to exile in Rio or Acapulco as a fortunate escape from a forced marriage to Helen.

She seemed to have gotten over her burst of temper. Casting him a doleful look, she sighed deeply and came to put her arms around his neck, resting her head against his chest. For the first time in all his encounters with her, he couldn't decide which role she was playing.

"I'm sorry I hit you," she said. "For a couple of minutes there, I totally lost it."

"I understand. You were upset. This is worrying for both of us."

She splayed her hand against his chest, stroking gently. "I've cooked dinner," she said. "It's a shame to let it go to waste. If you're not too upset, why don't we go and eat?"

Fretting about food wastage was certainly a first for Helen, but Stuart merely nodded. "Yes, let's. I'm looking forward to my first experience of your home cooking."

"I'm quite a good cook, actually—"

It was hard to believe, listening to her now, that minutes ago she'd been on the verge of hysteria.

"We can discuss our various options over dinner," she said. "You were right to say that we shouldn't overreact. I realize that now."

He didn't recall saying that precisely, but it was in his best interests not to alienate Helen. He would find it easier to escape if she was prepared to help pay for his departure. He'd just sent a huge check to Africa, and he would be scraping the bottom of the barrel to come up with funds to cover an airline ticket to Brazil and enough money to tide him over while he looked around for some new way to make a living.

Helen had cooked meat loaf and mashed potatoes, all part of the *Leave it to Beaver* scenario she'd been planning. Stuart found the meal oddly comforting—a flashback to the solid days of his mid-Western childhood, before he'd gone overseas and felt himself being driven mad by the weight of human suffering he was forced to observe.

For reasons he didn't fully understand, Helen seemed openly remorseful and went out of her way to be charming. They chatted in a desultory fashion about possible options that would permit them to carry on as before, but they both knew that if Marisa and Jimmy Griffin had uncovered irregularities in the operation of the Refuge, Stuart really had no choices other than fleeing the country or packing his suitcase for jail.

His cell phone rang when Helen was in the kitchen fixing dessert. Not many people had his cell phone number, and Stuart answered the call at once, instinctively fearing the worst. He was right to worry. The call was from Anya, who had strict orders never to phone him unless it was an emergency.

She was dead-on to consider this an emergency. Jimmy Griffin was in Castle Rock, she reported, along with Marisa Joubert and her son.

Anya was sobbing into the phone as she talked to him, and she seemed to have some insane idea that he was about to kill her, although with her imperfect English, made more broken than usual by sobs, Stuart couldn't be sure he understood what she was saying. Before he could confirm exactly what she'd been trying to tell him, he heard the sound of a child laughing, then a woman's voice speaking in the background—presumably Marisa Joubert's. With a strangled gasp, Anya hung up the phone, interrupting herself in mid-sentence.

But before she ended the call, Stuart did glean one final, stunning piece of news that he was confident he hadn't misunderstood.

Jimmy Griffin was Carole Riven's brother.

Several seconds passed before Stuart flipped his phone shut and set it on the table, next to his empty bread plate. How odd that he should feel that he was finally receiving just punishment for sins committed long ago and never quite atoned for. He was still sitting in the same position, staring blankly at the phone, when Helen emerged from the kitchen, carrying a tray laden with cherry cobbler and ice cream.

"Did I hear another phone call?" she asked, reverting momentarily to her cheery Mrs. Cleaver mode. "It was nothing worrying, I hope."

Stuart was too shocked and miserable to lie. "Yes, I had another phone call," he said. "It was Anya Dzhambirov."

"Anya Dzham—whatsit? Isn't she the girl who ran away from the Refuge?"

"Yes, that's what people thought." Given the circumstances, it seemed pointless to continue lying about Anya. "Actually, I knew where she was all along. It's rather complicated, but she thinks she's fallen in love with me, and she's been staying at my house in Castle Rock."

"Has she, indeed?" Helen sent him a look of utter contempt. "Another one of your destitute virgins that you couldn't resist impregnating, Stuart? You never could learn when it was important to keep your zipper zipped, could you?"

Stuart didn't bother to defend himself. He had more important worries right now than the fact that Helen seemed to be aware of his attraction to girls some twenty years younger than her. A hang-up that his psychotherapist traced back to high school. He forced himself to look straight at Helen as he told her what Anya had said. Maybe watching her reaction would bring reality to a fact he still couldn't fully comprehend.

"Anya says Jimmy Griffin is Carole Riven's brother."

Helen dropped the tray of cobbler. Paying the spilled food not the slightest attention, she sank down into a chair opposite him. "How can she know? Is she sure?"

"Yes, I think so." Stuart rubbed his eyes, trying to clear his vision, which had suddenly gone out of focus. "If Carole Riven was Jimmy's sister, that would make sense of everything, wouldn't it? That interfering bitch must have run tattling to Jimmy before she died."

"We have to think through what this means." Helen sounded feverish. "And how in God's name did Anya Dzh—whatever-her-name-is find out something so important, when Phil missed it?"

"She didn't exactly find it out, I guess. The information was thrust on her, so to speak. Jimmy and Marisa Joubert are at the house in Castle Rock right now."

Helen lost the color that had just returned to her

cheeks. "Well, now we know where they were going when they shook off Phil's tail," she said acidly.

"If Jimmy is Carole Riven's brother, he isn't going to give up." Stuart's voice sounded as forlorn as he felt.

Helen gnawed at her lip. "Jesus, this is a total disaster. There's no knowing what the police might uncover if Griffin's on their asses twenty-four hours a day, prodding them to search harder and deeper."

"I'll have to leave the country," Stuart said tiredly. "And even then, the chances are good that Griffin will nag the authorities to get me extradited."

"Brazil still doesn't have an extradition treaty, does it?" Helen spoke feverishly. "You'd be safe there."

"I guess. Right now, I feel as if I'm going to spend the rest of my life looking over my shoulder, wondering when the next knock at the door is going to be the police."

Helen paced the living room, still ignoring the upended dishes and the cherry juice seeping into the carpet. Despite the pacing, she appeared more in control than she had been earlier, as if the pacing were more to help her think than to calm her nerves.

"It isn't enough for you to leave the country," she said. "What we have to do is make sure that the police don't come after you."

"That's a great plan," Stuart said. "Unfortunately, I'm fresh out of ideas as to how we might do that."

Helen paced some more. "There is a way," she said finally. "I think I see how we could pull it off." She looked up at him, her eyes huge. "You have to commit suicide, Stuart."

She surprised a crack of morbid laughter out of him. "Yeah, that would take care of the problem, all right.

Unfortunately, I think I'd prefer a few years in jail to eternity in the local cemetery.''

Helen stopped pacing, and actually responded to his laugh with a smile of her own. ''I have to slow down and express myself better. We're going to fake your death,'' she said. ''You'll fly off to Brazil, but the police won't come after you because they'll think you're dead.''

''It's a nice thought, Helen, but if I'm in Brazil, the police aren't going to find a body. And without a body, they're always going to be suspicious. Besides, how do I fly off to Brazil without showing my passport?'' He shook his head. ''Those sorts of disappearing acts only work in the movies, where the director doesn't have to show the audience any of the details.''

''We can make it work.'' Helen spoke so quickly that the words fell over each other. ''How do you get out of the country? It's easy. You buy a plane ticket for cash to Dallas, or San Diego, or some other city close to the Mexican border. Then you pick up a rental car and drive it across the border. Your car probably won't even be stopped. It's getting into the States that's difficult, not getting out of it. And once you're in Mexico, you have all the time in the world to work out how you're going to make it to Brazil—if you decide it's even necessary to make the move.''

Stuart felt the faint stir of hope. He extinguished it. ''I'd need a fake driver's license, and a fake Social Security number, and lots of money. I don't have any of those things.''

Helen came and sat on his lap, leaning her head on his shoulder so that her hair brushed against his jaw. ''You know me, Stuart, and I'm not a good or a noble person, so I won't even pretend I'm willing to come with you. And I have to admit, once you're safely out of the country, I'm going to lie. I'm going to pretend that I know absolutely nothing about what you've been doing at the Refuge. I'm going to play the abused and naive victim to the hilt. That doesn't mean that I'm not grateful to you for offering to take the rap. I am.''

She drew in a shaky breath. "I'll give you the money you need, Stuart. I'm not giving you much other support, so I owe you that much."

He was surprised and touched by her unexpected generosity. "You can't afford to support me—"

"Not for long, no. That bastard ex-husband of mine just about cleaned me out. But I can help you to get started. As for the new driver's license and Social Security number—you know as well as I do that you can drive to downtown Denver and buy yourself a set of false ID within the hour."

"Thank you, Helen. I'm grateful, really I am, and I appreciate your offer of help. But there's still the minor problem of how we're going to convince the police I'm dead."

"That's more difficult to organize," she agreed. Her brow furrowed in thought as her hand stroked absently back and forth across his chest. "You need to leave a suicide note, of course, but then we have the problem of why nobody can find your body."

She pulled a little face. "Now if this were California, you could find a deserted stretch of beach and leave your shoes behind, and your wallet, and the police wouldn't necessarily be surprised if they couldn't find your body. Unfortunately, in Colorado we don't have any ocean."

"But we have Alpine Lake," Stuart said, feeling a sudden rush of excitement. "It's a glacial lake, and it's very deep. It's not as big as Lake Tahoe, obviously, but it's a decent size."

Helen frowned. "It might work... But they'd probably send in divers."

"So they wouldn't find me. But they'd never be absolutely sure."

"It needs something more," Helen muttered, half to herself. "How about if I claim that you came to me to say goodbye and hinted what you might do? Then you ran off into the night, and I was so worried that I came back to the cottage and found your suicide note—" She broke off. "It's not foolproof, Stuart, but at least it gives you a chance. Even if the police end up convinced you faked your own death, by then you'll be safely out of the country, and the trail will be cold. Remember how they always say that a detective's best chance of solving a crime is in the first twenty-four hours after it happens? A border guard might conceivably remember you or your car on the day you cross over into Mexico, but he's never going to remember you if the police aren't questioning him until three weeks later."

Stuart would never have expected her to be so helpful, and he folded her into his arms, kissing her with unusual gentleness. "Thank you, Helen. I'm truly grateful for your help."

She kissed him back, and he realized she was crying. He stanched the flow with the tip of his fingers. "Tears?" he said softly. "For me?"

"For you." She looked up at him, droplets trembling on her lashes. "I'll miss you, Stuart, I really will."

For the first time in their entire acquaintanceship, Stuart discovered that he genuinely wanted to make love to her. He took her in his arms and carried her into the bedroom. Instead of the voracious woman he was accustomed to, Helen made love with a sweetness that was almost elegiac. After they had reached completion, she lay in his arms for a long time, and he could feel the wetness of her tears against his chest.

Finally, she sat up in bed, wiping her eyes. "We don't have any more time for goodbyes, Stuart. We have to be practical. It's time for you to write that suicide note, and get your suitcases packed."

"You're right." Sighing, Stuart got out of bed and pulled on his robe. Padding over to his desk, he pulled out a sheet of writing paper and found a pen.

"Come and help me," he said. "What do you think I ought to say?"

Twenty

Finding where Stuart had stashed his ill-gotten gains was ridiculously easy, once Marisa and Jimmy persuaded Anya to let them search the files in the little room Stuart used as a study. Since he kept few papers in Castle Rock, they had only one small filing cabinet and the drawers in his desk to look through.

Leaving Anya to entertain Spencer, Marisa and Jimmy divided the file drawers between them. It took less than fifteen minutes for Jimmy to find the six folders that had originally been stored at the Refuge. Stuart had presumably moved them to Castle Rock the night he drove Anya here.

Ten minutes after celebrating that discovery, Marisa found a folder labeled "Cayman Islands." Inside were bank statements and correspondence that dated back to the fall of 1997. "I think I've found what we're looking for," she said, handing the folder to Jimmy. She wriggled her shoulders, relaxing her stiff muscles. "Who would have thought it could be this simple?"

He took the file from her, smiling. "Here's a third-grade riddle. When you lose something, why do you always find it in the last place you think to look?"

"I've no idea. Why?"

"Because once you find it, you stop looking." He grinned. "What I mean is, this only seems simple because we're finally looking in the right place. I'd been searching for over a month before you arrived, with almost no luck. It was the fact that you had access to Stuart's filing system at the Refuge that made all the difference.''

"Before we break out the champagne and set off fireworks, are you sure this really is what we're looking for?''

Jimmy sat at the desk and flipped through the file. "Yeah, this is the one—and Stuart's got his account number right on the first page. If I have to do some creative breaking and entering on the Internet, we've got everything we need right here.''

Marisa leaned against Jimmy, reading with him, as he quickly skimmed through the few pieces of correspondence and the pages of account statements.

"It doesn't look as if I'm going to have to break into his account,'' Jimmy said after a while. "Pity. I was hoping to dazzle you with my skill as a hacker. Stuart's got complete monthly bank statements here, going back to when he opened the account with an initial deposit of a hundred thousand dollars. That was in March 1998.''

"Presumably those were the profits from his first six months of operation at the Refuge,'' Marisa said. "He stepped up the pace these past two years, didn't he? I guess once his reputation got established, he managed to expand his client base and find more and more wealthy people willing to pay through the nose for his services.''

"He sure was raking in the bucks,'' Jimmy said, leaning back in the chair, as they reached the end of the file. "I figure that last year he deposited just over a million dollars. One million, one-hundred thousand, to be precise.''

"But what's he doing with the money?'' Marisa asked.

"I don't get it. Those account statements aren't hard to read, and, unless I'm missing something, Stuart isn't using Refuge funds to make more millions on the stock market or something. He just deposits huge checks from various people who've used his services, and then he pays out equally huge sums to a clinic in Africa. All to the same place, regularly as clockwork."

"The New Hope Clinic," Jimmy said. "He must have paid them close to two million dollars in less than two years."

They stared at each other in puzzlement. "New Hope Clinic? What does that mean?" Marisa asked. "Could it be a front for a plastic surgery mill? You know, one of those places that performs procedures that are illegal in the States."

"In Africa?" Jimmy shook his head. "Not very likely. It's far more likely that he's stealing body parts to provide kidneys and livers for rich folks in need of a transplant. That would tie right in with stealing eggs and selling babies."

"If that's what he's doing, why is he paying money *to* the clinic? He ought to be getting money back, not sending them massive checks every month." Marisa pondered for a moment. "Maybe the New Hope Clinic is just a fictitious entity. He's sending his money to Africa, and it's being laundered there and then filtered back to Stuart in the States."

"But he has no need to launder his money after it goes to the Cayman Islands," Stuart pointed out. "Once he's transferred it there, the IRS is never going to know about it, unless he tries to bring it back into the States. It's *before* it goes to the Cayman Islands that he ought to be worrying, not after."

Marisa let out an exasperated puff of air. "This guy is

driving me insane! Every time I think we have him nailed, he eludes our grasp again.''

Jimmy's brow furrowed. "Wait a minute, I've just thought of something. I remember seeing a picture on the credenza in the living room. I'll be right back.''

Jimmy returned, carrying a photo of Stuart standing outside a large, three-story building. The construction was inexpensive cinder block, but the blocks were freshly painted a gleaming white. *New Hope Clinic* was emblazoned in burnished letters across the portico, and Stuart stood in the entrance, surrounded by smiling doctors and nurses. He held a baby with a bandaged head, and two more young children, both wearing artificial limbs, were clinging to his legs. Stuart looked happier and more relaxed than Marisa had ever seen him.

"He has more pictures like this in his cottage," Jimmy said. "I paid them no attention because I knew he'd worked for the United Nations and I just assumed the photos were taken during his stint as a field director for the Commission on Refugees. But they take on a whole new meaning now we know about the money going out of his account each month.''

Marisa stared at the picture and gulped. "Is it possible this guy thinks he's some sort of modern-day Robin Hood?''

"It sure as heck looks like it, doesn't it?''

"No, that can't be possible. Surely to goodness, Stuart hasn't set up his whole horrible operation at the Refuge just to fund a hospital for orphans in Africa? Could he possibly be that crazy?''

"Stealing body parts and babies from one set of victims to pay for artificial limbs for another set of victims?'' Jimmy gave a crack of incredulous laughter. "Well, that has to be a first.''

"Good God, Jimmy, I think that's what he's doing!"

"Well, even if we're right about how Stuart's been using the money he makes, we obviously can't let him keep on selling babies. Not to mention the fact that he killed three women to protect his fund-raising projects."

"That's true, and it's terrible—but, Jimmy, the guy is clearly nuts. I have to say, I'm wondering if Stuart doesn't need to spend the next few years in a psychiatric hospital rather than in a jail."

"You're more generous than I am," Jimmy said tightly. "I don't care about his screwed-up motives and his crazy desire to save the world. I want to see him pay for his crimes."

"I'm not more generous than you. I guess more of my family background has rubbed off on me than I like to admit, and I try to avoid law enforcement officials as much as possible. Besides, you said it yourself—" Marisa pointed out. "Stuart's attempt to save the world is crazy. What he's been doing these past three years is the work of a deranged mind."

"It also happens to be criminal. Not to mention immoral. Since you're in such a forgiving mood, what excuses do you make for the fact that Stuart seduced Anya when she was destitute and utterly vulnerable? Or the fact that eighty-seven women have had what amounts to forced removal of multiple eggs from their ovaries? And that eleven women got over one pregnancy only to find themselves three months later carrying another child for some rich man who could afford to rent their wombs? Not to mention the minor fact that he murdered three women."

"I don't have any excuses. None. It's all horrible. But once you report what we know to the police, there's no turning back. If we bring law enforcement officials into this, they'll be forced to prosecute, even if they can't gather any evidence to pin the murders on him. They'll be so angry, knowing what he did, that they'll stick him with the toughest charge they can come up with for everything else he's done."

"That doesn't sound all bad to me," Jimmy said.

"Right now, you're furious with Stuart, but are you sure you'll still feel the same way six months from now? You already have to live with the grief of losing your sister to this lunatic." She took his hand, pleading with him. "Don't add regrets over the way you handle Stuart's punishment to the burden you're already carrying."

Jimmy paced the study. "I'm listening, but I don't want to hear what you're saying," he muttered. "I admit the guy is sick. The awful thing is that I bet he truly believes he's one of the world's good guys. But Jeffrey Dahmer was sick, too. Does that mean society should have said 'poor guy' and let him go on eating people?"

A gurgle of noisy laughter from Spencer in the kitchen attracted Marisa's attention, and she used it as an excuse to leave Jimmy to wrestle with the problem of how Stuart should be punished. "That cackle of laughter from my son doesn't sound good," she said. "It means he's up to serious mischief. I'd better check on him."

Coming into the kitchen, Marisa found her fears were justified. Anya was on the phone, paying no attention to Spencer. Her son, meanwhile, was having a grand old time. He'd found the cupboard where groceries were stored and had managed to open the door. Seated in the center of a circle of spilled noodles, he was alternately eating raw noodles and attempting to stuff them back into the torn cellophane pack.

Marisa scooped him off the floor. "Spencer, you know better than that."

Spencer looked at her sheepishly, but continued to crunch the raw noodles.

Anya finally noticed what was going on. She gave a whimper that sounded oddly guilty, and slammed down the phone. Anya should just have kept talking, Marisa thought wryly. With all the mess Spencer had made, Marisa had been paying no attention to Anya's phone call. But now she was on red alert.

"Who were you talking to, Anya?" Anya didn't know many people, and given her guilty expression, the list of potential callers narrowed even more.

"Nobody. I am saying nothing."

"You called Stuart, didn't you? For crying out loud, Anya, what got into you? What did you say to him?"

"Nothing. I tell him you are here. I warn him you are calling police." She sniffed, wiping her nose on a tissue. "You say Stuart will kill me. You are wrong. He is not perfect man, but he will not kill me. I know of killers, and he is not one."

Jimmy came into the kitchen in time to hear Anya's remarks. "What's up?" he asked Marisa.

"If you can believe it, she called Stuart."

"You have got to be kidding me!" Jimmy shook his head. "Damn! Do we have any clue how much she told him?"

"She says nothing. Nothing, that is, except that we're here, that we've accused him of murder, and that we're going to contact the police."

Jimmy sighed. "Well, I guess that puts our feet right smack in the middle of the fire. Now Stuart will probably make a run for it, which leaves us with no choice but to confront him tonight, ourselves."

Having argued in favor of not informing the police, Marisa found herself reversing her position. "Castle

Rock is a long way from Wainscott, which gives him almost a three-hour head start on us, assuming we don't run into Saturday-night traffic going through Denver. Maybe we have no choice but to call the police. They could get out there much faster that we can.''

"And you think they're going to trundle out to Wainscott with an arrest warrant for Saint Stuart simply on the grounds that the two of us claim he's murdered three women? Far from arresting Stuart, we'd be lucky if we could persuade them not to charge us with burglary. No, that isn't an option."

Jimmy was already walking back to the study, gathering up files and papers. Marisa followed him, holding Spencer. "But you were the one who said we should inform the police about what we've found out."

"Yes, on *our* schedule. Forty-eight hours from now, when I'd contacted our company lawyer and arranged for him to fly out here armed with enough legal gobbledygook to ensure that Stuart was the person who ended up behind bars, not us."

Marisa glared at a picture of Stuart surrounded by smiling orphans, steeling her resolve. "Whatever his motives, we can't let him fly off to some South American country without a lick of punishment for all the lives he's ruined." She thought for a moment. "What are we going to do about Anya? If we leave her here, she'll undoubtedly call Stuart and tell him we're on our way back to Wainscott."

Jimmy thought for a moment. "We'll take her with us and drop her off at Reg Donaldson's house. It's going to add a twenty-minute diversion to our journey, but he'll take good care of her. I'll call and ask for his help, while you supervise Anya's packing. It shouldn't take long to throw a few clean clothes and some toiletries into a case.

By the time I've finished explaining to Reg what's going on, Anya should be ready.''

Sullen and uncooperative, Anya spun out her packing as long as she could. His phone call to Reg finished, Jimmy wasn't prepared to wait any longer. He came into the bedroom, dumped the bag of toiletries on top of the clothes she'd already packed, and snapped the case shut.

"That's it," he said. "Let's go, Anya."

They drove to Reg Donaldson's and dropped Anya off, then continued the drive back to Wainscott, which was long but uneventful, and not delayed by any traffic jams.

Marisa knew that she couldn't possibly accompany Jimmy when he confronted Stuart. Spencer was already asleep, lying heavy in her arms, and she couldn't justify dragging him to any more strange places when it was long past his bedtime. There was also the chance that Stuart might turn violent or abusive when he knew he was cornered, and she had no desire to subject her son to any more scenes in which angry men raised their voices, hurled obscenities and made frightening threats. Evan had given them a lifetime quota of that in the first eighteen months of Spencer's life.

Jimmy escorted her up to her apartment, pausing in the doorway to kiss her goodbye. "It's going to be really late by the time Stuart and I are through. If you'd like me to, I'll stop by and let you know what happened."

"If I'd *like* you to?" In mock outrage, Marisa poked a finger at the center of his chest. "Unless you want to suffer grievous bodily harm next time I see you, buster, you'd better come and tell me what happens. I don't care how late it is."

"Yes, ma'am." He kissed her again. "Thank you for all your help, Marisa. Not to mention the loan of your car."

"You're welcome." She grabbed his sweatshirt and pulled him closer for a final kiss. "Take care," she said. "I'll be waiting for you."

The lights were blazing in Stuart's cottage, when Jimmy drew Marisa's Saturn to a halt in the driveway. He approached the front door warily, not wanting to scare Stuart off—but his caution was unnecessary. Helen Wainscott burst out of the cottage just as he was about to knock on the door. She was sobbing wildly, and her hair stuck out over her head as if electrified by grief. In her hand she clutched a sheet of paper.

She grabbed Jimmy's arm, although he wasn't sure if she even recognized him. "Oh, my God, you have to help me find him. I can't find him. I don't know where he's gone."

A leaden ball weighted Jimmy's stomach, and he cursed hard and long. Thanks to Anya's phone call, Stuart had obviously been able to fly the coop while Jimmy and Marisa were making the return journey from Castle Rock.

Sighing, he reached out and grabbed Helen as she tried to hurtle herself down the porch steps. "Ms. Wainscott, you can't go out there right now. You're not wearing shoes. You have to calm down."

She looked down at her feet, as if Jimmy's comment about her lack of shoes was the only part of his statement she'd heard. "I was wearing high heels. He ran too fast, I couldn't catch up with him."

She started to dart around the porch again, trying to get past him. Jimmy took her by the shoulders and forced her to stand still, putting his hand over her mouth to slow down her breathing and stop her from hyperventilating.

"Helen, listen to me. Are you talking about Stuart?

Why was he running? Did he take his car? Was he going to the airport?''

Helen blinked, as if Jimmy's string of questions had finally brought her back to awareness of her surroundings and his presence. ''Who are you?'' She stared at him. ''Oh, you're the janitor from the Refuge.''

''Yes.'' Given her state of mind, this didn't seem the moment to go into complicated explanations. ''Try to tell me what's happened here, if you can.''

She looked puzzled. ''Why are you here?''

''I've come to help you. Where's Stuart?''

''He's gone,'' Helen said dully. ''He had a phone call and he went mad. Insane.'' Now that she was calming down, her body seemed to lose the frantic nervous energy that had sustained her. She looked up at Jimmy as if she were going to say something more. Then her eyes glazed over, and she slumped against him. The piece of paper she'd been holding fluttered to the floor.

The yellow anti-bug light in the porch lamp made her color appear ghastly. Jimmy lifted her into his arms and carried her back into Stuart's cottage, where her pallor seemed a little less frightening.

Helen's color might look better inside, but everything else about the living room was a disaster. Jimmy stepped over wineglasses and plates, several of them broken, and picked his way around the fruit from some sort of pie that was splattered across the carpet, staining the pallid beige with slashes of vivid scarlet. A pair of candles had apparently been upended on the little dining table, and the smell of spilled, scented wax and charred linen napkins lingered in the air.

Helen was already stirring. Jimmy made her as comfortable as he could on the sofa, then went into the kitchen for some water. The kitchen was a little messy, showing that someone had prepared a meal there, but it was nothing like the wrecked state of the living area.

When he returned, Helen was sitting up, resting with her head in her hands. She took the glass of water from him with a murmur of thanks, but her hand shook so badly that the water spilled when she tried to carry the glass to her lips. Jimmy sympathized with her distress. If the state of the living room was anything to go by, Stuart's flight to freedom had been preceded by a pretty dramatic display of temper.

He helped her drink the water, then set the glass on a side table. "Do you want me to call a doctor?" he asked.

She shook her head. "No, I'm better now. I'm all right." She closed her eyes. "We need to call the police. They'll have to search for him."

Jimmy was a little surprised that she was so willing to turn her erstwhile fiancée over to the law. "Where do you think he's gone?" he asked. "Did he give you any indication if he was going to try to catch a plane? Did he take his car?"

She stared at him, reenergized by puzzlement. "Are you crazy? What in the world are you talking about?" Then she shook her head, muttering to herself. "Of course he's crazy. I forgot." She rubbed her eyes and looked at him warily. "You seem different tonight, Jimmy."

Apparently Stuart hadn't filled her in on any of the reasons he felt it necessary to skip town—Helen still believed Jimmy was mentally handicapped.

"It's a long and complicated story," Jimmy said. "But actually, I'm not a janitor, and I'm not learning disabled. I'm a private investigator. I specialize in working with large companies who suspect one or more of their employees of embezzlement or other illegal activities."

"Then what were you doing at the Refuge?" she demanded, but didn't allow him to continue. "I'm the chairman of the Wainscott Foundation, and I certainly didn't authorize your presence on Foundation property." She looked significantly annoyed and very haughty.

"You're right, and I apologize, sincerely. I know I've abused the kindness of a lot of people over the past few weeks. I had very good reasons, but again, it's a long story and time is of the essence if we're going to catch up with Stuart."

"Why do you keep talking about *catching up* with Stuart?" Helen asked. Her haughtiness vanished, and she shrank back against the pillows of the sofa, looking weary. "What do you think happened here tonight, for God's sake?"

A tremor of foreboding shivered down Jimmy's spine. "I assumed that Stuart had decided to cut his losses and make a run for it. After the phone call from Anya, he must have realized we were about to blow the lid on his illegal activities."

"So that's what that phone call was all about," Helen said. "He refused to tell me. Said there wasn't time." Her expression softened into deeper sadness. "The poor, foolish man. All this agony over a few legal difficulties."

She lifted her gaze to Jimmy's, and he saw that she was crying. "You haven't understood what happened here tonight, Jimmy. Stuart hasn't made a run for it, unless you want to say he's made the ultimate escape. Stuart committed suicide."

For several seconds, Jimmy had anticipated what Helen was going to say, but he still felt his stomach turn over at her words.

"I'm sorry for your loss," he said. He could offer that

much sympathy with perfect honesty, even though he couldn't pretend that he mourned Stuart's death.

"I don't want your condolences." Helen's response was tart. "Presumably, your investigation drove him to it, so I hope you're satisfied with the result."

Jimmy wasn't angered by her bitterness, in part because he felt he deserved her condemnation. He didn't mourn Stuart's death, but he regretted it. His conscience would have rested more quietly if it had never happened. Marisa had pointed out that Stuart was mentally unstable, and Jimmy wondered whether, if he hadn't been so hell-bent on revenge for Carole's murder, he might have foreseen how a fragile personality like Stuart's would react to the news that investigators were closing in on him.

An odd thought sidetracked him for a moment. It was surprising how he'd misread Stuart's character, despite five weeks of close, firsthand observation. He was usually good at psyching out how the targets of his investigations would react to the threat of discovery, and he'd been so convinced Stuart would run that the possibility of suicide hadn't crossed his mind. On the other hand, he'd never before encountered a criminal who was stealing and murdering in order to provide medical care for orphans, so perhaps he shouldn't be surprised that his predictive powers hadn't been working very well in Stuart's case.

There was no point in telling Helen that she'd had a lucky escape. That the man she'd agreed to marry would have spent the next several years either in prison or, at best, in a psychiatric institution, shut up behind bars. She was no longer hysterical, but it was obvious from her kneading fingers, her continued pallor and the constant drip of tears, that she was in a state of emotional turmoil. Still, Jimmy wanted to defend himself at least to the extent of letting her know that he hadn't been harassing

Stuart over a few hundred dollars missing from petty cash.

"Tonight's events must have been devastating for you, but you should know that the crimes Stuart committed weren't trivial ones. If he hadn't chosen to end his life, he would probably have spent the next several years in prison. If it's any consolation to you at all, Stuart may have made a rational choice that he preferred death to incarceration—"

"Rational?" Helen said witheringly. "Nothing Stuart did tonight was rational." She got up and started to randomly pick up china and glass from the floor. "Do you see this incredible mess? Stuart and I did that. My last memory of him is wrestling him on the floor, squirming and panting and trying to pull the gun away from him."

"He was going to kill himself in front of you?" Jimmy was startled into tactlessness.

"I don't know. I don't think that's what he planned originally. But I guess I came back into the living room earlier than he expected, and found him with the gun. When I tried to stop him from killing himself, he went berserk. We were on the floor, wrestling for control... It was awful. We were both so determined, it was as if we were possessed. There were a couple of moments when I thought I was going to get shot trying to get the gun away from him."

Jimmy had realized there must have been a struggle, but it was shocking to visualize it, nonetheless. "You were having dinner with Stuart tonight?"

She nodded. "We'd finished dinner. Then he got a phone call, just as I was going into the shower—" A mottled flush started at her neck and crept up her face. "Stuart and I had made love," she said, avoiding Jimmy's gaze. "Afterwards...afterwards, I took a shower, while Stuart answered his phone call. Stuart knew I would take a while, because I was planning to go back to the hotel tonight and that meant I had to get dressed again. While I was fixing my hair and putting on some lip gloss, I could hear Stuart moving around in here. After a while, I realized he was at his desk, writing.''

She broke off, and looked down at her hands as if surprised to find them empty. Her gaze roamed the room, a touch of her former wildness returning. ''His letter...where is it? I was carrying it. I had it in my hand, I know I did...''

Jimmy remembered the piece of paper she'd been clutching when he first arrived. Vaguely, he recalled seeing it flutter to the ground when she fainted. ''Calm down,'' he said, blocking her path so she couldn't start running around the room again. ''You dropped it outside, I think. Don't worry, I'll find it.''

He stepped outside, glad to draw some fresh air into his lungs after the oppressive emotional overcharge of the cottage interior. The night was cold but calm, and the note Helen dropped had drifted up against the side of the house. It lay there, a patch of crumpled white in the surrounding darkness.

Jimmy decided to read it before going back into the cottage, since there was no point in upsetting Helen Wainscott by reading it while she watched.

Dearest Helen. I tried to do good, to bring happiness and heal suffering, but the world wouldn't let me. Now, because of my efforts, I have no choices left except prison or death. I choose death.

    I will always love you, and I hope you will think of me with love, despite what I am about to do. Stuart.

Helen took the note from him, when he went back inside. She read it through again, her expression inscrutable, then she turned away from Jimmy, holding it against her chest.

"He finally grabbed the gun and ran out of the cottage," she said, not turning around. "I ran after him, but I was wearing stupid high-heel shoes and I couldn't keep up with him. It was dark, but I could see him in the distance, and hear him crashing through the undergrowth.

"He went into the lake. There's a shelf of shallow water that stretches out for about a foot before it drops off, precipitously. Stuart walked into the lake, and then he shot himself."

She turned around, her face ravaged. "I saw him fall in. I ran down to the shore, but it was hopeless. The water is black as ink, and fathoms deep in the spot he chose. I was too late. He was gone."

She'd told him that she didn't want his sympathy, but Jimmy couldn't help offering it. Most people didn't have to observe the gruesome death of even one person they loved. In her relatively short life, she'd already been forced to watch two loved ones die.

"I'm sorry," he said. "Helen, I'm really sorry."

She turned away again. "You'd better call the police. There's nothing more for us to do here."

Twenty-One

Through a haze of sleep, Marisa heard the ring of her apartment doorbell. Struggling to the surface of her dream, she sat up straighter in the chair and glanced at the clock above the TV. Four a.m. She'd been reading while waiting for Jimmy, but the last time she'd looked at the clock, it had been half-past midnight. She must have dropped off to sleep several hours ago.

Yawning, she pushed herself out of the chair and retrieved her book from the floor. Her muscles felt stiff and uncoordinated, and she shook herself, arms flailing, as she padded barefoot to the door.

Jimmy waited on the other side.

She smiled drowsily, the mists of sleep still swirling around her. "You've shaved off your beard."

"Yeah. I decided it was time to put Jimmy the janitor to rest."

"I never knew you were so handsome under the fuzz." Marisa ran her hand over his freshly shaved chin, letting her fingers trail along his jawbone until she touched his mouth. "Although I have to say, I'd begun to get quite attached to those weird little sprouts that stuck out every which way."

"Keep running your hand over my skin like that, and they just may spontaneously re-erupt."

She smiled, although the flash of desire she felt was

unexpected. A few seconds ago, she'd felt sleepy and a little bit flighty because their pursuit of Stuart was—hopefully—over. Now she discovered that with Jimmy, sexual tension always lurked no more than a millimeter beneath the surface.

"You should come in," she said. "It's cold out here at this time of night. Or rather, morning."

Jimmy stepped into the apartment. "You said to stop by whatever time I finished at Stuart's place, and I took you at your word."

"I'm really glad you did, although you must be exhausted."

"I'm better than I was thirty minutes ago. I detoured via my apartment and took a shower. Shaved off my beard. Found clean clothes." He gave a ghost of a smile. "Before the shower, I was catatonic. Now I'm inching toward comatose."

"Would a cola help? Coffee? Tea? Food?"

He shook his head. "I'm just about cola-ed and coffee-ed out." He caught her as she went past and folded her into his arms, sighing with relief as he rested his chin on top of her head. "You feel wonderful. It's been a rough night."

He didn't say that he needed to hold her to bring perspective back into his world, but Marisa could see that he was emotionally drained, as well as physically exhausted.

"What happened with Stuart?" she asked. Something about Jimmy's manner suggested she wasn't about to hear good news. "Did he finally confess? Has he been arrested?"

"None of the above." Beneath her cheek she felt the vibrations, as Jimmy drew in a ragged breath. "Unfortunately, I arrived too late to talk to him. He killed himself before I ever got to the cottage.''

"He committed suicide? Oh, no! I'm really sorry, Jimmy.'' Marisa had never warmed to Stuart, even before she learned the true measure of the man. Nevertheless, she felt a powerful wave of regret at the news of his death. Not only for the loss of a human life, but also because she knew that with Stuart gone, Jimmy would never be able to find closure in regard to his sister's death. Jimmy had been looking forward to the day when he would be able to tell his niece, Molly, that her mother hadn't been careless, hadn't neglected to fix the brakes on her car, hadn't thrown away her life in an accident that could have been avoided. But with Stuart dead, the chance of proving murder vanished. Jimmy would always have to live with a tiny niggle of doubt. Had Stuart really murdered Carole and the two women from Kosovo? Or were all three deaths a coincidence, as the police investigators insisted?

Frustrated by her inability to find the right words of comfort, she simply held Jimmy close. "Stuart wasn't a good man, but I'm still sad that it ended this way. If only Anya hadn't made that phone call! Were you the person who found him? That must have been terrible.''

"No, I didn't find him. Helen Wainscott was already at the cottage when I arrived. In fact, Stuart's body hasn't been discovered yet.''

"What?'' Marisa stared at him.

"That's part of the reason I'm so late. The police were hoping they'd be able to find him without calling in a special team, so I've been hanging around, doing what I could. Helen's pretty much a basket case at this point. In the end, the police couldn't find the body, so they gave up and went home an hour ago. I did, too. Helen's at the

Alpine Lodge. The cops rustled up some sleeping pills, so with any luck, she's sleeping.''

Marisa was astonished by Jimmy's attitude. Why wasn't he expressing any doubts about Stuart's death, given that no body had been found? Had he explained to the police that there were grounds to doubt Stuart's sudden, convenient attack of suicidal intent?

"Good grief, are you sure he's dead?" she asked. "Why is everyone so willing to believe he committed suicide, if nobody's seen the body? It sounds like a scam to me. The police need to consider the possibility that Stuart may be buying himself some extra time to get out of Denver and escape the consequences of what he's done. Faking his own death is just the sort of thing I'd expect from him."

"You're right, it's what I would have expected, too, but this isn't a scam. I'm not believing he's dead just because I read his suicide note." Jimmy folded her head back against his chest, stroking his hand slowly through her hair. "Helen Wainscott saw him do the deed, and it seems to have been pretty gruesome. Apparently, he ran out into Alpine Lake, shoved a gun into his mouth, pulled the trigger and toppled into the water, dead."

For a moment, Marisa couldn't speak. "That's the pits, Jimmy. How could he have done something that cruel to Helen? She's the woman he was planning to marry, for God's sake.''

"I don't think Stuart planned for her to see him die but he was desperate and Helen was chasing after him. You should see the living room in the cottage—it's a total wreck. Helen was wrestling with him for possession of the gun, and it looks like they really fought for it, tooth and nail. He was determined to die, and she tried like hell to save him. But he was stronger, obviously, and so, in the end, he won.''

Marisa shivered. ''Suicide is not only cruel, it's such a cowardly way out. Poor Helen. A week ago she was planning her wedding. Now she has to make arrangements for a funeral service, and there isn't even a body.''

''There isn't a body right now, but there should be one soon. The police have sent to Denver for a special rescue unit that's equipped to dive in very cold temperatures, and the team is expected to arrive by mid-morning. The lake is deep, and the water's mostly snowmelt, but the police don't anticipate any problems finding the body. We know exactly where Stuart went into the water, and the currents aren't really strong. They're optimistic they'll have him within four or five hours.''

''Helen was able to show the exact place on the lakeshore to the police?'' Marisa asked, torn between not wanting to hear too many vivid details, and needing to know what had happened.

''Yes. She was chasing Stuart all the way down to the lake, trying to stop him, so she knew exactly where he'd fallen in, even though she couldn't get to him in time.''

''This is getting worse and worse,'' Marisa said. ''Helen Wainscott is just about the last woman I ever expected to feel sorry for, but she's had a rough time of it, hasn't she? First she watches her sister bleed to death from a botched abortion, now she has to stand by and watch her fiancé—''

She shivered. ''Damn the man, anyway. His life was a mess, so why should his death be any less messy?''

Jimmy's mouth turned down in wry agreement. ''And now you and the rest of the Refuge staff are going to be left scrambling to pick up the pieces. Once word of Stuart's death leaks out, the Refuge staff will have to field a lot of inquiries. The local media will definitely call, since Stuart's something of an icon. Maybe even the national media, since he played such an important role on several national charity boards.''

She might even hear from the Coalition Service for Adoption Providers, Marisa thought. It was their annual board meeting that Stuart had supposedly been attending when Carole, Ardita and Darina all died.

''I guess I'll have to go in to the office,'' she said. ''Not only is it going to be hectic, it's also going to be really stressful for the expectant moms. They all adore Stuart, which isn't really surprising since he went out of his way to make each of them feel that he was their single best friend in the entire world. Anyway, I'll call the counselors first thing after breakfast and see if either of them can come in to help out.'' She shook her head. ''Jeez, what a mess.''

''A royal mess,'' Jimmy agreed, releasing his hold on her and crossing to the balcony doors. ''Given the mass confusion that you'll most likely be coping with, you should probably try to grab another few hours of sleep. You're going to need all the energy you can muster.''

Marisa followed his gaze outside, where the first flush of dawn already tinted the sky with soft pink light. Her mouth was suddenly dry. ''What about you?'' she asked. ''What are your plans for the rest of the night?''

He turned and gave her a friendly smile. ''If you don't mind, I'll bunk down on one of your living room chairs. I drove your car here, so I don't have my bike, and I have no enthusiasm for a five-mile hike back to my apartment right now. When you go in to the office tomorrow—later on today—I'll hitch a ride. I guess one of my tasks for Sunday morning had better be to rent a car.

Obviously, I'm going to need transportation for the next few days.''

"My living room chairs don't make very comfortable beds. I'm speaking from experience, since I just dozed off in one of them."

"I've slept in worse places."

His smile was friendly, but his body language betrayed him. It was costing him quite a bit to pretend that the thought of sharing her bed hadn't entered his head.

"I'm glad you're going to stay here for what's left of the night," she said. "I know you're grieving. With Stuart gone, you've lost the chance to find out exactly how your sister was killed."

Something in her tone of voice, something beyond mere sympathy, made his head jerk up. He looked at her through narrowed eyes. "It's not a night I'd choose to be alone," he agreed evenly.

She didn't plan how she would respond to him—the words just came. "Then don't be alone."

He went very still. "Are you inviting me into your bed, Marisa?"

She felt as if a yawning pit had opened at her feet and she'd voluntarily jumped into it. "Yes, I do believe I am." She gave a surprised laugh. "Fancy that."

Instead of crossing the room and taking her into his arms, he turned away, staring once again at the rosy-hued sky. "I want to make love to you, Marisa. I want that more than I've wanted anything for a very long time. But I can wait. When we do finally make love, you have to be absolutely sure. No looking at me and remembering Evan. No doubts about this being the right thing for Spencer. No hesitations."

"I'm sure, Jimmy." All at once, the confidence that

she was doing the right thing was bone deep. "I have no doubts. This is what I want to do."

He turned around, his eyes dark, intense. He didn't approach her. "Then come to me."

She walked slowly toward him. He didn't say anything as he watched her cross the room, but the leashed heat that emanated from him made her body yearn.

She didn't stop until she was inches away from him. Tension coiled in her stomach, tautened her spine. "Make love to me, Jimmy."

He gave a long sigh. Murmuring something incoherent, he put his arms around her and drew her hard against him. His hands twined in her hair, and she felt the wild beat of her pulse throbbing against his mouth. Then he found her lips and rational thought fled, as he kissed and stroked her body into a liquid slipstream of longing.

It was hours, or maybe only seconds, before he swept her into his arms, carrying her into the bedroom. But when they reached her bed and they'd shed their clothes he suddenly stopped.

Dazed, Marisa looked from him to the bed. "What's wrong?"

"Nothing's wrong, but it's been a difficult day for you. If you feel circumstances pressured you into this—" He stumbled to a halt, then started over. "If you want to just sleep, we can do that, too."

She laughed, a soft laugh of wonder and delight, because he'd asked, and because she was so sure that she didn't want him to stop. "You can't imagine how little I feel in the mood for sleeping right now."

His body relaxed slightly. "That's the best news I've heard in the past decade or two. And be warned—that was positively my last effort to play the gentleman."

She touched her hand to his face. "And that's the best news *I've* heard in the past decade or two."

He looked down at her, laughter fading. "Did I ever mention that you're beautiful when you smile?"

Unaccountably, she felt the prick of tears. "I believe you did. A couple of times, in fact."

He stanched the tears with his thumb. "You're beautiful when you cry, too." He kissed her. "I love you, Marisa."

I love you, too, Jimmy. She couldn't say the words. Not quite. Not yet.

If Jimmy was disappointed by her silence, he didn't show it. he reached out and pulled her close, and she cuddled beside him. Then she lay back against the pillows and, when he took her into his arms, she started to tremble. Not with fear that she was doing the wrong thing, but with longing.

After Evan, she had thought that making love would be difficult to the point of impossibility, that she would never again be able to trust her instincts, or allow herself to find pleasure in a physical act that had led to such devastating emotional betrayal. But she quickly discovered that the pyrotechnics Evan had been able to ignite in her had been empty displays of flash and glitter. She wondered how she had ever mistaken those technically perfect gymnastics for lovemaking. All she and Evan had ever shared was fireworks, with no meaning beyond the drama of the show.

With Jimmy, she felt a new and unsettling combination of tenderness and stark physical need. Her body ached with something hotter and sweeter than mere desire, and the completion she craved was more than a physical spasm of nerve endings. But the flash and glitter were there, too. So was the magic, stronger and more powerful than ever. She felt like quicksilver in Jimmy's hands, reshaping herself at his touch, the shining silver thread of pleasure growing brighter and stronger.

The pressure built, and she strained toward it, wanting to hold onto this sensation for ever, writhing because she couldn't bear the sensation to last a split second longer. For one moment more, Jimmy held her poised on the edge of the precipice. Then he murmured her name, and she tumbled over the edge.

Marisa woke to the aroma of brewing coffee and the sound of Spencer's laughter. Tying her robe, she pursued the smell of coffee into the kitchen. Spencer was in his high chair, eating dry Cheerios and drinking milk. He greeted her with a happy wave and a babble of chatter.

Jimmy was pouring out a mug of coffee. "Great timing," he said, adding milk and handing the mug to her. "Here you go. Would you like some cereal? Toast? You also have bagels in the freezer, but no cream cheese, as far as I can see."

She took the mug and cradled it in her hands, chasing away the morning chill. "You're obnoxiously cheerful for this ungodly hour."

He sent her a smile that electrified her clear through to her bones. "I figure I have lots to be cheerful about." He bent down and kissed the exact spot on her neck that was guaranteed to curl her toes. "Good morning. I can see that before breakfast isn't your very best time of day."

"When I was a teenager, my sister never spoke to me until noon. Trust me, Belle is a smart woman."

"I'm a doomed man," Jimmy said. "I even find you cute when you're grouchy."

The ring of the phone saved her from a reply. "Hello," she answered.

"Marisa? This is Helen Wainscott."

"Ms. Wainscott." Marisa paused a moment to gather her thoughts. With the wound of Stuart's death so raw, she didn't want to hurt Helen by saying the wrong thing. "I've heard the sad news about Stuart. Please accept my sincere condolences."

"Thank you." As was only to be expected, Helen's voice was somewhat shaky. "I didn't get much sleep last night, so I lay awake considering my options. The most important thing I realized is that the Wainscott Refuge is both my father's legacy and my sister's memorial. I'm determined not to allow Stuart's suicide to bring scandal and ruin to something entirely good and wonderful."

"I'm sure everyone on staff agrees with you, Ms. Wainscott. You can count on all of us to work hard to see that things run as smoothly as possible until you can hire a new executive director."

"Thank you. Whatever else Stuart may have done wrong, he certainly seemed to have the knack for finding dedicated employees. It's this question of finding a replacement director that's the reason for my call."

Helen gave an audible sigh. "As you can imagine, this doesn't promise to be a very pleasant day for me, so rather than sit in my room at the Alpine Lodge, worrying, I've decided to go in to the Refuge today and get a head-start on arranging a memorial service for his colleagues. It could be weeks before we can recruit the right person to take over Stuart's job, and in the meantime, it makes sense for me to act as the interim director. What I lack in experience, I can certainly make up for in determination to see that the Wainscott Refuge continues to provide the benefits and services that my father planned. As I said before, I refuse to see his legacy squandered."

"I understand exactly how you feel." Marisa admired Helen's ability to pick herself up and carry on in the face of real tragedy. "It would be great if you could come in today, Ms. Wainscott. If you're sure you feel up to it?"

"Please, why don't you call me Helen? Too much formality seems a little foolish when we're hoping to be working closely together for the next several weeks. Actually, what I was hoping was that you'd be willing to come in to the Refuge today and give me a quick rundown of the most important matters that need attention."

"Why, of course. I was planning to come in, anyway." Marisa stopped abruptly, deciding it wouldn't be tactful to mention the anticipated onslaught of media attention. "I'll be happy to help in any way I can. Unfortunately, since I'm such a newcomer myself, I'm afraid there will be quite a lot of things we're learning together."

"Well, at least you know your way around the filing system."

Helen was obviously unaware of the irony of her remark, but Marisa felt a twinge of guilt, anyway.

"Could you meet me at the Refuge at eleven o'clock?" Helen continued. "Is that too early? I'd like to call a meeting of the residents, and any staff who happen to be on hand, so that I can tell them personally about Stuart's death."

Marisa supposed there was no better way to ensure that all the expectant moms heard the truth, unpleasant though it might be. The inevitable wild rumors would undoubtedly be circulating soon enough, and there was no need for Refuge residents and staff to add fuel to the fire.

"I'll meet you at the Refuge, right around eleven," she said. "And, Helen, I'm truly sorry for your loss."

* * *

Even before Stuart's death, Helen had been fashionably emaciated. When Marisa met her at the Refuge later that morning, she looked skeletal, as if the trauma of the preceding night had sucked away what little flesh and blood she carried between her bones and her pale skin. Her eyes appeared sunken, and the shadows beneath them were so dark that they looked like bruises. She was, however, immaculately groomed, and since she'd chosen to wear stark, unrelieved black, her outfit for once seemed understated and elegant.

"I thought it would be a good idea if I spoke to the residents right before lunch, when they're all in the dining room," she said, after she and Marisa had exchanged greetings. "If any of the young women go to church, they should be back by noon. Is there some system for informing all the girls that they need to come out of their rooms and assemble in a general meeting place?"

"Only the emergency warning siren. But it's no problem. Jimmy's here, looking after Spencer for me. He can go room to room, informing all the moms-to-be that you want to speak to them."

"Speaking of Jimmy Griffin, I was not pleased when I discovered last night that he had been working here under false pretenses. He insists that you knew nothing of his masquerade. Is that true, Marisa?"

"Absolutely true," she said. "I was as angry as you must have been when I first realized that he'd been deceiving us all. The fact that he wasn't mentally handicapped bothered me a lot, because he played on our sympathies."

"I'm glad to hear you feel that way. I do, too." They were in Stuart's office, and Helen wandered over to the window, looking across the grounds to the guest cottage.

"The police have been working for three hours already," she said. "The divers are coming back to the truck. Look, can you see them?"

"Yes, I can. But maybe it's not a good idea for you to watch—"

"So many lies," Helen murmured. "So much dishonesty. Where did it all begin, do you think?"

Marisa debated whether to give her honest opinion, and then decided that Helen couldn't possibly be hurt by the truth any more than she had been already. "I think Stuart's mind must have snapped under the pressure of all the suffering he was forced to observe when he worked for the United Nations. He saw some atrocities that would have been enough to turn the strongest stomach. After that, he must have felt that any action on his part was justifiable as long as he didn't have to watch babies starving, and children hobbling about on one leg because they'd lost the other to a land mine."

"You're probably right, although I think it was even earlier." Helen tore her gaze away from the cottage, and from the divers, who seemed to have returned to the truck for a break and some refreshment. "It seems almost indecent that they're out there drinking coffee and eating doughnuts, while Stuart's body is waiting to be discovered."

Helen's thoughts had obviously taken a turn toward the morbid, and Marisa made a determined effort to steer them in a more positive direction. With a little chivvying from her, Helen managed to push her depression aside, and when the residents all finally got back from church, Helen delivered a simple and moving explanation of Stuart's death. Most of the girls were in tears, but Helen managed to offer comfort without getting maudlin, and she coped admirably with the torrent of questions, only rarely seeming overwhelmed by the variety of foreign accents and inner-city dialects.

Jimmy was waiting in the corridor, when Marisa and Helen finally left the dining room. His expression was so grim that Marisa knew he had bad news to report.

"Sgt. Flynn and another police officer arrived while you were talking to the residents, Ms. Wainscott. I showed them in to Stuart's office. They said they needed to speak with you urgently."

Helen was grief-stricken, but she was no fool. Her hand flew to the single strand of pearls at her throat. Her eyes were enormous. "Have they..." She swallowed and tried again. "Have they found Stuart's body?"

"I think the police sergeant wants to talk with you himself," Jimmy said gently.

Helen hurried back to the office, Marisa following in her wake.

"Sgt. Flynn." She'd apparently met the detective before, and she nodded to him in greeting.

"Ms. Wainscott." The detective inclined his head, sending her a look of deep sympathy. "Ms. Wainscott, I have to report that my dive team has been successful. They just retrieved the body of Mr. Stuart Frieze. As you reported, he'd been shot through the head."

"No!" Helen gave an anguished cry, as if—somehow—until this moment she'd been hoping to hear that it was all a mistake. That Stuart wasn't dead. That there had been no hideous tumble into the lake.

"I'm afraid there's no mistake, ma'am. The divers are back down in the lake now, looking for his gun." Sgt. Flynn cleared his throat, and his gaze slid sideways, fixing with relief on Jimmy Griffin.

"There are a lot of fish in the lake, and there's been some...destruction of facial tissue. I will have to ask for an official identification. Since you've worked here for the past five weeks, would you be able to make a positive ID, do you think?"

Marisa saw Helen sway on her feet. "Catch her!" she yelled.

Jimmy stepped forward just in time to prevent Helen falling to the floor in a dead faint.

Twenty-Two

Helen quickly recovered from her faint, and refused all offers to call for medical assistance. She was eventually persuaded to go back to the Alpine Lodge for a rest, but only after she'd drawn Marisa and Jimmy aside, out of earshot of Sgt. Flynn, in order to request their presence in her hotel suite later on that afternoon.

"You're the only two people in the world who have an overview of what Stuart was doing here at the Refuge. I need to know everything you've learned, so that I can be prepared to handle any rumors that might start to leak out within the next few days. From the little Jimmy told me last night when he was attempting to justify his undercover activities, it seems there may be any number of people willing to jump out of the woodwork and hurl accusations, now that Stuart is no longer with us and able to defend himself."

Helen's fingers kneaded restlessly with the button at the waist of her jacket. "I can't be caught napping. I feel I've been derelict in my duties because I allowed Stuart to blind me with his personal charisma, and I don't want to compound my mistakes by refusing to confront just how much damage he's done to the Refuge."

"At least I haven't uncovered any evidence that Stuart stole **Refuge funds**," Jimmy said.

Helen stared at him in bewilderment. "How could you

have found any irregularities in the accounts? It would take hours—days—of concentrated searching to go through the financial records of the Refuge.''

''But the accounts were all computerized,'' Jimmy explained patiently. ''I downloaded the entire contents of Stuart's hard drive, and then simply worked on the accounting files at night, in my apartment.''

''I suppose it's some small relief to know that the accounts pass muster.'' A mottled flush crept up Helen's neck, and she avoided their gaze as she continued. ''Still, I can't be blind to my own failings. I have a lot of regrets about my recent conduct. The board trusted me to keep a strict personal eye on activities here, and I allowed Stuart to charm me into a lack of vigilance. I can't fail the board again, or my father, or my sister's memory. I need you to be absolutely honest with me about how much damaging fallout there's likely to be in regard to Stuart's activities at the Refuge. I'm going to have to call in auditors, despite Mr. Griffin's hope that funds haven't been compromised. Naturally, I'd like to know in advance what they might find.''

Marisa and Jimmy both attempted to dissuade her from tackling more problems in the immediate aftermath of Stuart's death, but Helen remained adamant. ''No, I want to hear from the pair of you this afternoon. Frankly, I think I'm entitled to at least that much, after the tragic events of last night. After all, let's be brutally honest about this. You owe me. If you'd handled the situation more adroitly, Stuart wouldn't have learned that his crimes were about to be exposed in such a shocking and unexpected way. In which case, we can assume, he would be alive today.''

Leaving Jimmy and Marisa to stew over this parting

zinger, Helen accepted a ride back to the Alpine Lodge with one of the police officers.

"Phew! I see that Helen is a woman who doesn't mind piling on the guilt," Jimmy said, casting a rueful glance at her departing back.

"Is she right?" Marisa asked. "Are we responsible for what happened?"

"Of course not," Jimmy said. "Put that overactive conscience of yours to rest. Stuart killed himself, and we'd have stopped him if we possibly could. The choice to die was his, not ours."

"Yes, but we were so focused on finding his offshore bank statements that we didn't stop to consider how Anya would react, or what she might do. Stuart was her lover, her protector and the father of her child. We forced our way into the house—probably the only real home she's ever known—told her Stuart was a murderer, then paid her absolutely no attention whatsoever. I even left her to supervise Spencer, for heaven's sake!"

"You're right, we screwed up where Anya's concerned. Would I handle things differently if I had to do them over? Absolutely. Does that mean we forced Stuart to kill himself? No, not by a long shot. He killed himself because he had committed so many crimes that he couldn't see any other way to avoid the consequences."

Marisa envied Jimmy's ability to make clear-cut moral judgments. Her own nagging conscience always had to be wrestled into silence. "I want to believe you're right, Jimmy."

He crooked his finger under her chin and tilted her head back so that she was looking straight into his eyes. "Then trust my judgment on this. You have nothing to feel guilty about, Marisa. Anya had been missing for days, and we found her hidden in a house that nobody knew Stuart owned. We were afraid Stuart might kill her. Remember that? We had an obligation to warn her.''

Looking at him, the weight of doubt lifted. ''You're right. It would have been all too easy for Stuart to arrange another accident, just like he did with Darina and Ardita, and nobody would have been any the wiser. Anya needed to know that she was at risk.''

''You've got it.'' He kissed her lightly. ''That's my girl.''

His kiss warmed her clear through to her toes. Was she *his girl?* The idea didn't feel nearly as strange as it would have only two days earlier. She pushed the thought aside to be considered later, and asked another question. ''Speaking of Anya, did you manage to reach Reg and tell him what happened?''

''Yeah, I called him from your apartment this morning, while you were in the shower. He said that, having worked with Stuart on the United Way board, he would never have figured him for the suicidal type.''

Marisa shrugged. ''But then, if there's one thing that's clear about Stuart, it's that nobody had any real grasp of his true character, or the demons that drove him. How is Anya coping with the news of Stuart's death? I imagine she's pretty much shattered.''

''Anya still hadn't gotten up, when I talked to Reg. We agreed that we'd be in touch again later today. It's a fair guess that she's going to take it hard. Despite all the rational evidence to the contrary, the poor kid really did believe the guy was going to marry her.''

Sgt. Flynn poked his head around the door. ''Whenever you're ready, Mr. Griffin, we'd like for you to make an official identification of the deceased.''

Jimmy drew in a deep breath. ''I'll be right there.''

''Thank you. The medical examiner's van is parked in

the driveway of Mr. Frieze's cottage.'' The sergeant's radio crackled, and he backed out of the office, excusing himself.

"I guess I should start walking over to the cottage," Jimmy said. "No point in putting it off."

"Are you okay with making the identification?" Marisa asked. She suppressed a shudder at an involuntary image of how Stuart's face might look after his night floating with the fishes.

"I'd prefer not to have to do it. But better me than Helen."

There was no arguing with that. "What are you planning to do about Helen's royal command to present ourselves at the hotel this afternoon?" Marisa asked.

"We should go," Jimmy said. "Or, at least, I should go. Helen's right that I need to fill her in on everything we know about Stuart. I owe her that much. You, on the other hand, don't owe her anything, and you already look beaten up. Do you really need to put yourself through a grueling session with Helen Wainscott? I imagine it's not going to be a pleasant couple of hours."

Marisa considered for a moment, then nodded her head. "Yes, I need to be there. I can leave Spencer with Elsa, so he won't be a distraction while we're trying to talk. And Helen did ask both of us to come. Apart from anything else, I think it might make it easier for her if I'm there. She's still harboring quite a lot of resentment against you for getting yourself hired under false pretenses."

The phone rang before Marisa could say anything more, and it turned out to be the first of several requests for information from the media. Jimmy left to identify Stuart's remains, and the day resumed its frenetic pace. By two-thirty, Marisa had taken phone calls from every

TV station in Denver, as well as the major newspapers in Denver and Boulder. On hearing confirmation that Stuart was indeed dead, everyone expressed regret at the loss of a man they invariably referred to as "remarkable."

Stuart was certainly remarkable in his capacity to deceive everyone, Marisa thought with a touch of acerbity. The more other people praised him, the more she found her own attitude toward him hardening into hostility.

The phone rang yet again. A woman named Barb Burdine identified herself as the executive secretary of CoSaP, the Coalition Service for Adoption Providers. Marisa's pulse rate speeded up a little when she realized she was talking to the woman who would have recorded the minutes of the meetings Stuart was supposed to have been attending when Carole Riven died.

Barb Burdine had heard the news of Stuart's suicide from one of the Refuge trustees who happened to be a personal friend. Marisa answered the executive secretary's questions with her usual sanitized account of Stuart's death, and listened to the inevitable expression of sorrow on the loss of such a remarkable man.

Just as the secretary was about to hang up, Marisa decided that she couldn't let this opportunity pass. "Miss Burdine, everyone here at the Refuge really appreciates your expressions of sympathy. I wonder if you could help me with an administrative problem? As you can imagine, there are a lot of loose ends for me to tidy up in regard to Stuart's affairs, and some questions have arisen regarding his attendance at CoSaP's last board meeting."

"I can't imagine how I could help to resolve any of those questions, or why they would be important at this point, but I'm willing to give it my best shot."

There was no way to make her questions sound reasonable, so Marisa didn't try to invent plausible excuses.

She just asked. "I need to know if you have any way to check whether or not Stuart was actually present at those meetings," she said.

"He most certainly was. CoSaP is an umbrella organization, you understand, and I'm the only permanent staff member. I take the minutes of all board meetings, and maintain all the records, so I can assure you Stuart was there."

"Did he leave the room where you were holding the meetings for an extended period of time? Did he receive phone calls that he chose to take? Was there anything at all unusual about his conduct during the meetings?"

"None of the above. Stuart, as always, provided really valuable insights into some of the difficult issues that were raised. We're trying to get more widespread consensus within the adoption movement on the knotty issue of interracial adoption, and with his experience overseas, combined with his experiences at the Refuge, Stuart's contribution was especially invaluable. As for his attendance, he not only stayed through the actual board meeting, he also delivered two seminars at the conference that followed. He was also present at the dinner the night before the board meetings started, as well as the luncheons we arranged with some very interesting guest speakers, one of whom was a senior ambassador with the United Nations and a personal friend of Stuart's. In sum, Stuart would undoubtedly have to be considered the central figure at CoSaP's last board meeting."

"Thank you for sharing this with me, Ms. Burdine. I really appreciate the information."

The secretary hesitated for a moment. "I'm sure you know that there are a lot of rumors flying around. Stuart hasn't been dead twenty-four hours, and I've already heard that some irregularities have been discovered in the way the Wainscott Refuge has been run over the past few years. I'm not sure I believe the rumors, but whatever may have happened in Wainscott, from our point of view here at CoSaP, Stuart's wisdom will be sorely missed.''

Another jewel for the crown of Saint Stuart. Thanking the secretary again, Marisa hung up the phone, feeling mildly depressed. Somewhere at the back of her mind, she'd hoped to find out something new about Stuart's actions during the period of Carole's death. Something that she could take to Jimmy and say, *Look, here's the proof you wanted. Stuart killed your sister, along with Ardita and Darina.*

Instead, she'd confirmed that Stuart had been an active participant in the CoSaP conference. Which didn't mean that he was innocent of Carole's murder, of course. He could have hired somebody to push her car off the road, just as he could have hired somebody to stick a needle into Ardita's arm and stretch out Darina's body behind the garbage truck. But Marisa found it just a little surprising that Stuart had managed to contribute so much to the CoSaP meeting when his mind must have been full to bursting with worries about the triple murder he'd planned.

It was now almost two-forty. If she and Jimmy were going to be at the Alpine Lodge by three, as Helen had requested, they'd need to leave within the next five minutes. Marisa shut down her computer and went into Stuart's old office, where Jimmy had appropriated the desk and was attempting to make some small restitution for his undercover activities by cross-checking the Refuge accounts against the statements in Stuart's secret banking records.

Seeing Jimmy seated behind the impressive cherry-wood desk, working with fierce concentration at the computer, Marisa was struck by how at home he looked surrounded by the trappings of an executive office. It was hard to detect even a trace of Jimmy the janitor in this focused, high-intensity man.

Until he looked up at her and smiled. Then her stomach performed its standard lurch, and her heartbeat speeded up. She remembered how he'd looked in bed last night as they made love, and heat flashed through her body. "How's it going?" she asked, trying to sound brisk.

"Pretty well, except for the boredom factor, and that just took a giant turn for the better." He stood up and put his arms around her waist, resting his head against her forehead. "How about you?"

"Denver's movers and shakers are calling to express their regrets—a nice excuse for pumping me about the lurid rumors they're hoping I'll confirm."

He grimaced. "You'd better be prepared for a lot more of the same for the next several days. These are going to be rumors with legs."

"Anything in the accounts for Helen to worry about?"

"Not in anything I've unraveled to this point. So far, it seems that Stuart was smart enough not to mess with Refuge money." Jimmy's voice was tinged with cynicism. "He figured out that board members were more likely to notice faulty accounts than residents who were being exploited."

"At least we won't have to wake up to headlines screaming 'Charity Robbed of Thousands.' Did you get in touch with Reg again? How's Anya coping with the news that Stuart's dead?"

"Oops, I'm glad you reminded me. I've been so caught up in the accounts, I forgot to call back." Jimmy picked up the phone and dialed, pulling a face when he got the answering machine.

"Reg, this is Jimmy. If you're there, pick up, will you? Marisa and I are worried about Anya. How's she doing—"

The phone was picked up. "Jimmy, hey, I was two minutes away from calling you. Jesus, it's been a hell of a day here."

"Marisa's in the room with me, Reg. I'm putting you on the speaker so she can hear. What's up?"

"The short answer is that Anya ran away."

Over the phone, Marisa heard the drag of breath as Reg inhaled cigarette smoke.

"Oh, my God! I'm sorry," Jimmy said. "We were afraid she might pull something like that when she heard that Stuart was dead—"

"Yeah, but here's the real surprise of it. She ran away last night, before you told me Stuart had committed suicide. Anyway, the good news is that I have her back with me already. I picked her up at the airport a couple of hours ago."

"At the airport?" Jimmy said, sending Marisa a puzzled glance.

"Where was she trying to fly to?" Marisa asked.

"Mexico. With Stuart, if you can believe it."

"Whoa, Reg, stop right there." Jimmy held up his hand. "The short version isn't working. Can you start over with the long version? This isn't making much sense."

"Ha, glad you noticed that. Trouble is, the long version doesn't make much sense, either. But here goes. I got up around seven this morning. Came downstairs. No sign of Anya—but I didn't think anything of it, even though she'd gone to bed early the night before. I took your phone call, Jimmy, then hung around for a while, expecting her to join me any minute. When she didn't, I went for a jog. I like to convince myself that the cigarettes haven't totally eaten my lung tissue, so I pound around the block a couple of times most mornings. I met a couple of friends, chatted for a while.

"When I got back, it was nine-thirty—and still no sign of Anya. I waited until ten o'clock before I knocked on her door. No reply. I finally decided she was either seriously sick, or she wasn't there. So I went into the room to find out which, and discovered the bed hadn't even been slept in."

"But how did you track her down at the airport?" Jimmy asked. "That's the last place I'd have thought of looking for her."

"She left me a note on the pillow saying thank you for my hospitality, but she didn't need me anymore. She was going to meet Stuart, who would take wonderful care of her and their baby."

"Are you telling me Stuart conned Anya into believing he would ditch Helen and set up housekeeping with her?" Jimmy glared at the phone. "Jeez, the guy was a real prince."

"Wasn't he just?" Reg's voice was untypically grim. "After I got through swearing, I decided that even a kid with brains pickled in pregnancy hormones wouldn't have been crazy enough to wander out into the night with nothing more to sustain her than a vague plan of hitching a ride to Wainscott. I figured Stuart must have made arrangements to meet her."

"But if Anya's note didn't say where she was going, why did you decide to look for her at the airport?" Marisa asked.

"A lucky hunch, with a smidgen of logical deduction

to back it up. Stuart never struck me as a bus station kind of a guy, even in an emergency. So either he planned to pick Anya up in his car, or he'd arranged a meeting place at the airport. I decided to try the airport first, mostly because it offered a better chance of success. Since Stuart killed himself around dinnertime last night, he obviously didn't keep his rendezvous with Anya. On the other hand, she hadn't come home to my place, so it was a good bet she was still hanging around the airport waiting for him.''

''And was she?'' Jimmy asked.

''She sure was. I have a friend who's a cop with the airport police. Matt Mortimer. I found his son a job when nobody else could, and he's always figured he owes me one. I called the airport. I was really in luck, because Matt was working the shift. I gave him Anya's description and asked him to see if he could find her. Sure enough, he called me back thirty minutes later to say they'd found her sitting by one of the baggage carousels, looking pretty desperate.''

''But how did she get to the airport without your knowing?'' Marisa asked Reg. ''That's quite a long haul.''

''Apparently, she waited for me to go to bed and then walked to the nearest convenience store, where she called a cab and took it to the airport. She arrived there shortly before midnight, which was an hour later than Stuart had told her to get there, but he'd also told her not to let anyone know where she was going, so it was the best she could manage. Of course, the poor kid has spent the previous twelve hours wondering if she'd arrived too late, and he'd left without her.''

Marisa felt physically sick. It was mind-blowing to think that Stuart had been so selfish that in his final minutes on earth, he'd set out to deceive Anya into thinking they were going to have a wonderful future together. And yet, this cruelty had been perpetrated by the same man who'd been playing Robin Hood, sending thousands of dollars to rescue sick and abandoned children in Africa. Marisa shook her head. Stuart's mind and motives were twisted beyond comprehension—and almost beyond belief.

"Thank God, Anya's still technically a minor for another couple of weeks," Reg said. "That gave Matt an excuse to take her into custody while he waited for me to get to the airport and pick her up. Otherwise, I'm sure she'd have given him the slip. When I got there, she was all fired up, protesting that Matt had no right to detain her. She didn't want to come home with me, even though she was visibly exhausted. She was a hundred-percent certain Stuart was going to come and get her, and they would fly off to a life together in the tropical sunshine of Rio de Janeiro—which was going to be their ultimate destination after a detour through Mexico."

Marisa found the story disquieting on a number of levels, not the least of which was that Stuart had taken the time to invent such vivid details only minutes before going for his gun and blowing his brains out. "How's Anya doing right now?" she asked.

"Not so good. She's hostile. Angry. Terrified. I didn't even tell her that Stuart's body hadn't been found, or she'd have insisted that the absence of a corpse proved he wasn't dead."

"Well, if it's any help, you can tell her the body has been found," Jimmy interjected.

"Has it? That should help. In the past thirty minutes or so, she's progressed from refusing to believe that Stuart's dead to insisting that he was murdered as the result of a foul conspiracy by his enemies."

"Some progress," Marisa muttered.

"Yeah, for Anya, I think it is."

"I guess if you're from Chechnya, it's easy to believe in foul conspiracies," Jimmy commented.

"That's true. But according to Anya, she suspects foul play, because when she called to warn Stuart that you guys were closing in on him, he didn't even mention the possibility of suicide. Stuart told her he was going to cut his losses and make a run for it. He said that he finally understood what was important in life and that he really cared about her and the baby. He wanted to make a real home for the three of them, and to hell with Helen. He said he was going to Mexico. They'd wait for their daughter to be born, and from there he planned to go on to Brazil, taking her and their baby. As far as she's concerned, that's enough to prove he was murdered. He swore he was going to meet her at the airport, and— quoting Anya—she knows he was speaking the truth. At the time she hung up the phone, she insists, Stuart had no more intention of committing suicide than she did."

"Poor kid," Jimmy said softly.

"Yeah. Life sometimes sucks." Reg paused for a moment. "To be honest, I haven't tried too hard to persuade her to face reality. The kid's going through more than she ought to be. If she wants to delude herself into believing that Stuart was planning to take her to Rio and create a home for their baby, then, as far as I'm concerned, she's entitled."

"You're right. This is a case where insisting on the truth doesn't achieve anything. I really appreciate all your help," Jimmy said. "I owe you one, Reg. A big one."

"You owe me far more than one," he responded dryly. "I figure I have markers from you going back to kindergarten when I took the rap for the wad of bubble gum stuck under Miss Percy's desk. Fortunately for you, I'm lousy at keeping score."

"That's good news, because I have another favor to ask. Could you look after Anya for another couple of days, while we make some permanent arrangements for her? Obviously, she can't come back to the Refuge. Even if she'd be willing to agree, I don't think it's a good idea to thrust her in Helen's face. I'm sure we can find a permanent solution for Anya and the baby, but it's going to take some time, and time is the one thing we don't seem to have right now."

"I'll do my best," Reg said. "I'll take her to work with me tomorrow, and see if we can't find some odd jobs around the office to keep her occupied. Now that she knows Stuart's dead, her inducement to run away should be less."

"Thanks, Reg. I really appreciate your help. All of it, from the bubble gum wad on."

When the phone call ended, Jimmy got up and went to stand at the window. "Poor Anya. So much sadness flowing from one man's actions. Stuart has a lot to answer for."

"Oddly enough, Helen said much the same thing, just this morning."

"I'm sure she wouldn't be thrilled to know our minds were running on the same track." Jimmy glanced at his watch. "We need to get going. It's after three already, and Helen will be wondering what's happened to us. Are you going to drive—or shall I, now that I have my rental car?"

"Whatever." Marisa's response was as absent as her thoughts, and Jimmy turned to her.

"What's bothering you?"

"Anya," she said at once. "Jimmy, why did Stuart lie to her? What possible advantage was there to Stuart in having Anya rush out to the airport, unless he really planned to meet her there?"

"To get her off his back," Jimmy said, after a moment. "To give himself a chance to get her off the phone without confrontation."

"I guess so." Marisa picked up her purse and started to leave the office, then swung back, bumping into Jimmy.

"No, dammit, that's not a good enough answer. If Stuart wanted to avoid an unpleasant confrontation with Anya, all he had to do was hang up the phone. Why waste time making arrangements about a specific meeting place when he had no intention of being there? Why tell her that he wanted them to be a family, if he was planning to stick his gun in his mouth the moment he hung up the phone?"

"He seems to have been a person who wanted people to like him," Jimmy suggested, as they walked out of the Refuge. "It's not out of character for him to fabricate a happy ending for Anya even though he'd already decided to kill himself. The guy was capable of convincing himself that tricking Anya was the kind thing to do. Or it's possible that he really did plan to meet Anya, but then he changed his mind."

Marisa found her sunglasses and pushed them on as they left the tree-shaded steps and entered the bright sun of the Refuge parking lot. "But when you think about it more closely, Jimmy, neither of those explanations fits the story Helen told you last night. According to Helen, she came into the living room just as Stuart was hanging up the phone. Again according to Helen, Stuart was already on the verge of a complete breakdown—practically frothing at the mouth. She asked what was wrong, and he gave her an incoherent explanation about receiving a phone call from Anya warning him that he was going to be arrested for criminal misconduct. Helen expressed horror and surprise. Then she realized he was making a beeline for the writing desk where he stored his gun. But she happened to be closer to the desk, so she managed to get there first. She grabbed it. They fought for possession. Stuart won, and ran off to the lake with Helen hot on his heels.''

Jimmy turned to look at her. ''I don't see anything in that story to contradict what Anya told Reg.''

''I disagree. If Stuart could lie to Anya convincingly enough to deceive her about his plans, why did he suddenly go berserk? What was the precipitating event, after he hung up the phone, that caused him to lose control? One minute he's arranging to meet Anya at the airport. Next thing, *boom!* In the blink of an eye, he's going for his gun.''

''The timing's a bit off in Helen's account,'' Jimmy agreed, after a slight pause. ''She probably hedged the truth a little—and it's not so surprising, if she did. She's a proud woman, engaged to a man who's just committed suicide after thoroughly screwing up the administration of her father's legacy. Probably she didn't want to admit to me or the police that she and Stuart had argued right before he decided to go for his gun. But it makes sense if they did argue. Helen knew that Anya had been reported to the police as missing from the Refuge. It's possible—almost certain, in fact—that she demanded to know what Anya was doing living in Stuart's house, and why she had Stuart's private cell phone number. If Stuart decided there was no point in hiding the truth any longer and confessed that Anya was pregnant with his child, obviously Helen would be deeply hurt.''

"Hurt?'' Marisa repeated. ''Or angry? I would expect her to be infuriated by Stuart's deception. And she doesn't strike me as the sort of woman who'd react to betrayal by crumpling in the corner and sobbing into her handkerchief. She'd lash out.''

"Either way, whether she's hurt or angry, Helen's emotional outburst was most likely the final straw for Stuart. Faced with two women making irreconcilable demands, and armed with the certain knowledge that we were closing in on him, Stuart snapped. He went running for his gun—and you know the rest.''

"Or Helen could have snapped,'' Marisa said.

For a moment, her words seemed to hang in the air between them. They'd reached Jimmy's rental car in the parking lot, but neither of them got in. They stared at each other across the hood of the gleaming new Chevy, and the silence grew heavy.

"What are you suggesting?'' Jimmy finally asked.

Marisa realized she was shivering despite the bright sun. ''I'm not sure.'' She gave an impatient toss of her head, annoyed with herself for weaseling. ''No, that's not true. I know exactly what I'm suggesting. Anya described Stuart as a man who was getting ready to run, not as a man on the brink of suicide. Helen insists he heard Anya's news and instantly snapped. Those two stories are mutually incompatible.''

"You have to consider that both Anya and Helen are

viewing last night's events through the distorting mirror of extreme stress.''

"True. But the fact is, there are only two people who know for sure what happened in Stuart's cottage last night, and one of those people is dead. Why are we trusting Helen's account of what happened in preference to Anya's?'' Marisa rubbed her forehead. "Think about it, Jimmy. Who has more incentive to lie? Anya or Helen?''

"Helen has no reason to lie...unless she's hiding something.''

"Yes. Exactly.''

They stared at each other, then both backed away from pursuing their thoughts. "Maybe neither of them is lying in the strict sense of the word,'' Jimmy said, working hard to ignore the elephant of an idea that had suddenly imposed itself between them on the parking lot. "You saw how Anya behaved when we told her Stuart was engaged to another woman. She's willfully deluded where he's concerned.''

"Even for Anya, it's pretty hard to confuse suicidal incoherence on Stuart's part with a harried, but rational, discussion of where to meet for a flight to Mexico. That wouldn't be deluded on Anya's part—that would be psychotic.''

"She's been psychologically battered for years,'' Jimmy pointed out. "It's possible she *is* clinically delusional.''

"Maybe.'' Marisa expelled an unsteady breath. "But I'm not convinced. I learned when I was dealing with Evan that if someone tells a plausible story that's convenient for him, but all the people who could contradict it are dead, then you'd be real smart to take that story with a large handful of salt.''

Jimmy's fingers beat a restless rhythm on the hood of the car. He saw what he was doing and abruptly silenced the tattoo. "Okay, I'll say it. Are we seriously considering the possibility that Helen Wainscott might have murdered Stuart Frieze?"

"I am," Marisa said. "How about you?"

Twenty-Three

They'd been driving for five minutes, and the silence in the car was beginning to feel smothering. "Helen would never be convicted in a court of law," Jimmy said, as if responding to a question Marisa had asked. "Even if she shot Stuart, there isn't a shred of forensic evidence to prove it. No DA would bring charges, and if he was crazy enough to try, a good defense attorney would drive a double-wide trailer through the holes in his case."

"That doesn't mean we shouldn't confront her," Marisa said.

"I don't know if I want to confront her." Jimmy frowned meditatively at Wainscott's only traffic light. "If Helen did kill Stuart, there's a sort of poetic justice, don't you think? He murders three women and leaves no evidence that would convict him. Now the tables are turned. Stuart himself has possibly been murdered, and there isn't a shred of evidence to convict his killer."

"What if Stuart didn't kill your sister and the other two women, though? Then it isn't poetic justice at all." Marisa twisted in her seat belt, turning to face him. "Jimmy, remember how Stuart didn't stay at the main conference hotel when he went to that CoSaP conference in Maryland? Remember how he stayed at some country inn, with Helen Wainscott?"

"Yes, of course I remember. If you draw a triangle on

the map, connecting the locations where each of the three deaths occurred, then the inn is located right at the apex of the triangle.''

"Which makes it a very convenient lodging place for anyone wanting to drive to those three locations, wouldn't you say?''

"I sure do.'' The light changed, and Jimmy carried on down Main Street.

"But Stuart didn't take advantage of the convenience,'' Marisa said. "I had a long phone conversation with Barb Burdine this afternoon. She's the executive secretary for CoSaP—''

"I recognize the name. I talked with her myself, before I came to Colorado.''

"Then she presumably told you the same thing she told me. Namely, that she could personally vouch for the fact that Stuart was an active participant in all the conference sessions, and the board meetings that preceded them. He also introduced the speaker at the formal dinner that was held the very night your sister died.''

"I know, honey, I know. But I never thought Stuart committed those three murders in person. I always assumed he simply arranged for them to take place.''

"Then why not arrange to have them take place when he was miles from Maryland?'' Marisa asked. "If Stuart wasn't actively involved—if he took no part in the actual killings—why have them coincide with his attendance at the CoSaP meeting? Why allow the risk, however minuscule, that someone might connect his presence in the area with the deaths?''

"It's a good question,'' Jimmy admitted. "I don't have an answer. Except maybe that he was so anxious to silence all three women that he couldn't afford to wait.''

"Could be.'' Marisa stared straight ahead. "Helen

wasn't at the CoSaP meetings," she said. "Think about it, Jimmy. Helen was perfectly situated to see that your sister's car was run off the road, while Stuart was dazzling everyone with his brilliance at the CoSaP banquet. Same thing with Ardita and Darina. She had plenty of time to arrange their accidents. Unlike Stuart, who was under constant observation, there was absolutely no one keeping track of Helen's movements."

Jimmy's foot jerked down on the accelerator, and the car whizzed forward. Fortunately, this was Wainscott and there was no vehicle in front of him. He brought the car under control again, and turned to look at Marisa. "You think Helen might have had a hand in *those* killings, too? Christ, Marisa, with what possible motive?"

"That's easy. If Helen and Stuart were partners in crime for the illicit activities at the Refuge, she'd have a whopper of a motive. Anything your sister uncovered about Stuart would have threatened Helen directly."

Jimmy's expression became dubious. "It's one thing to speculate that Helen got pissed off at Stuart's affair with Anya and shot him in the heat of an argument. I can buy that. Maybe. It's another thing altogether to suggest that she's capable of carrying out three premeditated murders. Besides, why would she be involved in Stuart's illicit activities at the Refuge? Why would she set out to undermine a charity set up by her father, in honor of her sister's memory?"

"You were the one who told me this was all about money," Marisa said. "Maybe Helen needed the money."

"That's not likely," Jimmy said. "It's true her father left most of his fortune in various charitable trusts, but he left her a couple of million for her own personal use.

Not much if you want to play in the sandbox with Bill Gates, but not exactly chump change, either.''

"How much is the endowment for the Refuge?'' Marisa asked. "Did you have access to those figures when you were checking Stuart's handling of the accounts?''

"Sure. The finances of the Refuge are a matter of public record. Grover Wainscott left thirty million dollars in a charitable trust to be used exclusively for the health and welfare of single mothers and orphaned children. Eight million of that is set aside in a special trust to be expended on projects other than the Refuge. Another two million dollars were spent on renovations to the original homestead, and building an addition to house the mothers-to-be. The rest is divided between a small building fund, and a large operating fund, the income from which is used to support the running of the Refuge. As you can imagine, maintaining services to twenty-four pregnant women sucks up a hefty amount of money each year.''

Marisa steepled her fingers and pressed them against her mouth. "So in a nutshell, the final score from Grover's will was as follows: single moms and orphans, thirty million bucks. Helen Wainscott, two million. I'd say that might be cause for Helen being just a tad resentful. If she invests the two million conservatively, she might be receiving an annual income of $150,000. More, if she's willing to play the stock market, of course, but then she risks losing a lot of money, too.''

"She's single, no kids. A hundred and fifty thousand smackers isn't too bad.''

Marisa turned to look at him, her smile decidedly rueful. "Jimmy, in the circles Helen moves in, a hundred and fifty thousand bucks a year is *less* than chump change. I know because I've been there. It's how I grew up.''

"I never checked out Helen's finances," Jimmy said. "I had no reason to, or so I thought. *Damn!* She was divorced a few years ago—two? three? She could have come out of that with a few extra million. Or she could have been taken to the cleaners by the senator. In which case, she just might have been desperate enough to team up with Stuart to acquire herself a little extra spending money."

"Well, I know one thing for sure. Either she got money from the divorce settlement, or she has another source of income. Because, trust me on this, Helen is not living on a hundred and fifty thousand a year. Her travel and her clothes alone cost more than that."

They had arrived at the Alpine Lodge. Jimmy parked his rental car at the entrance and handed the keys to the valet. "We're here to see Ms. Wainscott," he said to the clerk in Registration. "Could you tell me the number of her suite?"

"Your name, sir?"

"James Griffin."

The clerk examined a sheet of paper. "Yes, I see you're on her list of expected visitors. And your friend is...?"

"Marisa Joubert."

"Of course. Welcome to Alpine Lodge, Ms. Joubert. If you take the elevators at the right-hand side of the lobby, just behind the fireplace, Ms. Wainscott's suite is on the third floor. Number 300. I'll call to let her know you're on your way up."

"What are we going to do?" Marisa said, as they waited for the elevator. "Quite apart from the minor fact that I've talked myself into believing Helen may have murdered four people, she clearly isn't a fit person to be running the Refuge. There are a lot of very vulnerable women who come to the Refuge expecting to be helped. If Helen really was in cahoots with Stuart, what's to prevent her from hiring another director, someone even more corrupt this time, who'll carry on exploiting the women and selling their babies to the highest bidder? She has to be stopped.''

"I agree, but the hell of it is, we have nothing to confront her with. I spent five weeks combing the file system and the computer database of the Refuge. If Helen was involved with Stuart, she's been incredibly smart. There's not a piece of paper in the Refuge file system, not a document, not a single piece of e-mail that implicates Helen in what Stuart was doing." Jimmy paced the lobby in front of the elevators. "You know the contents of those files as well as I do, if not better. I'm not missing anything, am I?''

''No, unfortunately, you're not missing anything,'' Marisa said. They let the elevator come and go. "If we confront Helen with what we suspect, she might break down and confess. It's a slim chance, but worth taking, maybe.''

"I don't think Helen's likely to crumble just because we toss a few unsubstantiated accusations at her. The most likely outcome would be a swift call to her lawyers and the threat of a lawsuit for slander. Even though she may be emotionally off balance in the wake of Stuart's death, if she's guilty of what we suspect, she obviously has iron self-control.'' Jimmy stopped pacing long enough to draw in a deep breath. "We're going to have to fake her out.''

"Great idea,'' Marisa said. "Have you any clue, even a small one, how we might manage to do that?''

"Anya,'' he said swiftly. "She's our trump card. And we'd better take the elevator next time it comes. The clerk in Reception called to say we were on our way up five minutes ago.''

"How is Anya going to help us fake Helen out?"

They stepped into the elevator, and Jimmy pressed the button for the third floor. "We're going to claim that Stuart confided the truth to Anya, who therefore knows for a fact that Helen was Stuart's partner in crime."

Marisa brightened, but gloom returned almost at once. "It's not enough. Helen's smart. She'll clam up and say it's Anya's word against hers. Then she'll call her lawyers and threaten all three of us with a lawsuit for slander.''

Jimmy's smile was predatory. "Then we'll have to squeeze the pincers a little tighter, won't we? We'll tell her Stuart left a document in his safety deposit box detailing Helen's role in the various illicit operations they were running at the Refuge. And Anya has the key to the safety box."

"Good grief, don't say that or Anya might meet with a fatal accident!"

"Okay. Anya had the key, but she's given it to Reg, who's given it to his lawyer."

Marisa gave a sigh of relief. "Yes, that's better. Jimmy, you're a genius."

"Or at least a really creative liar," he said.

They stepped out onto the silver-green carpeting of the third floor. Suite 300 was signposted to the left. "There's still one problem," Marisa said. "Since I'm the one who started all this speculation about Helen, I feel kind of obligated to point out that we've pulled this theory more or less out of thin air. Helen might be innocent as the driven snow. In which case, we're going for the jugular on a woman who just last night had to watch her fiancé blow his head off.''

"If Helen is innocent, I think we'll soon know it, and I'll back off." Jimmy shoved his hands into his pockets, too hyped to keep them still any other way. "I pulled some amazing cases when I was with the Bureau, but if Helen really did murder my sister, I'd have to say, this is one of the most amazing."

The door to Helen's suite was already open when they reached the end of the corridor. "Come in," Helen said, walking out into the hallway to greet them. "I've been expecting you."

"We're sorry to be late," Jimmy said. "Marisa was handling phone calls up to the last moment. A lot of people are very concerned about Stuart's death. He's certainly going to be missed in this state."

"He worked hard to improve the situation of a lot of people who didn't have anyone else to speak up for them." Helen looked away and her gaze fell on the photo she was holding. She held it out so that Marisa could see it. "This is my favorite picture of my sister, Prudence. It was taken the night of the junior prom. She was a pretty girl, wasn't she?"

"She was lovely," Marisa said, looking at the color photo, then extending it so that Jimmy could also see it.

"Very beautiful," he murmured. He looked across at Helen. "I can see the likeness to you."

"You flatter me, Mr. Griffin. Prudence was the pretty sister. I was the one with the brains."

Marisa looked again at the picture. Despite Helen's disclaimer, she could see the likeness Jimmy had mentioned. In the picture, Prudence Wainscott wore a flowing seventies-style dress in soft blue voile, with flowers scattered in her long, straight hair. Her face was turned slightly away from the camera as she laughed up at her escort. Or, at least, Marisa presumed her radiant smile was for her escort. She couldn't be sure, since half the photo had been cut away, so that only a masculine hand and the sleeve of a jacket remained visible.

"I plan to have it enlarged and refinished," Helen said, taking the picture back. "My father destroyed the negative years ago, in his first blaze of fury at my sister's death, but they can do such wonderful things with photo restoration nowadays. A bigger version would look good hanging in the entrance hall at the Refuge, don't you think?"

"I think it would look great, and it would be nice to have a picture of your sister in her old home." Marisa found the conversation faintly surreal. How were they supposed to segue from gossip about an old photo into an accusation of multiple murder?

"I should have thought of getting this copied and framed long before now. Stuart would have liked that." Helen's finger traced absently along the cut edge of the photo. "Prudence must have gotten pregnant right around the time this picture was taken. Her boyfriend skipped town six weeks later. He came from one of those grim mountain towns that mined silver in the eighteen-sixties and has been trying to justify its existence ever since."

"You knew him, then?" Marisa had never considered this possibility.

"Not really. My sister only brought him home on one occasion, and that was nearly enough to give my father a heart attack. What a dreadful waste it all seems now." Her shoulders drooped, and she seemed momentarily weighed down by the accumulation of grief. "I guess it was all over and done with a long time ago, but the Refuge never has seemed able to shake off the tragedy. First Prudence died there, then my mother and father

walled themselves up with their grief. Now Stuart..."
Helen's voice trailed away.

"Why did you kill him?" Jimmy asked, his tone of
voice conversational, as if he were making another comment on the old photo. "Was it because he'd screwed up
and couldn't deliver the money anymore? Or was it because you found out Anya was pregnant with his child?"

So that was how you segued into an accusation of murder, Marisa thought, with a tinge of hysteria. With all the
finesse of a sledgehammer hitting glass.

For a split second, Helen's body froze into absolute
stillness, then she looked up from her sister's picture, her
face congealed into an expression of utter disdain. "I
have no idea precisely what you're suggesting, Mr. Griffin, but I find the general tone of your remark deeply
offensive."

Marisa watched Helen with minute attention. She'd
learned to detect a myriad of small signs that revealed to
her when Evan was lying, but she'd acquired that knowledge over weeks and months of observation. A certain
sort of smile warned his temper was about to flare. A
faint tightening of his lips indicated that he was girding
himself to lie. But with Helen, she had little past knowledge to draw on, and she had no clue whether the woman
was genuinely outraged at Jimmy's accusation, or simply
turning in a very cool performance.

"If you really didn't understand what I just said, let
me spell it out for you." Jimmy's voice remained conversational. "Your father left almost his whole fortune
to charity, which in turn left you depressingly short of
pocket money. By what you must have considered a
stroke of great good fortune, Stuart Frieze found a way
to enhance operations at the Refuge to the profitable tune
of a million bucks a year—give or take a few thousand.

You were the only board member who visited often enough to catch on to what he was doing. By a stroke of what *he* must have considered great good fortune, you were willing to be paid off. So he bought your silence.''

Helen's contemptuous expression didn't waver. ''You're stepping seriously out of line in making such appalling accusations. I advise you not to repeat such slanderous statements, Mr. Griffin, because if you do, I certainly plan to take legal action.''

''As you must know, Ms. Wainscott, it's only slander if it isn't true. And I can prove that you and Stuart worked together in selling Refuge babies, and finding couples who needed to buy eggs or hire a surrogate mother. Stuart told Anya that you were his partner. He supplied her with copious details of your complicity.''

Helen raised an eyebrow, looking faintly amused. ''Her word against mine, Mr. Griffin? Not much of a threat. And somehow, I suspect the officers of the law are considerably more likely to believe me than some pathetic little immigrant.''

Hot damn, Marisa thought. *She really is guilty.*

''It isn't merely a case of Anya's word against yours,'' Jimmy said. ''There's also Stuart's written statement. Signed, notarized, and tucked away in his safety deposit box.''

''You're lying.'' For the first time, Helen's facade cracked just a little. She walked over to the bar and placed the photo of her sister on the counter. She visibly gathered herself together again. ''I would consider your accusations outrageous in any circumstance. In view of the fact that I had to watch my fiancé kill himself last night, I consider them totally beyond the pale. Leave now, both of you, or I'm going to call hotel Security.''

''That threat kind of brings us right back to where we

started this conversation, doesn't it? Stuart's death last night. Why did you kill him, Helen? My personal guess is that it was a mixture of motives. You knew Marisa and I were closing in on Stuart, and you were terrified he would implicate you in the mess. Anya was the last straw. The fact that Stuart got her pregnant while he was having an affair with you must really have stuck in your gullet."

Helen picked up the phone, but Jimmy intercepted her before she could dial. "Call Security if you want," he said. "But be warned. Marisa and I will drive straight from here to the police station. We'll tell them where Stuart has his safety deposit box, and we'll tell them what they can expect to find in there."

Helen's gaze narrowed. "Why haven't you gone to the police already?" She gave a choked gasp of relief. "You don't have any written confession from Stuart, do you? That's just a threat, to make me talk. You only have Anya's word to go on, nothing more." She turned her back on them and walked to the bar, then reached for a bottle of cognac and poured herself a stiff drink.

So much for faking her out, Marisa thought bleakly. Helen was even smarter than they'd anticipated.

Jimmy looked untroubled by Helen's skepticism. He gave a small laugh. "You couldn't be more wrong, Helen—but run with that theory, if it comforts you. I'm here instead of at the police station because I'm more interested in hearing the truth about my sister's death than I am in seeing you arrested for Stuart's murder."

"I know nothing about your sister's death."

"Try again." Jimmy moved very close to Helen, crowding her against the bar. "I used to be with the FBI, did I tell you that last night?"

"You mentioned it." Helen sipped the drink she'd poured.

Jimmy's hand whipped out, and he knocked the glass of cognac from Helen's grasp, taking her neck in a throttlehold. "Did I tell you why I left? No? Well, here's the main reason. I got real tired of following FBI rules about interrogating bad guys, and I'm still just about burned out on respecting the rights of criminal suspects. Especially when I'm talking to the woman who killed my sister."

Helen tore at his hands, gasping for breath, but Jimmy didn't loosen his grip. "Can't...talk," she gasped, her hands beating against the air.

Jimmy relaxed his hold on her throat, but he still held her pinned against the bar.

Massaging her throat, Helen looked into his eyes. "You're never going to give up, are you?"

Jimmy held her gaze. "No. Never."

She gave a little sigh, her shoulders slumping. "It's ironic, you know. We're here right now because you were convinced Stuart murdered your sister. But he didn't. He had nothing to do with it. If you'd understood Stuart better, you'd have known he wasn't the killing type."

"You killed Carole without his help," Jimmy said.

"Yes. Without his knowledge, even." There was resignation in Helen's voice and a weariness that went soul deep. "Carole came to me, you see, when Ardita and Darina complained to her about Stuart's attempts to force them to make egg donations. Stuart hadn't done anything illegal, as far as she knew, so she couldn't go to the police. Instead, she reported Stuart's abuse of his position to me—the daughter of Grover Wainscott, the great benefactor and noble protector of fallen women. Naturally, it never occurred to her that the last thing in the world I wanted was to defend that crazy old fart's legacy. I promised her I'd take care of it, and assumed she'd go away. After all, she was a busy woman and there was a good chance she wouldn't follow up.''

''Carole always followed up.''

''Yes, of course, she did. Unfortunately, your sister was as persistent as you are. With Ardita and Darina's help, she got wind of a very profitable baby sale we were about to make, and she closed in on the deal, ferreting around until she had all the details of the transaction.''

Helen shrugged. ''At that point, it was no longer simply a case of Carole knowing that women at the Refuge had been pressured to undergo dubious medical procedures. Now she had proof that Stuart was selling babies. Flagrant violation of the law. I didn't want to kill her, you know, but she didn't leave me much choice. And Stuart never knew for sure what I'd done, of course. God knows, I made a point of not telling him, or he'd have freaked out. Fortunately, he had an endless capacity for self-deception, and he was exquisitely careful never to enquire why Ardita, Darina and your sister all managed to meet unfortunate accidents within the space of a week. A week when I just happened to be hanging around a Maryland inn, a few miles from the scenes of the accident.''

Jimmy abruptly dropped his hold on Helen, moving away as if he couldn't bear to be in physical contact with her anymore, even for the purpose of restraining her.

''But how did it all happen, Helen?'' Marisa asked. ''Why did you ever get involved with Stuart in the first place? Was the money that important to you?''

''You sound so goddamn self-righteous.'' Helen sent her a scathing glance. ''If I had ever looked like you, or even close, maybe I could have afforded to be a martyr and give all my money to charity. Since I don't look like you, I have to buy my way into the places I want to go.''

''So it was all about money?''

''Only incidentally,'' Helen said. ''For Stuart, it was about the money. For me, it was about destroying the Refuge.''

''You're angry with your father,'' Jimmy said, finally turning around to look at her again.

''Angry?'' Helen gave a hard laugh. ''Oh, yes, I guess you could say that. When I was a teenager, my father decided that he was going to make me pay for every sin, real and imagined, that Prudence ever committed. You can't even begin to visualize what it was like growing up in that horrible house after my sister died. And then, when I'd put up with his nonsense for twenty years, he finally died. And left all his money to his fucking institute for pregnant whores.''

Marisa, normally a bleeding heart, found that her sympathies weren't touched by Helen's supposedly harsh home environment. ''Your father left you two million dollars,'' she said. ''After he died, you could have walked away and put everything connected with Wainscott and your family history behind you. Instead of building something new, you obsessed about destroying the old.''

''I don't need lectures from you,'' Helen said. ''I need a drink.'' She walked back to the bar, stooping to pick up a piece of shattered glass as she went—

''No! My God, don't do it, Helen!'' Jimmy lunged toward her, but she dodged behind the bar, slashing the broken glass across her wrists.

Not again, Marisa thought. *I'm not going to watch an-*

other person die violently. She crept quietly to the phone and dialed 9-1-1.

"Don't come near me." Helen pointed the jagged shard of glass at Jimmy, blood dripping from her wrists in a gruesome stream.

He ignored her order and moved in, kicking upward and sending the glass flying. She collapsed into his arms, and he grabbed a towel, then carried her over to the sofa and laid her down before ripping the towel in half and tying up both her wrists.

"Are you calling the paramedics?" he asked Marisa tersely.

"Yes. They'll be here in fifteen minutes."

"Fifteen minutes?" he muttered. "Jesus. Fetch me some more towels from the bathroom, can you?"

"Not going to let me take the easy way out, Jimmy?" Helen's voice was thready. "I think I may have out smarted you."

Marisa came back from the bathroom with an armful of towels. "Would ice help?" she asked, her stomach turning over at the sight of the blood-soaked kitchen towel.

Helen looked at her wrists with an almost abstract interest. "Prudence bled to death, too, you know. All because that bastard Stuart wouldn't stand by her."

Stuart? Marisa thought, looking at Jimmy. Helen couldn't possibly be referring to Stuart Frieze. Prudence had been dead for a quarter of a century by the time Stuart arrived at the Refuge.

"She bled and bled and bled, and nothing would stop it." Helen's eyes drifted closed. "Stuart was a senior and Prudence was a junior. He was the best-looking boy in the school. She was the prettiest girl. He wasn't called Frieze then. He used his stepfather's name—Hugget. Stuart Hugget.'' She laughed. ''Not very glamorous, was it?''

Marisa knelt on the floor alongside the sofa. ''Was Stuart Frieze the father of your sister's baby, Helen?''

''Of course,'' she said. ''That's where it all began, you know. With Stuart, when he walked away from my sister.''

''But you were going to marry him,'' Marisa protested. ''You were engaged to the man who abandoned your sister.''

''No, not really. I just made him get engaged to torment him, because I knew he was involved with Anya. But he could be so goddamn charming when he set his mind to it, sometimes I would almost forget how much I hated him. When we had sex, though, I always had to pretend to be someone else. It was the only way I could let him touch me.''

''Did Stuart know that you recognized him as the man who'd deserted Prudence?'' Jimmy asked.

''Oh yes, he tried to hide the truth from me at his initial interview, but when I told him I'd recognized him, he admitted the truth. He told me he'd come back to make restitution.'' Helen struggled to sit up, energized by a flash of potent anger. ''As if he could ever repay me for the total fuck-up he made of my life.''

''Don't move around,'' Jimmy said sharply.

''If they save me this time, I'll succeed next time,'' Helen said softly.

''Okay, that's your choice. But it won't be on my watch. I have a lot more questions to ask you. When you killed Stuart last night, was it an accident?''

''No,'' she said dreamily. ''I planned to kill him as soon as I knew you two were at his house in Castle Rock. It was all over for us then, and I was angry with him for

screwing everything up so badly. It was easy to manipulate him. He wrote the suicide note exactly as I dictated
it to him. Then he ran to the edge of the lake, with me
hard on his heels. Ironic, really, that he was so willing
to take himself to the place where I planned to kill him.
I told him we had to have footprints to tie in with the
story that I struggled with him, and that he ran out of the
house to escape from me. I was carrying the gun, for
God's sake, and he still didn't suspect anything. When
we got to the lake, I suggested we tussle some more, to
make it look really convincing. Then I said I needed him
to kiss me one last time. A wonderful goodbye kiss that
I'd remember forever when he was in exile in Brazil. He
seemed to like the idea of being remembered forever."

Helen fell silent, and Jimmy prompted her. "Was that
when you shot him?"

"More or less. I waited until he leaned in real close,
and then I shot him. Right smack in the middle of his
lying, treacherous mouth." Helen sighed. "Do you believe in ghosts, Jimmy? I never believed in ghosts, but I
could feel my sister standing right beside me. Prudence
was glad that I killed him."

Helen's eyes drifted closed and Marisa expelled a tight
breath. "Is she...still breathing?"

Jimmy nodded. "But I'm not having much luck in
stopping the bleeding. How much longer until those
damn paramedics get here?"

"At least another five minutes. She isn't going to make
it, is she?"

"No, I'm afraid she isn't."

For a moment, Helen opened her eyes and looked
straight at Marisa. A tiny but radiant smile transformed

her ravaged features into something younger and softer. "Prudence," she whispered.

Her head rolled toward the back of the sofa. "I'm cold," she said and closed her eyes.

Epilogue

The news of Helen Wainscott's suicide was greeted with short-lived surprise in the town that bore her name, and with polite indifference in the larger world. In life, she had invariably been identified as Grover Wainscott's daughter or, more rarely, Prudence Wainscott's sister. In death, she was identified as Stuart Frieze's fiancée, the shadow trailing at the heels of his brilliant obituary.

Marisa and Jimmy decided there was nothing to be achieved by revealing the truth about Helen's attempts to sabotage the work of the Refuge, and even less point in telling complicated stories about murders in Maryland. Officially, Carole's death remained an accident, and Stuart's death remained a suicide. Helen was assumed to have killed herself because of the stress and horror she'd suffered in witnessing his demise.

Two weeks after Helen's death, Marisa and Jimmy were eating dinner at *La Cafetière*. Marisa knew she ought to be enjoying every moment of this rare treat. The company was perfect, and not only was the food even better than she remembered, but this was also the first time in almost a year that she'd been out at night without Spencer.

It was hard, though, to do justice to squab stuffed with almonds and apricots when she knew that Jimmy had brought her here to say goodbye. He had spent the past two weeks working with law enforcement personnel and the Refuge trustees to identify the full extent of Stuart's abuses. The trustees were genuinely horrified when they discovered what their much-admired executive director had been up to. They were also terrified of facing a flood of lawsuits, and they were scrambling to establish rules and procedures, replete with checks and triple checks, that would prevent the recurrence of baby sales. A hastily passed amendment to the Refuge bylaws banned egg retrievals and surrogate motherhood in perpetuity. Hours were spent in consultations with lawyers, and an educational trust fund was established for Anya and her baby. An anonymous benefactor promised to continue funding Stuart's hospital in Africa. Only Jimmy knew that Marisa had approached her brother and set the wheels in motion for the Joubert Foundation to pick up the tab.

Marisa had known for days that Jimmy's work at the Refuge would soon be over. And now he was going to tell her he was leaving. Naturally, he was doing it in style. In a business setting, James W. Griffin strode through life with a focused intensity that was exhausting to watch. In leisure hours, Marisa had discovered more sides of Jimmy the janitor than she would have expected, from a sunny good nature to an easy ability for laughter and a quirky sense of humor. From Marisa's point of view, the combination was lethally attractive.

Jimmy waited for Kathleen to bring them coffee, before leaning across the table and covering her hand with his. His fingers felt cool, so it was odd that she should feel warmed by his touch.

"I have to go back to Washington," he said. "My partners have been covering for me for two months now. I can't ask them to carry me any longer."

"You have obligations. I understand." And she did

understand, perfectly. She'd been preparing herself all night to hear Jimmy say this. Unfortunately, she hadn't adequately prepared herself for the way her stomach lurched sickly and then plummeted. Only a short while ago, she had been convinced she would never again give a man the power to hurt her. Never take the huge risk of forming emotional bonds. Never make love again. Never need to feel the heavy warmth of a man's body lying next to her in bed. Now she tried to visualize her life without Jimmy, and found that she couldn't. It was simply too painful.

"Come with me," Jimmy said, his gaze watchful, his eyes holding hers so that she couldn't look away.

"I can't," she said swiftly. It was good that she didn't need to think about this. Good that her responsibilities made it impossible for her to consider leaving Colorado. She owed Spencer stability, quite apart from the fact that he deserved to be the prime focus of her life. She simply couldn't pick up and follow Jimmy to Washington, just because her heart felt as if it were shattering into small, jagged pieces.

"I have obligations, too," she said, firming her resolve. "I'm needed at the Refuge right now. Badly needed. Without me, there would be nobody to take care of all the administrative chores that keep the wheels turning."

"Administrative chores" suddenly struck her as a pretty pathetic counterweight to a shattered heart, but she didn't say anything more. Over the past couple of years, she'd made not expressing her deepest emotions into something of an art form, and she couldn't seem to find a way to escape the strictures of her habit. Instead, she stared at the foam on her cappuccino, watching the bubbles dissolve and disappear, one by one.

"The trustees have appointed an interim director," Jimmy said. "She'll be arriving next week. I'll admit you have a responsibility to stay until she arrives and gets settled in."

"I'm glad you understand—"

"I understand perfectly. Right now, you're needed at the Refuge. Two weeks from now, you're a free woman." He took her hand and carried it to his lips, pressing a kiss into her palm and then curling her fingers over the kiss. "Come to Washington, Marisa. Marry me."

She was terrified by how badly she wanted to say yes. "You make it sound so simple."

"It is simple for me. I love you. I want to be with you."

She smiled then, although she felt tears prick at the corner of her eyes. "I love you, too, Jimmy. But that doesn't make it simple. The idea of loving you scares the hell out of me."

"If you love me, then everything else is relatively unimportant. Just details that need to be worked out."

"Spencer isn't a detail," she said. "The fact that I love you doesn't change the fact that my son's needs have to come first with me."

"His only important need right now is to have you love him. You can do that just as well in Washington, living with me, as anywhere else." He took both her hands and enclosed them inside his. "Spencer and I are already good buddies. We could easily learn to love each other, if you give us the chance. Don't use Spencer as an excuse to shut me out."

His voice dropped. "I need you, Marisa. Last night, lying beside you, I couldn't sleep. I kept asking myself what I'd do if you refused to marry me, and I couldn't come up with an answer. It's not that I don't want to think about going back to Washington without you. It's that even when I try to think about it, I can't imagine having to live the rest of my life without you in it.''

His feelings were a perfect mirror of her own, and Marisa's battered heart ached in sympathy. Why was she so sure that she had to keep saying no? she wondered. Her first marriage had been a disaster, her first husband a monster. She thought of Helen Wainscott, who had allowed her whole life to be shaped by the single devastating fact that her sister had died in tragic circumstances. She wasn't going to make the same mistake, Marisa realized. She wasn't going to give Evan the ultimate victory of cutting her off forever from love and laughter and happiness.

She took Jimmy's hand and cradled it against her cheek. ''Let's go home,'' she said. ''I need to book a couple of seats on a flight to Washington.''

New York Times **Bestselling Author**

PENNY JORDAN

POWER PLAY

Eleven years had passed, but the terror of that night was
something Pepper Minesse would never forget. Four men
had taken from her something sacred. Now she was
determined that each should lose what he most prized.

Fury fueled her success. The files she held on each
would destroy them. For three men, her death is the
only solution. Only one man, who hides a truth more
devastating than Pepper's own, is capable of defusing
the time bomb she has set ticking....

"Women everywhere will find pieces of
themselves in Jordan's characters."
—*Publishers Weekly*

*Available the first week of
November 2000 wherever
paperbacks are sold!*

Visit us at www.mirabooks.com   MPJ587

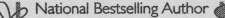

*From seduction in the royal sheikhdom to
high adventure in the hot Arabian desert comes a
breathtaking love story by international bestselling author*

DIANA PALMER

LORD OF THE DESERT

Gretchen Brannon was completely out of her element when she
aligned herself with Sheikh Philippe Sabon, the formidable ruler
of Qawi. They came from different worlds, but he made her aware
of her own courage. She, in turn, aroused his sleeping senses like
no other woman could.

But now that Gretchen's heart belongs to the Lord of the Desert,
she's become the target for vengeance by the sheikh's most
diabolical enemy. In a final showdown that will pit good against
evil, can love and destiny triumph...?

**"The dialogue is charming, the characters likable
and the sex sizzling..."**
—Publishers Weekly on Once in Paris

On sale October 2000 wherever paperbacks are sold!